Bolan charged from the building

"Starr, can you hear me?" he shouted into the mike.

"Got you," Starr said. "Go."

"We're coming out," Bolan announced. "My men will flank out and lay down cover fire into the vehicles. Tell your men to get into better firing positions as soon as we start."

Bolan ran on, dodging fire and returning it as he moved toward the trucks. "Where are you going, sir?" one of the voices asked.

Bolan's jaw tightened as he thought of Jackson and Gagliardi. These two warriors had mothers and fathers, maybe wives and children who would soon find out the loss of their loved ones.

"Where will you be going?" the voice repeated over the radio.

"Right up the middle," the Executioner growled into the face mike.

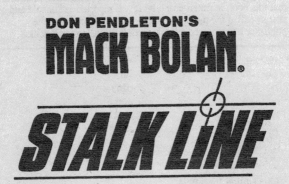

DON PENDLETON'S
MACK BOLAN®

STALK LINE

A GOLD EAGLE BOOK FROM
WORLDWIDE®

TORONTO • NEW YORK • LONDON
AMSTERDAM • PARIS • SYDNEY • HAMBURG
STOCKHOLM • ATHENS • TOKYO • MILAN
MADRID • WARSAW • BUDAPEST • AUCKLAND

First edition June 1995

ISBN 0-373-61442-X

Special thanks and acknowledgment to
Jerry VanCook for his contribution to this work.

STALK LINE

Printed in U.S.A.

Sow an act, and you reap a habit. Sow a habit, and you reap a character. Sow a character, and you reap a destiny.

—Charles Reade (1814-1884)

Some have, by their acts, chosen a destiny. My lot is to be the tool fulfilling that destiny.

—Mack Bolan

PROLOGUE

General Fajir Ham glanced to the light-skinned visitor standing at his side, then watched the four darker Somalian warlords prepare to enter the room. Only three of those four men would leave.

At least on their feet.

A cool breeze blew through the open windows of the house hidden in the foothills of northeastern Somalia. Ham remained standing at the head of the table as each of the leaders entered the room, casting quick, curious glances to the light-skinned man. They didn't know who he was. But they were about to find out.

General Ahmed Jabbar, who ruled Somalia's neighboring nation, Djibouti, entered first. A longtime ally of Ham's, Jabbar extended his right hand. A British gesture, it reminded Ham of the many years England had ruled sections of both countries.

Jabbar took the seat to Ham's right as Colonel James stepped forward. James, in control of Somalia south of the Juba River, extended both hands palm up, Kenyan style. Ham slapped the palms, then gripped James's curled fingers.

General Morris came next, his handshake firm and his eyes just as steady. Morris and his private army controlled everything between the Juba and Shebeli, including the southern half of the capital city, Mogadishu. Next to Ham himself, he was Somalia's most powerful warlord.

Ham's territory extended from the Djibouti border, around the northeast tip of Ethiopia, and now included the northern section of Mogadishu. He and Morris had been at war for years, at first for possession of the capital. Then the battle had grown personal as they fought over a woman.

Ham smiled inwardly. He had taken half of Morris's city. And he had not only taken the beautiful Aziza Mnarani, but he had given her body to both General Jabbar and Field Marshal Salih as a gift to solidify their alliance. This had added insult to humiliation for Morris, who still loved the woman, and the temporary truce that had allowed this meeting was far less stable than the grip of the two men's hands.

The last man to greet General Ham was Field Marshal Salih, and although his fingers curled tightly around the general's, the trembling of his lower jaw betrayed his fear. The youngest and newest warlord to come to power, Salih ruled the northeast corner of Somalia. His region was small but included Ras Hafun and Cape Guardaful, and was strategically vital since it offered northerly ports on the Indian Ocean.

Ham needed that region. And he intended to have it before the night was over.

Ham studied Salih's frightened eyes as he held the grip. The conference was taking place in the young man's premises, but Salih knew he had lost control. Each of the other four warlords had been escorted to the site by a contingent of soldiers larger than Salih's entire army. They waited now in their various camps outside.

General Ham waited as the warlords found chairs around the table. "Would anyone care for a cup of *shah* before we start?" he asked pleasantly.

All four heads shook in a negative response. "We are here to conduct business," General Morris said with the same counterfeit amiability. "Business must come before pleasure."

"Yes, indeed," Ham replied, still smiling. "But business can come *with* a certain amount of pleasure." He snapped his fingers, and a man appeared at his side, setting down a cup of tea in front of him. Ham took his time, spooning sugar into the dark brew, letting the men wait silently, making sure they knew they *must* wait until he was ready.

Finally, when he had tasted the tea, he said, "But perhaps you are correct. We should get on with it." He paused, clearing his throat. "We have had a very good thing here in Somalia. By controlling the food distribution, we have all become rich. Drugs, prostitution, the hijacking of goods sent by the West—all have added to that wealth." He paused, his eyes traveling from one man to the next. "But now that wealth is threatened by the Americans."

A cool breeze blew through the windows, causing the flame in the gas light on the table to flicker and cast ghostly shadows over the faces of the men. Outside the open windows, a hyena cackled in the darkness. "What I propose, gentlemen," he went on, "is that we cease all fighting between ourselves and recognize our true enemy. The Americans have become like dogs snapping at our heels while we attempt to do business."

"The United Nations—" Salih started.

Ham slammed a fist down hard on the table. "Make no mistake," he said. "It is *not* the United *Nations* that is behind this, but the United *States*. The United States *is* the United Nations."

Three other heads bobbed in agreement.

"Go on," said General Morris. "You obviously have something in mind."

"We must give up our arms as the Americans have demanded," Ham said simply.

"What!" General Jabbar screamed. "You are mad! We cannot—"

Ham held up a hand. "Relax, old friend," he said. "Hear me out. It will be a symbolic gesture—the type American politicians hold so dear. We will allow it to appear to the world that the U.S. has disarmed us and that we are now working together to form one of the *democracies* they love to initiate, then hold up to the world."

Snickers of disgust sounded around the table.

Ham lifted his teacup, took a sip, then shrugged. "Then the Americans will go home," he said nonchalantly.

"But," said Salih, "we will have no weapons! The people will rise against us and—"

Ham set his cup on the table. "Hardly, brother Salih," he explained. "We will receive new and better arms from our dear friend here." He turned to the light-skinned man, who nodded. "And then it will be 'business as usual,' as the Americans like to say."

"But how do we know they will leave?" James asked.

Ham chuckled. Next to Salih, James was the weakest of the warlords, but even he needed to be humored at this point. "America lost its will to fight with

Vietnam,'' Ham said. ''Oh, certainly they have enjoyed their little play-wars in Grenada and Panama...even in Kuwait and Iraq. But they no longer have the stomach for protracted engagements. Even as we speak, the American people cry, 'Bring back our *boys!* Bring back our *boys!*'" He said the word *boys* with such sarcasm that the others laughed.

Silence fell over the room. General Jabbar said, ''I must agree. America has become a nation more interested in appearance than reality. And if it *appears* to the world that we have given in to their demands, that is all they will require. They want only to claim victory, to save face. They will go home as soon as that has been achieved.''

''May I speak?'' Colonel James asked.

The heads around the table turned to him as James rubbed a hand across the smooth ebony skin of his face.

Ham watched him closely. He was a handsome man, this warlord of the south, and Ham was glad he was weak. It had not been necessary to bribe James with Aziza, as it had been with Jabbar and Salih. While strategically necessary, that gift had cut through Ham's heart like a dagger.

''What are we to do in the interim?'' James asked. ''This period after which we have turned in our rifles and before we receive new ones.''

''Yes,'' Jabbar agreed. ''We are outnumbered by the people. Without superior weapons, we would be cut to ribbons by their machetes the first time we attempted to hijack a food shipment.''

The light-skinned man cleared his throat, stood up and smoothed the tail of his light cotton sport coat over his thighs.

Before he could speak, General Morris finally voiced the question all of the warlords had been asking mentally. "Who *are* you?" he demanded bluntly.

The light-skinned man turned to Ham.

"His name is Ali Abu-Iyad," Ham said softly. "And he represents a man who hates the Americans even more than we do, if that is possible." The warlord watched the faces around the table as the man's identity sank in.

"As soon as the Americans have left," Abu-Iyad said, "I will provide you with more and better weapons. Instead of worn-out Soviet AK-47s, you will have FALNs, Heckler & Kochs, Galils—whatever you wish. I can provide rocket launchers, aircraft and other up-to-date technology."

"But *when?*" James asked. "When will these weapons be provided?"

"As soon as the Americans have left."

"Why not now?" General Morris demanded. "While we await the American withdrawal, we will be defenseless."

Abu-Iyad shook his head. "We cannot do it now. The Americans cover the ports."

"We have smuggled many things past them," Salih spoke up.

"Yes, and many things have been seized," said Abu-Iyad. "We cannot afford to take the chance." He paused, then went on. "Look, if you worry that your own people will attack during this temporary period of weakness, you create a problem where none exists. Your people are *starving*, gentlemen. They are more interested in where their next crumb of bread will come from than in seeking revenge. They are disorganized and will not find a leader who can change that in the few short days you will be without arms." He drew a deep breath. "But if it makes you feel better, keep a few of your best rifles for your personal protection. The Americans will not know, nor would they care. If you do this, and stay out of sight during this period, you will have no problem."

"Before I can agree," Field Marshal Salih said, "there is one thing I demand to know." His hands trembled on top of the table. He laced his fingers together, but the trembling continued. "How is the country to be run after the Americans leave?" He glanced suspiciously at Ham. "Will we redivide the sectors more equitably?"

"The divisions will be the same as they are now," Ham said. "Any changes will be made between individual leaders ... as they are now." He glanced toward Morris, who stared grimly back.

Salih shook his head. His face hardened, and Ham could see the inward battle the young warlord was waging as he struggled to gather his courage.

The time had almost come. The time to seize control of Salih's portion of Somalia, and solidify Ham's superiority over the other warlords.

"The most efficient port to bring in the new weapons is in *my* sector," Salih said. "For its use, I demand a reward."

Ham suppressed the smile that threatened to form on his face. Salih was in no position to demand *anything*. He glanced to his sides, seeing amused tolerance on the faces of Jabbar and Morris.

General Ham kept his face deadpan as he said, "And what is it you would like as your reward, Field Marshal Salih?"

Salih frowned, and Ham could see the young fool had not thought that far ahead. Finally the younger man said, "The Nagel Valley to the south. Down to and including the port of Eil."

An uneasy silence followed his words. General Morris was the first to laugh. He was followed by Jabbar and finally James. Salih's frightened face turned angry, his black skin paling to a moldy gray.

Ham kept a straight face, but his voice took on a mild sarcasm. "Perhaps you would also like General Morris and myself to throw in Mogadishu?" he said. Out of the corner of his eye, he watched Morris, Jabbar and James. He could see that they had now branded Salih as a liability to the plan.

It was time to act.

Ham turned to the door and shouted, "Captain Sadiki!"

A black man of medium build in a short-sleeved khaki uniform shirt entered the room and saluted. He wore a thick Garrison belt around his waist, and the black rubber grips and polished stainless steel of a Colt Anaconda extended from the holster on his hip.

"Have you spoken to Field Marshal Salih's lieutenant?" Ham asked.

Sadiki grinned. "I have," he said. "We are in agreement."

A quizzical expression covered Salih's face.

"Excellent, Sadiki." Ham turned back to Salih. "I am afraid I cannot give up that much of my land, Field Marshal Salih."

Salih stood up angrily. "I will not be laughed at," he said. "This meeting is over. You will now leave. I will have no part of your coalition. Go back to your own lands."

General Fajir Ham rose, as well, letting his face show the anger and contempt he felt for the young man. "I *am* in my own land," he said.

Salih's eyes flew from Ham to Sadiki, then back again as he realized what was happening. "A coup?" he said incredulously. "My men have sided with you?"

Both Sadiki and Ham nodded.

Salih curled his fingers into tight fists, his eyes electric with anger and hatred. "A coup," he repeated under his breath. "A bloodless coup."

Ham turned to Sadiki, drawing the Colt Anaconda from the man's holster. He turned back to Salih. "No, *not* bloodless," he said, then double-actioned the trigger and sent a .44 Magnum slug drilling through the young warlord's nose.

CHAPTER ONE

The scent of danger drifted up through the air with the ocean mist.

Mack Bolan couldn't see the threat below. He couldn't hear it, feel it, touch it or taste it. But the stench of danger in the nostrils of the man known as the Executioner was as strong as the salt sea of the Indian Ocean.

Bolan pulled the rip cord, and his parachute flowered out above his head as the hum of the Archer II PA28-181 faded into the darkened sky. As the chute caught, jerking him momentarily upward, he glanced down. Directly below, indistinct in the darkness, he could see the rolling waves. He glanced up. Blurred in the distance ahead of him, the craggy shoreline of the East African coast was barely visible.

He pulled the mask over his face and shoved the air regulator between his teeth a second before his feet hit the water. He took a deep breath as the weight of his pack pulled him under, then unclipped the Spyderco Civilian knife from his belt. Drawing the serrated edge through the parachute cords, he freed himself from the soggy chute, then tapped a button on the scuba console and sent a burst of air shooting into his buoyancy unit.

Bolan achieved neutral buoyancy, twenty feet below the surface, the flotation vest pressed tight against his chest. He tapped another button, bleeding some of the air, and dropped ten feet farther. Then he pulled the fins from his pack and slipped them onto his feet.

With another deep breath, he found his flashlight, adjusted the beam, then started forward through the black waters.

Bolan reviewed the whirlwind events of the past few hours as he made his way toward the Somalian shore. A CIA informant—a low-ranking man in the employment of General Ham—had informed his contact of a meeting to take place between Somalia's five major warlords. The snitch had also seen an unexplained lighter-skinned man—possibly Arabic, Iranian or Jewish—in the company of the general.

The information had gone through the usual channels: snitch to contact, contact to supervisor, then up the bureaucratic chain to the CIA director.

The director had deemed it important enough to contact the President.

Bolan moved through a school of fish, his flashlight beam bouncing over their striped fins and sending them scurrying in all directions. The water warmed against his skin as he rose above a shallow reef, swimming carefully over a growth of fire coral.

He had just finished a joint assignment with Stony Man Farm's three-man counterterrorist unit, Able Team, when he'd been contacted by Hal Brognola, Stony Man's director of the Sensitive Operations Group. Things were heating up again in Somalia. What had begun as a "peacekeeping mission" had turned into a hit-and-run war between U.S. forces and the warlords. General Ham was at the top of America's Top Ten Wanted List, and although reporters interviewed him almost nightly, the United States Army seemed unable to find the man.

Which, of course, made no sense. Bolan knew that if the news hawks could locate Ham, the Army's Criminal Intelligence Division could, too. This and other discrepancies made it obvious that politicians rather than soldiers were running the show. In short, the whole bloody business was threatening to turn into another Vietnam.

Bolan felt the anger grip his stomach as he moved toward the shoreline. He remembered the Vietnam atrocities all too well. He had watched good men— thousands of good men—die because bureaucrats had decided that America *should not win*.

The water grew more shallow as he neared the coast. His ears popped as he rose, and he reached up, pinching his nosepiece and blowing through his nostrils to equalize the pressure. When he reached a depth of six feet, he pulled the mask from his face and cautiously rose to a standing position beneath the surface.

Cool ocean zephyrs blew through the Executioner's wet hair as his head poked tentatively out of the water. His eyes scanned the shoreline under the quarter moon. It looked deserted, but the sense of threat— the danger he had smelled the moment he leaped from the Archer—filled his nostrils even more than before.

Moving toward the sand, he pulled the air tank and other underwater gear from his back. He crept quickly and silently into a grove of palm trees fifty feet from the water. Dropping his gear, he opened a plastic envelope from his pack and pulled out a pair of hiking boots. From another of the envelopes came an olive green T-shirt, khaki safari jacket and pants. A third watertight pack held his weapons.

As soon as he dressed, he slid into the ballistic nylon shoulder holster that carried his sound-suppressed

Beretta 93-R 9 mm pistol. Threading a strong-side hip holster through his belt, Bolan shoved the huge Desert Eagle .44 Magnum into leather, then added extra magazine carriers to his waist before clipping the Spyderco Civilian knife inside his pants at the small of his back.

His perception of imminent threat increased as he buried the scuba gear in the sand. Bolan's personal-warning senses had been forged long ago in Vietnam, then polished to a razor's edge as he subsequently battled the mafia, international terrorists, and other enemies of the U.S. His senses were as real a weapon as the firearms he had just secured to his sides and incalculably more valuable. Early on he had learned to trust them, and although they might sometimes defy logic, that defiance had kept him alive on too many occasions for him to ignore his senses.

Tonight was no exception.

Bolan had just finished burying his gear when a volley of rifle rounds broke the still night. He dropped instinctively to one knee, the Beretta leaping into his hand as if by magic. More bursts of fire erupted, the bullets striking the tree trunks in front of him with wet, slapping sounds. Down the beach, perhaps a hundred yards away, he saw the muzzle-flashes. Five rifles—AK-47s by the sound. The men behind the assault weapons had spread out across the sand at a 135-degree angle around the grove of trees.

Three certainties hit Bolan as he crouched behind the tree trunks. First, it would be useless to return fire. True, the Beretta had a range of over a hundred yards, but his only targets were the muzzle-flashes spotting the shoreline. The chances of a hit were slim, and the 93-R's own muzzle-flash would pinpoint him within the trees. Second, he realized that his attackers were only semitrained. At that distance and in the darkness, they could not possibly have seen his movements within the trees. To know he was there, they had to have spotted him on the beach earlier. The fact that they hadn't fired then meant that they had been out of range even for their rifles. They had had plenty of time to completely surround the grove.

But they hadn't. Which marked them as amateurs.

The third realization that dawned on him now was that even though the men trying to kill him were novices, they had the advantage. If they didn't move into pistol range—and so far, they showed no inclination of doing so—they *might* just get the job done. Sooner or later, with enough lead flying around him, one of the wild 7.62 mm slugs was bound to find its mark.

Bolan huddled within the trees as more rounds sang past. The fire came in long bursts with little time in between. What he needed was a lone shot, followed by a break in the noise. His plan allowed only one chance, and if the men with the AK-47s failed to hear him, all would be lost.

Rifle rounds continued to riddle the trees as Bolan steeled his nerves against the onslaught. Finally it came. A single rifle round. Then the only sound was the metallic snap of a fresh magazine being shoved into the Soviet assault rifle.

Bolan switched the Beretta to his left hand and drew the Desert Eagle with his right. Letting out a blood-curdling scream that pierced the sudden stillness along the shore, he fell from cover. His chest and face hit the sand.

Muffled voices drifted along the beach. Then footsteps began moving toward him over the wet sand.

Five men. All coming from the same direction. But he had no idea of their formation. Again he would get one chance and one chance alone.

Bolan tightened his fingers around the Desert Eagle and Beretta. Both weapons were out of sight, wedged between his body and the sand. The footsteps drew closer.

The Executioner waited.

AROUND THE AGE OF TWENTY, Don Elliot had begun to suspect that he'd been born a century or so too late.

By forty he was sure of it.

His lungs screaming for air, Elliot slowed his pace as the cave appeared in the distance. Unslinging the AK-47 from his back, he slowed to a walk. His breath returned quickly to normal, and he silently congratulated himself for the countless miles he had jogged down the steaming African paths that passed for roads. His past few years in the fish-canning business had presented him with a sedentary life-style, and had it not been for his personal commitment to physical fitness, he'd never have made it this far.

Elliot vaulted a narrow stream, looked down and caught a brief glimpse of his face in the clear water. Damn, he was grinning. What the hell was wrong with him? Regardless of his physical condition, there was every chance in the world that he'd be shot in the next few hours. But he was in the best mood he'd been in since...well, for nine years.

The smiling man ducked into the cave, and the temperature dropped a good ten degrees, sending a quick chill over his sweat-drenched body. He laid his rifle down, dropped to a seat against the cool wall of the cave, and an even deeper chill shot through his shirt and up his spine. Closing his eyes, he relished the sudden respite from the heat outside.

Well, he had always said he'd rather face the entire horde of Genghis Khan with a penknife than have to walk into a bank and ask for a loan. Now, if you substituted General Fajir Ham for Genghis and the warlord's men for the horde, he was pretty much getting his wish.

Elliot opened his eyes. The fish-canning business was history. Ham had taken it now, as he'd taken almost everything else in this part of Somalia. The factory was gone, Elliot's money was gone and he was pretty much back where he'd been nine years before, when he'd quit the CIA.

The words came out before he could stop them. "Thank God," Don Elliot said, and now the smile on his face become a beam.

Footsteps sounded at the cave entrance, but Elliot didn't bother to reach for the rifle. He knew those steps. Benjamin Barkari—or "Friday," as Elliot had called the man for the past fifteen years—had been less than a hundred yards behind him during their flight from the wrecked Mercedes along the road. The big Swahili was an adventurer at heart, too, and Elliot knew that the years they'd spent as partners in the canning business had been as hard on Friday's nerves as they'd been on his.

A large, round head poked into the cave, scanned the small cavity, then entered. Sweat beaded Friday's ebony forehead, and the armpits of his light chambray shirt were soaked. A scowl covered his face as he leaned his rifle against the wall and took a seat across from Elliot.

"Beat you," Elliot said simply.

The scowl on the black man's face turned instantly to a smirk. "Only because I allowed it," he said. "Someone had to stay behind to slow them down."

"Right." Elliot said and chuckled. "I didn't hear any shots."

Friday tapped the machete at his side, and Elliot looked down to see fresh blood seeping through the canvas sheath. "I left him propped against a tree where the others will find him," the black man said. "It will not stop them. But they will slow down." He crossed his legs in front of him on the cool stone floor.

Elliot nodded, closed his eyes and took in a deep breath of the refreshingly cool cave air. They were safe—at least for the moment. Ham's men would find the cave eventually, but it would take time. He and Friday had covered their tracks as well as they could under the circumstances, and they should have a few hours' respite before their pursuers picked up the trail. By then they'd be rested and on their way across the plateau, toward their more permanent hideout in the mountains of northern Somalia.

His eyes still closed, Elliot reviewed the chaotic events of the past few days. General Ham had been after the East African Fish Canning Company since the fall of Siyad Barre. When his troops had finally come to the factory, Elliot and Barkari had fled to the safehouse they'd kept in Mogadishu since their CIA days.

Elliot relaxed as his body temperature continued to drop. It hadn't taken Ham's men long to find the house, and Elliot and Friday had been forced to flee once more. They'd been one step ahead of the warlord's men and might have made a clean getaway if the damned Mercedes hadn't blown its water pump.

"German efficiency," Friday said sarcastically, as if reading Elliot's mind. "Piss on it."

Elliot grinned but didn't answer. Perhaps Friday *could* read his mind. Sometimes he felt as if he knew what the big Swahili was thinking. Elliot had first met Benjamin Barkari when he'd been with the Company, as the CIA was often called. He'd recruited the black mercenary to provide intelligence within a terrorist faction of the Swahili tribe.

Elliot opened one eye and squinted at his friend across the cave. Friday looked as if he might have fallen asleep.

When Elliot had left the CIA, Benjamin Barkari—by then Elliot was calling him Friday, after Robinson Crusoe's right-hand man—had gone with him, becoming his partner and the chief foreman of the fish cannery. They had worked together in one capacity or another for almost fifteen years now, and Don Elliot trusted his friend as he never had another man. That trust, he knew, went both ways.

"Does it make you miss it?" Friday asked suddenly.

"I *always* missed it," Elliot said.

"So why did we leave?"

"To get rich. We were told that wealth made one happy."

Friday opened his eyes, then closed them again. "We were misinformed," he said.

Elliot looked at his watch. "How long do you suppose we have before they find us?"

"An hour. Perhaps two."

"When was the last time we cleaned the weapons?"

Friday frowned in thought. "Before Ham took the factory." He paused. "The AKs will be all right. You could pour mud into the receivers and let an elephant stomp them into the ground and they'd still work. But this—" he drew the faded blue Argentine-made .45 automatic from his belt "—I am not so sure."

"I wouldn't be, either," Elliot chided. "Ugly damned gun."

Friday laughed. "It shoots the same bullets as that gaudy spectacle on your hip," he said. "And the men it has killed are as dead as the ones you have shot."

Elliot drew the customized Colt .45 Government Model from his belt, held it up and saw the bright blue finish sparkle in the sunlight drifting into the cave. "A point well taken, my man Friday," he said.

He rose and moved deeper into the cave, rounding a corner and pulling a small flashlight from his pocket as the light faded. He found the small green metal ammo box where he'd left it years before, amid the other supplies he'd stocked in the cave when it had first begun to look as if things might go bad for Somalia.

Lugging the box back into the light, he set it between him and Friday and flipped the latches. Pulling out two clean rags, he tossed one to Friday, then spread out the other across the floor of the cave and sat down.

A feeling of warmth came over Elliot as he dropped the 10-round Ramline magazine from the Colt. Working the slide, he caught the chambered round in his left hand as it came out the port. The former CIA man studied the empty weapon.

Friday was right—it *was* a spectacle. And from a strictly combat point of view, it was arguable whether or not the time and expense he had put into the customization had been worth it. The Mexican silver grips with inlaid turquoise did nothing to enhance the weapon's efficiency, nor did the match-grade Bar-Sto barrel amount to much at the distances at which pistol combat usually took place. True, the Hartt's recoil reducer, King combat hammer and beavertail grip safety, polished ramp and sear, lowered ejection port, front-strap checkering and Wilson extended thumb safety and slide release all increased the gun's smoothness and reliability—but only marginally when compared to the piece as it came out of the box.

Elliot separated the slide from the frame, then began setting pieces of the weapon on the cloth. Combat efficiency—that had been the excuse he'd given for spending so much time customizing the .45. The real reason he had done it was *therapy*.

Working on the Colt, changing this, changing that, testing each new part along the way—it had kept him going. Kept him from losing his sanity during the monotonous years of canning fish and making more money than he knew how to spend.

Elliot sprayed a liberal dose of a cleaner-lubricator over the pieces of the .45 and sat back to let it soak in, his mind returning momentarily to the past once again. He had spent two tours of duty in Vietnam. During the last stint he'd been recruited by the Agency, and he had stayed with them until finally convinced he should grow up, make some money and settle down. Even though Barre's government had been socialist, Elliot had known the country was still wide open for enterprise.

But the former CIA operative's interest in business hadn't lasted long, and Don Elliot soon developed a narcoticlike addiction to adventure. Sure, the fish-canning business brought wealth. But it also brought high blood pressure, ulcers, borderline alcoholism and an occasional mild curiosity as to what the back of his head would look like if he stuck the barrel of the customized Colt into his mouth and pulled the trigger.

During his years with the CIA, Elliot had taken one bullet in the thigh, and another had passed so close to his ear that it left a red burn. He'd been cut with a knife three times and beaten once with a cue stick in an out-of-the-way tavern near Lima. But all in all, Elliot had to figure that the fish canning business was the most dangerous job he'd ever had.

The former CIA agent lifted another rag from the box and began wiping down the slide of the .45. He'd quit trying to figure himself out years ago. Right now, even though he really *was* about to come face-to-face with "Genghis Khan," he felt the way he imagined an alcoholic must feel falling off the wagon after staying sober for nine years. Adrenaline was pumping through his body as if propelled by a fire hose, and it felt like the embrace of an old friend.

Elliot finished wiping down the slide and went to work on the frame, then the other components. When he was finished, he held the weapon up for inspection. As it sparkled in the light drifting in through the mouth of the cave, it was truly a thing of beauty.

Elliot holstered his weapon and looked across the cave to see Friday reloading his Argentine .45. The big Swahili smirked as he looked at the gun on Elliot's side. "I've heard that some people in your country accuse *black* people of gaudiness." He laughed, shaking his head.

Elliot returned the laugh. "Touché," he said. He had started to speak again, when the rustling of leaves sounded outside the cave.

Both of the .45s suddenly returned to the men's hands as their laughter faded.

HIS FACE HALF-BURIED in the sand, Bolan allowed one eye to half open as the footsteps neared. A well-worn pair of Nike basketball shoes appeared at the top of his field of vision, followed by the cuffs of a ragged pair of blue jeans. The man in the Nikes came to a halt as his knees entered the picture.

Low voices whispered in what the Executioner recognized as the Somalian dialect of the Cushitic language. Although he couldn't understand their words, it was obvious there was some disagreement. Probably over who would move in first to check the body.

Bolan waited as the men continued to bicker. Although he couldn't see them, he could feel the barrels of the men's AK-47s aimed at his back.

Finally the man in the Nikes shuffled forward and dropped to one knee. Reaching gingerly forward, he grasped Bolan by the shoulder and rolled him onto his side.

As the Desert Eagle came into view, the Executioner shoved the barrel into the man's face and pulled the trigger. The blast from the .44 Magnum blew the back of the man's skull from his head, sending a shower of blood and bone fragments over the sand.

The other men froze.

Bolan rolled onto his back, squeezing the Desert Eagle's trigger again as the front post sight drifted across the chest of a man gripping a Soviet assault rifle. A massive Magnum cut a swath through the gunner's sweatshirt and sent him flying to his back on the wet sand.

The other three men fumbled with their weapons as the Executioner raised the Beretta. As his fingers tightened around the hard plastic grips, his thumb dropped the selector to 3-round burst. A trio of 9 mm subsonic rounds found a home in the midsection of a gunman wearing a tattered blue shirt. The slow-moving 147-grain bullets, combined with the Beretta's sound suppressor, made the weapon sound like a toy after the roar of the .44.

Scraps of the blue shirt were driven into the entry wound, and blood sprayed out the front. Bolan rolled across the sand, and return fire hit the spot where he'd been a split second before. Wet grains of sand stung his face as he came to a halt.

Bolan stayed prone, presenting as small a target as he could. Two men still stood. Dropping the Beretta's barrel onto the chest of a man wearing a Miami Dolphins baseball cap, the Executioner moved the Desert Eagle over to the last AK-toting gunman, then pressed both triggers simultaneously.

The Desert Eagle's solo roar drowned out the 93-R's soft coughs, but the Beretta continued to jerk even after the big .44 had come to rest after the recoil. The .44 Magnum hollowpoint slid across the hand holding the AK-47, then entered the face behind it. The Beretta's 3-round burst struck the other man in the chest, throat and mouth as Bolan allowed the weapon to climb with the kick.

Suddenly silence returned to the African shore.

Bolan leaped to his feet. He moved to the nearest body and ripped the AK-47 from the dead fingers. A quick inspection of the rifle showed an empty 7.62 mm casing stovepiped in the breech. He dropped the malfunctioning weapon, and it was then that he first noticed the arm bands.

He stared down at the dead man whose rifle had jammed. A pale blue arm band was tied around his left biceps. In the center was the wrinkled white five-point star. The flag of Somalia, it was also the symbol of General Ham and his warriors.

Bolan moved quickly to the dead man with the Dolphins cap and lifted the AK-47 from the sand next to him. It appeared to function well, and another quick inspection turned up half a magazine of Russian hardball with one round still waiting in the chamber.

Flipping the selector up to Safe, Bolan pulled a full mag from the back pocket of the dead man's faded khaki work pants, then gathered several more spares from the other bodies littering the sand.

He turned and looked up the beach in the direction from which the men had come. Soft waves broke over the sand, and a cool breeze was blowing in from the ocean. But the peace that now reigned along the northeast African shore wouldn't last.

The Executioner intended to make sure of that.

Returning to the trees, he slid into his backpack, then started down the beach, jogging over the footprints Ham's men had left in the damp sand. While Somalia had some of the most beautiful beaches in Africa, trees such as the ones that had sheltered him earlier were rare, and he could expect little cover if he encountered another of Ham's patrols.

But one more meaningless shoot-out with the general's flunkies was hardly on his list of priorities. He would take on any comers who got in his way, but he had no intention of wasting more time fighting along the beach. He had bigger fish to fry. Or, he thought, as a hard smile played at his lips, under the circumstances, he supposed he should say bigger *Hams* to fry.

For ten minutes he followed the tracks back to a gravel road bordering the sea. A 1992 Toyota Land Cruiser had been parked in the short grass to the side, and the Executioner could see the footprints where the five men had left the vehicle to begin their patrol. The doors were locked.

Bolan didn't have time for games. Drawing the Desert Eagle, he drove the butt through the driver's-side window. Sliding behind the wheel, he cracked the plastic on the steering column, connected the proper wires and listened to the Land Cruiser sputter to life.

A moment later he was on his way over the gravel toward Mogadishu.

And another new war.

THE FIRST RAYS of morning sun broke over the horizon as Bolan neared the checkpoint a mile north of the Mogadishu city limits. He slowed the Toyota as he fell into line behind a red Buick Regal Estate Wagon. His eyes scanned from the cars ahead of him to the guard shack on his right. Hastily constructed of scrap lumber, it was nevertheless sturdy enough to support the M-60 machine gun mounted on the roof.

The U.S. Marines around the shack wore desert cammies and the new "Fritz hats" that were gradually replacing the older steel helmets. All of the men wore M-16A-2 battle rifles slung across their chests in assault mode, and most looked ready to hit the desert battlefield at a moment's notice. Water bottles, first-aid gear, extra ammo magazines and pistols hung from their web gear.

Guard duty in many places around the world was considered a vacation. In Mogadishu it was a half step away from the front lines.

Bolan turned his attention back to the Buick ahead of him as the line moved forward. He watched a young Marine carrying a clipboard move to the driver's side of the vehicle and lean down to speak through the window. The head behind the wheel bobbed animatedly as papers were produced.

The young American studied them, then waved the car on through.

Bolan pulled up to the place the Regal had vacated, producing the passport from the pocket of his safari jacket. Both the passport and press credentials had been prepared hurriedly, but should have no problem withstanding the scrutiny of a simple Marine untrained in detecting forgeries.

The young American leaned toward the open window of the Land Cruiser. "Passport, sir," he said.

Bolan handed the document through the window.

The Marine looked from the picture to Bolan's face, then jotted the number on the clipboard before returning the passport. "The vehicle?"

"Rented," Bolan answered.

"Please state your business in Mogadishu," the young Marine said in a practiced voice.

"I'm a writer," Bolan said.

The Marine smiled wearily. "Who are you with?"

"Free-lance. Doing research for a book."

A slight frown fell over the young man's face. "You have any press credentials?" he asked.

Bolan handed him the card.

The Marine glanced at it, then handed it back. "What kind of book you working on?"

"It's a war story."

The weary smile returned. "You came to the right place," he said. "Watch your ass, sir." He waved Bolan on through.

The Executioner drove on into the city. He had encountered one of Somalia's few surfaced roads shortly after leaving the beach, but now pulled off it for a combination of dirt roads and ancient cobblestones.

Mogadishu's downtown area reminded Bolan of Beirut. The only people who ventured from the relative safety of their homes were those whose business outweighed the risk. These included the drug pushers selling marijuana, heroin and particularly khat. When chewed, the leaves of the khat bush produced a mild amphetamine high. Although officially illegal, the substance was flown in from Kenya and driven across the Ethiopian border daily by the warlords' smugglers.

Many of the buildings had fallen victim to shelling. Other structures stood in ruins from ground attack. Here and there sandbags had been set out in front of stores and offices, and bars covered the windows and doors of the businesses that could afford them.

Bolan shook his head as he drove on. Beirut might no longer be the "Gem of the Middle East" as it had once been, but at one time there had been wealth in Lebanon and at least some of it remained. But Somalia had not seen prosperity since the early sixteenth century, when a newly discovered sea route to India cut the ports of Mogadishu and Brava from the Arab-controlled trans–Indian Ocean trading network. Since then the people of Somalia had lived in relative obscurity. And now all but the warlords starved. Most were even too poor to afford the sandbags and bars that might provide a modicum of safety.

Bolan glanced along the dusty road and saw the sign he was looking for—an artist's rendering of a man sitting cross-legged and wearing a turban, coaxing a python out of a basket with a flute. Beneath the picture were two words in Arabic that the Executioner couldn't read. But he knew what they meant. The Dancing Viper.

Pulling the truck up next to the curb, Bolan got out and locked the doors. With a quick glance up and down the street, he started for the paint-chipped wooden door beneath the sign.

On the surface, Bolan's objectives in Somalia sounded like a simple three-part mission. First, check out the informant's report that the warlords were conspiring to create the illusion that they were complying with UN demands in order to take over once again as soon as the troops pulled out. Second, if that proved correct, he would make the rounds of the country, first locating and then eliminating the warlords. The third part of the mission was to discover the identity of the mysterious light-skinned man who was keeping company with General Ham these days.

Bolan opened the door and stepped inside into semidarkness. Simple? Only on paper. Each step of the way would present obstacles that would have to be overcome.

He stood beside the door, scanning the bar and dark booths as his eyes adjusted to the dim lighting. Cigar, cigarette, marijuana and opium smoke hung in the air like fallout clouds after a nuclear explosion, combining with the stench of cheap wine, sweat and stale urine to assault his nostrils.

In order to complete his mission, Bolan had known he would need the help of someone who could be trusted—and who knew the country. While those two virtues certainly weren't mutually exclusive, men who possessed them rarely just fell into your lap. Hal Brognola had known a man who at one time had been among the best, but when the Stony Man director had contacted Hans Heinz, the former French foreign legionnaire had been the first to admit that times had changed. If he wasn't looking at the bottom of a bottle these days, it was because he was uncorking a fresh one.

Heinz had, however, agreed to take Bolan to a former CIA agent he knew who might be willing to help. For a price, of course. And that man, the former legionnaire said, knew the ropes within the embattled East African nation as well as Heinz himself.

As Bolan's pupils dilated, the figures within the Dancing Viper began to take shape. Along the bar he saw a series of elderly men slumped over glasses of foul-smelling wine and strong Arabic coffee laced with opiates. An emaciated man with a heavily waxed mustache stood behind the bar in an apron, making a halfhearted attempt to wipe grime from a glass. A dark fez sat on his head, and his ratlike eyes moved from Bolan to the rear of the room, then back again.

Bolan followed the man's gaze, seeing more human residue at the tables between the bar and back wall. All eyes within the room were upon Bolan as he spotted the man in the Australian bush hat propped against the dirty stucco wall.

Bolan started that way, stepping around a woman even more gaunt than the bartender who moved into his path. Huge, gaping sores covered her face and neck. Smaller ulcers—the result of too many needles being stabbed into her arms—covered what Bolan knew would be collapsed veins. What looked to have once been smooth sable skin had turned a pale, pallid gray.

Bolan wondered what had happened to the men and women in the Dancing Viper that they had chosen this path to total ruin. People didn't just simply sit down one day and decide they'd become disease-ridden, dope-shooting derelicts. What had happened to these people?

The answer came suddenly, and the sorrow in his heart changed to anger. He didn't know the details of these wasted lives, but he knew the general reason they'd become what they had. And the word *general* would be spelled with a capital *G*.

While the people of Somalia starved and died of disease, men like Ham, Morris and Jabbar hijacked the shipments of food and medical supplies donated by the United Nations, Red Cross and other charitable organizations. The goods never reached the masses that needed them, but were diverted to the black markets or sold to other countries.

Bolan stopped in front of the man in the chair, realizing suddenly that his fists were clenched. He would put a halt to this destruction of the innocent Somalian people by the warlords, he vowed silently. And the only thing that would stop him would be death.

The man whose chair was tilted back against the wall wore a filthy, ribbed undershirt, soiled slacks and scuffed brown combat boots held together with gray duct tape. The face beneath the battered Australian hat hadn't seen a razor in several days. His eyes were closed, and the odor of alcohol on his breath sliced through the general foulness of the rest of the room.

Bolan's anger now became disgust. According to Brognola, Hans Heinz had worked closely with both the CIA and DEA in the past, and at one time had been regarded as a reliable hand. Unlike the others in the room, Heinz was not a native Somalian who was stuck here. He was a transplanted German who still owned property in his homeland and could have gotten on the first ship or plane heading northwest if things had gone wrong for him in Somalia.

Bolan lightly kicked the sleeping man's calf with the toe of his hiking boot. He got no response. A harder kick brought only a drunken grunt, a short break in the snoring, then more sleep.

Bolan took a half step back and swept his foot beneath the rear legs of the chair.

Hans Heinz collapsed in a cursing heap on the floor.

Bolan watched the man look up through foggy eyes, then reach clumsily for his back pocket as he hauled himself to his feet. The knife came out just as clumsily, and the Executioner grabbed the wrist holding it. "Take it easy, Heinz," he said softly.

The murky eyes tried to clear as Hans Heinz looked up. "You the guy Brognola told me was coming?" he slurred with only the remnants of a German accent.

Bolan nodded.

"How about you buy me a drink?"

"Not now. Let's get out of here."

Heinz scratched the stubble on his chin. "You got the money?"

Bolan nodded again.

Heinz stepped past the Executioner and stumbled toward the door.

Bolan followed, silently praying that Hal Brognola had known what he was doing when he picked this man to lead him to Don Elliot.

CHAPTER TWO

By 0900 hours the African sun was already threatening to burn holes through the war-torn streets of Mogadishu. The window on the driver's side of the Land Cruiser was still broken, and Bolan had rolled down the window on Heinz's side as soon as they'd left the Dancing Viper, not only because the truck's air conditioner didn't work but to help fight off the rank body odor and smell of stale alcohol that followed the German like a loyal dog.

Bolan guided the vehicle down other dirt streets, occasionally turning onto potholed concrete or asphalt according to Heinz's semisober directions. Clarity of thought was no longer the German's long suit, and they lost their bearings twice before he recognized landmarks that got them back on track again.

Bolan drove patiently, hoping they'd stumble onto Don Elliot's safehouse soon, or that Heinz would sober up enough to make sense, or both. But he held little hope of ever getting much use out of the man sitting next to him. But since Heinz appeared to be his only link to Elliot, and Elliot his only link to the warlords, Bolan would just have to work around the man's alcohol-dazed condition.

"God, I've got a conk," Heinz said as they turned into a residential area. Bolan saw him holding his head in both hands. "You wouldn't happen to have a beer on you, would you?"

Bolan shook his head. "There's aspirin in my pack," he said. "I'll get it for you when we stop."

"Like putting a Band-Aid on a severed artery," the German said, his face still hidden behind his fingers. "What I need is a drink."

Bolan shook his head again and steered the conversation to more relevant concerns. "Tell me, Heinz, how is it you know Elliot?"

Heinz rubbed his face again, then looked up at the windshield. "Don't you mean how is it that Elliot would trust a skid-row drunk like me with the knowledge of the location of his safehouse?"

The Executioner shrugged. "That's another way to phrase it, yeah."

The German chuckled, then groaned as the movement brought more pain to his head. His hands returned to his face as he said, "You haven't even told me your name yet."

"You can call me Pollock. Rance Pollock."

Heinz nodded. "Well, Pollock, Don's had the place for at least ten years that I know of. I've only been trying to drink the ocean dry for the last couple or so." He paused, closing his eyes and rubbing the top of his head. "I did some free-lance work for the CIA right after I left the legion, and I got to know Elliot then. We were pretty tight once, the three of us."

Bolan frowned. "The three of us? Who's the third?"

"Big black fellow Don called Friday. You know, I can't even remember his real name anymore. Swahili, though, I remember that. He went into the canning business with Elliot." He glanced up. "Turn right at the next corner."

Bolan twisted the wheel. "The three of you worked together for the Company?" he asked.

Heinz nodded.

Bolan felt Heinz's eyes on him as he drove. The German turned back to the windshield, pointing at a complex of run-down apartment houses on Bolan's side of the road. "There it is."

Bolan turned left into the complex, following the German's directions to park in front of the third in a row of two-story buildings. He threw the truck into Park, killed the engine and got out, waiting while Heinz struggled from the passenger's seat.

Bolan led the way up three crumbling concrete steps to a common hallway. The door had been propped open with a piece from one of the broken steps, and a small diamond-shaped window sat at eye level in the upper half. Another set of steel stairs led to the second floor, and Heinz followed Bolan up.

"Better let me go first," Heinz said as they started down the second-floor hallway. "If he's hiding, he'll be antsy. He'll recognize me."

Bolan followed the man down the hall. He let his right hand fall to his belt, curling his thumb casually over the buckle. The position of his hand looked natural, but from it he could quickly reach either the Desert Eagle or Beretta.

The two men stopped in the hall in front of a door bearing the Roman numeral VIII. Heinz rapped several times on the rotting wood, then stepped back so as to be clearly visible through the peephole.

"Who is it?" came an African-accented voice through the door.

"It's me, Friday," the German said. "Hans Heinz. Open up."

The door opened a crack, and Bolan could see a dark set of eyes flicker from Heinz to him, then back to Heinz. He didn't let it upset him. It seemed only reasonable that Elliot's partner would be cautious under the circumstances.

The door closed again, and Bolan heard the chain being slipped off the lock.

The yellow caution light in his brain suddenly turned red as the door swung open to reveal the bore of a sawed-off 12-gauge shotgun.

The Desert Eagle came out of the hip holster reflexively, traveling in an arc to strike the shotgunner under the chin and drive him back into the apartment. Bolan lowered the big .44, dropping the sights on the man's chest as the shotgun clattered to the floor and the man who had held it went sprawling onto his back.

Bolan's thumb found the safety and flipped it to Fire. As the man on the ground fumbled for a short-barreled revolver in his waistband, Bolan's finger started back on the trigger. It stopped in midstroke as six more men suddenly appeared in the living room of the safehouse apartment. Each wielded either an AK-47, a shotgun or a submachine gun.

And each wore the light blue arm band with the white star that told Bolan they were from the ranks of General Fajir Ham.

The man Bolan had struck finally got the revolver out of his belt and scrambled to his feet, his free hand cupping his chin. Blood oozed from the gash left by the Desert Eagle's front sight. He moved toward Bolan, staring up at the taller man, his eyes burning with anger. "You will drop your weapon immediately," he said through clenched teeth, "or you will die."

Bolan studied the shorter man's face. He meant business. So did the other men scattered around the room. And even the Executioner couldn't gun down seven armed men who were less than five feet away and flanking him.

With a deep breath he released his grip on the big .44 Magnum and let it roll forward to hang in the air from his finger. As the black man in front of him ripped the pistol from his hand, he glanced to his side.

Hans Heinz finally looked sober.

DON ELLIOT had always been impressed by the native warriors of Somalia. They came from various tribes, with Afars and Issas predominating in the north, and the Kikuyu, Luo, Baluhya and Kamba more common in the south. But regardless of their tribal heritage, they were expert woodsmen to the man. Most could track a mosquito from Cape Town to Tunisia if called upon to do so, and the history of warfare between the tribes had instilled in the men a ferocity in combat that equaled nothing Elliot had ever seen.

Elliot admired the tribes immensely for these skills. But Africa had changed, and not all of the men had changed with it. Many still utilized a combat strategy more amenable to spear-and-bow warfare than to firearms.

Not that Elliot was complaining about it at the moment. The fact was, that archaic system was probably about all that was keeping him alive.

The first of Ham's men to charge through the cave entrance barreled in head down, bellowing like an angry water buffalo. Elliot squeezed the three-quarter-pound trigger on the Colt, and a .45-caliber Eldorado Starfire jacketed hollowpoint hit the center of the man's chest, blossoming to nearly twice its original size before lodging just in front of the spine.

The AK-47 that the man had gripped in both hands went flying as his muscles spasmed in death, and he fell to his knees, then sprawled forward.

As the customized .45 rose with the recoil, Elliot saw a second man abruptly halt in the mouth of the cave. Elliot started to fire again as the sights fell on the man's bare chest. He didn't need to. Another explosion sounded within the confines of the cave, and the second warrior fell on top of his comrade. Out of the corner of his eye, Elliot saw the muzzle of Friday's Argentine .45 bounce in the big man's hands.

A third man moving toward the cave entrance suddenly did an about-face. Both Elliot and Friday fired, narrowly missing as the figure disappeared to one side of the entrance.

Elliot holstered his gun and reached over his shoulder, grabbing his rifle and crawling toward the right side of the opening. Friday moved to the left. The former CIA man thought briefly of the rear opening in the cave.

Ham's men weren't likely to have found it yet. Even if they had, it was barely wide enough for a man to squeeze through, and there were heavy munitions boxes blocking the way. No one would be coming in that way without making enough noise to alert them.

Elliot's ears rang as the explosions echoing off the stone walls died down. Outside, the excited voices of the warlord's men sounded muffled and distant. He flipped the AK-47's selector to full-auto, curved it around the edge of the opening and pulled the trigger. A blind burst of fire sprayed the sparse vegetation surrounding the cave.

Peeking around the corner, Elliot saw the bushes rustle as the attackers dived for concealment. He pulled back to cover as return fire ricocheted against the outer wall of the cave.

"These men are faster trackers than we gave them credit for," Friday said from the other side of the entrance.

"How many were there altogether?" Elliot asked.

"I counted eight." He looked down at the two men on the floor between them. "There are at least six left."

Elliot nodded, his grin fading as the initial excitement of combat wore off and the seriousness of their situation set in. He waited, listening, as the return fire died down. Voices outside the cave started to mumble.

"You think they—" Elliot started to say.

Friday held up his hand, stopping him. The big Swahili pressed an ear into the opening, listening as the voices outside continued to argue in one of the native dialects. "Their leader just ordered another man to radio for reinforcements," he said. "But they forgot the walkie-talkie. Left it back in the car on the road."

Elliot chuckled lightly. That helped their position. Not a lot, but some. He edged close enough to the opening to get a partial view of the thinly treed desert outside.

More fire from outside suddenly pelted the sides of the cave, driving him back. Several of the rounds entered the opening, ricocheting throughout the room as Elliot and Friday hugged the floor. When the assault died down, the two men extended their AK-47s outside and fired long bursts into the trees.

After another exchange of fire from Ham's men, the fireworks quieted again. The voice of the leader returned.

Elliot moved back to his viewpoint, while Friday strained to hear what was said. When the voice halted, Friday whispered, "He's sent a man back to the car for the radio."

"It'll take him over an hour to get there," Elliot said.

Friday nodded. "Yes, but when he does, others will come."

Elliot sat silently, pondering the predicament. Friday was right. Ham would send more men. Men who would bring plenty of supplies with them to wait things out. He and Friday had food and water stashed in the cave for three, maybe four days, max.

And there was another possibility. Ham might even send one of his squads of stupid young khat-chewing dope heads. A few leaves of the amphetaminelike plant—one of the few stimulants sanctioned by Islam—and the troops would come after them like stoned kamikaze pilots.

Either way, it didn't look promising. The cave was only a temporary hideout, and simply wasn't equipped or fortified for a siege.

"We better do something, then," Elliot said. "If it comes down to fighting a hundred men instead of six—five, I guess, if you consider whoever goes for the radio—I'd rather take my chances with the five."

A rustling in the bushes twenty yards in front of the cave prompted a sudden burst of fire from both Elliot and Friday. They heard a scream, the bush rustled again, and a dark-skinned arm fell into sight.

More rounds battered the rock wall in front of them.

"Call it four," Friday said when the gunfire stopped. "But you're right. Even if we take out the rest of them here, we'll have more than we can handle when the reinforcements hit our trail. We've got to stop the guy before he reaches the radio."

"Any ideas?" Elliot asked.

Friday turned. "How about if I run out front?"

"Perfect," said Elliot. "Hey, bud, I'd do it myself, but I'm the wrong color." He glanced down to the arm bands on the dead men lying between them.

Friday followed his eyes, then nodded. He took the arm band from the sleeve of the nearest dead man, then rolled it up his own arm.

"After you take out their runner, circle back," Elliot said. "Give me the signal. We'll take these guys in a cross fire."

"All right," Friday said. He stood up and moved toward the back of the rocky chamber. "I doubt they've got anybody positioned to see me when I leave," he said. "But how about laying down a little diversionary fire just in case?"

Elliot studied the back of the man he had grown to love like a brother over the years. "Be careful, okay?"

Friday snorted. "The thought *had* occurred to me," he said. Friday threw the AK-47 sling over his shoulder. "Here's another fine mess you've gotten me into," he said, then turned toward the rear exit of the cave.

A moment later Elliot heard the munitions boxes slide across the rock floor. Leaning into the opening, he held the AK-47's trigger back against the guard.

THE MAN who reached out to take the Desert Eagle from Bolan was short, maybe five foot five, and if he weighed a hundred thirty pounds Bolan would have been surprised. Knocking him to his back a moment earlier had taken little more effort than swatting a fly.

But the Desert Eagle .44 Magnum, whose bore was now pointed up at Bolan's face, increased the little man's size tenfold.

Blood still dripped from the gash on his chin as the man stared at Bolan, his eyes filled with anger. Slowly, methodically he brought the Desert Eagle back behind his hip, then swung it forward with all the power of his body.

The barrel struck Bolan in the jaw. He staggered back, barely keeping his feet as his vision blurred. His eyes closed involuntarily as sharp daggers of pain shot through his skull. They opened again as he fought to maintain consciousness.

The little man stepped forward, patting him down and finding the Beretta 93-R in the shoulder rig. He ripped it from under his captive's arm and stepped back. "We are now even," he said. "But soon I will be ahead." Turning to a taller man holding a shotgun, he said, "Blanco, bring them both inside."

Bolan turned toward the man with the shotgun. Through hazy eyes he saw a tall, thin figure with negroid features. But the man's skin had lost its black pigment, leaving it a light chalky gray.

The man's rough hands reached out, jerking Bolan inside the apartment. Behind him he heard a quickly muted protest from Hans Heinz as the drunk was brought in behind him. More hands joined Blanco's on Bolan as he and Heinz were dragged through the living room into the kitchen. Two metal chairs scraped away from the dinette table and were placed back to back in the center of the room.

His brain still foggy, Bolan found himself being pushed unceremoniously into the chair facing the living room. A moment later he was being bound to the backrest with a coarse hemp rope.

As his vision began to clear, Bolan took the place in. His immediate surroundings consisted of a modern kitchen, complete with stove, refrigerator and microwave oven. Five men stood around him, their shotguns, rifles and subguns all aimed his way. Squeezing his eyes against the pain in his head, he forced himself to concentrate.

The dilapidated exterior of the building contradicted the well-equipped interior and provided the perfect disguise for a safehouse. Besides the modern appliances in the kitchen, he could see furniture in the living room. Good furniture. Not extravagant, but certainly livable.

His eyes returned to the kitchen. The door to a large pantry was open, and inside he could see shelves overflowing with canned food. The labels were faded. The cans and packages had been there a long time, maybe years.

Added to the rest of what he'd seen, the cans told Bolan what he wanted to know. This had been Don Elliot's fail-safe spot, his hideout should he ever need it. Here he could live in decent comfort for months without so much as ever venturing outside.

What had happened to the plan also became clear as Bolan's vision finally returned to normal. Ham's men had found the place, but Elliot and Friday had already left. Now it would be the warlord's men who ate the canned food while they searched the place for clues as to where the former CIA man and his friend had gone.

Blanco appeared in front of Bolan, turning his head to the side. "Ilaoa," he said. "Do you wish me to question this one?"

The short man stepped into Bolan's vision, shaking his head. He had quickly bandaged his chin with gauze and tape and now pulled on a pair of black leather gloves. "No," he said simply. "*I* will take this one. You will question the rummy." He turned toward Bolan as Blanco disappeared to the rear.

Bolan saw the Desert Eagle stuffed into Ilaoa's waistband on the right side. The Beretta rode opposite, also jammed into Ilaoa's belt. The small man raised his hand slowly, purposefully, then slapped Bolan across the face. "This can be easy," he said. "Or it can be difficult." He paused. "The choice is yours."

The slap hadn't been hard, but it had landed on the same spot where Ilaoa had struck Bolan earlier with the Desert Eagle, and now all of the pain returned to shoot through his head. Through gritted teeth, Bolan said, "If the choice is mine, let's keep it easy. It's been easy so far. My mother used to spank me harder than that."

Anger twisted the little man's face. He slapped Bolan three more times. "We know that your friend Elliot has another hideout. Somewhere in the mountains. Where is it?"

Bolan heard another slap directly behind him, followed by a low moan. He looked up at Ilaoa. "I don't know," he said, then braced himself for the blows he knew would follow.

They did. But this time Ilaoa curled the fingers inside his gloves into tight fists, driving punches over and over into Bolan's mouth, nose and jaws.

Bolan tasted the blood in his mouth as his lips split. He had no idea how long the beating would go on. But when it was over, and their captors realized he and Heinz had no information to give, they would be killed. It was that simple.

More punches stung him, snapping his head back and finally replacing the sharp pains in his skull with a dull ache. He fought to remain conscious, fully aware that his only chance of survival was to stay alert. Ham's men were human, and somewhere along the line, they would make a mistake. They would leave Bolan an opening, a chance for escape.

Bolan knew he had to stay cognizant enough to recognize and take advantage of that opening when it came.

Finally the fists stopped. "I will ask you once more," Ilaoa said. "Then, if you do not answer, my *questioning* will begin in earnest. Where is Elliot's mountain house?"

Bolan shook his head.

"So you choose that this be difficult?" Ilaoa said through gritted teeth.

"I haven't made any choices since I came through the front door," Bolan told him.

Ilaoa smiled, tugging the gloves tighter on his wrists. Then, methodically drawing back his arm as he had done earlier, he drove his fist into Bolan's stomach.

Bolan saw it coming. He tightened his abdominal muscles, and the little man's fist struck a wall of stone.

Ilaoa's wrist bent painfully, and he drew back his arm, cursing. Anger flooded his eyes as he drove his other fist into Bolan's chest. Bolan tightened instinctively again, but the little man's focus was on target this time. New pain filled his chest.

Bolan pushed painfully out with his stomach muscles, trying to reverse the vacuum that had been created in his lungs. He blew out, waited for the pain to subside, then looked back up at Ilaoa. "Tell me something," he said. "If we knew where Elliot was, why would we have come looking for him *here?*"

The expression on Ilaoa's face indicated that the little man hadn't yet had time to consider that obvious discrepancy. That realization, combined with the knowledge that his punch had not had the effect he'd desired, heightened the fury in his eyes.

With an sudden scream, Ilaoa bent forward, striking his prisoner over and over. Face-stomach-chest... face-stomach-chest. Finally exhausted, he stepped back and dropped his arms to his sides, then lashed out at Bolan's shins and knees, his movements wild and maddened flurries of frustration.

Bolan took the blows, hardening himself against the aches and stings that shot through his body. Behind him he could hear Blanco performing a similar beating on Hans Heinz.

Ilaoa didn't stop until he was out of breath. Then he stepped back to survey his work.

The sounds of bone striking flesh and the cries and moans to Bolan's rear suddenly stopped. Blanco's voice sounded in the silent room. "They are lying, Ilaoa."

Ilaoa disappeared behind Bolan. A moment later Ilaoa said, "No. The big one, perhaps. He is hard. But not the drunk. He would have told us all he knew long ago."

"What should I do?" Blanco asked.

"We will take them both to General Ham," Ilaoa said. "We will let him decide. Cut them loose."

Hazy again from the beating, Bolan felt the pressure as a knife blade wedged between the backrest and his flesh. A second later the rope snapped. Two of the men holding subguns let their weapons fall to the ends of their slings and reached forward, jerking him to his feet.

Bolan turned around and saw Hans Heinz's back. The ropes had been cut from his chair, as well.

"Stand up," Blanco ordered the German.

Heinz didn't move.

"Stand up, swine!" Blanco commanded. He leaned forward and slapped Heinz across the face.

Hans Heinz twisted onto his side as he fell to the floor from the blow. Bolan saw the man's cuts and bruises and realized his own face must look similar. But there was one major difference between Bolan's face and Heinz's as the German hit the floor.

Hans Heinz's wide-open eyes stared vacantly into space, unblinking.

Ilaoa squatted next to the man, his fingers pressing against the carotid artery in Heinz's neck. "Bah!" he said when he got no pulse. He stood up, brought his leg back and kicked the German's body in the ribs. Then, turning to Blanco, he said, "Dispose of this."

Bolan stood unsteadily as the two men who had pulled him to his feet let his arms drop and moved to the body on the floor. He watched them hoist Hans Heinz's body unceremoniously into the air, then carry him into the living room.

The barrel of a shotgun jabbed Bolan in the ribs. "Move," he heard Ilaoa command, and turned to see the little man holding the scattergun. He let himself be pushed into the living room as Blanco opened the front door to the hall.

"Wait," Ilaoa said, coming around to Bolan's front. "Bind his hands first."

Bolan felt a sudden rush of adrenaline fill his veins. This was not the ideal chance for escape, but it might well be the only one he got. Only Ilaoa and Blanco stood between him and the open door, and even in his weakened condition, Bolan knew he could take them both. He could be past them and halfway down the hall before anyone knew what had happened.

But what of the five other men bearing the shotguns and other weapons behind him? They would come out of their shock and catch up to him in the hallway, where they would cut him down with a barrage of bullets and buckshot.

Unless he had a shield.

Knowing he would get no better chance, Bolan made the decision without further debate.

As he felt the man behind him begin to loop another rope around his wrists, Bolan slipped his hands back through the rough hemp and shot a right cross out from his body. The knuckles of his big fist struck Ilaoa's jaw solidly, and the man's eyes closed.

Before Ilaoa could slump forward, the Executioner had scooped him over his shoulder and started toward the door.

Blanco reacted quicker than Bolan would have expected. Stepping in front of the door, he fumbled to raise the rifle in his hands.

Bolan ducked as he sprinted forward. Ilaoa's back struck Blanco in the face, knocking the black albino to the side. Blanco rebounded off the frame as Bolan raced on through, bounced off Bolan's side, then fell back against the door frame.

Bolan pivoted just outside the doorway, turning toward the stairs. In another few seconds Blanco and the other men would rush after them. They would not want to take the chance of hitting their leader, and would avoid shooting above Bolan's waist.

But his lower extremities were wide open. Were these men good enough marksmen to risk a leg shot? Were they quick-minded enough to even think of it?

Bolan reached up, ripping the Beretta 93-R from the waistband of the man over his shoulder as he sprinted toward the stairs.

His questions were answered as the hallway suddenly exploded with shotgun and rifle rounds, and the frayed carpet around his feet split under the onslaught.

CHAPTER THREE

Benjamin Barkari shoved the heavy munitions cases away from the opening in the rock and peered through the dried vegetation. It had been years since he and Elliot had equipped the cave, and the plants they had brought in to conceal the rear exit had long ago died from lack of water. But even in death, they still did their job, and the Swahili saw no indications that Ham's men had located the narrow hole.

Barkari felt the thrill in his chest as the adrenaline pumped through his body. After nine tedious years canning fish, he was about to face danger again. It was what he had been trained for, perhaps what he'd been born for.

The Swahili's keen eyes scanned the desert right to left as his mind flew backward in time. During his forty-four years of life, he had been a soldier in the Kenyan army, a free-lance mercenary in Africa and South America and finally a contract agent for the CIA and DEA. These jobs had brought with them the obvious dangers.

Barkari grinned. Over the years he had been shot at with bullets, arrows, and even once with a bazooka. None of the missiles had found their mark. Other men had come after him with knives, swords and spears, but none of the edged weapons had been any more successful than the guns. True, he had suffered one glancing blow from a baseball bat in a cantina in Nogales, Mexico, but he'd absorbed the brunt of the force with the fleshy part of one forearm, then wrapped his other around the throat of his attacker and crushed the life out of him.

Barkari slung his AK-47 over his back. Parting the dried vines, he crouched, preparing to exit the cave. As soon as he heard Elliot open up with diversionary fire, he dived from the opening to the concealment of a bush ten yards away.

The Swahili crouched behind the outgrowth, searching the sparse cover of the desert for any sign of Ham's men. As his eyes moved from bush to bush, the memory of the Mexican incident came back. He had killed the man and been promptly arrested by *federales*. To his horror, he soon learned that the man had been the son of a prominent Mexican politician. And no amount of baksheesh was going to get him off the hook.

Elliot had flown to Mexico from Cairo. When he too became convinced that bribery stood no chance, he had recruited a group of down-and-out mercenaries and broken Barkari out of the run-down prison where he awaited trial. Two of the mercs had died in the firefight that ensued, and Elliot himself had taken a bullet in the leg for him.

That was what Benjamin Barkari called a friend.

Satisfied that he had not been seen, the big Swahili turned and crawled farther away from the cave. He kept to his belly until he reached a shallow ravine that circled the area, then rose to his feet and began circumnavigating the cave.

As soon as instinct told him he had passed the area where Ham's men waited, Barkari rose. Far behind him he saw the rocks of the cave. He would not be seen across the desert if he stayed low, and he left the shallow canyon, jogging in the general direction of the road.

Barkari breathed easily as his eyes scanned for signs of the man sent back for the radio. He was an experienced tracker and knew that the desert held many illusions, some natural, others man-made. The apparitions of nature were mostly visual, like imaginary oases and similar mirages. Those of mankind's invention were mental. They included such foolish notions as the desert being a lifeless, useless place that supported only small amounts of life—all of it malevolent. True, there were needle-thorned cactus, scorpions and insects that killed or made life so painful that death became wishful thinking. But the desert was vast, and such creatures were few and far between.

Sweat broke on the big Swahili's face as he ran on. He tried to clear his mind, letting his unconscious take over to search the ground for the trail. But the woman—the damned *whore*—kept popping into his mind, and he felt the depression sink into his chest like a hundred-pound rucksack.

Do not think of her, Benjamin Barkari ordered himself. She is gone, and you are better off without her. He ran on, trying to make himself believe the lie.

Parallel rows of closely placed commas appeared in the sand where a centipede had crossed his path. A furry scampering under his running feet Barkari chalked up to a desert mouse—too small to be a rat. The woman crossed his mind again. He drove her away. But the beautiful black vision was a persistent visitor, and did not leave until he saw the shoe print in the sand.

Barkari stopped and knelt. Angling slightly to the north of the path he himself had been pursuing was the imprint of an athletic shoe. He examined the track as he caught his breath. A moment later he was up and running again.

Here and there as he ran, the Swahili saw more prints. Interspaced between them, he passed clumps of dry grass mashed down by the same shoes. Whoever the man ahead might be, he had a slight limp that favored his right leg. Depending on how serious the injury or deformation was, it would slow him down.

Barkari slowed slightly himself. He was entering an area of the desert he remembered from the race away from the highway. Ahead he knew he would encounter more jagged rock formations, gaping canyons in the earth and large sand deposits. They would afford splendid ambush sights if the man ahead realized he was being pursued, and it would not pay to tip him off too soon.

Ahead the Swahili saw a star-shaped outcropping of rocks. Beyond the formation would be a series of stair-step uplands that he and Elliot had mounted as they fled into the desert. In reverse now, the steps would lead back down to the road where both the Mercedes and the Land Cruisers that had pursued it were parked.

Barkari took a deep breath and increased his speed. He had to pace himself carefully, walking the fine line between a gait that would leave him too shaky to shoot and one that brought him to the road too late to stop the radio transmission. The man ahead had made better time than Barkari would have guessed, and would be close to the radio by the time the Swahili found him.

Benjamin Barkari broke into a sprint and pulled his rifle from his back as he passed the rock formation. Sedentary rock, battered and pitted by countless centuries of erosion, gave way beneath his feet as he dropped down to the series of natural steps beyond the rock outcropping.

Barkari dropped two more levels, and suddenly the road appeared ahead. A hundred yards farther down, he saw a running man. Another hundred yards beyond that, at the bottom of the steps, the Land Cruisers and Mercedes were still parked at the side of the road.

Barkari ran on, careful not to stumble each time he dropped to the next level of the giant staircase. His chest heaved for air now, and he wondered briefly how he would ever hold the rifle steady enough to shoot.

By the time Ham's man reached the road, the gap between him and Barkari had narrowed to seventy-five yards. Barkari kept running as he saw his prey reach into his pocket and hurry toward one of the vehicles.

The Swahili stopped abruptly. There was no way he could get into range in time to take the man out, certainly not with the shaky arms and sputtering breath the run had produced. He'd be lucky to hit a target the size of the Land Cruiser....

Okay, if he'd be lucky to hit the Land Cruiser, then that's just the kind of luck he would call upon now.

Barkari took a deep breath as he brought the assault rifle up to his shoulder and flipped the selector to full auto. Sixty yards, give or take.

As the man ahead shoved the key into the door, Barkari held the trigger back.

Round after round peppered the vehicle, driving the man away from the door. The thirty bullets in the weapon emptied, and the bolt locked open.

The man ahead heard the silence and dived back to the door. As Barkari's practiced hands dropped the magazine and replaced it with thirty more 7.62 mm rounds, his eyes saw the figure wrench open the door and lunge into the front seat. The Swahili held the trigger back again.

If he counted right, it was the fourteenth round of the second magazine that was the magic bullet.

Barkari let the rifle fall from his aching shoulder as the gas tank, then the entire Land Cruiser, went up in flames. He watched passively as the doors blew open with the explosion and a fiery figure leaped screaming from the vehicle. The flaming man ran toward the Swahili, looking more like something out of a comic book than a human being.

Benjamin Barkari let the man get within thirty yards, then mercifully emptied the rest of the magazine into the flames that enveloped him.

BULLETS AND LEAD SHOT sang off the steel of the top step as Bolan dashed down the stairs. Then the low-aimed fire of Ilaoa's men stopped abruptly as they temporarily lost the angle of fire at his legs. The only targetable area endangered their leader's unconscious body draped over Bolan's back.

The steel stairs sang softer now as Bolan's boots hit each rung on the way down. When he reached the ground floor of the apartment house, he would have to sprint for the door. And with Ilaoa bogging him down, it would be a very *slow* sprint.

The other six gunners would be close behind, and the angle of trajectory would change again when they reached the first floor. Clear shots at Bolan's lower half would again be possible.

Ham's henchmen had missed Bolan's legs a moment earlier through a combination of luck and astonishment. With the odds stacked so high against him, they had not expected him to attempt escape. But Bolan knew he might not be that lucky the second time around.

Once he reached the first floor, Bolan saw that the ten-foot stretch to the exit was a death trap. He had to change the rules of the game, fast.

As he had done so many times, the Executioner made the life-and-death decision in an instant. Turning, he raised the Beretta, which he still carried in his right hand.

Blanco's face appeared at the top of the steps. With no time for the sights, Bolan aimed the 93-R upward and snapped a shot up the steps.

The round took the black albino square between the eyes.

As Bolan turned toward the exit, he caught a glimpse of the rainstorm of red that blew up toward the second-floor ceiling. Above him he heard the pursuing footsteps stop and excited voices scream in Cushitic. Then the remaining five men continued down the metal stairs.

Through the open doorway, Bolan saw the Land Cruiser parked in the lot outside. It was less than twenty yards away, but he knew instinctively he could never reach the vehicle, get it started and get out of the line of fire in time.

Killing Blanco had slowed the men down—but not by much.

Reaching the door, Bolan snatched the Desert Eagle from Ilaoa's waistband and let the man slip from his shoulder. The unconscious form fell to the side of the doorway. Bolan sprinted five yards on through the opening for the benefit of the eyes behind him, then cut suddenly to his right as if to make a break for it away from the building. As soon as he was out of view through the doorway, he back-tracked to the entrance.

Pressing his back against the wall next to the door, the Desert Eagle in his right hand and the Beretta in his left, he took a deep breath as he heard footsteps pound down the hall toward him.

Bolan had done his best to make it look as if he was dropping his shield and making a run for it. If things went well, his pursuers would dash past him into the open before they realized he was actually still beside the door.

If things didn't go well...

Bolan's teeth ground together. He had no inclination to consider what would happen if the men with the shotguns and assault rifles approached the doorway cautiously.

The first man through the door carried a Mossberg 500 12-gauge pump gun. He followed Bolan's earlier path, cutting sharply to his right a few yards outside the building.

The second gunner, wielding one of the favorite AK-47s, was less than a step behind the leader.

The third gunner through the door toted another of the Soviet assault rifles. Overweight and slower, he was huffing and puffing loudly.

The fourth man followed with another 12-gauge. Bolan saw his eyes register a passing glimpse of the danger at his side as he passed into the open.

One man remained in the hallway, probably having stopped to check on Ilaoa. But the last man had seen Bolan.

It was time to act.

The Beretta 93-R spit a muffled 3-round burst into the nearest man's chest as he turned and opened his mouth to warn his partners. The shotgun slid from his hands as he was thrown back inside the door.

Although sound suppressed, the Beretta wasn't silent by any means. The three men in the front yard turned toward the noise.

Bolan turned the Beretta toward the overweight man. Another trio of 9 mm hollowpoints sliced through his fat belly as the 93-R danced in the Executioner's hand. In Bolan's other hand, the Desert Eagle roared, and the second gunner took a speeding Magnum round in the lungs, blood spurting from his mouth as he hit the ground.

Bolan swung both weapons toward the first man who had exited the hallway as the gunner got off a blast of 12-gauge buckshot. In his excitement the warlord's man sent the lead shot sailing high over Bolan's head, and as he pumped the slide again, Bolan's Beretta dispatched subsonic hollowpoints that found their mark in the man's throat and face.

Bolan dropped to a knee, edging toward the doorway again, low. The fifth man still lurked inside, and by now Ilaoa had probably regained consciousness, as well. Peeking around the corner, Bolan jerked back as a full-auto burst of rifle fire struck the door frame above his head.

Keeping the Desert Eagle trained on the door, he dropped the partially spent magazine from the Beretta. He shoved the weapon into his belt and pulled a fresh double stack from the carrier still on his belt. The full load of 9 mm slugs went up the butt of the 93-R, snapping into place with a satisfying click. Redrawing the weapon from his waistband, he waited.

Ilaoa wanted him. So let Ilaoa come to *him*.

The Executioner crouched against the wall, his eyes unblinking. He heard whispering voices on the other side of the door, and sent five .44 Magnum messengers drilling through the rotten wood toward the sound.

Silence followed.

Bolan continued to wait. Had his blind rounds found their mark? Maybe. Maybe not.

Five minutes later nothing had changed. An eerie silence still lingered on the other side of the doorway.

Bolan frowned. Ilaoa hadn't struck him as a patient man, and he couldn't picture the warlord's lieutenant having the discipline that this kind of stressful interval required.

Finally he moved away from the door. If he showed his head around the corner again, and Ilaoa was still alive, a bullet would be waiting. Backing out into the yard, Bolan moved a good twenty yards from the door before he crept into sight of the doorway.

The legs of a prostate man in khaki slacks were visible through the opening. But it wasn't Ilaoa.

Bolan moved forward cautiously, both guns at the ready. When he finally reached the opening, he scanned the hallway left to right. Empty. Dropping his eyes to the man on the floor, he saw that two of the blind .44s he had fired through the wall had found their mark.

But Ilaoa was nowhere to be found.

Bolan's eyes traveled down the hall. At the other end of the building, the rear door to the crumbling apartment house stood open. The hot African wind whistled slightly as it blew through the opening.

THEY'D COME for him soon. They had no other choice.

Don Elliot checked the chamber of the AK-47 for perhaps the twentieth time as he waited inside the cave. The man who had been sent to radio General Ham for reinforcements had had plenty of time to return. He hadn't. That meant Friday had gotten him, and that in turn meant that the big Swahili was now either on his way back or already hidden somewhere behind Ham's men in the desert.

Through the mouth of the cave, Elliot could see the sun lowering on the horizon. If they hadn't realized it already, it would soon become as apparent to Ham's men as it was to him that their man wasn't coming back. They'd have to attack on their own. If they had any brains at all, they'd probably wait until dark.

Probably. That was the operative word, and Elliot kept his rifle trained on the opening. The men General Ham and the other warlords hired came from all walks of Somalian life. Some had served in various African armies, but others were simply ruthless criminals recruited for that very ruthlessness. They thought differently than well-disciplined soldiers, and they were often emotional in their strategy. That emotionalism made them unpredictable, and made human killing machines that could be every bit as dangerous as the most well-trained Navy SEAL, Green Beret or Soviet Spetsnaz trooper.

Elliot tightened his grip on the rifle. He had to be ready for *anything,* whether it seemed reasonable by military standards or not. He would be just as dead from a daytime attack that seemed illogical as one lifted directly from Sun Tzu's *Art of War.*

The former CIA man watched as the sun fell below the horizon. One by one the sounds of the desert night broke the stillness of the Somalian desert. Elliot listened to their beauty.

In the distance an owl hooted its lonely lament. Elliot chuckled. He knew that owl, knew him well. A damned big owl, it stood well over six feet tall, weighed a good two hundred thirty pounds and about the only thing it *couldn't* do was fly.

The owl hooted again, and Elliot's eyes narrowed as he stared at the mouth of the cave. The first call had meant Friday was in place. But the second could only mean he'd seen something that caused him to risk another warning signal.

Elliot moved farther against the wall, out of the direct line of sight of anyone who burst through the opening. He waited silently, listening, straining to hear footsteps, breathing, anything that might give him a second's advantage over the men he knew were about to storm the cave.

Instead, he heard a voice. Strong and clear and speaking in English, it was nevertheless tinged with the accent of the northern Afar tribe that dwelt in Ham's province. "Mr. Elliot!"

Elliot didn't answer.

A moment later the same voice said, "Mr. Elliot! Mr. Barkari! We must speak!"

Again Elliot remained silent.

"Mr. Elliot and Mr. Barkari," the voice said again. "I know you can hear me. This problem we find ourselves in can be solved without bloodshed!"

Elliot analyzed the new development. The fact that Ham's men were trying to coax him out into the opening meant they had lost confidence in their ability to take the cave. And they still thought Friday was inside with him. That was good. *Damned* good.

But it didn't mean they'd just give up and go home. Elliot had heard stories about what happened to anyone who failed General Fajir Ham, and the punishment the warlord dealt out made death look like the easy way out.

No, they would come. And soon.

Elliot listened for footsteps. Nothing. Voices whispered again. As he waited, he glanced to the rear of the cave, and a thought suddenly struck him.

Turning back to the mouth of the cave, he looked up at the sky. A quarter moon. Not too bright yet not too dark.

It just might work.

Rising swiftly to his feet, Elliot moved around the corner to the small cavern he and Friday had used as a storage area. The heavy munitions cases the Swahili had moved still partially blocked the rear exit. Elliot squeezed past them and out of the cave.

Turning back to the rocky outcropping, he slung his rifle over his shoulder and began hoisting himself up the outer wall of the rock formation.

He could never have pulled it off while the sun was still up. But if he moved slowly, making sure not to draw attention to the top of the rocks, the surface just might be ragged enough to afford adequate cover in the semidarkness.

Elliot dropped to his belly, worming up and over the irregular formation. Out of sight to the front, he could still hear the whispering voices, and he silently thanked God that they had no professional leadership. That lack of direction—added to the confusion that resulted from all the bickering between the men—was all that allowed him to pull off a grandstand stunt like this, perhaps all that had kept him alive so far.

Five minutes later Elliot pulled himself up behind a large boulder near the front of the hill. Looking down now, he could see the path the attackers would have to take to reach the cave. From this vantage point, he could even see two of them behind some wild scrub. The two heads were indistinct in the darkness, but they appeared to be the ones who were doing all the arguing.

Elliot pulled the rifle slowly over his shoulder and waited. He could take out these two men before they knew what happened. But the final two were invisible, somewhere in the scattered underbrush surrounding the cave. Friday might get them, but he might not, too. And if he didn't, they would be in for another round of waiting that they simply couldn't afford. Sooner or later, radio or no radio, Ham would wonder what had happened to his men and send more to find out.

Suddenly one of the two men below raised his head. "Elliot!" he called out again.

Unable to answer now even if he'd wanted to, Don Elliot waited.

The man rose to a standing position, waving the man next to him to do the same. They crept slowly forward, keeping low and taking advantage of the rare cover and concealment that offered itself along the way.

Elliot fought the temptation to fire as they drew nearer. Instead, his eyes scanned the dark night behind them in search of the remaining two gunmen.

He saw nothing.

When the two men got within ten yards of the cave, they parted, going right and left. On another hand signal from the leader, they broke into a sprint, stopping on each side of the opening that led inside.

Not twenty feet above them, Elliot watched it all, again fighting the urge to take the easy shots and rid himself of at least two of the would-be killers. No, he reminded himself again. He couldn't afford to alert the other two men still hidden behind them.

A moment later two more heads appeared from behind the underbrush. They followed a similar route, splitting at the same spot as the other two and then racing to the sides of the opening.

Elliot started to fire, but by the time he had the sights in place the four men had disappeared beneath a narrow rim of rock that ran along the top of the opening. He could see the occasional foot or arm as they prepared to storm the cave, but nothing vital.

A flicker of movement out in the desert drew Elliot's attention, and he saw a dark shadow creep forward. The shadow was twenty yards from the cave when Elliot saw it duck behind a thicket of dried brushes.

The former CIA man smiled grimly. The owl had returned to its nest, and Elliot felt like hooting himself.

Below, Elliot heard one of Ham's men whispering in Cushitic. "One, two, three..." The arms and legs he'd seen disappeared now, and the next sound he heard were the explosions of full-auto weapons and their echoes in the cave below.

Elliot jumped to his feet and leaped from the ledge as Friday sprinted forward. The former CIA man's boots hit the ground and he landed in a semicrouch next to the opening.

Inside, the steady stream of autofire continued.

Friday arrived next to him a second later. He nodded toward the entrance to the cave. They turned and stepped silently into the cave just as the men inside realized the cavern was deserted and let up on their triggers. All four started to turn back toward the entrance.

But before they could do so, those four men in General Fajir Ham's employment lay dead on the cool rocky floor.

HOT DRAFTS of the late-afternoon wind blew through the open windows of the Land Cruiser as Bolan guided the vehicle north over the pitted African road. The smell of baked asphalt filled his nostrils as the hot steering wheel bit into his callused hands.

Bolan watched the sides of the road as he drove, seeing occasional herds of gaunt cattle and emaciated sheep doing their best to scratch sustenance from the thin grass. The animals' chances of survival, he knew, were even less than those of the humans who inhabited this war-torn, impoverished nation.

Bolan drove on. The pain in his head and chest had subsided in the hours since the beating he had taken at the hands of Ilaoa, and he silently gave thanks that Ham's little lieutenant had been no stronger than he

was. Bolan knew he would be sore for a few days, and
the rearview mirror told him his face looked as if he'd
just spent fifteen rounds with George Foreman. But
the bruises and cuts would heal, and no permanent
damage had been done.

The all-terrain vehicle rolled precariously across the
rotting wooden planks that spanned a long-dry creek
bed. The cratered earth below the bridge looked like
the pebbled surface of a worn-out basketball. A
weathered road sign on the right side of the road announced the village of Johar, and Bolan slowed as he
passed through the miserable cluster of huts and clay
buildings.

Old men with open sores sat along the narrow path,
their eyes void of hope. Several barefoot women in
ragged robes had gathered around a community well.
Their children, ribs exposed from malnutrition, bellies bloated with air, moved listlessly about the area.

Bolan shook his head. Even with the U.S. forces at
work, food, medical supplies and other goods from
the United Nations rarely reached the villages. The
warlords saw to that, and as a small boy stared into the
passing Toyota, his eyes as lifeless as those of the old
men, Bolan renewed his vow to see that changed.

The Land Cruiser picked up speed again as he left
the village. From the bits and pieces of conversation
he had heard from Ilaoa and his men, he knew that
they suspected Elliot and Barkari of having some
mountain hideout in Somalia's north. The town of
Erigavo had been mentioned, and with no better leads
to follow, he'd headed that way.

Bolan's eyebrows dropped low in concentration as
he drove. It sounded as if Elliot and Barkari had left

the Mogadishu apartment a half step ahead of the men who had come for them. If so, they would have taken any route that afforded escape. But sooner or later, assuming they were indeed headed for the Erigavo area, they would come back to this road leading north.

He passed a small oasis of fan palms that stood amid a forest of bristling cacti. The ground flattened ahead, and in the distance, just over a slight rise, he saw thin lines of rising smoke. A moment later he topped a rise and saw smoke drifting up into the air just above the next hill.

Bolan leaned harder on the accelerator, and as he reached the crest, he saw a Land Cruiser similar to the one he was driving parked on the side of the road. Thirty yards ahead of it stood the smoldering remains of what looked like another of the black vehicles, and just beyond that stood a brown Mercedes.

The Executioner drove past the first Land Cruiser and stopped next to the wreck. The gas tank had exploded, and bits and pieces of the vehicle scattered the ground. Pulling off the road onto the narrow shoulder, he left his own vehicle running and got out.

Smoke filled Bolan's nostrils as he neared the wreckage, taking in what had happened as he walked. Bullet holes were visible in what remained of the Toyota, and on what remained of the back seat he saw the burned and blackened stock of an AK-47.

His eyes moved across the road to where a trail of burned grass led down a steep slope. As he followed the trail, the smoke took on another stench—an odor that had filled his nose too many times in the past to go unrecognized now.

Burning flesh. Human flesh.

Bolan came to a halt at the edge of the slope and looked down to see a scorched corpse in the ravine. It was burned beyond recognition, but a small wisp of blue on the body's left biceps had escaped the fire.

A Ham arm band.

Bolan let out a breath. At least it wasn't Elliot or Barkari. He moved on down the slope, saw splattered blood and what looked like a piece of intestine a few yards from the body.

The man had been shot after he'd caught on fire. Someone, probably the same man who had drilled the Land Cruiser with autofire until it exploded, had performed a mercy killing.

Bolan hurried back to his own vehicle. Sliding behind the wheel, he drove quickly to the Mercedes. Someone had demolished the Land Cruiser with a barrage of well-aimed rifle fire. Had it been Elliot and Barkari? Probably. Ham's men could have caught up with them here, on the road.

But if that was the case, where were the rest of the warlord's troops? Bolan could see no other bodies with or without the blue arm band.

He pulled to a halt behind the Mercedes. A moment later he was sitting in the passenger's seat digging through the glove compartment. Finding both a title and insurance form, he studied them.

Both bore the name of the East African Fish Canning Company.

Bolan walked back to the rear of his truck and pulled out his backpack and the AK-47 he had seized along the beach.

He didn't know the details of what had happened here. But of one thing he was certain.

Somewhere beyond the jagged stair-step rock formations he was now climbing, he would find more of General Ham's men.

And with them he suspected he would find Don Elliot and Benjamin Barkari.

CHAPTER FOUR

Night fell across the desert, casting an eerie glow over the cacti and rock formations on the dry ground. Bolan followed the trail of the man he guessed had blasted the Land Cruiser. He used his flashlight sparingly, fully aware that it pointed him out like an accusing finger to anyone who might be watching. But with the dim moon overhead, it was either that or lose the trail and wait until morning.

The AK-47 slung over his shoulder in the assault position, he marched slowly along. He had encountered several sets of tracks leading away from the roadway, and two sets—a man wearing lug-soled boots, another with the ripple-print soles of athletic shoes—had doubled back. The lug soles had made a third trail leading back from the road, and Bolan had to assume the feet wearing them belonged to the man who had shot up the Land Cruiser.

As Bolan moved on through the night, what had happened became a little clearer with every new bit of evidence he uncovered. Elliot and Barkari had to have had a lead on the Land Cruisers since, with the exception of the charred remains in the ravine, there were no signs of combat along the road. That meant the Mercedes had stopped here for other reasons. Probably engine trouble—not an uncommon occurrence in the hot African climate.

But Ham's Land Cruisers had been close enough behind that the men inside had given chase on foot across the desert, and unless he missed his guess, they had caught up with Elliot and Barkari somewhere up ahead. For some reason, one of Ham's men had returned to the road. Why? For a forgotten weapon?

Whatever that mission, it had been important that Elliot and Barkari see that it failed. One of them— heavy, judging by the depth of the tracks the lug-soled boots were making—had trailed the warlord's man back to the road, destroyed the Land Cruiser and then shot the man as he burned.

The sound of automatic rifles in the distance broke through the quiet desert night, and Bolan stopped in his tracks. Gunfire was hardly unusual in Somalia, but these rounds came from the direction in which he was heading.

The gunfire died down as quickly as it had begun. After a few seconds there was a second volley.

As Bolan broke into a jog, the distant explosions stopped once more.

Bolan skirted several large rock formations, scanning their cracks and crevices for signs of ambush. The speed at which he ran was just short of reckless under the circumstances, but he sensed somehow that whatever had taken place ahead was already over.

Which meant that Elliot and Barkari had either killed the remainder of Ham's gunmen or been killed themselves. If they were dead, he had lost his sole access to the warlords. But even if they had been victorious, they would hurry out of the area and be just as lost to him as if they'd been killed.

The sooner he reached the site of the gunfire, the more likely he was to find them.

Bolan spied a body propped against a tree in a sitting position. His head nearly severed from his body with a machete, the man had been dead long enough that his body had bled dry. Caked blood covered his white T-shirt and the blue arm band on his upper arm.

Another body appeared behind a thicket of bushes some twenty yards away, the gaping exit holes of high-powered rifle bullets visible in his back.

Dropping to one knee, Bolan rolled the man over, noting another blue arm band with the white star. The gunner had been dead several hours, too, and the bullets that had pierced his heart had allowed the blood from his body to flow into a dull black pool that surrounded his corpse.

Bolan stayed on one knee, his eyes searching the night. Two other bodies lay nearby in the bushes. All of them had been looking up toward a nearby hill when they'd died.

Rising to a crouch, the Executioner flipped the AK-47's selector to full auto as he cautiously moved on. As he drew closer to the hill, the dark entrance of a cave appeared.

His gut instincts told him only the souls of the recently departed now inhabited the cave. He approached cautiously anyway, staying low as he neared the dark, gaping entrance. He dropped the rifle to the end of its sling and drew the quiet Beretta as he sprinted the rest of the way.

A weird feeling that someone was watching caused the hair on the back of his neck to stand as he reached the entrance. Bolan pulled the Mini Maglite flashlight from his pocket, twisted it to activate the beam but held it tight against his palm. For a moment his skin glowed an eerie red in the desert night, then he squatted, set the flashlight on the ground with the beam aiming inside the cave and rolled it out into the opening.

He stepped back to cover.

The only sound was the hard aluminum flashlight rolling across the mouth of the cave.

Bolan moved cautiously into the opening, found the flashlight and aimed the beam into the cave. Six bodies were scattered on the floor, all but one wearing the now-familiar blue arm bands. Kneeling next to the man without the band, Bolan studied the body. Like the dead men outside, this man had died hours earlier.

Benjamin Barkari? Possibly. But Bolan didn't think so. He had the feeling Barkari had pursued Ham's man back to the Land Cruisers and put an end to the man's mission.

Bolan rose, shining the light down on the other dead men. All had taken high-caliber rifle rounds in the back at close range. And *these* men had died in the past few minutes—undoubtedly victims of the weapons fire he had heard.

Bolan looked up, shining the light around the cave and seeing the recent chips in the rocks where the heavy rounds had made their marks. He twisted the Mini Maglite until the wide beam allowed him to see the entire cavern. A dark area farther on suggested another cavity hidden from casual sight.

Following the light, Bolan turned the corner and entered a smaller room. Green metal ammunition boxes and wooden storage crates were stacked haphazardly along the walls, some of them open as if they'd just been rummaged through.

Storage. Elliot and Barkari hadn't carried these heavy boxes as they made their mad dash from the road. Obviously they had set this place up as a temporary hideout and restocking site sometime in the past.

Bolan noticed the open crates and boxes on the floor. After killing Ham's men, Elliot and Barkari had hurriedly replenished their supplies, then taken off. They couldn't have much lead on him, and if he picked up their trail now, he might catch them by morning.

And go after them, he would. Just as soon as he'd replenished his own dwindling ammo supplies.

Bolan quickly searched through the boxes, finding extra 7.62 mm rifle rounds and several more spare magazines that appeared to be serviceable. He hadn't expected to come across any .44 Magnum ammo but breathed a silent sigh of relief when he found the lone box of 9 mm full metal jackets. Not what he'd have wished, since 9 mm full-metal-jacket slugs drilled through their target too fast and did too little damage on the way. But under the circumstances, he could hardly protest.

Bolan pulled the partially spent Beretta magazines from under his arm and inspected them. Six rounds of the 147-grain subsonics remained in one of the boxes, four in the other. Stripping the rounds, he dropped five hardballs into the bottom of one mag and topped it off with the hollowpoints. The other magazines he loaded with the overpenetrative full-metal-jacket rounds.

Bolan moved back to the front of the cave, then stepped out into the night. Elliot and Barkari had proved to be able warriors so far, and they'd be hiding their trail as they went. Seeing through their cover wouldn't be easy in the darkness, and the sooner he got started, the sooner he'd—

Bolan stopped in his tracks as the metallic click of a rifle bolt chambering the first round sounded in the still desert night. The sound had come from the bushes directly in front of him, and it was followed by an identical sound to his left.

More rifle bolts slammed home. Men in camouflage fatigues, their rifles aimed at him, began stepping out of the darkness all around.

Bolan's eyes moved clockwise. At least thirty men had surrounded him.

Then a voice to his rear said, "Keep your hands in plain sight and turn around."

Bolan turned. Five men were aiming rifles at him on top of the hill, just above the cave entrance.

TWO HUNDRED YARDS from the cave, his back flattened against the rocks, Don Elliot pressed the infrared binoculars against his eyebrows and watched the dark form move from bush to bush outside the cave. The lone man carried a rifle in assault position but slung it over his back as he hurried to one side of the entrance and stopped.

Elliot handed the binoculars to Friday and rubbed his eyes. He gave Barkari a moment to focus, then said, "Any idea who it is?"

"No. But he's a *big* son of a bitch." He let the binoculars fall from his face. "And he knows what he's doing. He rolled a flashlight across the entrance to draw out any fire before he went in."

Elliot felt relieved that they were at least temporarily safe. "But who is he—one of Ham's men?"

"Perhaps," said Friday. "Ham has employed a few white mercenaries in the past. But it makes no difference who he is. What *does* make a difference is that we get going."

"Agreed," Elliot said. He raised the binoculars for a final glance and caught a glimpse of movement to the left of the cave. He turned the lenses and saw perhaps three dozen men in camouflage fatigues moving in to surround the hill. More cammie-clad men climbed the rear of the cave, taking advantage of the same hand- and footholds Elliot had used earlier in the night.

Friday could see what was happening even without binoculars. "Well, whoever he is, he won't be lonely."

"No, and chances are good he won't be *alive* much longer, either," Elliot said. He opened the leather binocular case on his belt and shoved the glasses inside. "Let's go, Friday," he said. "We'll learn to live with the fact that we never knew who he was."

BOLAN SQUINTED in the darkness, trying to focus on the man-shaped configurations on top of the cave. He remained frozen, his hands away from his body. He estimated that over thirty rifles were aimed his way, which meant this was no time to disobey the orders that had just been given him. AK-47s fired the 7.62 mm Russian rounds and they made a big hole.

One of the men on top of the rocks shifted slightly, and Bolan saw the silhouette of his rifle. He frowned. Instead of the curved Kalashnikov banana clip he'd expected, he saw the straighter box magazine of an M-16A-2.

At the same time he recalled that the man who had spoken from the top of the cave had done so with a deep Southern accent.

Bolan relaxed. Americans.

Footsteps behind him indicated that the men to his rear were closing in. A moment later the AK-47 sling was ripped from his shoulder. A rifle barrel poked into his spine as several sets of hands patted him down, then a man moved in front of him to pull the Beretta and Desert Eagle from under his jacket.

Light brown hair stuck out from under the man's Kevlar helmet as he looked down at the big .44 Magnum. "Holy Mother of Jesus, Sarge." he said. "This guy brought his own field artillery with him."

The men on top of the rocks began descending. The man who had spoken stepped up, and Bolan saw the U.S. Marine sergeant's stripes on his sleeves. "Who the hell are you?" he asked Bolan bluntly.

"A friend," Bolan said. "You can call me Rance Pollock, or anything you want. But I'm on your side."

"What's your *real* name," the sergeant asked.

"That's the one thing you *can't* call me," Bolan replied.

"How come?"

"Because I have no intention of giving it to you."

The sergeant stepped back and looked him up and down. "Pollock will do for now," he said. "You know, I may be crazy as a fuckin' loon, but I'm inclined to believe you. At least my gut instinct tells me you *are* a friend."

"Your gut instincts are right," Bolan said.

"Yeah," the sergeant said. "Sometimes they are, sometimes they aren't. I'm still gonna have to check you out."

Bolan hesitated. No one except the President and
Hal Brognola even knew he was in Somalia. If the
sergeant went through the normal channels, it would
be days before he was cleared. He'd be in some stock-
ade until then, and by the time he got out it would be
too late to stop Ham and the other warlords.

Bolan wasn't big on grandstand plays, but under the
circumstances, he had no other choice. "You have a
comm link direct to the U.S., Sergeant?" he asked.

The sergeant frowned, then nodded. He snapped his
fingers, and a corporal carrying an armored field
briefcase hurried up. He opened the case and produced a pair of cellular phones.

"We relay to Mogadishu, then bounce off some
fuckin' satellite or something," the sergeant said.
"Don't know how it works, but I know it does." He
handed one of the phones to Bolan, then glanced at
the watch on his wrist. "You're in luck. The space
bird's in range." He paused, his face hardening. "But
I've got to warn you, Pollock. There isn't anyone
much short of the U.S. President who's going to convince me to let you go without checking further."

Bolan nodded, taking the phone and tapping in the
number. "Okay," he said simply.

The sergeant pressed the other cellular phone to his
ear as the line rang twice, then was answered.

"Oval Office, Mrs. Specklemeyer speaking," said
the voice on the other end.

The sergeant's lower lip dropped open.

"Baker, Frog, Buck and Wendy," Bolan said, giving the President's secretary the prearranged code that
would get him through to the man behind the desk in
the next room. "Tell the President that it's Striker."
He waited.

A second later a voice familiar to millions of people around the world came on the line. "Trouble, Striker?"

The sergeant's awe turned to skepticism. He held the phone away from his mouth, whispering, "How do I know it's not just a good impersonation? Rich Little or somebody?"

Bolan held up a hand. "Give me a second," he said to the side. Then he spoke into the phone, "Mr. President, I'm in-country. But I've run across some of our boys who aren't sure I should be. I'd appreciate it if you'd have a word with Sergeant..." He looked up at the man in front of him.

"Er, Starr, sir. Sergeant Dennis Starr."

"...with Sergeant Dennis Starr, Mr. President."

"Put him on," said the man in the Oval Office.

The sergeant pressed his phone tight against his ear. He listened for a moment, then his face took on a smile of relief.

Bolan pressed the disconnect button on his phone and handed it back to the corporal.

Starr continued to listen. "Yes, sir...yes...thank you, sir," he said, then hung up and let the corporal return the instrument to the case.

"Cleared?" Bolan asked.

Starr laughed happily. "Oh, you're cleared all right, Colonel Pollock. And I'm to give you whatever help you require. Just tell me what you need."

"Directions," Bolan said. "And maybe a ride."

Starr nodded toward a tall, slender black man in a colorful robe who stood to the side. "Khalid can take care of the directions and advice," he said. "He's been working with us as a guide. As far as the transport goes, we're about to break off patrol long enough to deliver a shipment of supplies to a village just north of here. You heading that way?''

Bolan nodded.

''Terrific!'' Starr beamed.

Bolan studied the man. He didn't know what the President had told Starr, but it must have been good. ''You seem happy enough about all this,'' Bolan commented.

''I am.'' Starr nodded. ''As soon as we're done, I get a two-month leave to go home.''

''Then let's get going, Starr,'' he said. ''Your family is waiting.''

THE JEEP in which Bolan and Starr rode was roughly in the center of the convoy of supply trucks, personnel carriers and support vehicles. As they turned off the cracked pavement and onto a dry gravel road, Bolan glanced to the man seated next to him in the back seat of the open vehicle.

Although Bolan had taken advantage of the drive to doze as best he could while bouncing over the rough roads, Sergeant Dennis Starr had been awake all night. Now, as the sun broke over the horizon, he turned to Bolan and grinned.

''It shouldn't take long once we get to Garoe,'' he shouted over the whine of the engine. ''We just guard the blue floppies—'' he gestured over his shoulder to the men and women in the transport vehicle behind, all of whom wore the powder blue floppy boonie hat of the United Nations ''—and make sure the warlords don't swoop in and steal the supplies. Then we'll head toward Erigavo.''

Bolan nodded, turning to the side of the road as the day began to dawn. A recent drought had added to the hell in which the Somalians lived, and as the sun began to illuminate the landscape, Bolan saw the results. There were no indications of agriculture whatsoever, and the only signs of life were occasional herds of sheep, goats and camels. The animals, as well as the men who tended them, looked scorched and thirsty and appeared to be in constant search for the water that would relieve their misery.

Bolan saw a series of short hills ahead and settled against the seat. They were in the plateau country of Somalia now, and less than a hundred miles from the V-shaped border with Ethiopia. On the other side of the border lay the Ogaden Desert. Ethnically part of Somalia, the vast stretch of land had been annexed by Ethiopia's Menelik I, and had been the cause of hostility and warfare between the two countries ever since.

The Executioner sighed silently. It didn't seem to matter where you went in the world; everyone had at least one enemy that predated recorded history. The Arabs had the Jews, and the Jews had the Arabs. The Japanese had the Chinese, and they both had the Koreans. In America, before the coming of the Europeans, the Seneca Indians had the Catawba and the Iroquois. And the Shawnee and Tuscarora had been fighting *everybody* since before anyone could remember.

Hatred, jealousy and bigotry, Bolan thought as they neared the hills, were traits that led to warfare. Would these characteristics be weeded out as man evolved, or were they so basic that they would remain forever?

He didn't know, but he didn't expect things to change much in his lifetime. So he would spend what remained of that lifetime fighting the evil that led to violence and injustice for the weak.

The yellow caution light in his brain broke suddenly into his thoughts as the convoy drew abreast of the hills. The desert acoustics being what they were, it was impossible to tell where the first shot came from. Only that it found its mark in the forehead of the driver seated directly in front of Bolan.

He dived forward as the jeep swerved toward a drop at the side of the road. At the same time a second sniper round exploded in the hills to their side. Behind him Bolan heard a scream.

"What the fu—?" Starr exclaimed.

Bolan leaned past the driver, grabbed the wheel of the jeep and guided it to a halt a foot from the edge of the plateau. Five feet below the ridge, he saw a yard-wide shelf that followed the lip. Beyond that the earth fell two hundred feet to another of the endless plateaus.

"Over the side!" Bolan commanded as more rounds peppered the jeep and the vehicles in front and behind it. "Get down."

None of the troops needed to be told twice.

The first two shots had been carefully placed, but now the Somalian desert became a battlefield of automatic fire. Bolan dived over the side of the jeep and sprinted around the vehicle. Dust blew up in clouds as first his feet, then his legs, skidded over the ridge. Twisting as he fell, he reached out to grasp a partially exposed root. The root crackled but held as his momentum carried his feet on over the deeper drop.

Bolan pulled himself back against the earth, drawing the Desert Eagle from his hip. Dennis Starr dived over the edge of the embankment, misjudged the width of the shelf and started to fly on.

Bolan reached out, circling his arm around the man's waist and slamming him back against the rocky side of the ledge.

More fire flew over their heads to land harmlessly somewhere below. On both sides of Bolan men jumped over the side to the ledge, their hands clawing frantically to keep from plummeting over the drop. Two men didn't make it, and their screams rose eerily back up the side of the cliff as they fell to their deaths two hundred feet below. Out of sight on top of the ridge, several screams sounded as slower Marines were mowed down by the autofire from the hills.

Bolan pressed his chest against the hot rocks that shielded him from the attackers. His lungs heaved as he caught his breath. "Ham's men?" he asked Starr.

Starr was too winded to speak. He simply nodded.

Bolan looked over his shoulder. Three feet behind him the world dropped off. A descent might be possible, depending upon how many footholds and handholds they could find. But it wasn't practical. As soon as the men hidden in the hills realized what they were attempting, they'd hurry down to the edge and pick them off one by one like flies on a wall.

Bolan turned back toward the hills, rising up slightly over the edge of cover.

A barrage of 7.62 mm bullets whizzed above his head.

Starr had nearly caught his breath now. He glanced over the edge of the cliff, then to the rocky plateau behind him. "This is...what they call...being between a rock and a hard place," he gasped.

Bolan smiled grimly. At least Starr was keeping a cool head, proving to be a good man to have on your side during battle.

"Any ideas, Pollock?" Starr gasped.

Bolan nodded.

"Hope it's a good one."

"Not particularly," Bolan said. "Just the *only* one."

"I was afraid you might say that," Starr said. "Let's hear it anyway."

The gunfire above them continued. Bolan looked over the cliff as he spoke. "Down is our only way out."

Starr had had the same thought. "Yeah, but we'd never get away with it," he said. "They'll figure out—"

"We don't have to get away with it," Bolan said. "We just have to make them think we're trying it."

Starr's face went blank for a moment. Then realization dawned like a light bulb flashing on. "Decoys?" he asked. "An ambush?"

The Executioner nodded.

"You're right," Starr said. "It's *not* a particularly good idea."

"If you've got a better one," Bolan said, "I'm all ears."

Starr shook his head. "No, I don't." He drew another deep breath, his chest heaving. "Let's have a go at it."

"Tell the man next to you," Bolan said. "Have him pass it on down the line, and tell them to get a count of how many men we have left. Don't count the UN people who aren't armed. And tell them we need volunteers for the decoys. Men who have climbing experience."

The rounds raging overhead died down a bit as Starr nodded, then turned and crawled to the man nearest him. Bolan turned the other way, finding a frightened young private on his other side.

The boy's green eyes were wide in shock, the skin of his face drawn tight over the youthful freckles that sprinkled his nose and cheeks.

Bolan told him the plan, then ordered him to pass it down the line.

The barrage had ended now that most of the Americans were below the ridge, but sporadic fire still came from the hills. But Bolan knew what was happening. Ham's men were trying to decide whether or not to come on down and take possession of the supplies in the trucks. They would have reconned this ambush sight carefully and knew that the only escape route was *down*. Eventually, they knew, the Americans would have to give it a try.

But how soon? Until the Americans began the descent, they could rise up over the ledge, return fire and pick off Ham's troops when they tried to take the trucks.

Word came back down the line on both sides of Bolan. Eighteen men were scattered up and down the ledge to Starr's side, four of them noncombatant UN workers. All but two of the Marines had followed their training, bringing their rifles with them as they fled the death-trap vehicles. Five were mountain trained.

On Bolan's side there were eight marines, all with weapons, and an equal number of unarmed "blue floppies." Only two of the warriors had volunteered for the descent, but one of the UN workers—a man who had made several difficult ascents on some of the world's most challenging peaks—had offered to go down, as well.

Bolan sent word back each way for each of the mountaineers to begin the descent, making as much noise as possible. He sent the rest of the men crawling both ways, spreading out to leave the area in the middle open.

"I hope you know what we're doing," Starr said as he turned to head away.

Bolan didn't answer. The military strategy he had just put into operation—the pincers movement—was as old as fighting itself. Like all classic military movements, it would be well-known by anyone who had studied warfare.

Would that include any of General Fajir Ham's men in the hills? And if so, would they recognize the tactic in time to counter it?

Bolan rose to his feet, stooping to remain hidden as he followed the private along the ledge. He didn't know if the plan would work or not. But it was all they had.

Bolan moved on. Over the edge he could see the two Marines and the UN man in the floppy blue hat slowly working their way down the side of the cliff. He passed over them, then stopped fifty yards farther. Leaning forward, he tapped the private on the shoulder.

The young man turned. Terror still radiated from his eyes.

"First fire?" Bolan whispered.

The private gulped. "Yes, sir," he whispered back.

Bolan nodded. There was nothing he could do or say to remove the man's fear. "Pass the word along to stop," he said. "And tell everyone to get ready."

The private turned, whispering to the man in front of him.

Bolan turned back to his rear. Far up the ridge now, roughly two hundred yards away, he could see Starr. Beyond him, crouched behind the wall of earth that led to the top of the plateau, were more men.

The area between them, where the Americans had jumped over the edge after deserting the vehicles for cover, was now bare. But with any luck, it was to this area that Ham's men would come.

Bolan stuck the Desert Eagle back in his holster and drew the sound-suppressed Beretta. He raised his sleeve to his forehead, wiping the sweat from his brow, and waited.

It took thirty minutes for the first head to peek over the edge, sixty yards away.

Bolan dropped the Beretta's front sight on the target, then lined up the rear. Slowly, as the man in the blue arm band peered curiously over the side of the cliff, Bolan squeezed the trigger.

The Beretta jumped lightly in his hand as a cough sputtered from the barrel.

Bolan pulled himself up over the side of the cliff as the man in the blue arm band tumbled down. Rolling on up into a combat crouch, he saw at least forty of the men in blue arm bands scattered around the vehicles. Another twenty had come to the edge of the cliff, their AK-47s ready to pick off the Americans on their downward climb.

Bolan left the Beretta on semiauto as he sprinted forward. Raising the pistol as he ran, he tapped a round into the first arm-band-clad man who turned his way.

The man fell silently.

Then the others turned.

Automatic fire pierced the still plateau as the U.S. Marines on his side of the pincer rolled up over the edge of the cliff and spread out behind him. In the distance Bolan heard more chattering shots as Starr's side of the movement opened fire.

Some of the AK-47s in the hands of Ham's men turned toward Bolan. Others turned toward Starr. Shocked at what had happened and unable to make a decision, some of the enemy troops wavered, uncertain where to aim.

Bolan flipped the Beretta to 3-round burst as he closed to within twenty yards of the men in the middle of the pincer. He sent a trio of rounds hammering into the chest of a gunner wearing a blue T-shirt and torn khaki pants. The Soviet assault rifle fell from the man's hands as he dropped to his knees, then sprawled forward onto his face.

More of the men with the arm bands fell as fire flew from the Americans' M-16s.

The Executioner heard a truck engine roar and turned toward the convoy. He caught a glimpse of the young private to his side. He saw the young man's teeth bared in an animal snarl as he sprayed the enemy with a blanket of rounds, then slammed a fresh magazine into his weapon as the rifle ran dry.

Drawing the Desert Eagle behind his back with his left hand, Bolan aimed at the left front tire of the sputtering truck and fired. The vehicle dropped to an awkward angle as the tire exploded.

"Come with me!" Bolan ordered the young private as he sprinted toward the convoy. The private fell in behind him.

Bolan raised the Beretta again, taking out a man in a straw hat as the man tried to swing his AK-47 toward them. Two more fell to Bolan's fire as he neared the first vehicle in line.

Beside the trucks, between the convoy and the cliff, the war raged on.

"Go left!" Bolan ordered the private. "Clear each vehicle, then move on!"

Bolan headed to the driver's-side door of the jeep at the front of the convoy. The private raced to the passenger's side, opposite. As the roar of gunfire filled their ears and burned cordite invaded their nostrils, the young man swung his rifle barrel up and over the side of the jeep.

Bolan traded the Beretta for the big .44, aiming into the jeep as he slowed. Satisfied that none of the warlord's men was hidden on the floorboard, he and the private moved on to the supply truck behind it.

A man wearing an arm band suddenly darted around the rear of the truck as Bolan neared. His eyes opened wide in surprise as Bolan lifted the Desert Eagle slightly and fired a round that split his skull.

Bolan moved on, leaping into the air to see into the cab as he passed. "Clear!" he shouted to the private, who was sprinting up to the other window. "Move to the rear!"

Bolan slowed again, scooping up the AK-47 that had fallen from the hands of the man at the side of the truck, then stopped just short of the rear tires. He edged slowly around the back of the truck, then waited for the private to show himself on the other side. Bolan looked into the young man's face as the Marine skidded to a halt.

The fear was still there. But it was under control. The kid had learned the first lesson of battlefield psychology: the fear didn't leave. So you had to make it work *for* you, rather than against you.

Bolan nodded to the kid. The kid nodded back.

Leaning around the rear of the truck, Bolan jerked the green canvas curtain from its rings and let it fall to the ground. His eyes quickly scrutinized the cargo area.

Two men in arm bands inside the truck raised weapons. One held one of the favorite AK-47s, the other a sawed-off double-barreled shotgun.

The Kalashnikov in Bolan's hands rose steadily as a burst of rounds stitched the first man from gut to throat. As he fell, Bolan heard the softer chatter of the private's M-16.

The man with the shotgun was thrown back against a stack of crates. The shotgun barrels flipped upward, exploding simultaneously. A fist-sized hole appeared in the roof of the truck.

The two warriors moved on down the line, clearing the rest of the trucks and jeeps, the young private paralleling Bolan on the other side of each vehicle. More fire erupted from their weapons. More of the enemy fell in death. Together they left four more bodies on the ground. Three more men in the blue arm bands met their maker inside the vehicles.

Bolan bent at the waist, grabbing a fresh magazine from the vest of a fallen man as they neared the last truck. He was about to shove the new load into the rifle when he heard the soft crunch of gravel behind him.

He ducked instinctively as he whirled to the rear, jamming the magazine into the AK-47. With no time for sights, he shot from the hip, sending a steady stream of fire into one of Ham's men.

The first round caught the man in the chest, then the burst worked its way upward, spitting into his face. As he turned back to the front, Bolan saw the young private drop another of Ham's men with a point-blank volley.

Four more shots exploded to Bolan's side. Then, as he left the convoy and turned back to the battle by the cliff, the plateau suddenly quieted into a ghostly silence.

Bolan surveyed the scene. Bodies were scattered across the flat land, most of them with blue arm bands. But here and there some had on the desert cammies worn by Starr's men. One of the unarmed UN workers had foolishly ignored the orders to remain below on the ledge, and now lay in a pool of his own blood, his floppy blue hat still on his head.

Bolan heard footsteps behind him and turned to see the young private staring up at him. The same eyes from which fear had emanated earlier now held a world-weary sadness that defied the boy's tender years.

The kid had done well. He would never again be the innocent young boy who had entered the battle, and his eyes now reflected the remorse that comes with war. But the rest of the young private's face was beaming with the broad smile of triumph.

CHAPTER FIVE

As the pilot next to him coaxed the helicopter into the air, General Fajir Ham felt anger and hatred shoot through his body as if he'd injected it with a syringe. He pressed the cellular phone tighter against his ear, listening to Sadiki's voice.

"They tracked the two men to a cave on the plateau," Sadiki said. "But our men are all dead."

For a moment Ham didn't speak, trying to get a grip on the anger that could only hamper his decision making. Don Elliot and Benjamin Barkari had escaped the fish factory. They had escaped the safehouse in Mogadishu. Now they had escaped once again in the desert.

Ham kept his voice even and controlled. "I keep hearing that they have a house in the mountains," he said. "Have you located it yet?"

"No. But we know it is somewhere near Erigavo," Sadiki said. "At least Erigavo is where all of the building materials they purchased were shipped."

Ham glanced down at the ground as the helicopter continued to gain altitude. "They will go there next," he said. "Find the house. And find *them*." He held the phone away from his mouth, cleared his throat, then said, "Lead this expedition yourself, Sadiki, and *do not fail*."

Now it was Sadiki's turn to pause as the subtle threat sank into his consciousness. "Yes, General," he said.

That finished, Ham changed the subject. "What of the military convoy on its way to Garoe?" he asked. "Are the food and medical supplies now in our possession?" Another interval of silence gave him the answer.

"General—" Sadiki finally started.

"I am very disappointed," Ham interrupted. "We must speak seriously about your position when I return from Mogadishu. Soon I plan to move into the south, then on to Kenya and beyond. A strong man must lead my troops. Tell me, Sadiki, if you no longer feel you are that man, could you suggest someone who might be more capable?"

As the helicopter leveled off and began moving toward Djibouti, there was another long gap in conversation. Ham took a perverse pleasure in the crackling of static that was the only sound in his ear.

Sadiki finally broke the silence. "I will fly to Garoe with a contingent of men immediately," he said. "We will try again."

"Do not *try,* Sadiki," Ham said. *"Succeed."* He disconnected the line and returned the phone to its case.

The warlord sat back against the seat. The military convoy delivering food and medical supplies to Garoe wasn't a large one, and it made little difference in the overall spectrum of his operations. But success, in all operations both big and small, was vital to the morale of the troops. And it was essential to the mind-set that kept the Somalian citizens subservient.

As the Hughes 500D crossed the border between Somalia and Djibouti, Ham concentrated on the soothing rotor blades above his head. The sound was peaceful, comforting. It calmed him, and he realized that the half-million dollars he had paid the French aviation distributor had been well worth it, even if only for the tranquilizing effect it had on his soul.

Ham sighed contentedly as the helicopter continued to follow the ragged coast of northern Africa. Besides, he thought, the Frenchman had thrown in the new fleet of all-terrain vehicles. And a half-million dollars was a mere pittance considering the growth he had seen in the khat trade recently. Importation of the mild amphetamine, along with heroin and more serious drugs, combined with the hijacking of the UN supplies and prostitution, had changed him from a moderately wealthy man to one who could no longer keep track of his holdings.

The warlord chuckled silently. Taking a lesson from the American Mafia, he had now moved much of his wealth into legitimate investments outside Somalia. He felt like an Arab oil sheik. His money was beginning to gather interest faster than he could spend it.

Ham looked out of the helicopter's glass bubble. To his right he saw the rising waves of the Gulf of Aden as they broke over white sand beaches.

The voice of the light-skinned man sitting directly behind the warlord broke the silence. "It is beautiful, yes?" Ali Abu-Iyad said. "I can see why my people wanted it."

"Make no mistake," Ham said without emotion. "Your people did not *get it* in the past, and they will not *have it* in the future, regardless of what you are willing to trade."

"Of course," the man said quickly. "I only meant that of which we have already agreed."

Ham nodded as the Hughes neared the capital city of Djibouti and the Gulf of Tadjoura appeared just beyond. "Of course you did," he said.

The warlord continued to stare ahead through the glass. Across the Gulf of Tadjoura he could barely make out the shallow skyline of the city that had been named after it. He looked down again, at the contorted rock-and-lava formations along the coast. Large salt deposits were scattered here and there, and tiny figures moved among the deposits.

Ham shook his head in disgust. Afar tribesmen were collecting the salt they used as currency. The Afars, a nomadic people who inhabited Djibouti's north and had strong links to Ethiopia, were even more destitute, miserable and stupid than the Issas in the country's south.

The Issas at least showed their loyalty to Somalia. But for the most part they were a witless race, as well, and Ham was ashamed that his mother had been one of them.

For a moment the warlord's thoughts returned to his childhood. He had entered the world in 1940, roughly nine months after the Italian army had moved from Ethiopia into Somalia. The fascists had immediately taken what little the country had of monetary value and, not satisfied with the spoils of war, had begun concentrating upon the women. Tall and lithe, with mysterious aquiline features and smooth ebony skin, the dignified women of the Issas had always ignored strangers.

Except, of course, when being raped.

A confusing mixture of sorrow and hatred filled Fajir Ham's breast as the helicopter began to descend over the Djibouti airport. He had heard the story only once, as a ten-year-old child, huddled within his blankets under the stars of the great plateau. While the men of the tribe tended the sheep and the women believed him to be asleep, his mother and the other women had become crazed on a blend of khat and bootleg wine.

Ham had listened with closed eyes to the stories of the women as they spoke in whispers, recounting tales of the degradation to which the Italian soldiers had subjected them. Ham's mother was no exception, a victim of faceless, grunting soldiers who satisfied themselves, then moved on to join in the drunken laughter with the other men.

Sweat broke out on Ham's forehead as the helicopter set down on the pad. He had relived his mother's nightmare a million times over the years, overcome by anguish and outrage.

"He comes," said Abu-Iyad, pointing through the glass.

Ham pushed the painful memories from his mind as he turned to see General Jabbar come out of the terminal with his six bodyguards. Resplendent in a long, flowing robe, the warlord of Djibouti waved his guards away as he stepped up to the open door of the Hughes 500D. "I will be safe with my good friend General Ham," he shouted over the whirling blades. "You will follow in my helicopter."

Of course you will be safe, Ham thought. At least for the time being.

As Jabbar boarded the Hughes, Fajir Ham got out of the helicopter, trading places with Abu-Iyad in the rear seat. He slapped a hand onto Jabbar's knees as the Warlord settled in and the Hughes rose back into the air. "Are you ready to capitulate to our new Uncle Sam?" he asked the man.

Jabbar burst into laughter. "But of course," he said. "The white man must save us poor kaffirs from ourselves."

Ham smiled. "Yes, we are far too stupid to be trusted with weapons—perhaps even sharp objects. But I believe you are mistaken about one thing, dear friend Jabbar."

Jabbar frowned. "Oh? And what is that?"

"It is the South Africans that call us kaffirs. To the Yanks and other white Westerners, I believe we are known as niggers."

Both men laughed.

The light-skinned man in the front seat turned around. "Not all of us refer to black men in such terms," he said. "Nor do we think of you that way, either."

Ham reached forward, patting the man on the shoulder. "No, of course not, my dear friend," he said, making sure the sarcasm he felt stayed out of his tone. "You are here to aid us. You are our friend."

Abu-Iyad smiled.

Ham returned the smile, but behind his closed lips his teeth were clenched. They were playing a game, this light-skinned man and he. They each needed something from the other, and both were willing to feign respect for the other on behalf of that need.

At least until those needs had been fulfilled.

Ham nodded. "We are all businessmen here," he said. Still smiling at the man in front of him, he went on. "But I will happily concede that you have a better basic understanding of the strange operation of the American mind." He turned back to Jabbar. "Only one aspect of our plan worries me, my brother."

"And I suspect," Jabbar said, "it is the same aspect that worries me."

"Yes," Ham went on. "The Americans may be animals, but they are not *stupid* animals. We must keep enough of our rifles to protect us from the people until our friend here can resupply us. The Americans are bound to know we will do this."

Both Ham and Jabbar turned to the front seat.

Abu-Iyad chuckled. "As you yourself pointed out, General Ham, I have studied the American political mind. The politicians of the United States have become actors on a world stage. They care far more how things *look* than how things *are.*

"It is all quite simple, if you understand how they operate," he continued. "Let me predict exactly how the next few days will go. You will agree on camera to turn in your weapons. The Americans will say thankyou and act as if they believe you. Then you will all turn to the news cameras and the Americans will say, 'See, we have stopped the dictatorship of the warlords in Somalia.' Then they will go home."

Ahead the city of Mogadishu appeared through the glass. "This is insanity," Jabbar said. "They will know that we have kept our weapons, but pretend not to know?"

"Precisely," Abu-Iyad said. "No one in their right mind expects someone to give up all means of self-defense." He chuckled, then added, "The Americans only demand that from their own citizens at home."

Out of the corner of his eye, Ham saw a puzzled look come over Jabbar's face. "I do not understand," the Djibouti warlord said.

Ham patted his knee. "Our friend is referring to the American government's current attack on its own Second Amendment. Its attempt to disarm the Americans citizens of their firearms and take away their ability to defend themselves from criminals."

All three men laughed. "As I said," Jabbar repeated, "they are insane."

"Perhaps *not* so insane," Ham said. "Can you imagine the problems *we* would have had conquering our own country if the Somalian citizens had possessed guns?" He turned back to the front seat. "Let me make sure that General Jabbar and I have this straight in our minds, because it is a way of thinking that is foreign to us. The Americans will know we have held out weapons to defend ourselves."

The man in the front seat nodded. "Yes."

"But they will act as if they do not know."

"Yes, again."

"This will give them an excuse to go home?"

Abu-Iyad nodded.

Ham frowned. "America does not know that you will rearm us as soon as they are gone. But even without that knowledge, they *must* know that the same weapons we keep to protect ourselves can be used to again subordinate the population as soon as they are gone." He shook his head. "Do the American people not care?"

"Perhaps the American people do," said the man in the front seat. "But they no longer matter. The American *politicians* are running this operation. And all that politicians require is a good show."

As the helicopter reached Mogadishu, General Jabbar looked at Ham and shook his head in awe. "With this foolish system of thinking, brother Ham, how did the United States ever become a world power?"

Ham shrugged.

The rotor blades slowed as the Hughes descended to the helipad. A limousine driven by an American sergeant pulled up ten yards away. Ham and Jabbar traded the rear of the plane for the back seat of the limo as Abu-Iyad took the seat next to the driver.

Two jeeps filled with well-armed American Marines led the way into Mogadishu. A third jeep filled with the camouflage-clad Americans brought up the rear.

Ham grinned as he watched his American bodyguards fall into place. Yesterday he had been the most-wanted man in Africa. But as soon as he had sent word that he would sign the treaty and turn in his rifles, he had been given an immediate amnesty. Abu-Iyad was right. Appearances *had* become more important than reality to the Americans.

The limo stopped in front of the Hargeisa Hotel on Italiyo Street. Ham and Jabbar nodded a goodbye to Ali Abu-Iyad and got out.

Surrounded by their contingent of U.S. Marines, they smiled into the popping flashbulbs and video cameras of the newspeople as they made their way up the steps and into the dining room.

Television cameras lined the walls, reporters were speaking into microphones and the camera operators struggled to take it all in at once. General Morris and Colonel James were already waiting with smiles.

Five minutes later James, Morris and Jabbar had all signed the treaty in which they agreed to turn all armament over to the American troops during the next three days. General Ham smiled into the camera as he dramatically picked up the pen. "Together with my friends, I will strive to make Somalia into a democracy of which our big brother America will be proud," he said.

A round of applause went up around the room.

Ham leaned over the table and scrawled his name below the others.

An American wearing three stars on his dress uniform stepped forward, and Ham saw that his name tag identified him as General Walker. Walker shook the warlords' hands. When he came to Ham, he held the grip as he turned to the cameras. "It is a historic day for the peoples of both the United States and Somalia," he said as the press stabbed their microphones closer. "Together we are opening the door to democracy in northeast Africa."

Flashbulbs popped. Questions assaulted the men from all directions. "When will you be pulling out, General?" shouted a woman standing in front of a CNN camera.

"Within the week," said the man with the stars on his hat.

General Jabbar fell in next to Ham again as the Marines escorted them out of the hotel toward the limousine. "How did these people ever rise to strength?" Jabbar whispered into Ham's ear, shaking his head in disbelief.

Before he could answer, Ham saw the rear door of the limo opened by the light-skinned hand inside the vehicle. He slid onto the seat, then across it, letting Jabbar in beside him.

"You did not answer my question, dear friend," Jabbar said as the limo pulled away. "How could a nation that assigns more importance to symbolic gestures than reality ever become a world power?"

Ham frowned, thinking about it. "My only guess would be that they behaved differently in the past," he finally said. Then, looking up at the smiling light-skinned face in the front seat, he said, "We begin turning over our guns tomorrow morning. When will the new weapons arrive?"

DON ELLIOT LED the way from the road down the rocks. "You *sure* somebody's coming?" he called over his shoulder. "We haven't seen a car since we've been on this road, Friday." A minilandslide of pebbles trickled down around his ankles as he crab-walked toward the bottom of the gully.

Behind Elliot, Benjamin Barkari cursed as he lost his footing. He slid past Elliot, then stopped as he caught his balance. "Yes, I am *sure* somebody is coming," he said. "In fact, I am sure there are *many* somebodies coming."

At the bottom of the canyon, Elliot paused to catch his breath. He had watched Friday drop to his belly a few minutes earlier and press his ear against the road. It looked like something out of an old Western movie, and Elliot half expected Friday to say, "Comanches. Maybe a hundred of them."

The former CIA operative turned to his partner. "You don't suppose Ham got his whole posse on us this soon, do you?" he asked.

Friday shook his head, drops of sweat flying from his cheeks and forehead. "It's too soon. More likely it's a supply shipment headed north."

Elliot nodded. That made more sense. The man who had tried to radio for help had never done so, thanks to Friday. By now Ham would have figured out something was wrong—maybe even gotten a report on the bodies they'd left outside the cave—but it was still too soon for him to have put a search party into action so close.

"So," Friday said, "what do we do? Hide here until they pass, then go to Garoe and steal a car like we'd planned?"

Elliot hesitated. With the UN workers and U.S. Army in town, stealing a car was going to be very difficult. The soldiers would be there to protect the supply shipment, not prevent auto theft, but they'd be watching things.

A sudden idea hit Elliot, and he turned to his friend again.

"Uh-oh," Friday said. "I've seen that look before. It usually means you've just thought of something that borders on insanity."

Elliot chuckled. Far in the distance he heard the hum of the approaching vehicles. "Hide your rifle," he said.

"My God, Elliot, you aren't planning to—"

"Relax, Mr. Barkari," Elliot said as he squeezed his AK-47 between two boulders and began covering it with sagebrush.

Barkari began pulling thick handfuls of the dry vegetation from the cracks in the rock and covering his rifle.

As the hum of the oncoming convoy grew louder, Elliot and Friday climbed back to the top of the gully, dropping behind an outgrowth of rocks next to the road. Covering his head with the sagebrush, Elliot peered through the dead vines and scanned up and down the route.

The former CIA man smiled. They had unwittingly picked an excellent place for what he had planned. Fifty yards back the way they had come, the road made one of its few bends around another formation of rock. They would have a good view of the vehicles as they came around the curve. Looking the other way, Elliot saw that the road dipped sharply a hundred yards farther toward Garoe.

He nodded. If their timing was right, they'd be able to pull it off.

Elliot drew the customized Colt as the hum became a roar. He studied the first vehicle as it came into view—a jeep. He hoped the last vehicle in the convoy would be a jeep, as well.

Only two men sat in the lead jeep, both in the front seat, and he hoped that was repeated in the vehicle that brought up the rear.

Elliot watched the vehicle pass, eyeing the corporal stripes on the man in the shotgun seat. The man stared blankly ahead. They were close to their destination now, and the man didn't expect trouble.

A supply truck passed, then another. Another jeep—in the center of the convoy, Elliot guessed—rounded the curve next. Elliot saw the young, fresh-faced driver and an older man wearing sergeant's stripes next to him.

The former CIA operative frowned. A man wearing khaki slacks and a safari jacket sat in the back seat. Big guy with dark hair and a hard face. His head didn't move as the jeep passed, but his eyes scanned the road like a hawk searching for prey.

Elliot's abdominal muscles tightened. The guy in the back seat might be wearing civvies, but he was about as much a civilian as George Patton. The fact was, he showed more military professionalism under the circumstances than any of the soldiers who had passed.

Elliot's stomach didn't relax until the jeep had passed and disappeared down the incline.

Next came a personnel vehicle, then more supply trucks. Finally another jeep rounded the bend and started toward them.

"You suppose that's the rear guard?" Friday whispered.

"I damn sure hope so. If it isn't, we're going to look mighty foolish to whoever comes around the mountain after it."

Elliot waited until the jeep was twenty yards away, then suddenly rose to the top of the rocks. The soldiers in the front seat of the vehicle turned toward him as the sagebrush fell from his head and shoulders. But before they could react, he was flying toward the back seat of the jeep.

The former CIA man saw the pair of M-16s lying across the back seat a second before his boots hit the floorboards. He twisted, letting the jeep's forward momentum throw him back to a sitting position over the rifles.

As he looked back up, Elliot saw Friday fly through the air like some giant black bird. His knee caught the man riding shotgun in the side of the face, then he fell into the back seat next to Elliot.

Beneath him the sharp edges of one of the rifles bit into the back of his thighs. It was a welcome pain. They'd been forced to leave their AKs behind, and Elliot suspected a couple more assault rifles would come in damn handy before this party was over.

The sergeant riding shotgun recovered from Friday's knee and turned toward them, his hand fumbling with the canvas flap on his hip holster. Elliot leaned forward, shoving the barrel of his .45 into the man's cheek. Next to him he saw Friday aim his pistol at the driver.

Elliot leaned in, reached around the sergeant and jerked a Beretta 92 from the flap holster. He handed it to Friday, then relieved the driver of a similar weapon.

Both men in the front seat were still stunned. Coming out of the semistupor, the sergeant stared at Elliot with cold, hard eyes, rubbed his cheek and said, "All right. You assholes are holding all the aces. What do you want?"

The driver started to slow.

"Keep driving," Elliot ordered, switching his .45 from the sergeant and pressing it into the back of the driver's head.

The jeep resumed speed.

The other vehicles in the convoy had disappeared over the rise, but Elliot knew this was not the place to desert the pack. Open country lay between them and Garoe. They had been damned lucky no one was looking into the rearview mirror as they leaped from the rocks, and the chances of no one seeing them take an alternate path across the desert were about fifty thousand to one.

Elliot studied the sergeant in detail for the first time. Short, thick, muscular, he looked like a career NCO. A tough son of a bitch, he showed no fear. He could be trouble.

"Just keep driving like you were until we tell you differently," Elliot said. "If you don't follow my directions precisely, we'll shoot you both. Try to signal the others, we'll shoot you both. In fact, do *anything* I don't like—"

"And you'll shoot us both," the sergeant growled. "I think we get the picture, you fuckin' traitor."

Elliot cringed at the word. "I'm not a traitor," he said softly. "And I'd hate to kill a fellow American. But I will if it comes down to that. Now turn around, face the road and shut the fuck up."

The sergeant glared at him another few seconds, then turned around.

Elliot crouched down farther, shifting positions so he could see between the two men in the front. The convoy was continuing as before, with no one evidently the wiser that the rear jeep had been hijacked. The former CIA man squinted at the truck ahead.

Someone had shot the hell out of it. And recently. Bullet holes, their edges still a bright untarnished silver, were scattered about the vehicle.

A few minutes later a weathered wooden road sign announced Garoe in ten kilometers. Friday leaned over to whisper in Elliot's ear, "We may have overlooked the obvious."

"How's that?"

"Did you ever consider just telling these guys who we are, that we're the good guys, that the *bad* guys are trying to kill us, and then letting them take care of us?"

Elliot hesitated. He'd thought of it, all right, but one major problem had prevented him from even suggesting it to his friend. He shook his head. "They'd just ship me back to the U.S.," he said.

"Call me crazy, Don," Friday said irritably, "but that really doesn't sound all that bad at the moment. I mean, if it comes down to a choice between Ham's men blowing our brains out and drinking rum and coke on Miami Beach—"

"I said they'd ship *me* back, Friday," Elliot said. "Who the hell knows *what* they'd do with you? You aren't an American citizen."

"Political asylum?" Friday asked.

"Maybe," Elliot said. "But in the confusion you could just as easily wind up with an earful of political double-talk, a 'good luck, Mr. Barkari' and a fast escort from the consulate back to the street. Want to risk your life on it?"

Friday thought for a moment. "Things are bad but they're going to get worse, Don. Tell them who you are, what's going on and get the hell back to the States." He paused. "I'll be fine."

Elliot turned angrily to face the Swahili, his voice rising. "Fuck you, Friday. We've been together too long. We'll either get through this or we won't. But we'll do it together."

The sergeant in the front seat half turned as Garoe appeared in the distance. "Go ahead and kiss the son of a bitch," he said. "We won't look."

Friday jammed the barrel of his .45 into the man's neck, knocking his head forward. "You just keep facing the front, you bastard," he said. "And you might get out of this alive."

The driver followed the truck in front of him as they entered the village. Elliot leaned out of the jeep, risking exposure to scan the area ahead. The road led into the downtown core, and it would be somewhere in this area that the supplies would be unloaded. "Go on to the next intersection, then turn," he ordered the driver.

"Which way?" the driver asked.

"I don't give a shit which way!" Elliot screamed in his ear. "Just turn and get out of sight and do it *fast!*"

The jeep moved on, slowing as they reached a narrow dirt crossroad. Crumbling houses lined both sides of the road. Men, women and children with hungry faces and bloated bellies were hurrying after the convoy as fast as their malnutritioned legs would carry them.

"Now!" Elliot yelled into the driver's ear as they reached the intersection.

The driver turned sharply to the left, narrowly missing a group of starving Somalians bent on following the trucks.

"Now you better drive like a bat out of hell until we get to the road leading north," Elliot ordered as they started past more of the collapsed dwellings. "Or all your work so far will have been for nothing and you'll die right here with a .45 behind your ear."

"Gardo or Erigavo?" the driver asked in a trembling voice.

Elliot hesitated. He had forgotten there were two roads leading north out of this village. The winding trail that eventually led to Erigavo would be the quickest route, but telling these men to go that way would leave a hell of a clue as to where he and Barkari were headed.

On the other hand, if they took the road to Gardo, they'd have to cut back west and south after that village and ultimately add a good hundred miles to their journey. That meant hours over roads that were slow going at best.

What it boiled down to was that they couldn't afford to make the choice either way.

"Pull over," Elliot ordered suddenly.

"Sir?"

"Pull over! Now!"

The young soldier stomped the brake. Dust flew through the air as the jeep fishtailed to a halt at the side of the narrow street.

Elliot and Barkari grabbed the M-16s beneath their legs, leaped over the sides of the jeep and pointed their rifles at the two men in the front seat.

The driver looked up at the former CIA man with terrified eyes. "Are you gonna kill us?"

"You're damn right they're gonna kill us," the sergeant said, his face a mask of hatred. "They've got to. It won't take us fifteen minutes to get back into town and let the others know what went on. They know it and they need more of a start than that." He glowered at Elliot, unafraid.

"Right and wrong," Friday said. "Take off your boots, both of you."

"What?" the driver asked.

"Just do it!" Elliot screamed.

Both of the men in the front seat quickly unlaced their boots and pulled them off.

Friday took the boots as they were handed over the seat. Then the stock of Elliot's rifle flashed through the air, striking the back of the sergeant's head with the crack of a baseball hitting the bat.

The man slumped forward, unconscious. The driver's mouth opened wide in surprise, and his hands moved protectively to the back of his neck.

"Get out and take your buddy with you," Elliot ordered.

A second later the driver had pulled the sergeant out of the jeep and laid him on the ground.

Elliot and Barkari crawled over the seat to the front as a group of uninterested natives hurried past in search of the supply trucks. Elliot threw the transmission into gear, then looked over to the driver, who now stood over his unconscious sergeant next to the jeep.

Mouth agape, the young man stood staring at him, awaiting further orders.

The former CIA man stared back. "You got a choice, kid," he said. "You can leave your NCO here and run for help. That'd be the fastest." He paused and glanced at the ragged natives that continued to hurry past. "Of course, if you do, he'll be stripped naked and maybe even have his throat slit before you and the other troops get back." He paused. "Or you can wait for him to come to. Or carry him. I'll leave it up to you."

He let the clutch out and drove away.

Elliot knew the kid would never leave his sergeant—particularly after the seed that the former CIA man had just planted in his brain. And it made no difference whether the young Marine chose to carry the man or wait. The delay would afford him and Friday the head start they needed.

Elliot turned the corner and started north through the village. Next to him he heard Friday sigh.

"Too bad you had to coldcock the sergeant," he said. "Tough guy. Seemed like a good man. Even if he did call you a traitor."

Elliot nodded. He had gotten over the initial anger at the word. "He didn't know what the hell was going on," he said. "You or I would have thought the same."

Friday returned the nod as the road leading north appeared ahead.

BOLAN WATCHED the sides of the narrow road as the convoy rolled toward Garoe. He had noticed a lessening in awareness on the part of most of the soldiers since the ambush, and recognized it as a natural posttrauma response many semitrained warriors went through after battle.

Human beings were programmed to take only a certain amount of stress before their brains relaxed. The brain's mental and emotional survival mechanism worked much the same as a release valve on a pressure-driven piece of machinery. When the level of stress exceeded a certain threshold, the mind simply went on vacation. If it didn't, it would explode and shut down completely. Bolan had had the training and combat experience to avoid this stress reaction. These men didn't.

A large formation of boulders appeared to the right of the road ahead. Bolan watched the rocks as the convoy neared, knowing it was up to him to remain alert while the others dealt with the trauma of battle. Learning to fight was one thing. Learning to avoid the natural tendency to relax immediately afterward was another. In the jungles of Vietnam Bolan had seen men fight valiantly one minute, only to die through inattention to detail during a downtime a few minutes later.

Bolan glanced at the back of the head of the young man driving the jeep. As with most other soldiers in the convoy, this had been his first taste of battle. His limit had been reached, and he was rejoicing that he was still alive rather than realizing that death might lurk around the next curve.

The Executioner studied the thick growth of vegetation the Somalian wind had blown over the tops of the rocks as the convoy passed. His gut tightened momentarily. Several roots of the dried sagebrush were visible in the tangled mess. They had been recently uprooted.

Could a sudden windstorm jerk the plants from the ground? Maybe. It happened sometimes. But it seemed unlikely that so much of it would get caught at the top of the rocks.

Bolan turned, his eyes still glued to the rocks as the trucks and other vehicles passed. He thought he saw a brief flicker of movement in the vines. Then, nothing.

He turned back to the road, rubbing his weary eyes. Years of battle stress, sleepless nights and staring death in the face had raised his own "release valve" to the highest possible degree, but Bolan knew he was only human. He had gone several days with little or no sleep. Maybe his eyes were playing tricks on him.

Bolan closed his eyes, then opened them. This wasn't the time to nap. Even in his state of semiexhaustion, he was more likely to notice any new dangers that presented themselves than the other men.

Soon the convoy topped a hill, and the village of Garoe appeared ahead.

A slight dejection crept through Bolan as he saw the semiruins of Garoe. Like most of the other villages and cities of Somalia, Garoe was a combination of the ruins of civil war and the looting of the warlords. Men like Ham, Jabbar, Morris and James had destroyed the socialist government of Siyad Barre. However bad that government might have been, at least *some* order had prevailed when Barre had been in power. But as soon as he'd been overthrown, it had become dog-eat-dog, with only the biggest and meanest of the canines surviving.

Bolan pushed the melancholy from his heart as the convoy headed for the downtown area. Men, women and children looked up from the sides of the road, then began moving listlessly after the trucks.

Passing through the rundown shacks and huts, the convoy entered what had once been an area of commerce. The ruins of a two-story government building stood at the center of the town, the shambles reflecting what must once have been an elegant example of Africanized Roman architecture.

The convoy curved around the ruins, then halted. Starr jumped down from the jeep and hurried toward the front of the line as the other men began exiting the vehicles.

Bolan dropped to the ground, scanning the area as the residents reached the convoy. Several of the Marines began unloading cases of provisions. Others took up positions around the circled trucks, rifles held in front of them like riot batons, doing their best to create some order as the starving Somalians tried to break through the trucks toward the food.

The gloom that had filled Bolan's soul a moment earlier changed to anger. Ham. Jabbar. Morris. James.

The warlords had reduced their own people to the level of scrounging, begging dogs, stripping away all remnants of human dignity. If allowed to continue, these men would eventually cause the genocide of their own people.

Bolan's jaw tightened. He intended to hold the warlords accountable for the degeneracy he saw here.

Suddenly, Bolan saw the face of a GI with a wooden crate in his arms disintegrate. A split second later the sound from the rifle shot reached his ears.

Bolan hit the ground, the Desert Eagle leaping into his hand as he tried to pinpoint the origin of the shot. A second shot followed, kicking up dirt to his side.

Bolan rolled under the jeep, his eyes turning toward the crumbling building at the center of the convoy. Screams from the men, women and children who had come for food echoed as the natives scattered. Hearing a thud, he turned to see the emaciated, ulcer-ridden body of a Somalian woman lying on the ground.

He turned back to the center of the convoy. Snipers. Ham had sent men to Garoe ahead of them, and now they were nestled safely in the ruins where they could pick off the Americans one by one.

Sporadic gunfire continued to emanate from the decaying two-story building. The shots were carefully placed singles—probably from scoped bolt-action weapons—and far more effective under the circumstances than the full-auto M-16 fire that the Marines responded with.

With no visible target, Bolan held his own fire. The warlord's men were safely covered by the bricks and blocks of the crumbling structure, so there was no use wasting ammunition.

The sniper fire from the building halted momentarily. Bolan felt that there could not be more than a dozen snipers hidden in the ruins. They were outnumbered and, if he led the Marines in a rush, could be overtaken. But that would mean American casualties.

The alternative was a tactical retreat. But for that, the Americans would have to return to the vehicles, and anyone showing his head right now ran a high risk of getting it blown off.

Bolan had no time to decide which of the two alternatives was preferable. A second later the snipers opened up again with a new fury. Then more fire, this time from fully automatic rifles, sounded behind him. Rolling to his side, he saw holes appear in the dirt next to his feet.

He twisted, jackknifing to the opposite side of the jeep. He saw five of the now-familiar black Toyota Land Cruisers racing toward the convoy from the south. Four more came from the north.

Men wearing blue arm bands, AK-47s blazing in their hands, leaned out of all of the warlord's vehicles.

CHAPTER SIX

The U.S. Army jeep sped across the plateau. Life, both animal and vegetable, had been scarce as the jeep crossed the dry north-central area of Somalia's interior, but as Don Elliot and Benjamin Barkari neared the upward slope that would eventually take them into the mountains of the north, they began to pass the occasional oryx and small herds of wild donkeys.

The sun had begun to fade by the time the jeep started up into the foothills. Elliot held the steering wheel in one hand, watching his partner out of the corner of his eye. Friday faced the road. His face had taken on the deadpan look that Elliot had seen frequently. The former CIA man knew that the lack of expression was a cover for the agony in Friday's soul.

"Stop thinking about her," Elliot finally said. "It won't do you a damned bit of good."

Friday snorted. "I wasn't thinking about her," he lied.

"Good," Elliot said. "Make sure you don't start." He raised his elbow and sniffed the armpit of his shirt. "Son of a bitch," he said, changing the subject to make sure his friend did the same. "I could use a shower."

"I know."

"You too, huh?" Elliot said.

"No, not *me*," Friday said.

Elliot looked over to see the black man grinning.

The jeep sped along the bumpy road. Ahead and to the right, Elliot saw the camp of a small tribe of nomads. Feeble sheep mingled through the impromptu hamlet of worn tents flapping in the wind. Elliot tapped the horn as they passed, but no one bothered to look up.

The listlessness that had infected the villagers had also struck the nomads.

Elliot heard the jeep's engine start to whine as the road began to steepen. He downshifted, his eyes focused on the trees that were beginning to appear as they grew nearer to water. He didn't think there was much chance that Ham or his cutthroats knew exactly where they were, but they'd know the general vicinity of their destination.

Glancing up, Elliot caught his reflection in the rearview mirror. He saw the crow's-feet at the corners of his eyes and the loose bags of skin that hung under them. Wrinkles crossed his forehead like lanes on a racetrack. More wrinkles had begun to groove into his cheeks at the corners of his mouth, and the hair around his temples could no longer be called salt-and-pepper. It was gray.

It suddenly dawned on Don Elliot that he had lived far longer than he'd ever expected. The wrinkles and gray hair above his ears were like badges of honor representing the careful planning and execution of countless dangerous missions. They hadn't come from being careless, and if he expected to have any more wrinkles and watch the rest of his hair turn gray, this was no time to start taking unnecessary chances.

Elliot's eyes returned to the trees.

The sun had fallen when the jeep entered Erigavo an hour later. The village reflected a stronger Arab influence than Garoe, but its haggard men and women had the same drawn look of despair. The same signs of civil war and subsequent lawlessness—empty shell casings, crumbling buildings, the burned remains of houses—lined the streets.

Elliot guided the jeep through the center of town, remembering that it had once been the major trade center of this part of the country. At one time the gold and silver jewelry of Somalia's craftsmen had been sold in booths along the street. Finely woven cloth, baskets and leather goods had been available. While the village, like the country itself, could never have been called affluent, at least the trade and other enterprises had provided food and shelter for most people.

Now all the former CIA operative saw was poverty and despair.

The road led north, and ahead Elliot saw several men and women walking indifferently in that direction. His mind returned to the big man who had been in the jeep when the convoy had passed the rocks before Garoe. He couldn't be sure, but he thought it was the same man he and Friday had seen at the cave.

Elliot had thought the big man was a mercenary in Ham's employ when he'd first seen him through the binoculars. But if it was the same guy, that no longer seemed likely.

The former CIA man felt a shiver run up his spine. If the truth were known, the guy gave him the willies. He had looked into the sagebrush as the convoy passed, and although Elliot knew it was impossible, he got the feeling the guy knew they were there. Or at least that the big man had sensed *something* was out of place.

Elliot cast the thought aside as they passed the people alongside the road. He glanced into the jeep's mirror and saw a young man staring after them.

As the man reached for the pistol in his belt, Elliot noticed the blue arm band. Anger and frustration suddenly overcame him, and he struck the steering wheel with both fists.

Friday saw him look in the mirror and turned in his seat. "Floor it!" he screamed, his lug-soled boot shooting across the jeep to stomp on top of Elliot's foot.

The jeep shot forward as they both heard the explosion.

The round went wild, hitting a rock and sending sparks glittering down the road in the twilight. Elliot kept his foot on the pedal, not slowing until they were well out of pistol range. "Can you see anything?" he asked.

Friday was sitting sideways in his seat. "He gave up after the first shot," he said. "He's running toward one of the houses."

"To a radio or phone," Elliot said. "Dammit, Friday, I'm sorry. I didn't see him." He downshifted as they started higher into the mountains.

Barkari shrugged. "Ham must have scouts covering the villages by now," he said. "The one who saw us is going to notify men who are standing by. We should have thought of that."

"We damned sure should have," Elliot said. The wind blew hot against his face as they rose into the mountains. "We're rusty, Friday. We're missing little things that could get us killed."

Friday shrugged and faced forward. "It doesn't matter. We're less than ten miles away now. We'll be there before the scout contacts Ham."

"Sure, we will," Elliot said. "But now they'll know we're somewhere around here."

"We had the building materials shipped to Garoe, Don. They knew it already."

"No, they *suspected* it. Which meant at least some of Ham's men would stay busy checking other possibilities. Now they can concentrate everybody here, and I hate to remind you, old buddy, but we've used up all our hidey-holes. This is *it.* They find us here, we got no other place to run." Elliot twisted the steering wheel, guiding them around a curve as they neared the safehouse in the mountains.

"Oh, well," Friday said. "Nobody lives forever, right?"

Elliot chuckled. He always liked working with Friday more than with other agents and informants. Something about their combined chemistry had resulted in an ability take things seriously but still remain light. "Right," he finally said. "Nobody lives forever, and who the hell would want to?"

A broad grin spread across Friday's face, and Elliot could see that at last the woman was no longer on his mind. "It's good, really," the Swahili said. "Think of what happens in your last years. Strokes. Sexual impotence. Dialysis machines."

"And in your case," Elliot said, "advanced Alzheimer's."

ANOTHER VOLLEY of automatic fire from the oncoming trucks drove Bolan back under the jeep. On the other side of the vehicle, a sniper round fired from the crumbling old government building slapped into the front fender as if to remind Bolan that he and the entire column of Marines were still caught in the carefully planned cross fire.

Somewhere down the line of vehicles, Bolan heard a scream. Then a voice screeched, "I'm blind! My God, I'm blind!"

Pressing his face low to the ground, Bolan looked between the front tires. Under the chassis of the truck ahead, he saw the legs of several men. He bellycrawled forward, then yelled, "Starr!"

One of the men rolled over. Then Starr said, "Pollock?"

Bolan scrambled out from under the jeep as a burst of autofire cut swaths of grass from the ground around his feet. The bullets singing in his ears, he dived forward, squirming under the truck and crowding in with the other men.

He came to rest on his belly, facing Starr. The sergeant's face was white. But his eyes were clear, in control. "Looks like my R&R to the States may get canceled." He smiled weakly.

"Just postponed," Bolan said. "But it'll be canceled if we don't act quick."

"Okay, Colonel," Starr said as more rounds struck the truck over their heads. "You outrank me. What do we do?"

The Executioner pointed toward the walkie-talkie headset over Starr's ears. "Get on the horn and divide us into two detachments. I'll take half the men and rush the building. The rest of you stay here, work yourselves into positions where you can return fire and wait for us to get back."

He rolled toward the outside of the circle and saw that the enemy vehicles had come to a halt. Their passengers had exited the vehicles and taken cover behind the engine blocks, where they continued to assault the convoy.

By the time he had rolled back to face Starr again, the sergeant had given his orders. "I've got you six men ready to go," he said.

"I need *half* of the men," Bolan said.

"That is half," Starr explained. "Of what's *left.*"

A young private scrambled under the truck and crawled toward them. "Sergeant Starr," he began, "I—"

Bolan reached up and ripped the headset from the man's ears. Wrapping it around his head, he spoke into the face mike. "This is Pollock," he said. "Count off."

"Jackson—ready, sir!"

"Faulk."

"Gagliardi!"

"Nance."

"Redwine, sir."

"Cobb."

Relentless fire from both sides continued to pound the convoy. Bolan reached out and tore a grenade from the combat harness of the young private. As he spoke again, Starr and the young man both moved to the edge of the truck and began firing at the enemy vehicles.

"I want one frag grenade from each man into the building on the count of three," Bolan ordered. "And I want us all inside before the smoke clears." He paused, said, "One," and rolled toward the center of the circle.

Bolan pulled the pin from the grenade and held the handle down. "Two," he said.

Rolling from under the truck and to his feet in one smooth motion, he brought his arm back behind him. As he threw the grenade toward the crumbling old building, he yelled, "Three!" into the face mike, then sprinted after the missile as it flew through the air.

Although the snipers were still invisible, their surgical shots continued as Bolan and the six Americans raced toward the ruins in the center of the convoy. Bolan saw the other grenades sail toward their marks as he ran.

His grenade hit first, opening a new hole in the front of the crumbling structure. The other six grenades all struck within a half second of each other, sounding like one giant explosion as the men neared the building.

Dust, blood, chips of stone and body parts filled the air as Bolan leaped up over the rubble and entered what was left of the edifice. He saw a man leaning back against a partially standing interior wall, blood pumping from a stub where his arm had once hung.

The arm lay a yard to the sniper's side. A blue arm band was still tied around the biceps.

Bolan fired as the man reached for the pistol in his belt with his remaining hand, sending a lone .44 Magnum missile to split the sniper's eyes. He heard a shot somewhere to his left, and a chip of stone struck him in the ear.

Bolan felt blood drip down his neck as he turned toward the sound of a bolt-action rifle chambering a round. Through the smoke and dust that hung in the air, he saw a man wearing a ragged green shirt ten feet to his right. His hair singed, angry red splotches covering his skin, the man looked like something from a postholocaust movie as he turned the scoped rifle toward Bolan.

Bolan twisted, his finger moving back on the trigger. The Desert Eagle roared in his hand as he fired from the hip, snapping another of the massive .44 Magnum slugs up into the man's chest.

The chatter of M-16s split the air as the other men reached the ruined building and went to work on the snipers. As dust settled and visibility returned, Bolan saw a man in a blue arm band fire his rifle point-blank into a soldier wearing a camouflage sweatband above his eyes.

The American's eyes opened wide in surprise as blood poured from his chest. Bolan turned toward the man with the arm band, triggering a double-tap of .44 bullets that entered his neck.

Racing to the fallen American, Bolan knelt and grasped his head. "Come on, Marine," he said, starting to lift the kid into his arms. "Let's get you out of..." He looked into the boy's sightless eyes, and his voice trailed off.

Bolan glanced up to see another of the warlord's men wearing a makeshift khaki uniform and athletic shoes. The man gripped an M-16 in both hands, firing semicontrolled blasts Bolan's way with the unfamiliar weapon.

Bolan shot from the kneeling position, watched the M-16 fall from the gunner's hands. The man hadn't had the GI rifle before; he had been sniping with a bolt-action rifle. But he had the M-16 now, which meant that the kid on the floor wasn't the only American casualty.

Keeping his eyes up, Bolan looked through the haze to see a red-haired American drop one of the snipers with a 3-round burst. To his side, another man from the convoy cut a figure eight of .223 ammo between two more of the enemy.

Slapping a fresh magazine into the Desert Eagle, Bolan rose to his feet. He was reaching for the M-16 in front of him when two more of Ham's men rounded the broken corner of what had once been a room and faced their personal Executioner.

Bolan lived up to his name. Both men took chest shots that traveled on through their spines. Chunks of flesh the size of tennis balls blew out through the exit wounds.

Suddenly the firing inside the pulverized building was over.

Bolan scooped the M-16 from the floor and turned back to the convoy. The war to his rear hadn't let up. The Marines beneath the jeeps and trucks were still pinned down by autofire from the Land Cruisers.

He checked the chamber of the M-16, then moved to a wall. Through a gap between a jeep and one of the transport trucks, he could see part of a head above the hood of a Land Cruiser.

Bolan steadied the rifle against the wall as he flipped the selector to semiauto. He dropped the sights on the head behind the truck and took a deep breath.

It was time to see to it that Sergeant Dennis Starr boarded the next plane home to see his family.

The lone round from the M-16 removed the top of the head as neatly as if the man behind the Land Cruiser had been scalped. A high-pitched scream echoed as what was left on top of the neck dropped from sight.

Bolan flipped the selector back to full auto as he charged from the building. "Starr, can you hear me?" he shouted into the face mike as he ran.

"Got you, Pollock," Starr said. "Go."

"We're coming out," Bolan announced. "My men will flank out and lay down cover fire into the vehicles. "Tell your men to get into better firing position as soon as we start."

. "Got you, Pollock. Everybody read him?"

Several affirmatives came back over the airwaves.

Bolan ran on, dodging fire and returning it as he moved toward the trucks. "Who's left inside?" he asked.

Faulk, Nance, Redwine and Cobb all sounded off.

"Faulk and Nance, go right," Bolan said into the radio. "Redwine and Cobb, take the left. Take up positions flanking the enemy vehicles. Let me know when you're in place."

"Where are you going, sir?" one of the voices asked.

Bolan dropped down behind a truck. His jaw tightened as he thought of Jackson and Gagliardi. Both had died in the attack, and he wondered which one he had briefly held in his arms. These two warriors had mothers and fathers, maybe wives and children who would soon find out of the loss of their loved ones.

"Where will you be going?" the voice repeated over the radio.

"Right up the middle," he growled into the face mike.

THE BLOODIED DEAD BODIES of Americans in desert cammies, the lifeless forms of African men and women, the screams and moans of the wounded who lay mixed with them on the ground—all these things registered in Bolan's mind, fueling his anger as he moved along behind the column of vehicles.

A voice sounded in his ear as he spotted Starr beneath a truck. "Nance in place, Colonel."

"Affirmative, Nance. Stand by." Bolan dropped to a knee behind the engine block of a truck. "How many men are left?" he asked the sergeant.

Starr leaned around the hood and fired a quick burst into the nearest of the warlord's trucks. Jumping back away from the return fire, he said, "Us or them?"

"Both."

Starr shook his head. "Us, I don't know. But we've taken casualties." He blew air between his clenched teeth. "Them—"

Bolan held up a hand as another voice came over the airwaves. "Redwine, sir. Ready when you are."

"Affirmative, Redwine," Bolan said. He turned back to Starr.

"They had nine of the Land Cruisers," Starr said. "And as best I can tell, four men in each one. I'd say we've taken out a third or so."

Bolan moved forward to peer around the bumper as the gunfire continued. If Starr's calculations were accurate, that left roughly two dozen of Ham's men still firing from behind the trucks parked in an arc on the other side of the convoy.

"Cobb in place," came over the radio.

"Stay put, Cobb," Bolan answered. He moved back to the Starr. "Any natives still in the area?"

"Just the dead ones," Starr replied. "The rest scattered like a covey of quail."

"Faulk, sir," said another voice.

Bolan told the final man of the team to get ready. Holding the face mike in one hand, Bolan spoke into it. "Listen up." He waited for the American gunfire to die down, then said, "This is Pollock again. When I give the word, I want every man here to hit the nearest vehicle with a grenade. Is that clear?"

Several affirmative responses came back. But not nearly as many as he had hoped for. Starr was right. The Americans had taken casualties, many casualties.

"Nance, Faulk, Redwine and Cobb," Bolan said. "You read me?"

All four men answered again.

"Same song, second verse," Bolan said. "As soon as you hear the explosions, go in for the cleanup. Start at your ends, and we'll meet in the middle. Everybody clear?"

Again the four Americans answered.

Bolan dropped the half-empty M-16 magazine from his weapon and took the full box Starr handed him. He shoved it into the mag well.

"I'll go with you," Starr said.

Bolan shook his head. "You stay here and cover us."

"Look," Starr argued. "You *need* me to help clear the vehicles. Just because I'm getting ready to go home doesn't mean I don't have a job just like the rest of—"

"You're wrong," Bolan interrupted.

"Dammit, Pollock, it's *my* job as much—"

"That's not what you're wrong about," Bolan explained. "It's your job, all right, but so is staying here with the rest of the men. What you're wrong about is me needing you." Before Starr could answer, he spoke into the mike again. "Toss 'em, guys."

A second later two dozen fragmentation grenades flew through the air toward the crescent of enemy vehicles.

Bolan leaned around the truck. Some of General Fajir Ham's men saw the grenades in the air.

At least he figured they must have. He heard two quick screams a second before the explosions decimated the enemy trucks.

Bolan rose, circled the front of the truck. The near-simultaneous roars were almost deafening, and sharp shards of steel and glass still flew through the air as he moved cautiously forward. He ducked a flying piece of tailpipe as the gas tanks that hadn't blown with the initial blasts caught flames and began exploding.

Bolan took up a position ten yards in front of the center vehicle, the stock of the M-16 pressed hard against his shoulder. A screeching, flaming form came twisting from behind a truck.

Bolan dropped it with a 3-round burst.

Two more burning men appeared, running frantically away from the vehicles on the other side. Bolan raised the sights to his eyes and ended their misery.

In his peripheral vision, he saw the men of the cleanup team at opposite ends of the crescent. As he scanned the vehicles for more survivors, Nance took out another enemy with a quick burst.

Bolan waited as the final gas tank erupted into flames. When no more of Ham's men appeared, he turned back to the convoy.

Far from being over, the work was just beginning.

"Assign a damage-control detail to check the wounded," Bolan said as soon as he reached Starr.

"And post a guard while it's going on." He turned a full circle, scanning the area. "I don't think there'll be a second wave, but there's no use taking chances."

Starr nodded, gave orders into his mike, then turned back to Bolan. "You staying or going on?"

"Going on," Bolan said. "And I need to borrow this Khalid, if he's still alive."

Starr nodded, then called the man on the radio. Khalid answered promptly and a moment later appeared in front of the trucks, holding a hot M-16 in his hands and appearing no worse for wear.

Bolan shook Starr's hand. "Thanks," he said.

Starr nodded wearily. "Anything else I can do for you before you leave?"

Bolan frowned, thinking. "No. You and your men have already done enough. You've got good soldiers, Sergeant."

Sergeant Dennis Starr was smiling as the Executioner and Khalid walked away.

Bolan examined the nearest jeep. A few bullet holes were visible, but didn't look as if they'd punctured any vital area. A quick look under the hood confirmed his judgment.

"You know the Erigavo area?" he asked Khalid as the tribesman took the passenger's seat while Bolan took the wheel.

"Certainly," Khalid said. His speech sounded formal, learned from textbooks.

"Ever heard of a guy named Donald Elliot?"

"Fish canning."

"That's him."

Bolan threw the jeep into gear and pulled away from the convoy. "He's supposed to have a place somewhere in the mountains."

"Correct."

Bolan turned toward the man next to him as they left the village of Garoe and sped up the darkened highway leading north. "You sound sure of it."

"I should say I am," Khalid said, smiling. "I helped him build it."

"How did you get to know him well enough that he'd trust you like that?" Bolan asked.

"I don't actually know Elliot that well," Khalid said. "My connection is more to his partner, Benjamin Barkari."

Bolan turned to the man at his side again. "You're of the same tribe? Both of you Swahili?"

"I should hope so," Khalid said, a wide smile spreading across his face. "We had the same mother and father."

Bolan didn't answer for a moment. Then the smile on Khalid's face spread to his own. Once in a while— once in a *great* while—you got lucky.

"Why didn't you tell me before that Benjamin Barkari was your brother?" Bolan asked.

Khalid Barkari shrugged. "You did not ask," he said.

DON ELLIOT SAT DOWN on the bed, untied his boots and pulled them off. His feet still on the floor, he fell back, looked at the ceiling and sighed.

Since General Ham's henchmen had chased him and Friday from the fish-cannery office three days ago, this was the first easy breath he had drawn, and he hoped it would be the beginning of a whole line of easier breathing.

Down the hall Elliot heard Friday settling into the other bedroom. They were here for the long haul, it appeared, and he needed to get settled, too. But not immediately. Right now all he wanted to do was close his eyes and sleep for about eight hours. Or eight days, or eight months...

The former CIA man felt himself nodding off, and it took every bit of willpower he had to pull his legs onto the bed and stretch out. He felt the taut muscles in his face begin to relax, and his lips curl upward. The past three days had been one life-and-death situation after another, but in many ways he'd had more fun than he'd had in the past nine years.

Elliot closed his eyes, still smiling. But enough was enough. The past few hours had reminded him that the life of an adventurer had its drawbacks. Like getting shot at repeatedly. And rarely sleeping.

Elliot let himself slip into a half sleep, then suddenly opened his eyes as his body jerked him back to consciousness. Fully awake again, he rose to his elbows as his eyes skimmed the room uneasily. Had he forgotten to activate any of the security devices? Was there *anything* he had forgotten to do?

No. He had done it all. Elliot fell back on the bed again and closed his eyes, but sleep didn't come. He went over the mental list of security precautions he had taken as soon as they'd arrived at the house. He and Friday had hidden the jeep under a pile of brush ten miles away, then hiked on in, carefully covering their trail. They had moved slowly into the narrow crack in the rocks that led to the hidden canyon, their rifles ready on the off chance that Ham's men had located the hideout.

Elliot felt his pulse quicken at the thought. No, he told himself, it was almost impossible. The chances had to be a million to one. Keeping the *fact* that he had been building a house confidential had been impossible, of course—there had been lumber and other equipment to buy, and word of the project had gotten out as he knew it would. But he, Friday and Friday's brother, Khalid, had picked up each shipment personally, and no one else had been to the location. The framing, plumbing, the installation of the alarm systems—they had done it all themselves. Besides Elliot and Friday, Khalid Barkari was the only other person who knew how to get to the place.

So what if Ham got hold of him and tortured the directions out of him? Khalid was tough like his brother, but every man had his breaking point.

No, dammit, that was stupid thinking—again a million-to-one shot. Khalid had been working as a guide for the Americans for the past six months. And even General Ham wasn't going to go up against the Marines to get a man who *might* know where to find them.

Elliot forced his mind back to the security system. The magnetic sensors started at the opening in the rocks, the only entrance and exit to the canyon. More of the hidden electrical circuits cut across the trail to the house at different heights. Sound discriminators circled the building for fifty yards, the doors and windows were guarded by vibration sensors and pressure mats lay under a quarter inch of earth around the house.

Anything out of the ordinary would trip a silent alarm, thus notify Elliot that they had visitors without letting Ham's men know they'd been alerted. That way, Elliot and Barkari could get their other little surprises ready....

Again Elliot tried to force himself to relax. The noise from the other bedroom had quieted. Now the only sound Elliot heard was a low snore drifting down the hall.

It took all of the strength the former CIA man could muster to reach over and kill the lamp on the bed stand. He flopped back on the bed and closed his eyes a final time, drifting into a deep, dreamless sleep.

Don Elliot didn't know how long he'd been asleep when he felt the rough hand on his shoulder jerk him to a sitting position. All he knew was that he was looking down the barrel of the biggest damned gun he'd ever seen in his life.

CHAPTER SEVEN

Moonlight flowed through the windows, casting a soft, eerie glow over the interior of the house. The only sound was the snoring—two sets of the deep nocturnal breathing—that drifted to the rear of the building.

Bolan drew the Desert Eagle as he slid silently down the hall over the carpet, Khalid at his heels. Khalid had explained the various aspects of the alarm systems he had helped install and they had experienced little difficulty deactivating the sensors as they made their way into the hidden canyon and on to the house. But Benjamin Barkari's younger brother had also warned that he hadn't visited the hideout for nearly a year, and there was always the chance that Elliot and his brother had added new security of which he would be unaware.

Bolan moved on silently. At the very least, Elliot and Barkari would have guns close at hand. And since there was no way of calling ahead to announce that it was "family" coming to visit, the only answer lay in getting the drop on the two fugitives before Elliot and Barkari mistook them for Ham's men and blew their heads off.

Reaching the open door to the bedroom, Bolan stopped. Inside the room, not three feet away, he saw a white man lying face up on the bed. Elliot.

Bolan turned and silently waved Khalid on down the hall. Turning back to the open door, he eyed the nightstand next to the bed. The lamp was the only thing on the surface. He swung his gaze back to the bed itself. Elliot lay on top of the covers, evidently having been too tired to even roll them down before he went to sleep. Bolan had a clear view, and no weapons were visible there, either.

But the Executioner had not survived the years through naïveté. Don Elliot had been a pro, and he had *something* waiting. Whether it was a gun, knife, club or whatever, the former CIA operative had some kind of weapon ready for that one-in-a-million chance that somebody beat the odds, found the house and made it inside without tripping the alarm.

Bolan's attention now turned to the man himself. Elliot still wore the clothes he must have arrived in— loose-fitting khaki slacks and a shirt that could hide any number of weapons.

Bolan moved suddenly, swiftly, silently. As he closed the distance to the bed in one quick stride, he saw Elliot's body stiffen as the former CIA man sensed his presence. Before the former CIA operative could open his eyes, Bolan shoved the barrel of the Desert Eagle into his face.

Bolan watched the man come fully awake. As his eyes cleared and he took in the situation, Don Elliot said, "I'm exhausted. And I'm sick of running, asshole. Just shoot me and let me go back to sleep." Ashe spoke, his left hand moved to his face to scratch his chin.

Bolan recognized the diversion as Elliot's other hand began moving behind his back. Smooth. Well done. Elliot had practiced it.

He reached out, grasping the hand and holding it in a viselike grip. "Don't do it, Elliot," he said in a clear calm voice. "I'm a friend."

The CIA man hesitated.

"I've come with Khalid Barkari," Bolan added quickly.

The use of the name extended the pause. Before Bolan could speak further, a voice he assumed to belong to Benjamin Barkari came down the hall. "Don't kill anybody, Don. I don't know the details yet, but it's my baby brother and some friend of his."

A moment later Benjamin and Khalid Barkari entered the room. Benjamin flipped the light switch. His lips were stretched across his face in good humor.

Bolan released Elliot's arm and stepped back, dropping the Desert Eagle to arm's length at his side.

Elliot sat up on the bed, rubbed his eyes with his free hand, then brought the hand that had been behind his back around to the front.

Bolan saw the stainless steel of the customized parts on the bright blue finish of the Government Model .45. A pro's gun. Every combat advantage, however slight, had been added to the weapon. Elliot took this pistol seriously.

The former CIA man dropped the .45 on the nightstand and said, "Damned thing digs into your back when you try to sleep, anyway." He got groggily to his feet, looked up at Bolan, then started for the hall. "I'll put the coffee on." He yawned over his shoulder. Then, stopping, he turned back. "Cream and sugar?" he asked.

"Black," Bolan replied, deadpan.

BOLAN SET the steaming mug on the coffee table and leaned back on the couch. He was probably as exhausted as Elliot and Barkari, but he couldn't afford to sleep. Not yet. With each passing minute, General Ham and this mysterious light-skinned man were closer to carrying out their plan.

It was time the Executioner did some planning of his own.

He glanced around the living room, noting the knotty-pine walls, the cedar-beamed ceiling, the sturdy oak furniture. This was a man's house, with far more emphasis put on function than decor. Don Elliot had prepared well for emergencies, and Bolan had no doubt that he and Friday could have lived safely within the canyon for months, if not years.

The modern appliances ran off a generator, and Bolan knew that the pantries would be stuffed with canned food. Bolan watched Benjamin Barkari—now wearing a white apron—sprinkle garlic powder over the four porterhouse steaks sizzling on the indoor grill.

Bolan turned back to the men, seeing that the sky through the picture window was began to lighten. In the distance he saw the eastern wall of the mountains take on a hazy purple hue.

Elliot had designed this place with all the benefits of a hideout without the drawbacks. By relying on a combination of high-tech security and invisibility, he had been able to include picture windows that provided a startling view.

"Hey, Friday," Elliot yelled over his shoulder into the kitchen. "Breakfast about ready?" He lifted his coffee mug and took a sip.

"Almost," Benjamin Barkari yelled back.

"Tell me, how'd you come across this valley in the first place?" Bolan asked.

"A little bird told him," Friday called out from the kitchen.

Elliot laughed. "Inside joke," he said. He raised his coffee mug again. "Friday and I used to come up to this area bird hunting. They've got a breed of pigeon in this region that's right up there with pheasant if you cook it right. Anyway, we shot this bird, and it disappeared behind the rocks. Next thing I know, Harpo—he was our bird dog at the time—*disappears* into the side of the mountain."

Bolan nodded. "The entrance is hidden until you're already on top of it," he said. "You've got to know it's there or you'd never see it."

Elliot nodded back. "That's what we're counting on, anyway." He rose, went to the kitchen and returned with the carafe from the coffee maker. "Khalid tell you about the history of the canyon?" he asked, filling Bolan's cup.

"Just that this was where ancient religious ceremonies were performed."

Elliot moved to fill Khalid's cup, then his own. "Somewhere in history, people lost track of this place. The legend remained, of course, but most people—me included, until we blundered onto it—believe it's *just* that. A legend."

Benjamin Barkari appeared with a huge wooden tray. The thick porterhouses sizzled as he leaned over and placed a plate and utensils on the coffee table. Bolan looked down to see a veritable feast of steak, toast and hash brown potatoes.

"Please excuse the bread and potatoes," Friday said as he moved on around the room giving the other men their breakfasts. "They are canned, and I'm afraid they taste like it."

"I'll try to overlook it," Bolan said, cutting a piece of steak. It had been cooked to perfection and was hardly the kind of meal he'd expected in this remote area of war-torn Somalia. As soon as he'd swallowed, he said, "Elliot, we've got to talk."

"No."

Bolan looked up.

"Eat first, Pollock," Elliot said, taking a bite of toast. "We'll talk then." He paused for a sip of coffee. "But I've already figured out why you've come, and the answer is no."

Bolan nodded. "We'll eat first," he said. He cut another slice of the porterhouse.

Bolan frowned as he ate. Elliot was smart. *Damned* smart. He didn't know who Bolan was exactly— probably assumed he was CIA himself. But he knew Bolan wanted his help. Wanted to use his knowledge of the country to find a way to get close to Ham and the other warlords.

All four men were famished from their journeys, and breakfast went down with lightning speed. As soon as Elliot and Friday had taken the plates back to the kitchen, the former CIA man came back into the living room and said, "Okay, Pollock, any friend of Khalid's is a friend of mine. And you're a fellow Yank, and maybe that counts for even more." He paused, then said, "So consider this place yours for as long as you'd like to stay." Another pause brought a harder expression to his face. "But don't expect me to leave and go looking for Ham or anybody else with you."

Bolan crossed his legs and looked the man in the eyes. "You wouldn't like to get a little revenge on Ham?"

"For what?"

"Stealing your fish-cannery business, for starters. How about taking all you've worked for for the last nine years?"

"Best thing that ever happened to me," Elliot said. "My blood pressure's probably dropped twenty points, and my appetite's come back." He nodded toward the kitchen. Turning back, he said, "Not everybody was cut out to can fish. I learned that the hard way." He dropped into the chair where he'd sat earlier.

Bolan sat silently, forcing him to go on.

"Ham and the other warlords are none of my business," Elliot said. "I don't have any intention of getting involved. Friday and I are going to stay here until the food runs out, then leave the country."

"Really?" Bolan said. "Where do you plan to go?"

"Home, maybe. Haven't decided yet."

"What do you plan to do when you get there? Any idea on how you're going to put the porterhouses on the table since Ham has all your money now?"

Elliot laughed. "I *like* living well," he said. "But I don't *need* it. Porterhouses beat the hell out of balogna, Pollock, but it's been my experience that wealth doesn't have a damned thing to do with happiness."

Bolan waited. Elliot was a tough nut to crack. He'd have to try another angle. Leaning forward, Bolan stared at the former CIA man. "All I need is an in. Get me close enough to Ham and the others, and I'll take them out myself."

Elliot shook his head. "Killing the bastards doesn't bother me, Pollock. They deserve it a thousand times over. Fact is, if I went to all the trouble of helping you, I'd probably *insist* on pulling a few triggers myself."

"You've got a deal," Bolan said.

Elliot lowered his eyes, shook his head and laughed softly. "You're good, Pollock, I'll give you that. But I said *if,* not *will.* The answer is still no."

Still staring at the man across from him, Bolan sat straight again. "Okay, if you aren't upset about what Ham did to you, how about what he and the other warlords have done to the Somalian people?"

The look that came over Elliot's face told Bolan he'd hit a nerve. The man's face flushed pink, and the anger seemed ready to boil over any second. "That's not my business, either," he said.

Bolan ran with the ball. "Of course not. None of it's your problem, is it? Not the children with bloated bellies dying of starvation. Not the women being raped. And certainly not the men who get shot because they accidentally step in the way of one of Ham's gunmen, or look at them wrong, or maybe just because the warlord's men haven't killed anyone in a day or two and they're bored." Bolan glanced dramatically around the room. "No, it's not *your* problem, Elliot. You're living just great." He nodded toward the kitchen. "Got any steak left?"

By now Don Elliot's face had turned beet red. He jumped to his feet. "Listen, you son of a bitch," he yelled. "You don't know *shit* about me or Friday or what we've done. Our fish business kept more people from starving than Barre's whole pinko government. We donated money to every fucking Tom, Dick and Harry relief organization that came into the office, and we built maybe half of the housing you saw in Mogadishu. *Why the fuck do you think Ham came after us in the first place?*" He stood there staring at Bolan, his eyes blazing.

"That was a nice speech, Elliot," Bolan said calmly. "And I don't doubt that every part of it is true. But what it boils down to is that in the past you did everything you could to help the Somalians." He leaned forward and lifted his coffee mug. "I guess what I can't understand is why don't you do what they need *now?*" He took a sip of coffee. "Something that won't just help relieve a little of their misery, but *end* it."

Elliot pivoted away from Bolan and faced the picture window as the sun tipped over the mountains. "We're out of practice," he said without conviction. "We've lost the edge."

"Elliot," Bolan argued, "the two of you escaped the attack on your factory, you escaped another in Mogadishu and a third at the cave. You've made it all the way across Somalia with Ham's men chasing you every step of the way, and all I had to do to find you was follow the trail of bodies you left behind. You want to tell me you've lost the edge? Sorry, but I don't buy it."

There was a long silence, finally broken by Benjamin Barkari. "He's right, Don," he said softly from the kitchen.

Another silence followed. Finally Elliot's barely audible voice drifted back. "Yeah, dammit, I know."

The former CIA man turned back around. His eyes drilled holes through his audience, but they were eyes filled now with the intensity of purpose rather than anger, confusion and conscience. "I've thought about killing Ham and the others for years," he said. "And

I've already come up with the only plan I think has a chance in hell of working."

BOLAN ADJUSTED the hot-water tap and stepped into the shower, feeling the fiery needles of water wash away the dirt and grime of the Somalian roads. He shook his head in amazement at the modern comforts Elliot and Barkari had been able to install in such a remote site. The generator produced enough power to offer a hot shower at the same time his clothes were being washed and dried in the laundry room.

He thought about what Elliot had said earlier. The former CIA operative was a good man, and it hardly surprised Bolan that he'd been unable to grow rich in the fish-canning business and ignore the poverty in which the average Somalian lived.

But financial aid hadn't been enough. Don Elliot had already started planning to assassinate the warlords by the time General Ham ran him out of business.

He hadn't heard Elliot's plan yet. All four men had fought the fires of hell to reach the mountain hideaway and were at the point of exhaustion by the time Elliot had finally agreed to assist Bolan. They had opted to catch two hours of sleep before sitting down for a war conference.

Bolan wrapped the towel around his waist and walked from the bathroom down the hall to the laundry room. As he passed the bedrooms, he heard the other men waking up.

Bolan pulled his clean clothes from the dryer and got dressed. Five minutes later he joined Elliot and the Barkari brothers in the living room. The former CIA man had made more coffee and handed out the mugs as the others took their seats.

Bolan dropped down onto the couch where he'd sat earlier. He saw no reason to waste time. "Okay," he said, looking at Elliot, "you've thought about it already. Let's hear what you have in mind."

Elliot adjusted his position in the armchair. "The different warlords have different degrees of security," he said. "Morris is probably the most lax, but even he travels with several of his best men as bodyguards. Colonel James has what amounts to a fort in the south, and he rarely leaves. Jabbar in Djibouti is more like Morris. He gets out a lot, but during this period where they've turned in their guns, my guess is he's staying pretty close to home. I've also heard that both he and Ham have hidden compounds complete with top-notch security systems, metal detectors for visitors and the like. That's where they'll be until the Americans go home, is my guess." Elliot lifted his cup to his lips, sipped, then set it down on the coffee table. He made a face. "I drink any more of this crap and my eyeballs will float away."

Khalid spoke up. "So what are you saying, Don? That we'll have to infiltrate these compounds and kill them there? Where they're the most protected? This is the craziest idea I've ever— "

Benjamin Barkari reached over and grasped Khalid's arm. "Not as crazy as you might think," he told his brother. "It will not be easy. But not *impossible,* either."

Bolan leaned forward. "You know where these compounds are?"

Elliot shook his head. "No, and finding out would have meant a risk of tipping our hand to the warlords. So Friday and I were waiting until we were *sure* we were going to do it before we took the chance." He shrugged. "All this was before Ham chased us out of business, of course. Just staying alive has taken over as top priority since."

Bolan nodded. Elliot and Barkari were impressive, competent operatives, and Khalid had proved himself, as well. These would be three good men with whom to go into battle. "Let's hear the rest of it," he said.

"In short," Benjamin Barkari said, "I think Morris will be the easiest since he's the most visible. James, at least to my knowledge, pretty much depends on brute force to keep people out of his place, and we can find ways around that. But Ham and Jabbar—they're another matter. Neither Don nor I are too excited about trying to deactivate alarm systems we're not familiar with. Too much chance to screw up and get caught. So we felt a snitch introduction was the only way to go. We'll need a story and a reason to meet the two men. The actual hit will have to be one of opportunity once we're inside, and because of that we'll pretty much have to play the escape plan by ear, as well."

For a few moments Bolan didn't speak. There were weaknesses in what the two men had planned. For instance, getting inside the compounds didn't mean they would encounter opportunities to strike. And it was far easier to *plan* playing an escape "by ear" than it actually was to pull one off in the midst of armed men whose leader you'd just killed. But any plan had flaws, calculated risks that were necessary if it ever went past the planning stage and became a mission.

"What about just hitting them all at the next news conference?" Khalid said. "They'd all be together and—"

Bolan shook his head. "The news cameras," he said. "If they happened to catch a shot of Elliot or your brother, they'd eventually uncover their connection to the CIA."

"Can you imagine the headlines?" Elliot said. "CIA Assassins Kill U.S. Political Enemies."

The room fell silent. Bolan closed his eyes and rubbed his temples. Elliot was right. They might get away with taking Morris out in public, but the other three warlords would have to fall behind their own walls. He would have to enter the lair of each lion in order to kill him.

Bolan opened his eyes and looked up. "So," he said, "let's begin with the first stage. We need a snitch. Do you have one?"

"No," Benjamin Barkari ansered. "We have been trying to think of someone—"

"I did last night," Elliot broke in. He looked at Friday. "Aziza."

Barkari shook his head. "No," he told his partner. "We could never trust her. He has chosen her path, and she no longer—"

"I don't think so," Elliot said with mild irritation in his voice, and Bolan could sense there was something of a personal nature going on. "Aziza, I strongly suspect, has her own reasons for what she's done. Look, Friday, we need *one* person with connections to *all four* warlords. We're talking about killing four very powerful men who have connections to one another. The minute the first one goes down, the others are going to get paranoid as hell. By the time the second one is lying in his grave, they'll insulate themselves with bodyguards and won't see anyone they don't know well."

"Well, they damned sure know Aziza well," Benjamin Barkari said sarcastically.

Bolan could see from their faces that both Elliot and Khalid knew why Benjamin Barkari seemed so adamant that this Aziza not be involved. But when Friday didn't volunteer to explain, Bolan saw no reason to ask. Barkari's personal life was of no interest to him unless it might somehow jeopardize the mission. Right now, however, he needed to know who this woman was and why Elliot thought she could get them into the compounds.

"So who is this Aziza?" Bolan asked.

"A whore," Barkari replied. "Just a whore."

"No, she's not," Elliot said. "She's smart. She's been the lover of three of the four remaining warlords, and she's become a rich woman in the process."

"So she's a high-priced whore," Friday said.

Elliot ignored him. "There's a story behind her, but what it all boils down to is that she's our best bet. Maybe our *only* bet. Colonel James is the only one she's never slept with, but he'll know her."

"Then with a good story she could get us close to all of them?" Bolan asked.

Elliot smiled. "With Aziza, even a half-assed story might work. Aziza isn't just another whore to these guys—particularly Ham and Morris. They *love* her. Fought each other over her for a while. You'll understand what I mean when you meet her. She's . . . she's like a prize. A princess."

"Okay," Friday said. "Then she's a *royal* whore."

Bolan frowned. Whatever the deal was, it *was* personal. And serious. He made a mental note to get the Swahili warrior alone at the first opportunity and find out what was going on.

"All right," Bolan said. "Let's assume for a minute that she agrees to help. We need a story that'll not only make sense, but one that assures us the warlords won't get together and compare notes. After the first one goes down, if they make any connection to this Aziza, the mission won't only be over, she'll be dead."

"Any ideas?" Elliot asked.

Bolan nodded. "First I want to ask you a question. Rumor is that there's a light-skinned man—maybe a Caucasian, more likely an Arab—hanging out with Ham these days. Any idea who he is or what he's up to?"

Elliot shrugged. "Word on the street is that he's an arms dealer. Some guy who's behind the fact that Ham and the others are finally ready to turn in their rifles. He's going to resupply them all after the U.S. goes home." He paused, chuckling. "A variation of the foolish idea that you can stop crime by controlling guns."

Bolan frowned. That could be right, he supposed. If the light-skinned man was a gun dealer, he stood to make a substantial profit. But something in his gut told him there was more to it—something bigger than just a business deal. He stood up. "Okay," he said. "An idea's beginning to form. We'll work on it on the way." He rose and started toward the hall.

The other men in the room jumped up. "On the way where?" Don Elliot asked.

"To meet Aziza," Bolan said.

GENERAL FAJIR HAM WAVED goodbye to General Jabbar as the helicopter rose into the sky, turned and started back toward the Somalian border.

"The man trusts you," said Abu-Iyad, who was in the front seat next to the pilot.

"Of course he does," Ham said, the false smile of friendship he had shown to Jabbar as they took off still on his face. "Why shouldn't he trust me?"

The man in the front seat laughed. "Because I suspect that as soon as you receive the new weapons, you will take over Djibouti."

The smile faded from Ham's lips. That was *exactly* what he intended to do. But he had told no one of his plan. Were his motives so easy to read?

"You are a white man," Ham said as the chopper crossed the border. "You know nothing of our ways, let alone the sense of loyalty that African tribesmen have for one another."

The light-skinned man turned to face him, and in the man's eyes Ham could see that he knew the comment had been offensive. "I am sorry," the man said. "Perhaps I was wrong. But should that be your intention, I would have you know that it would be supported by me—and our mutual benefactor. We want only what you and I have discussed, but we would like to see a competent man in charge of all of Somalia. One we could continue to work with."

Ham leaned forward. "You do not feel you could work with Jabbar?"

Abu-Iyad shrugged. "Perhaps. But you are far wiser. Far stronger. Things would go more smoothly if you were in charge of all of Somalia and Djibouti."

Ham sat back. He knew what the man had just said was the most blatant of flatteries, spoken to massage his ego. Yet even with that knowledge, the words were effective, and he felt the pride surge through his soul.

He was, of course, the strongest of the warlords. And no doubt he had gotten that way by being the wisest.

The plateaus of Somalia appeared, and the helicopter began to descend. "We will speak of this matter again after the weapons arrive," Ham said.

The man in the front seat nodded. "We should," he said. "I believe it would be most beneficial to both of us."

The Hughes 500D flew low over a large boulder. Ham remained quiet as the helicopter landed next to the rock, then opened the door and placed a foot on the boarding step. "You wish to come with me?" he asked Ali Abu-Iyad.

The man in the front seat shook his head. "I must return to my country and make certain there has been no delay in the shipment."

"There better not have been," Ham said. "If there has, it would not be wise for you to return."

The light-skinned man smiled politely. "There will be no problems," he said. "But please, you must remember. We are helping *you* as much as you are helping *us*."

Ham watched as the lighter man stepped out of the cabin and dropped to the ground. The man's expression told Ham that he wasn't afraid, that he knew his country held five hundred times the power Ham did and that while they might need something that Ham could offer, the warlord needed them even more.

He was right. And that knowledge infuriated Fajir Ham.

"I will see you when you return," the warlord said through clenched teeth.

The man next to the pilot was still smiling as the helicopter rose into the air.

Ham watched it become a tiny speck high in the air, then looked out over the plateau. The anger still burned in his chest as he scanned the flat horizon for curious eyes.

Perhaps at the moment General Fajir Ham controlled nothing but a section of a poverty-stricken Third World country. But it was by far the largest section, and it would grow even larger. He had already disposed of Field Marshal Salih. Next he would take over Djibouti, then move south to overrun General Morris and Colonel James. With the additional troops he had picked up from Salih, added to the men he would inherit from Jabbar, the two southern warlords would fall quickly. Then he would rule both Somalia and Djibouti.

And men like Ali Abu-Iyad would treat him with *genuine* respect rather than the counterfeit esteem they did now. Or they would die.

Ham turned to the man-made boulder and pressed the button in its side. The squeaking sounds of gears and pulleys broke the silence over the plateau as the boulder slid aside to reveal a doorway.

Ham's war club tapped against the concrete as he descended the flight of steps. He flipped a switch on the wall at the bottom, and the door above him began closing, the rock sliding back into place. Two men wearing well-starched khakis and holding AK-47s nodded as Ham passed through the metal detector, the steel inserts in the war club setting it off. He turned down the hall to his left. From the kitchen at the end of the hall came the fragrant odor of roasting kid and spiced rice. As he walked toward it, he could see several black women peeling bananas and washing mangoes and papayas. He followed the smell and sight as far as an adjoining hallway, then turned right.

Small bedrooms lined this side of the underground complex—quarters for the staff, guards and the two women besides Aziza that Ham kept on hand. More armed guards stood watch at both ends of the hall, and he passed them and a dozen identical doors before turning left again to cut between the living and dining rooms to his office.

Ham entered the office and closed the door, dropping into an armchair beside his desk. The anger still flowed through him as if his veins had been injected with a molten lava, and he tapped the war club against the floor.

Respect would come, he·told himself. It would come soon. It would come with power, and that power would come through the weapons he would soon receive.

A soft tapping sound caused the warlord to open his eyes. He looked up to the door that connected his office to the master bedroom. The tapping sounded again, and he said, "Come."

The door opened slowly. Then the most beautiful face Fajir Ham had ever seen appeared as she leaned around the doorway, showing the expanse of her caramel-colored swanlike neck.

"You have returned?" Aziza said, her voice like a symphony of flutes.

Ham didn't answer. He simply stared, taking in her beauty, feeling the anger in his heart give way to the desire that now overcame him.

"I have been waiting," Aziza said, and stepped around the corner into the office.

Ham felt himself gasp for breath. The woman wore nothing but a necklace.

Painstakingly carved ivory elephants, lions, tigers and other beasts dangled from the gold and silver around her neck as Aziza walked forward, her small, rounded breasts bobbing gently with each step. The warlord's eyes dropped from the firm breasts to the smooth muscles in her thighs, then returned to her face. Her entire body was covered with a light sheen of sweat, and Ham guessed she had been on the treadmill in the bedroom when he'd arrived.

Aziza's lips pouted, her eyes playful, as she stopped in front of Ham. She leaned forward, grabbing a handful of the hair on the back of his head and pulling his face to her tight belly.

Ham's tongue shot out, flickering over the caramel skin. He tasted the salty sweat mixed with the fine, feathery hairs on her abdomen, then his mouth moved lower toward the thicker patch of hair between her legs.

Above his head, he heard Aziza purr. "Do you want me?" she asked. "Do you want me *now?*"

A mental image of Ali Abu-Iyad flashed through Ham's brain. The anger returned to mix with his lust. "I will have you," he growled.

Ham stood up, his lips moving to hers. He kissed her hard, feeling the woman's lips press back against his. He felt desire flood his soul as Aziza pulled his robe over his head and threw it to the floor.

The warlord pressed his body into her, waiting for the lust in his heart to reach his groin. He threw his head back to face the ceiling, screaming in anger and frustration when nothing happened.

Aziza reached up, gently cupping his face with both hands. "Quiet," she whispered. "Quiet, my master. It will work. We will make it work." She took his hand and led him around the desk and through the door to the adjoining bedroom.

CHAPTER EIGHT

The two jeeps had been hidden within twenty yards of each other, yet Bolan hadn't noticed the one Elliot and Barkari had hidden when he and Khalid arrived.

Now, as the four men began to throw the branches and other camouflage from the vehicles, Bolan reminded himself that sometimes you really *did* have a stroke of luck thrown your way.

He had worked with many men over the years, both competent and incompetent. Don Elliot and Benjamin and Khalid Barkari were professionals, and Bolan was pleased that fate had thrown these men on his side for the mission.

Bolan slid a heavy branch from the hood and let it roll to the ground. When she wasn't shacked up with one of the warlords—Ham being her latest semipermanent companion—this Aziza lived in Mogadishu. Which meant that unless they came across an aircraft of some kind, they were about to make another whirlwind drive across the plateau.

Elliot threw the final branch from the other jeep, then walked to the one Bolan and Khalid were uncovering. "Why don't you hop in with your brother, Khalid?" Elliot suggested. "I need to talk to our new fearless leader, and the trip down is as good a time as any."

Khalid looked up. Bolan saw the two men's eyes meet and saw the understanding that passed between them.

Bolan slid behind the wheel as Khalid got into the other jeep with his brother. Elliot took the passenger's side, and a moment later the two jeeps were heading out of the mountains.

Bolan shifted gears. "Let's hear it."

Elliot didn't waste any time. "Okay. You may have noticed a bit of a change in Friday's attitude whenever the subject of Azizi comes up."

"A man would have to be brain-dead not to."

Elliot chuckled. "Yeah, I guess so. Anyway, to make a long story short, they used to be in love."

Bolan nodded. He could understand it. It wasn't that uncommon for good men to fall in love with prostitutes. The same drive to right wrongs and see that justice was done often instilled in these warriors an urge to save the women from themselves. "So what happened?" he asked as the jeep whined down the steep incline.

The former CIA man shrugged. "She left him."

"Why?"

Elliot looked over his shoulder, and even though he knew the men behind them couldn't hear, his voice lowered. "You want the truth or the story Aziza gave Friday?"

"How about both? I need to know the truth, but I also need to know anything that might affect your partner's reactions while we're working this thing."

Elliot nodded. "Well, in short, Aziza told him she didn't love him anymore. That he was gone too much and that he bored the living shit out of her when he wasn't gone."

"But that's not the truth?" Bolan probed.

"Not only no, but *hell no*. I knew the woman well. She loved him, all right." Elliot glanced over his shoulder again. "Aziza was a performer. A good one. She was walking home from a club where she'd been singing one night, and a dozen or so of General Morris's men followed her out the door. They knew she was going with a Swahili, and they gang-raped her."

Bolan's fists tightened on the wheel. There were few crimes—maybe none—that bore a stigma the way rape did. As unreasonable as it was, in many parts of the world the woman was still blamed. She had been "soiled," and at best was considered to be "used goods."

Bolan could figure out the rest. "She never told Friday what had happened because she was afraid he'd get himself killed seeking revenge."

"Good guess," Elliot said. "And she made me promise not to tell him, either."

"His brother knows, though, doesn't he?"

Elliot nodded. "Yep. How'd you know that?"

"I saw the look that passed between you earlier. But tell me this. What's this woman doing hanging out with the warlords after all that's happened?

Elliot shrugged. "I don't know," he said. "Maybe she's found a way to get rich." He paused. "But like I said, Pollock, I knew her pretty well myself. If you ask me, she's using what works for her and planning her own revenge."

Bolan didn't answer, and silence fell over the jeep.

They rolled up over a rise in the road, then the terrain began to level out. Gradually the mountains grew smaller, finally becoming foothills. The afternoon sun climbed high in the air, and the scorching African heat began to soak the men's shirts.

Elliot broke the silence as they neared the plateau again. "As soon as we get to Mogadishu, we'll check her mother's house," he said. "If she isn't there, it'll mean she's with one of the warlords again. Her mother might know how to reach her without alerting anyone."

Bolan nodded. "Good idea. But I think there's something we'd better take care of first."

Elliot turned to him. "What's that?"

Bolan reached over the seat, grabbed the sling of one of the AK-47s and swung it over to Elliot. Turning back to the road, he nodded to the curve a quarter mile ahead.

A Toyota Land Cruiser had just rounded the bend.

Four more similar vehicles were behind it.

EVEN AT AN EARLY AGE, David Sadiki had seen something in himself that many men with the same problem never realized.

His verbal skill exceeded his capability.

Sadiki learned young that his gift was speech, and by the time he had reached the age of fifteen he had talked his way under the skirts of most of the available girls of his tribe and even several of the wives of the Issa warriors.

As he grew older, Sadiki found that with a little modification, the same techniques worked in nonsexual matters. Consequently he had gotten every job he'd ever sought.

But David Sadiki had never sustained a relationship with any woman for longer than six weeks. Most of the jobs he had talked his way into had lasted less than a year. He could get the woman but he couldn't keep her. He could get the job but he couldn't do the job.

In short, David Sadiki could "talk the talk" but he couldn't "walk the walk."

And he knew this.

The hot wind blew through the open windows of the lead vehicle as the search party drove north out of Erigavo. Sadiki didn't bother to watch the road—he had assigned other men to such trivial duty. Instead, he thought back to *The Peter Principle,* a book he had read many years ago.

For the past month he had been in charge of General Ham's military strikes, and things had not gone particularly well. Had he talked himself past his level of competency, as discussed in *The Peter Principle?* Perhaps. No, *probably.* He had been successful in creating distrust between the warlord and Ham's former right-hand man, Taza. He had climbed the back staircase to take both Taza's place and his title of captain. But now, as Taza lay in his shallow grave on the plateau, Sadiki found he had another problem.

Quite frankly he didn't have the foggiest idea of how to run an army.

The line of trucks moved on across the plateau. Far in the distance, Sadiki could see the mountains. Elliot and Barkari had been spotted in an army jeep, heading north, which seemed to confirm the rumor that they had a hideout somewhere north of Erigavo. But did they really? Or was Sadiki pursuing another dead end that would mean he had to return and report another failure to General Ham?

If so, this would be his *last* failure. If he didn't locate Don Elliot and Ben Barkari, and locate them fast,
his body would be feeding the worms next to Taza's.

The grade grew steeper as they reached the foothills. Gradually what had been a flat, straight road
began to curve around small rock formations. Sadiki
closed his eyes, concentrating.

A story. He needed a story. With the right words he
could convince General Ham that this failure had not
been his fault.

Sadiki felt his body shift as the Land Cruiser
rounded another curve. But what story? It would have
to be far better than the last if he expected to live and
keep his position.

"Captain?" The driver's words broke into Sadiki's
concentration.

Sadiki didn't open his eyes. "Not now, Kafu," he
said in irritation. "I am thinking."

"But Captain—"

"Not *now,* dammit!" Sadiki felt the Land Cruiser
slow but paid no attention. A scapegoat, that was
what he needed. It had worked with Taza, and it
would work again. If he could put the blame onto one
of the other men in the search party, he could—

"Captain, please..."

Sadiki closed his eyes tighter against the intrusion.
"If you interrupt my thoughts again, Kafu," he said,
"you will be shot." Yes, a scapegoat. He would pick
one of the men out, then create the illusion that he had
helped Elliot and Barkari cover their tracks. It would
take intimate planning and perhaps planting some
false evidence, but it would work.

After all, had not speech—the ability to talk his way into what he wanted and out of what he didn't—always been his gift?

"Captain!"

Anger filled Sadiki at the driver's failure to heed his warning. Kafu would pay a heavy price for this insolence. Not by being shot as he had threatened, but by becoming the scapegoat Sadiki needed.

David Sadiki opened his eyes and started to turn to the driver. He stopped when he saw the two jeeps barreling toward them less than fifty yards up the road.

A hailstorm of automatic fire shattered the windshield of their truck. "Stop!" Sadiki screamed. Then he flew forward against the dash as Kafu stomped the brake.

The warlord's right-hand man felt numb all over. He looked down to see his shirt soaked with blood. He opened his mouth to speak again, but only more blood poured forth, and David Sadiki suddenly realized that it didn't matter.

It was far too late for talk.

BOLAN DOWNSHIFTED the gears and hit the accelerator. "Wait until we get within range," he told Elliot as the wind whipped his hair back over his head. "Then give them the whole magazine."

Elliot had already turned his back to Bolan. His left leg was extended and braced against the floorboard as his other knee dug into the jeep's seat. Strapping the seat belt over his calf to secure himself, he glanced over his shoulder, then nodded toward the low hills on both sides of the road ahead. "You gonna try to reach the rocks?" he shouted into the wind.

Bolan shook his head as the jeep zoomed on. "I'm not going to *try* to get there, Elliot," he said. "I'm going to *do* it."

The former CIA operative buckled the seat belt across his calf, twisted toward the road and brought the stock of the AK-47 up against his shoulder. Sighting down the barrel at the oncoming vehicles, he said, "Thank God for the power of positive thinking, eh, Pollock?"

Bolan didn't answer. Looking up into the rearview mirror, he raised his hand, waving for Benjamin and Khalid Barkari to follow. The motion was unnecessary. The following jeep had increased speed and was matching their pace. As they neared the oncoming trucks, Bolan pointed toward the hills on the left side of the road.

In the mirror he saw Benjamin Barkari nod behind the wheel. He raised his hand, his thumb and index finger circling into the "okay" sign. Next to Barkari, Bolan could see Khalid strapping himself into the passenger's seat as Elliot had done.

"Something's wrong," Elliot shouted over the wind and grinding engine. "They *have* to have seen us by now. But they aren't even changing speed."

Again Bolan chose not to answer. It was true. The convoy was behaving as if they hadn't seen the jeeps. They hadn't sped up, slowed down or made any change since rounding the curve.

Had they mistaken the two jeeps for an American patrol? It wasn't likely. In view of the size of the warlords' own armies, Uncle Sam never went out this light. No, there had to be another reason.

But that reason didn't matter. In another few seconds the convoy would be upon them. And the reasons for the lax behavior on the part of Ham's men would be the least of Bolan's concerns.

Fifty yards from the advancing trucks, Bolan tapped the brake. In the corner of his eye, he saw Benjamin and Khalid Barkari pull up next to him in the oncoming lane.

"Let's do it!" Bolan yelled, and as the words left his mouth the explosions from two AK-47s met his ears.

Bolan saw the windshield of the lead vehicles vaporize as he cut the wheel hard to the right.

The Barkari brothers' jeep shot toward the rocks on the opposite side of the convoy.

Elliot twisted, firing over his head into the second of the warlord's vehicles as Bolan stomped the brake and brought the jeep to a halt next to the rocks. He reached over the seat, grabbing the other AK-47. He was halfway out of the vehicle when he heard Elliot behind him.

"Pollock! I'm stuck!"

Bolan leaned back into the jeep, whipping the Spyderco Civilian knife from his belt. He saw Elliot struggling with the buckle on the seat belt.

The tip of the Spyderco's serrated blade slid under the belt as the first of the return rounds peppered the jeep. Bolan sliced up and back, snapping the nylon in two and diving across the seat as more fire fell over them like a hailstorm. Finding the handle, he threw open the door, shoved Elliot out to the ground, then scrambled across the seats after him.

The sharp cracks of the rifle rounds were punctuated by dull thuds as the bullets struck the other side of the jeep. Bolan crab-crawled backward, pressing his back against the fender. From the road he heard the screech of rubber as the fleet of Land Cruisers slid to a stop.

Bolan didn't know who was leading this pack of wolves, but whoever was in charge was either incredibly stupid or had little experience. By stopping where they had, the warlord's men were between the rocks on both sides of the road. Now, if he and Elliot could make it to cover, with the Barkari brothers on the other side of the road, they'd have the enemy in a cross fire.

Bolan turned to Elliot. "You hurt?"

The former CIA man shook his head.

"Then let's go." Slinging the AK-47 over his back, he rose to all fours and hurried to the front of the jeep. The boulders at the foot of the hills stood ten yards past the vehicle, but if they could make it across the gap, they'd be shielded by walls of rock that would laugh at the AK-47's 7.62 mm rounds.

Bolan waited for a lull in the fire, then shot forward. He reached the nearest boulder a split second before a string of fire followed his tracks. A louder explosion blasted over the bullets as he ducked down behind the rock.

One of the Land Cruisers' gas tanks had exploded.

Turning back toward the jeep, Bolan saw that Elliot had moved to the point where he'd been a moment earlier. The former CIA man squatted now, waiting for another lull in the battle before chancing the sprint that might mean life or death.

Bolan decided to help him.

Unslinging the AK-47, Bolan rose from cover and saw the other four vehicles parked in line along the road. Forty yards farther, just off the pavement, flames leaped from the vehicle that had led the convoy.

The men in the other Land Cruisers had abandoned their vehicles. Shadowy forms were visible through the tinted windows. Other partial figures could be seen beside the hoods and bumpers.

Bolan cut loose with a full-auto volley that shattered the glass of the nearest truck. He let up on the trigger as his rifle barrel moved to the vehicle behind it and did the same. The shadowy figures behind the glass dropped behind the cover of their vehicles.

Elliot sprinted to safety at Bolan's side.

"Want me to head for higher ground?" the CIA man puffed, out of breath.

Bolan shook his head. "I don't think it'll be necessary," he said. "Another minute or two and Friday and Khalid ought to be in position."

It was more like seconds.

Full-auto fire came from the other side of the road, and Bolan raised his head again to peer over the rocks. He couldn't see the Barkari brothers across the road. But he could see the empty brass 7.62 mm casings flying up into the air from behind the rocks. And he could hear the result of their handiwork in the moans and screams of terror that came from the road between them.

"Get ready," he said. He shoved a full magazine into the AK-47.

A split second later the men who had survived the Barkari brothers' surprise assault came flying around their trucks.

Bolan and Elliot took aim.

Bolan's first 3-shot burst blew the lungs from a man wearing a ragged red T-shirt as he rounded the bumper of the second vehicle in line. Bolan swung the rifle barrel slightly to point at the hood of the next truck as a man in a blue chambray work shirt dived over the front of the vehicle. Another burst of fire stitched red buttons onto the back of the shirt.

Bolan heard Elliot open fire at the two vehicles at the rear of the line. At the same time Benjamin and Khalid Barkari continued their attack from across the road. More of the warlord's cutthroats fled between the trucks.

Bolan dropped a man leading two others between the first and second vehicles, then tapped the trigger lightly again and sent a lone round into the chest of the man behind him. The third man in the party was already limping from a bullet in the leg, and the next squeeze of the trigger sent a burst of fire into his multicolored dashiki.

Confusion now reigned around the enemy trucks as the gunners who had tried to escape the Barkari brothers realized they had forgotten the men on the other side of the road. Bolan turned in time to see Elliot drop a man with long, braided hair and a beard, then swing his weapon smoothly to another gunner.

More of the dazed gunmen stopped in their tracks, uncertain of which way to go. One man, wearing blood-spotted khaki slacks and a matching shirt, ran first one way and then the other, the AK-47 in his hands firing stupidly into the air.

Bolan dropped the front sight on the khaki and pulled the trigger.

The AK-47 emptied, and another magazine took its place. More bullets flew from the rocks toward the warlord's hirelings.

Then suddenly silence descended on the foothills.

Bolan and Elliot stood from behind the rocks, their rifles still trained toward the line of trucks in case any of the downed men were playing possum. Slowly, they made their way around the rocks to the road.

Bolan waved Elliot to the rear of the convoy and took the left. He saw Benjamin and Khalid Barkari make their way down from the rocks on the other side of the vehicles.

Bolan kept the AK-47 ready as he made the cleanup walk. He found no survivors, just the war-torn remains of the men General Fajir Ham had sent to kill them.

Meeting Elliot in the middle, the Executioner led the way between the vehicles. The Barkari brothers were conducting their own cleanup on the other side, and as they passed between the Land Cruisers, a lone shot broke the stillness.

Bolan stepped from between the vehicles and saw Khalid standing over one of the warlord's men, his rifle a foot away from what had once been a head.

Benjamin Barkari's voice came from the other end of the convoy. "There are a few holes in the body," he said as Bolan turned and saw him looking under the hood of the last Land Cruiser in line. "But I believe it will run. And we will make better time than in the jeeps."

The men boarded the warlord's vehicle. Bolan twisted the key, and the Land Cruiser roared to life.

THE DOWNFALL of the government had brought chaos to the nation of Somalia.

And with the chaos had come the inevitable crime.

The few people who had grown wealthy in the socialistic environment created by Siyad Barre had been chased from their homes by the angry masses who could no longer be restrained. Some had been murdered, and others had fled to Kenya, Ethiopia or other places of refuge.

Few of the frenzied rioters had been foolish enough to try moving into the large homes and settling. Those who did had fallen victim to the same fate as the previous owners, and the streets of Mogadishu had run red with the blood of both rich and poor alike.

By the time the dust of sudden anarchy had settled, the people of Somalia had gladly accepted the military organizations led by men such as Ham, Jabbar, Morris and James. At least *some* order would be the result, they told each other. At least *some* good would come from the megalomaniacal Third World potentates. The warlords would take the best for themselves, of course, but they would leave the scraps for the people.

The people of Somalia had been surprised when the warlords finished looting the cities and countryside, for the scraps had been taken, too.

Because he was aware of all this, the man known as the Executioner was equally surprised as he pulled up in front of the home of Aziza Mnarani's mother. The one-story redbrick house might have blended in perfectly in a middle class suburb in Colorado Springs or Davenport, Iowa. Surrounded as it was by the rubble of shanties patched with grass and cardboard, the house seemed like a mansion.

Bolan brought the truck to a halt as the first rays of sunlight crept over the horizon. Why hadn't the people of Mogadishu torn this house to shreds like they had others down the block? Why hadn't the lamppost in the center of the lawn or the porch swing next to the front door been stolen? Why were all of the windows intact?

He knew the answer was simple.

The people of Mogadishu knew of Aziza's connection to the warlords. Which meant her mother was under their protection.

To steal something from one under the protection of a warlord meant death.

"You go first," Don Elliot said in the back seat. "She's an old woman. The four of us together will scare her."

Bolan glanced up into the rearview mirror and saw Benjamin Barkari shake his head next to Elliot. "No," the Swahili warrior said. "I will stay in the car."

"Come on, Friday," Elliot said. "She'll recognize you."

"You have met her," Barkari said. "You can do it."

Elliot's voice took on the tone of a patient parent talking to a child. "Yes, I've met her. Once. She's not going to remember me. Now go on up and ring the doorbell, Friday. Tell her you've come looking for her daughter."

"No."

Bolan turned around, resting his arm over the seat. The drive from the north had been long and hard. They had been forced to keep their eyes open for more of Ham's search parties, and none of them had gotten any sleep. They were all tired again, and that fatigue was affecting Benjamin Barkari's judgment.

"Friday," Bolan began, "I understand how you feel, and I can sympathize with those feelings. But you're a professional, and you can't let them get in the way of the mission." He paused, glanced back to the front, then turned back again. "You're the most likely candidate to break the ice here. Now go do it."

Benjamin Barkari's dark eyes shot daggers for a moment, then softened. Nodding his agreement, he got out of the back seat and walked toward the front door as another day broke over Mogadishu.

Bolan turned to watch him out of the side window.

"What if she's not here?" Elliot said. "You thought of that?"

Bolan nodded. "We find out where she is."

"And if she can't be contacted without alerting whichever warlord she's shacked up with *this* week?"

"Then we go to Plan B," Bolan said.

"Which is—" Elliot started.

"Not yet formulated," Bolan finished for him.

He watched the front door of the house open. A crack at first, then wider as the woman inside recognized her visitor.

"This is very painful for him," Khalid said from the seat next to Bolan. "He was…still is…very much in love with her."

Bolan nodded. "I understand that," he said. "And if there was any other way we could do this, that's what we'd do. But there isn't."

Khalid nodded back. "I know," he said. "And Benjamin knows, as well."

Bolan turned back to the house in time to see Benjamin Barkari speaking through the door. A moment later the tall Swahili turned and waved them toward him.

Bolan, Elliot and Khalid got out and crossed the lawn to the open door.

A moment later Bolan found himself seated next to Elliot on a modern Western-style divan in the living room. Benjamin Barkari had found a chair to the side.

Bolan took a quick glance around. The walls had been painted the typical American off-white. The divan and chairs had been imported, but had originally been purchased from some discount furniture outlet. Framed prints, evidently purchased to fit the color scheme rather than for artistic content, were spread across the walls. In short, the interior of the house was like the outside—livable, but hardly elegant by U.S. standards. But it spoke volumes about the Mnarani family's connections.

Aziza Mnarani's mother was the only thing in the house that looked out of place. Although dawn had just broken, she looked as if she had been awake for hours. Dressed in a robe that differed slightly from that of the Issas and Afars Bolan had seen, she reminded him of a tiny black bird. Deep gray wrinkles crossed her forehead and cheeks, and the skin beneath her chin sagged loosely with age. But the old woman's brown eyes sparkled with youth and vitality as she gracefully sat down.

Her eyes stayed glued to Bolan as Benjamin Barkari spoke in a strange tongue. When he'd finished, she looked to him briefly, spoke a few words, then turned back to Bolan.

"Before we begin," Friday said, "Mrs. Mnarani wants you to know she is originally from Kenya. She is Masai and very proud of her heritage." He paused, then added his own words. "It is the traditional way many of the tribes begin a formal conversation."

Bolan nodded. The Masai were one of the many nomadic tribes of the area, and he now recognized the language the two spoke as being one of the Nilotic dialects.

The old woman spoke again.

"Mrs. Mnarani wants to know if you are a leader of the American Army," Friday translated.

Bolan smiled at the small woman. A precise answer would not only violate the security he needed to be successful, but it might also take years to explain through translation. Leader of the army was close enough. He nodded.

Mrs. Mnarani spoke again.

"She thought so," Friday translated. "She could tell. She wants to know if you are here to get rid of General Ham and the other warlords."

Bolan hesitated. The downfall of the warlords might well mean the end of the comfortable life this woman was leading amid the misery of the rest of the nation. For her to help him might mean her own demise. Yet something in the old woman's eyes told him that the truth was the best answer.

Something else told him that she would detect any answer that was *not* the truth.

"Tell her that's exactly what I intend to do, and that we need her daughter's help."

Benjamin Barkari translated.

The old woman's wrinkled face broke into a smile. Now when she spoke, the words fairly tumbled from her mouth.

Bolan listened, hearing the name *Aziza* several times. He watched Benjamin Barkari's downtrodden expression fall lower. Finally the Swahili warrior held up his hands. "Wait, please," he said. "I will not remember it all." Turning toward Bolan, he said, "She will help you but she doesn't know about Aziza. She thinks her daughter has come to love the life of sin she now leads. But in any case, we can ask her ourselves." He paused, took a deep breath, and Bolan could almost feel the pain sweeping through Friday's heart. "She is to arrive for a visit later this morning."

Mrs. Mnarani spoke again.

"Yes, she wanted to make sure that you know that she doesn't approve of her daughter's actions."

Bolan nodded. "I understand," he said. "Does she know how long it will be before her daughter arrives?"

"No. Sometime before noon, she hopes," Friday answered.

"We'll come back," Bolan said.

Benjamin Barkari translated, and the tiny woman leaped to her feet, shaking her head and speaking hurriedly again.

"She says no, we will stay," Barkari said. "We look tired and hungry. She has three extra bedrooms, and we must sleep while she prepares food."

With his words, the accumulated fatigue of the past few days finally had license to fall over Bolan. He wearily nodded his approval. "Tell her thank you," he said as he forced his exhausted limbs to function.

Mrs. Mnarani looked up into his eyes. A sly grin quivered on her lips as she spoke out of the side of her mouth to Benjamin Barkari.

Friday forced a small laugh, the pain of the experience still evident on his face. "She says it will be especially delicious food she prepares, since it was purchased by General Ham."

Bolan chuckled. "Yes, it will be."

The little birdlike woman led the four men down a short hallway. She ushered Bolan into one room,

Khalid into another, then grabbed Elliot and Benjamin Barkari by the arms and moved on.

Bolan saw her look up at Friday and whisper in a kind, gentle voice as she stopped in front of another bedroom. He looked across the hall to Khalid.

"She said that at one time she had thought she would have my brother permanently," Khalid said. "She still wants him as her son-in-law, and she just asked him to forgive Aziza for her mistakes."

As he turned to enter his bedroom, Bolan saw Benjamin Barkari shake his head and turn toward the door down the hall. As Friday disappeared from the hallway, Bolan saw the tears in the Swahili warrior's eyes.

CHAPTER NINE

Bolan opened his eyes to the smell of strong coffee drifting down the hall into the bedroom. Rolling to his side, he saw that his watch on the bed stand next to him read 10:45.

He rose to a sitting position, rubbing his eyes. Three hours' sleep was hardly enough—especially for a man who had gotten only two hours the day before and none for the previous two days. Yet he felt a hundred percent better than he had upon his arrival back in Mogadishu. Relaxed. Alert again. The three hours' rest would have to do.

Rising to his feet, Bolan walked to the closed door. Soft, semiwhispering voices floated down the hallway. The pleasant chirp of Mrs. Mnarani he recognized immediately. The other voice sounded younger. Lower, but still feminine.

It could mean only one thing. Aziza had arrived.

Bolan looked down at the wrinkled clothes he had slept in, ran his hands across his thighs, then opened the door. He followed the voices into the kitchen, stopping in the doorway. He was a guest in this house and he didn't want to overstep his boundaries. He would wait for an invitation.

Another reason for Bolan to stop in the doorway came to him as soon as he caught sight of Aziza Mnarani. The beautiful black woman could have stopped a charging rhinoceros with those eyes, and

Bolan now saw why the mere mention of her name had
sent Benjamin Barkari into a near-catatonic state.

Seated across the kitchen table from her mother, the
young woman smiled politely at him. She had inher-
ited her mother's deep chocolate eyes, but the skin
surrounding them was smooth, the color of soft caramel. Aziza's long black hair had been straightened
and hung to the sides of her aquiline face like locks of
coal-black silk. The woman exuded a sexual charisma
that only a dead man could overlook, and it was easy
to see how she could work her way into the heart of
any warlord she chose.

Bolan's eyes fell involuntarily to the long, sleek neck
left bare by a red V-neck T-shirt, then returned to the
face as the full red lips opened to reveal a perfect row
of ivory teeth. "You are the one called Pollock?" she
asked.

He nodded.

Aziza Mnarani lifted a porcelain coffee cup from
the saucer and held it up. "Would you like some coffee?"

Bolan nodded again.

Mrs. Mnarani started to get up, but Aziza reached
across the table and patted her shoulder. "I'll get it,
Mother," she said, then rose from the table and glided
toward the kitchen counter as if in the middle of some
graceful ballet. Bolan saw that the red T-shirt had been
tucked into a pair of black jeans that might as well
have been painted onto her shapely buttocks. Her hips
swayed suggestively as she floated to the cabinet, her
movements natural rather than contrived.

Bolan studied her as she poured a cup of coffee,
then turned to hand it to him. "My mother told me
that a man named Pollock and three others had

come," she said, leaning back against the counter and crossing her arms across her breasts. "That they wanted to see me." Her voice was still pleasant but now betrayed a trace of suspicion. "So tell me. What can I do for you?"

Bolan took the cup. "Did she tell you who the other three men were?" he asked, taking a sip.

Aziza shook her head. "Just that I would know some of them and not to worry." She moved back to her chair and gestured for Bolan to sit down between her and her mother. "Please."

He did so. "The other three men are Don Elliot, Khalid Barkari and—"

"Benjamin Barkari," Aziza interrupted, her lovely face suddenly aging ten years and taking on the same painful look Bolan had seen on Friday's. "If Elliot and Khalid are here, the third man would be Ben."

Bolan nodded.

Aziza glanced to the door. "They are still asleep?"

"I assume."

The pain on Aziza's face flashed to anger. "Then you and I must talk," she said. "Have you been told what happened to me?"

"Elliot told me," Bolan said.

Aziza's voice took on a tone of irritation. "I should have known he couldn't keep his mouth shut. Has he told Ben?"

Bolan shook his head. He watched Mrs. Mnarani out of the corner of his eye. "Does your mother know?"

"No," Aziza said. "But don't worry, she speaks no English." She dropped her eyes to the table. "I am sorry. I haven't been fair about Don. He is a good

man, and it was in his arms I cried when I couldn't do
so in Ben's.''

Bolan didn't answer. He could see she wasn't finished.

Aziza looked up suddenly, an expression of concern overtaking her face. ''Ben hasn't found out about
the rape some other way, has he?''

''No,'' Bolan replied. ''But I'm not sure you
shouldn't tell him. Thinking you don't love him may
be even more painful.''

Aziza shook her head violently. ''At least this way,
he stays alive.''

Again Bolan didn't answer. But this time it was because there was no answer. Nothing Benjamin Barkari did could erase the pain and humiliation Aziza
had suffered at the hands of the warlord's men. It was
a judgment call whether or not Friday should be told.
Bolan knew what *he* would do—what he *had* done—
when the family he loved had been the victims of brutal, violent animals like those who had molested Aziza
Mnarani. He suspected Friday would be compelled to
seek the same justice, and as Aziza believed, that quest
might well cost him his life.

Bolan studied the beautiful face next to him. ''I'm
sorry to have to ask this,'' he said, ''but you were
raped by General Morris's men, Aziza. I think I know
the answer to my next question, but I have to ask.
What made you—''

''What made me become a whore?'' Aziza asked,
staring up into his eyes.

''I wasn't going to put it that way.''

''No, but that is what you are thinking.'' Aziza
didn't give him time to argue. She shrugged. ''You are
tall and strong,'' she said. ''And I suspect you are

skilled in the use of weapons. I am not. I am a woman. I have nothing but the weapon all women have at their disposal.'' Her eyes narrowed suddenly, and Bolan saw a coldness that had been missing a moment earlier. "So I am using that weapon, and I *will* obtain my justice.''

"You want Morris dead?'' Bolan asked.

"Of course. And the other warlords, as well.''

His gut instinct told him the woman was telling the truth. But while his instincts were rarely wrong, he knew he wasn't infallible. There was another answer he needed before he completely trusted her, and the only way to get that answer was to ask the question. "Aziza, you've already gotten close enough to these men to kill them a thousand times over. Why haven't you?''

Aziza surprised him by laughing. "A reasonable question,'' she said. "And I will answer it. But first...'' She reached over, patting her mother's arm, and speaking in the Masai language.

Mrs. Mnarani stood up, kissed her daughter on the cheek, and left the room.

When Aziza spoke again, her voice was somber, almost as if she had gone into a trance. "At first all I wanted was revenge on the men who had raped me,'' she explained. "And I got it. I slept with General Morris and I made him fall in love with me.''

Bolan had no trouble accepting that fact. He watched the beautiful face, the exquisite body. Aziza Mnarani exuded a sexual magnetism that would be hard, if not impossible, for *any* man to resist.

Aziza took another sip of coffee and set her cup down. "One by one,'' she said. "I convinced Morris that the men who had raped me were disloyal to him.

They are now all dead by Morris's own hand. But during the time I was with him, I not only heard about but *saw*, the rapes of other women." She folded her hands on the table in front of her, and Bolan saw the knuckles turn white.

"Morris would see a woman on the street he desired, his men would kidnap her and bring her to us. He would—" Aziza suddenly choked, stopped talking and took another sip of coffee. When she had composed herself, she said, "I was forced to witness acts I cannot even bring myself to describe."

"There's no reason you have to," Bolan said.

Aziza looked up, tears in her eyes. "Do you know the depths of depravity to which the human soul can sink?"

"I've seen my share of it."

Aziza dabbed at her eyes with a napkin. "So I decided I wanted Morris dead, too. Then I realized that it was even larger than that." The beautiful woman's graceful hands balled into tight fists, her voice rising. "All over Somalia this happens," she said. "Women are taken by the warlords and their men with no more thought than when they butcher a sheep." Her tears threatened to burst forth any moment in a thunderstorm of anguish. "I live only to avenge myself and other women. And I will sacrifice myself, if necessary, to kill all four of the warlords."

Bolan started to speak but stopped when he heard footsteps. He turned to see Benjamin Barkari standing behind him, his face a mask of impotent suffering.

Friday stared at Aziza. "Why?" he asked. "Why didn't you tell me?"

Aziza's tears burst forth now, her chest jerking spasmodically with sobs. "You heard it all?"

Barkari nodded. "Why?"

"Because you would have tried to kill them," Aziza whispered.

Friday's eyes filled with a rage Bolan had not seen yet in the tall black man. "I *would* have killed them," Barkari said.

Aziza closed her eyes and wrapped her arms around her body, shaking with misery. "And they would have killed *you*," she whispered.

Silence fell over the kitchen. Bolan didn't speak. Now that Friday knew the truth, the two of them needed time to work things out, decide where their relationship was headed. Bolan stood up to leave.

"Can you forgive me?" Aziza asked as he started for the door.

The tears that flowed forth from Benjamin Barkari's eyes matched those still rolling down Aziza's cheeks. Crossing the kitchen in front of Bolan, he pulled the beautiful woman to her feet. "I love you," he declared as he crushed the woman to his chest. "I love you."

Bolan left the kitchen and entered the living room. He hadn't gotten a chance to come right out and ask for Aziza's help, but he had no doubt now what the answer would be. The beautiful Masai woman had been through hell at the hands of the warlords, and she shared a common goal with Bolan.

They both wanted the warlords dead.

And if he had anything to say about it, they were going to get their wish. *Soon.*

Bolan started down the hall to find the shower.

LIKE BERLIN when divided between East and West Germany, the city of Mogadishu had two distinct sectors. Somalia's capital city had no Berlin Wall, but the boundaries could have been no more clear to the people of Somalia than if the Great Wall of China bisected their city.

The people of Somalia just *knew.* Knew that everything north of the obelisk on Shire Warsme, and east of Somaliya Boulevard belonged to General Fajir Ham. The rest of the city, the southwest half, fell into the domain of General Morris.

The Land Cruiser was parked at the corner of Bin Idriis and Roma. Behind the wheel, a pair of binoculars in his lap, Bolan looked back at the beautiful woman seated behind him. "Tell me about Ham," he said. "Exactly what's he planning?"

Aziza shrugged. "He and the other warlords will be resupplied with weapons as soon as the American troops go home. They're coming from America's old friend, Saddam Hussein."

Bolan felt his blood run cold. No matter what happened in this part of the world, the Mad Dog of the Gulf always seemed to have a thumb in it somewhere. "What's Saddam getting in return?"

"A port. What else?"

Bolan turned back to the front and nodded. Of course, what else. A port was what Iraq had been after in Kuwait, among other things. If he could get one on the coast of Somalia, it would be almost as good, and he'd even have his archenemy Saudi Arabia sandwiched in between.

"Ham's planning to take over the rest of Somalia right after the new arms arrive," Aziza said. "Then Djibouti."

Bolan frowned. He hadn't thought about Djibouti, but it made sense.

Aziza faced him. "But it doesn't stop there, Pollock," she said. "He hasn't made up his mind yet, but either Kenya or Ethiopia come next. And he won't stop there."

Bolan shook his head. "He's biting off more than he can chew by himself. He ought to know that." He thought for a moment. "Unless he's going to have Iraqi help."

Aziza shrugged. "Maybe he will, I don't know. But even if he doesn't get troops from Iraq, the fact is he thinks he can do it. He thinks he can do anything. He's mad, Pollock, and he won't stop until he's dead. Death will come, but before it does thousands of innocent Africans will lose their lives." She drew a deep breath. "He's been reading up on his African history. You're familiar with the 'scorched earth' policy of the Zulus?"

Again Bolan's blood ran cold. Africa's angry Zulus of the last century had indeed scorched the earth, moving across the continent and leaving an all-encompassing wake of death behind them. No man, woman, child or animal had been left standing. Indeed, the scorched-earth theory maintained that every blade of grass was to die.

"That's how he plans to 'chew what he bites,' as you say," Aziza said. "At least at first. Ham's theory is that enough dead women and children in the first few villages will influence the ones down the road to surrender peacefully."

A flicker of movement jerked Bolan's attention back to the street. He pressed the binoculars to his forehead and watched four men in light tropical suits get out of a Rolls-Royce. Each of the men looked as if he could play defensive line for any NFL team he chose, but there was one distinct difference.

Bolan didn't know too many tackles or guards who toted submachine guns.

One of the four men, the sides of his head shaved high, a circular carpet of curly hair topping his head, opened the back door of the Rolls. A short, squat man struggled out.

Next to Bolan in the Land Cruiser, Benjamin Barkari mumbled something unintelligible under his breath.

"That is him," Aziza said from the back seat. "Morris."

Bolan watched Morris sandwich himself in the middle of his escorts and begin waddling down the sidewalk. Bolan squinted, concentrating. Morris appeared to be observing no special security precautions during this period in which the U.S. forces were collecting weapons. But the subguns slung over the shoulders of the bodyguards told Bolan that, as he'd suspected, the warlords had no intention of giving up *all* their firepower. "That all the men he usually brings with him?" Bolan asked Aziza.

"It's about average," the voice in the back seat said. "His treaty with General Ham came several weeks ago. And he knows the rest of Somalia is afraid to try to harm him."

Bolan nodded. "What was the war with Ham about?"

There was a long pause in the back seat. "Me," she finally stated.

Benjamin Barkari mumbled again.

The party on the sidewalk stopped at the door to a small concrete building. Bolan raised the binoculars to read the sign over the door: Lido Royale. "Morris own the club?" he asked Friday.

Before the man could answer, Aziza said, "He owns everything in Mogadishu that isn't owned by General Ham."

Bolan watched Morris and his men disappear into the Lido then turned toward Barkari, studying the man. Friday's face, his mannerisms, his entire demeanor betrayed the mixture of emotions that had assaulted him ever since he'd overheard Aziza talking of her rape. Now Friday and Aziza held hands, and Barkari had turned toward the back seat to stare at the beautiful black woman like a teenage boy who'd just been told his girlfriend's parent were leaving town for the weekend.

Bolan frowned inwardly. He was all for love, happiness, joyful reunions and living happily ever after—so long as they didn't interfere with business. But he had a sneaking suspicion that the shock of hearing Aziza talk about what had happened to her had prevented Friday from thinking things through. Sooner or later that shock was going to wear off, and the Swahili would start to question the route his woman had taken to get her revenge.

Bolan turned back to the street. What it all boiled down to was that regardless of her motives, Aziza had willingly slept with other men. No man had an easy time coming to terms with such things. And as soon as Barkari would start trying to sort it all out, he could become a liability. Bolan would have to monitor the situation closely. If Barkari didn't handle things well, it would affect his performance and might get him and the others killed.

Aziza broke into Bolan's thoughts. "Morris will be inside for perhaps thirty minutes," she said. "He will eat lunch, check the books, then move on."

"Where will he go?" Bolan asked.

"It depends. He eats here every day. But after that his schedule varies."

Bolan looked at his watch. Figuring on nothing more than a recon mission, he had seen no reason to awaken Elliot and Khalid and had left the two men asleep at Aziza's mother's house. But now, with the light security Morris was running, he could see an opportunity to get the first warlord out of the way without a lot of time-consuming planning.

Bolan twisted toward the back seat. "When he comes back out, I'm going to kill him," he announced simply.

Aziza's eyes opened wide. "Now?"

"There won't be a better time," he said, "and we've got to move on. After the first warlord goes down, security will tighten up on the others. There's nothing we can do about that, and we'll just have to adjust to it as we go. We might as well take advantage of the easy one while we can."

"No," Benjamin Barkari said.

Bolan turned toward him and saw the hatred in his eyes.

"*I* will do it," Barkari argued.

Bolan shook his head. "You're too personally involved. Don't worry, he'll be just as dead if I—"

"*Neither* of you will do it," the voice from the back seat said. "I have waited many months for this. If the time has come, *I* will do it."

Bolan turned back to Aziza. She could do it. And maybe easier than he could himself.

"Morris is mine," Aziza said. "Ham is the worst, but Morris was the most disgusting. I will not ask to kill the others if it is not possible." She paused for breath, her chest heaving with emotion under the tight T-shirt. "But you must let me do this myself. If you don't, I will not help you with the others."

Bolan studied her eyes. She'd help him regardless of whether or not he let her take out Morris herself. She wanted all the warlords dead as much as he did. But she had a point, too. She *deserved* the privilege if she wanted it.

Bolan rested an arm over the seat. "You know how to shoot a gun?" he asked.

Aziza opened her purse and pulled out a gold-plated Walther PPK .380. A beautiful leaf-scroll pattern had been etched into the golden frame and slide and, combined with the engraved ivory grips, had turned the weapon into a true work of art. "A gift from Morris himself." She smiled.

Bolan nodded. "Go kill him with it," he said.

Aziza put the Walther back in her purse and started to get out of the car.

Bolan reached over the seat and took her arm, stopping her. "Do it on the street where we can cover you," he said. "Don't go inside."

Aziza nodded, then turned and started across the street toward the club.

Bolan turned toward Benjamin Barkari. The look of love on his face had been replaced by anger and hatred as soon as the personal relationship between Aziza and Morris had entered the conversation. Now a veil of confusion had fallen over him.

Bolan could see that the party was over. Reality had sunk in, and Friday had realized the truth he would have to live with if he were to reestablish his relationship with this woman. He no longer knew whether to be ecstatic at Aziza's return, or to hate her for what she'd done after the rape. He didn't know whether he wanted to hold her in his arms for the rest of his life or slap her across the face, call her a whore and kick her as far as he could.

"Friday," Bolan said softly.

Benjamin Barkari didn't answer. He continued to watch Aziza cross the street.

"Friday!" Bolan said louder.

The Swahili turned.

"Get ready," Bolan ordered. "Set up on this end of the street and take out the two gorillas closest to the building."

Friday nodded silently.

"I'll cross and go to the other end of the block. I'll take the two on his other side."

Again the Swahili nodded dumbly.

Bolan reached up and grabbed the man by the collar. Staring into the deep brown eyes, he saw a vacant look. "Friday, are you at home in there?" Bolan asked.

Benjamin Barkari nodded again.

Bolan took a deep breath and let the air rush out between his teeth. "When we get back to Mrs. Mnarani's," he said, "you and I need to talk."

A fourth nod was the only answer he got.

Bolan opened the door and got out, crossing the street and walking to the end of the block. He stopped at the corner in front of a burned and looted store that looked to have been a pharmacy before the war.

Aziza had stopped by the door to the Lido Royale. She nodded toward Bolan, then leaned back against the wall.

Benjamin Barkari stood two doors down, gazing blankly into the window of a dress shop.

Ten minutes later the door opened, and two of the bulky bodyguards emerged, their subguns slung over their shoulders.

Morris walked behind them with the other two men bringing up the rear. He stopped in his tracks when he saw the beautiful woman.

Aziza said something to him, and the warlord melted visibly.

The lovely young black woman reached up, wrapping an arm around Morris's neck. But as she pressed her lips against those of the fat man, her other hand disappeared into her purse. The Walther came out in one fast, smooth movement and jabbed into Morris's jiggling belly.

Bolan heard the muffled explosion.

The two men now on the warlord's left reached up for the straps to their weapons. But before they could unsling the guns, Bolan had dropped them both to the sidewalk with a double-tap from the Desert Eagle.

As the explosion from the second massive Magnum round died down along the street, Bolan heard the crack of Benjamin Barkari's .45. One man on the warlord's right fell face forward to the cracked concrete.

The other turned toward Barkari and pulled the trigger. A burst of fire chipped the concrete of the building next to the Swahili.

Bolan planted a third .44 Magnum slug between the man's shoulder blades, and he fell sprawled face-down on the hot street.

Bolan raced forward. General Morris had fallen to his knees. His pudgy hands were crossed over the hole in his belly, and bright streams of crimson seeped through his fingers. His eyes looked up, confused as they stared at Aziza Mnarani.

"My love...why..." the warlord said.

Aziza's answer was simple. She shoved the barrel of the Walther between the fat warlord's open lips and pulled the trigger again.

Morris was thrown to the ground on his back, and by the time Bolan reached the man, the eyes that had been filled with such adoration a moment earlier were glazing over to stare lifelessly at the heavens.

Bolan watched Benjamin Barkari walk forward. The Swahili stopped three feet in front of the dead warlord, his face a mask of fury that bordered on insanity as he aimed his weapon downward.

The .45 began to dance in his hand.

Friday emptied the magazine into the man, then dropped to both knees and broke into tears.

ALONE IN HIS OFFICE in the underground compound, General Fajir Ham sat back in his chair and tapped the Issa war club on the floor next to him.

He didn't like what was going on around him. Or inside him.

Around him Ham saw his empire at a crossroads. He had changed his mind about moving through southern Somalia first. As soon as the new weapons arrived, he would move directly into Ethiopia, his first act the return of the Ogaden Desert to its rightful owners. The village of Jijiga would fall first, and the blood of every man woman and child would run through the streets.

An almost sexual thrill rushed through his body as he closed his eyes and pictured the carnage in his mind. Like a modern-day Genghis Khan or Attila the Hun, he would leave nothing alive in Jijiga. Word would travel fast to the other villages, and soon all he would have to do was send in a few men to cart off the spoils of war. From there, Kenya and beyond, and if he did meet resistance too great, he would call upon the new alliance with Iraq. They would help him. At least if they wanted their port they would.

Ham came out of his brief reverie and back to reality. All that was in the future. At the present he had problems. His empire was teetering on the very edge of disaster, and all because of a lack of leadership below. Sadiki had failed, and Sadiki was dead. Elliot and Barkari had slipped through every net he threw out for them, and now he was hearing stories that Barkari's brother and some other American had joined them. From the descriptions that had come in, it sounded like the same man who had escaped Ilaoa at Elliot's safehouse.

Well, he could handle what was going on around him, given time. All he had to do was replace men like Sadiki with others, and Elliot and Barkari and the other two would be history.

But what about the turmoil raging *inside* him?

Ham lifted the framed photograph of Aziza from his desktop. God, she was by far the most beautiful woman he had ever seen. As he looked at her now, resplendent in a canary yellow bikini, her smooth ginger skin standing out in bold relief against the white sand along the coast of northeast Africa, he felt his pulse quicken.

Ham set the picture back on the desk, shivering involuntarily as he thought of the soft, secret places hidden beneath that bikini. Until meeting her he had never successfully coupled with another human being. His attempts with prostitutes had been humiliating disasters, and the only sexual pleasure he had taken from them was when he took their lives.

But Aziza...Aziza had found a way to bridge the gap between his lust for blood and more conventional love.

Ham sat back, closing his eyes. He knew that the sexual awakening Aziza Mnarani had spawned in him was only part of his feelings for her. There was more, far more, and it terrified him. Was this what men called love? If so, he both loved and hated it. He liked the way it made him feel, liked the warmth it provided that until now he had experienced only through imposing pain and suffering on others. He had always kept women around, but they had been nothing more than window dressing.

Ham opened his eyes and stared at the photograph. He found that more and more he was allowing Aziza to get away with things that he would never have permitted with another woman. She sometimes disagreed with him. Once or twice she had even raised her voice to him in anger and gotten away with it without so much as even a slap. Yesterday she had told him she would be leaving the compound to visit her mother in Mogadishu. Not *asked* him. *Told* him. And he had allowed her to go.

What was happening to him?

Ham placed the picture facedown on the desk. He had wanted Aziza the first time he had seen her on the arm of General Morris. At first he had simply wanted to take her away from the little fat man who controlled the southwest portion of Mogadishu—to show the weaker warlord that he could. But those feelings had changed.

Fajir Ham righted the picture and took one last look as the telephone to his side began to buzz. He lifted the receiver and pressed it into his ear. "Yes?" he said.

"Ilaoa has arrived."

Grateful for the interruption in his confusing reverie, Ham said, "Send him in."

The door opened and Gregory Ilaoa entered the room.

Ham's eyes fell to the bandage on the short man's chin. Ilaoa had sustained a nasty gash from one of the two men who had come looking for Elliot and Barkari at their Mogadishu apartment. "You requested my presence, General?" Ilaoa said.

"No, I *ordered* it."

"Yes, of course," Ilaoa said. He stood straight as a flagpole.

"Sit down, Gregory," Ham said, pointing to a chair across from his desk. "It is your turn."

Ilaoa raised a nervous eyebrow as he took the seat. "I do not understand, my General. My turn for what?"

Ham smiled widely. "To either live or die."

The man in the chair gulped.

After his confusing thoughts about Aziza, the sight pleased Ham beyond measure. "Are you aware that Sadiki has been killed?" he asked.

"Yes, General," Ilaoa said. "They were ambushed by Elliot and Barkari near Erigavo. It is a tragedy. My heart—"

"It is no tragedy, Gregory," Ham said. "Sadiki was all mouth. He spoke well and convincingly but never came through with what he promised." He paused. "You will do better, I am sure."

A mixture of shock and pride came over Ilaoa's face. "You mean I am—"

"You will take Sadiki's place," Ham said.

Ilaoa started to speak, but Ham waved a hand in front of his face and stopped him. "The four men were spotted later as they drove south. I suspect they were heading for Mogadishu."

Ilaoa reached up and touched the gauze on his chin. "My first act as your commandant will be to find and kill them all."

"Good," said Ham. "Very good. Be *successful*, Gregory. You failed at the safehouse. Do not fail again. Do not forget that Sadiki failed one too many times, and it cost him his life."

Ilaoa fairly leaped from his chair and saluted.

Ham nodded back to him, then again toward the door. He waited until Ilaoa had his hand on the knob, then said, "Gregory?"

"Yes?"

"Had Sadiki survived the attack on the road, I would have killed him myself."

The knot that formed in Ilaoa's throat this time was satisfying to Ham. His spirits rising, he heard the buzzer on the phone as Ilaoa left the office. He lifted the receiver and pressed it to his cheek.

"A call from overseas," the warlord's secretary said simply.

Ham tapped the button and heard the crackling sounds come over the wire.

"Good day, General," said Ali Abu-Iyad. Then, without further preamble, he said, "I have been watching the Americans help your men load the weapons. On CNN. You have kept enough rifles and ammunition to protect yourself, I assume."

"Of course," Ham said, the suspicion that some problem had arisen suddenly flooding his chest. "But only if I remain in the compound. We had to make it look convincing." He paused. When Abu-Iyad didn't reply, he said, "What is the problem?"

"Oh, nothing drastic," said the voice over the crackling line. "But there has been a delay in the shipment."

Fajir Ham felt his fingers tighten around the receiver. "What do you mean, a *delay?*" he shouted into the instrument. "You assured me that—"

"Please, General, calm down," said Abu-Iyad. "Two days at the most. You demanded the best— Heckler & Kochs, Galils, FALNs from Belgium. The timing is a little off, that is all."

Ham snorted, then slammed down his fist onto the desk. "If the people of Somalia learn of our temporary weakness, do you know what they will do?" he demanded. "Do you? They will seek my men out and cut us to shreds with their machetes."

"You will be safe in your compound, General."

"Of course I will, you fool!" Ham screamed into the phone. "But I cannot get all of my men into the compound with me! And if I have no one left to fire the weapons when they arrive, where will we all be then?"

"We will be fine," the voice said. "Two days at the *most,* and you will have more rifles and other small arms than you had before."

"Call me immediately when the shipment is to start," Ham said. "Until then I will remain here."

"You have my word, dear friend," said Abu-Iyad. He said goodbye and hung up.

Ham set down the phone down. He would wait. He would have to. And the weapons would arrive. Saddam Hussein not only wanted but needed a port from which to launch his ships. He would come through soon, and Ham would move on Ethiopia.

The warlord frowned. Perhaps he should demand some of the chemical agents that his new friend was famous for to spray on pesky Ethiopians.

Ham opened his mouth and cackled at the ceiling. Yes, he had problems, but they were small and they would be overcome. Aziza would soon be back, and he would begin the slaughter of anyone who opposed him.

The warlord sat back once more, closing his eyes. His breath quickened as again he pictured his men running through the streets of Jijiga, blood flowing like tiny streams over their ankles.

Soon his empire would enter its expansion phase.

CHAPTER TEN

"Slow down a second, Striker," Bolan heard "Cowboy" John Kissinger say as he pressed the receiver to his ear.

"I need it *now,* Cowboy," Bolan said. "I can't afford to slow down."

The chief armorer of Stony Man Farm—America's top-secret counterinsurgency base from which Bolan sometimes worked—chuckled. "You can't afford not to," he said. "The weapons system you're asking for...yeah, sure, I've been working on it. But it's still in the experimental stage. I haven't field-tested—"

"I need it now," Bolan repeated. "I don't have time for your field test. When I'm through, you can have mine." He paused, listening to the line crackle as it connected him over the thousands of miles to Stony Man in the Blue Ridge Mountains.

Finally Kissinger said, "I've got two of them ready in 9 mm. But you said .45, right?"

"Right."

"Hang on and I'll check."

Bolan heard Kissinger set the phone down. In the background soft clicks sounded as the dial on the huge vault door next to the wall phone spun. A moment later the heavy steel lock thudded open.

Kissinger came back on the line. "Okay, there's a Glock 21 .45 I've been playing with." He took a long, deep breath. "And one of the new Hellweg speed rigs that just came in will fit it. But the holsters have got spring-steel guts, Striker. They'll set off a metal detector as fast as a gun unless I replace the metal in them with ceramics, too.''

"You cut the ceramic for it yet?" Bolan asked.

"Yeah. It'll take me maybe ten minutes to swap it out and sew it back up. But I won't have time to test how *that* works, either."

"If *you* do it, I'll put my faith in it," Bolan said. "Just do it fast, Cowboy, and get it to me even faster."

A long sigh came over the line. "Okay. Give me thirty minutes total, and I'll fit the Glock with a laser, too. And I've got four hundred rounds of ceramic-cased .45 hollowpoints loaded up. How much—"

"All of it," Bolan said.

A click sounded on the line, and then the voice of Barbara Price, Stony Man Farm's mission controller, said, "Grimaldi's been playing around with a Pana-via Tornado F2 all morning. He's on the ground refueling right now." She paused. "I'll tell him to prepare for takeoff."

Grimaldi was the Farm's number-one pilot. And the Tornado, of German-Italian-UK origin and design, had a top speed of fifteen hundred miles per hour. With that combination the only faster way to transport the modified weapon system he wanted would be for Captain Kirk to beam it from the Blue Ridge Mountains to Somalia.

"Tell Jack to toss everything out along the Juba River, just south of Bardera."

Bolan supplied the coordinates, and Price repeated the numbers.

"Thanks," Bolan said, and hung up.

Killing four warlords in a row wasn't going to be easy. Somalia was a small country. Word of the assassinations would travel faster than Bolan could, and with each death the remaining warlords would tighten their security even further.

Which meant that while Aziza could be used as the door key to each warlord's stronghold, a different approach, a different angle, would be necessary each time. And the Glock would serve as at least one.

Bolan turned to others seated in Mrs. Mnarani's living room. The war council had commenced as soon as Bolan, Benjamin Barkari and Aziza had returned from taking General Morris out in front of the bar. Bolan had carefully laid out the situation as he saw it, then the steps that would be necessary to get the remaining three warlords. As he spoke, it had become increasingly clear that the strikes he was about to undertake would require two elements: stealth and speed. And while those elements weren't mutually exclusive, they didn't always walk hand in hand, either.

Bolan knew it would take slow, painstaking role camouflage to get close enough to the warlords. He would have to count on Aziza's getting him through the warlords' tightening security, which included metal detectors on the parts of Ham and Jabbar. In other words, the steel Beretta and Desert Eagle would be useless.

That had prompted his call to Stony Man Farm.

The first problem was simply transportation. Word of Morris's assassination would travel fast, and Ham, Jabbar and James would batten down their hatches. He had to move from one warlord to the next as fast as possible, and that didn't mean bumping over the rocky roads of Somalia in a truck.

"We need air transport," Bolan said, looking at Elliot. "You mentioned the helicopter you had at the fish cannery. Is it still there?"

Elliot shrugged. "Far as I know. From what little I've heard, the business is still running. The only difference is that Ham's taking the profits instead of Friday and me."

Bolan nodded. "What kind of chopper is it?"

"An '83 Aerospatiale," Elliot said. "Astar, 1450 TT."

Bolan frowned. He wasn't familiar with the model. "Will it seat us all?"

"Oh, yeah. With room for an extra shirt and socks," Elliot said.

"Anybody but you and Barkari know how to fly it?"

Khalid nodded. "I can."

"The only problem is it's Ham's, now," Elliot said.

"Not for long," Bolan said. "Did you hear the coordinates I gave out over the phone?"

Elliot nodded.

"Take the Land Cruiser and head that way. You'd be too easily recognized at the fish cannery, anyway. There'll be a package coming down on a chute. If it gets there before we do, take charge of it for me."

Elliot nodded. "Who's *we?*"

"Me, Khalid and Aziza," Bolan said. "We're going after the chopper and we'll meet you with it. Then we'll all head south to pay Colonel James a visit."

Out of the corner of his eye, Bolan saw Benjamin Barkari frown. "It seems unwise to take Aziza with you to the fish cannery," he said. "She will be recognized. If that happens, she will be of no further use.

Why not let her come with Elliot and me? It makes far more sense.''

Bolan turned. It was obvious what Friday was after, and it had nothing to do with what made sense. He wanted his newly reunited girlfriend with him and out of danger.

Bolan couldn't blame him. And it would be nice if things had worked that way—but they hadn't. "Elliot," Bolan said. "Go get the truck ready."

Elliot stood up. "You want Friday to—"

"Just do it," Bolan said. "Friday, come with me."

Bolan led Friday to the bedroom where he had slept earlier that morning, ushered him inside and shut the door. "I'm going to make this short and sweet," he said, turning to face the Swahili warrior. "Before Aziza came into the picture, you impressed me as a well-trained and talented professional. Since then you've been acting like a junior-high kid who's afraid the captain of the football team is out to steal his girlfriend."

The tall black man stiffened angrily, his fingers curling into fists. "Listen to me, you—"

Bolan shook his head. "No, Friday, *you* listen to *me*. Right now you're a mixed-up mess of emotions. I can understand it but I can't allow it. You're judgment is bad and likely to get us all killed if you don't clear your head."

Barkari tried to speak once more, but Bolan cut him off again. "Now that you've gotten over the initial shock of learning that Aziza was gang-raped, you're confused about the way she's acted since. Right?"

Slowly the Swahili nodded. "Yes," he said under his breath.

"Okay, right or wrong, she started using her body to get close enough to the warlords for revenge. What that boils down to is that she slept with them. That knowledge bothered the hell out of you when we saw Morris today and it affected your work.

"Here's the bottom line, Friday. Either forgive the woman for what she's done or call her a whore and tell her you never want anything to do with her again. But make up your mind before you leave this room. Otherwise, you aren't coming along with the rest of us."

"I will go where Aziza goes," Barkari said, gritting his teeth.

"Not unless you come to terms with this situation, you won't."

"You would stop me?"

Bolan looked at him steadily, his expression clearly stating his resolve.

For several seconds the men's eyes stayed locked. Then little by little the anger began to fade from Benjamin Barkari's face. "You're right," he said. "But it is difficult to admit."

Bolan nodded. "I'm sure it is." He paused. "Which will it be?"

"I love her," Barkari said. "I can't let her go again."

"Then learn to live with what she's done. We're getting ready to kill three more men, and two of them have slept with her, too. The third one *wants* to, and the way things are going to be set up, he'll get a chance to try. Can you handle that?"

"I will try."

"You'll have to do better than try," Bolan said.

Bolan studied the Swahili's face. Benjamin Barkari was in a spiritual hell, but Bolan thought he saw the resourcefulness in those dark brown eyes to get through it.

Without another word Bolan opened the door and stepped out into the hall. He had another quick phone call to make.

Then it would be time to go steal a helicopter.

EAST AFRICAN Fish Canning Company stood one block inland from Mogadishu's Old Port, approximately halfway between the Torino restaurant and the Anglo-American Club.

Seated next to the driver in the minibus, Bolan saw the entrance two blocks away. A low rock wall surrounded the grounds. A narrow gravel drive led through the opening that served as a gate.

Behind him Khalid suddenly yelled, *"Jojii!"*

The miniature bus, Mogadishu's only semireliable means of public transportation since the fall of the government, screeched to a halt. Aziza, wearing a blond wig, sunglasses and lots of makeup, got off, followed by Khalid and Bolan.

The strong odor of fish assaulted Bolan's nostrils as the minibus pulled away. Turning toward the cannery, he could see the top half of a one-story concrete office building above the wall. Twenty yards behind the offices stood the structure Elliot had said was the warehouse. Although he couldn't see it from here, Bolan knew that the packing building was located on the other side of the warehouse.

And just beyond that would be the helipad.

He turned back to Khalid and Aziza. "Give me five minutes, then start toward the cannery office. Find a good vantage point but stay off the grounds until you see us leave the office building and head toward the helipad. Then make your way to the chopper as unobtrusively as you can."

"They think you are an importer from England?" Khalid asked.

Bolan shrugged. "That's what I told them over the phone, and they seemed to buy it. In fact, the guy I talked to sounded anxious for me to come in."

"He would be," Khalid said. "Ham's men are killers not businessmen, and I suspect the place has been in chaos since Elliot and my brother were chased away. The have lost many customers already, I imagine."

Bolan nodded, then turned toward the cannery. "Five minutes," he said over his shoulder.

He kept a moderate pace as he walked along the port-side street. As he neared the entrance to the cannery grounds, Bolan adjusted his bush jacket. He had awakened earlier to find it washed and ironed and hanging in his room. With a fresh pair of brown slacks from his pack and an empty briefcase for effect, he now looked the part of the English business entrepreneur in Africa.

The difference lay beneath his clothes, which concealed the Beretta 93-R and Desert Eagle .44 Magnum.

Bolan entered the gate on the gravel drive and saw the discord Khalid had predicted. All over the grounds, men walked aimlessly, argued or stood scratching their heads. Two forklifts were being driven around the grounds with no apparent destination, and several of Ham's killers-cum-fish-canners had simply given up all pretense of enterprise and sat against the walls smoking cigarettes.

Bolan studied the men as he neared the office building, seeing the bulges under the tails of their shirts. They might not know what they were doing when it came to running a fish cannery, but that didn't mean they weren't dangerous.

He pushed through the glass door into a dingy front office. The walls of the room were scarred with several recent bullet holes, but the blemishes on the desk facing the door had come from years of use. Stacks of paper covered the desk, spilled onto the floor and reflected the same confusion that reigned outside of the building.

Behind the desk sat a pudgy black man wearing a food-stained tie over his short-sleeved sport shirt. Loose folds of flesh, sporting two days' growth of tiny black hair, hung from under his chin. The man looked up as Bolan entered.

The Executioner's eyes flickered up to a row of hooks on the wall behind the desk, where several sets of keys dangled. Dropping his eyes quickly, he smiled. "Mr. Kafwala?" he said in a British accent.

The lumpy man struggled to his feet and extended his hand. "Yes, Mr. Marks-Hall? I am pleased to make your acquaintance. You are interested in importing our products to England?" He smiled widely, not waiting for an answer. "I'm sure we can reach an agreement that will be attractive to both of us. Let me tell you about—"

Bolan cleared his throat, stopping the man. Sticking with the accent, he said, "Please, before we begin. Have you a gentlemen's room I might visit?"

"Certainly," Kafwala said, pointing to a hallway at the rear of the office. "Last door...wait, I will show you." He moved out from behind the desk, the loose skin under his chin dancing in time to each step as he waddled toward the hall.

Bolan followed the man out of the front office into the hall, past two empty smaller offices, toward a closed door at the end. The fat man pushed the door open.

Bolan had verified what he wanted to see—Kafwala was the only person inside the small building. Bolan's hand moved under his jacket to the butt of the Beretta 93-R under his arm.

Kafwala began turning back toward Bolan. "I will wait for you in the off—" he said, then stopped in midsentence as the sound suppressor attached to the Beretta touched the side of his nose. The fat man's eyes opened wide in shock and fear as they tried to focus on the weapon. Then his mouth closed, and the jowls started dancing.

"Get the keys to the helicopter," Bolan growled, the British accent now a thing of the past.

"But—"

"Do it. Or you'll die before you hit the ground." He pressed his back against the wall and waved Kafwala toward the front office with the Beretta.

The corpulent man waddled past. Bolan kept the Beretta tucked close to his side as they retraced their steps. No plan was without flaws, he knew, and each strategy, no matter how well thought out in advance, always carried with it a certain amount of calculated risk. The chance he had taken in his plan to repossess Elliot's helicopter was that someone would walk in from the outside in the middle of finding the keys.

And Murphy's Law, Bolan now saw, was in full effect.

The glass door swung inward as Kafwala reentered the front office. Two men wearing blue chambray work shirts, their ebony skin shining with sweat, hurried inside.

"Kafwala!" the shorter of the two said loudly. "We can't find the—" He stopped in his tracks when he saw the expression on his supervisor's face.

The taller of the men, wearing a shaggy mustache and goatee, stopped next to him.

Bolan stepped out from behind the fat man, aiming the Beretta at the two workers. "Freeze," he ordered quietly.

Had the two men followed the command, they might have lived. Instead, they both pivoted back toward the door.

Bolan thumbed the selector to semiauto and triggered. The short man moaned as the first round entered the back of his head and exited the front of his face, showering the glass door with a thick coat of blood and flesh.

The second quiet 9 mm hollowpoint caught the taller man in the spine, paralyzing him a split second before he fell to the floor. His dying eyes looked up at Bolan.

A third semiauto round closed the eyes.

Bolan looked through the blood dripping down the glass door and saw another figure stop ten feet from the office. Wearing a ragged straw hat with a blue-and-white band, the man stared in shock.

Bolan aimed through the glass, but before he could line up the sights, the man had sprinted out of sight to the side of the door.

Bolan twisted to Kafwala, grabbing the man's jowls and shoving the Beretta under his nose. "Get the keys and get them quick," he ordered. He twirled the fat man around and shoved him toward the desk.

Kafwala bumped into the desk, recovered and moved slowly around the side toward the wall. *Too* slowly for Bolan's taste.

Bolan dropped the 93-R's front sights on the desk, flipped the selector to 3-round burst and pulled the trigger. The suppressor coughed, and the ancient wood next to Kafwala split, throwing splinters into the air. One sharp sliver shot into the fat man's leg like an arrow, and Kafwala screamed, thinking he'd been shot.

"You're okay," Bolan growled. "But you won't be if you don't hurry."

Kafwala suddenly looked like an old-time movie as he raced to the keys on the wall.

Bolan took the key ring he was handed and dropped it into the side pocket of his jacket, then grabbed Kafwala by the jowls again. "One of your men saw us through the door," he said. "When we get outside, you're going to tell them that everything's okay. This gun will be in your ribs, and if anything goes wrong...it goes off. Got it?"

Kafwala nodded. He opened his mouth to say something but couldn't find the words.

Bolan looped his free arm through the other man's, jabbed the Beretta into his back and pushed him toward the door. They stepped over the body blocking their path, then moved to the glass.

No one was visible outside.

Bolan reached around the blubbery man and opened the door, jostling Kafwala outside. Walking his hostage to the corner of the building, Bolan then turned him toward the warehouse.

The pretexts of work that had been going on around the fish cannery when Bolan arrived had now stopped. The men seemed to have disappeared into thin air. Bolan escorted Kafwala past the warehouse and across the short span of grass to the cannery proper. They continued along the building toward where the helipad was located.

The odor of fish grew stronger as they passed the cannery. Bolan heard the machines inside shut down. Excited voices drifted through the windows in a language he couldn't understand.

When Bolan and Kafwala reached the rear of the cannery building, Bolan squeezed the fat arm hard. Kafwala stopped. Still gripping the soft flesh of the man's biceps, Bolan moved past Kafwala to peer around the corner.

The men who had been scattered throughout the grounds had now grouped in a bunch behind the cannery. Bolan saw the man in the straw hat talking excitedly in the middle of the mob.

Twenty yards directly behind the building, at a forty-five degree angle from where the men stood, the Astar 1450 TT stood on the helipad. Right where Elliot had said it would be.

Bolan turned back to Kafwala. "They know *something* is going on," he whispered. "But they don't know what. You and I are going to walk to the helicopter, and you're going to yell at them to get back to work. Is that clear?"

Kafwala nodded, his chin flesh flapping again.

Bolan stuck the Beretta under his jacket. "Don't forget it's still here," he warned. "And it's pointed at your heart." He pushed the fat man around the corner.

He stayed close on Kafwala's far side, planning to use the fat man's bulk as a shield if necessary. So far, everything that could go wrong *had,* and there was no reason the losing streak had to end here.

It didn't.

Halfway to the helicopter, two dozen heads turned toward Bolan and Kafwala. The hands beneath the heads shot under their shirts and reappeared with a variety of handguns.

"You better talk and talk fast," Bolan growled softly.

Kafwala shouted something in the native tongue. Bolan didn't know what it was. But it wasn't a get-back-to-work order.

A shot sailed over Bolan's head. More rounds followed, narrowly missing them both.

Kafwala screamed something else. The firing stopped.

Bolan ducked, looped an arm around the fat neck and pulled Kafwala tightly to his side in a headlock. He jerked the Beretta from under his jacket and pressed the suppressor into the fat jowls. As two dozen pistols pointed his way, he walked on toward the helicopter, dragging Kafwala. The fat man spoke a mile a minute now, tears streaking down his cheeks as he screamed at the men.

Across the yard, on the other side of the assembled killer-workmen, Bolan saw Khalid and Aziza sprint from behind a small shed. He nodded toward the helicopter pad, and the two headed that way.

Several of the men saw Bolan nod toward the helicopter and turned in that direction. One of them spotted Khalid and Aziza and brought his pistol up.

"Either of them gets shot, *you* get shot," Bolan yelled into the ear of the man he had in the headlock.

Kafwala screamed more orders.

Bolan stopped. The chopper would take a few minutes to warm up, and they needed Kafwala until then. He pressed his lips close to the fat man's ear. "Tell them to move back and drop their guns. Tell them if they shoot at all—me or the people getting on the chopper—I'll kill you."

Kafwala's lips flapped like a flag in the wind.

As Khalid and Aziza reached the helicopter, the men hesitantly laid down their weapons and began backing up.

Aziza disappeared into the chopper. Khalid stopped and turned toward Bolan, who reached into his pocket, found the keys and sent them arching through the air into Khalid's hand.

A moment later the helicopter's engine revved up. Slowly, careful to keep Kafwala between him and the other men, Bolan began moving toward the Astar. The door opened as he reached it, and he looked inside to see Aziza reaching over the back seat.

Bolan backed into the opening, pulling Kafwala after him. Still using the fat man as a shield, he climbed into the seat next to the woman in the blond wig and dragged Kafwala into the passenger's seat next to Khalid.

He kept the Beretta against Kafwala's head. "We warmed up yet?" he asked Khalid.

Khalid Barkari, a headset wrapped around his ears, turned to the instrument panel, then nodded.

A second later, as the helicopter was about to lift off, Bolan pushed Kafwala out of the chopper. Khalid took the chopper straight up, hovering high over the cannery. By the time the men on the ground had recovered their weapons, the chopper was safely out of range.

BOLAN GAZED OUT the small window of the Astar as they neared the village of Bardera. They were above Somalia's tropical southern lands now, about to leave the area that had been dominated by General Morris until a few hours ago.

Bolan knew that Morris wouldn't be dominating anything anymore, unless you counted the coffin in which he'd be buried. Within a few hours Bolan expected to be able to say the same about Colonel James. Ham and Jabbar were the strongest of the warlords, and their deaths would require more planning and effort. But Bolan fully intended that they, too, would fall before he left Somalia.

Bolan turned to the terrain below. The ground was far greener than Somalia's north central plateau but every bit as flat and monotonous. The only breaks in the dreariness were occasional corn and banana fields that appeared as they neared the Juba River. With its headwaters in the Ogaden region of Ethiopia, the Juba flowed through Kismayu into the Indian Ocean, on the way providing moisture for cultivation.

Here and there Bolan saw small bands of semi-nomadic tribal farmers tending their meager plants. Carrying hoes and sickles, as well as spears and machetes, the men looked little different than their ancestors might have looked five hundred years ago. They were starving, dying of disease, and moved lethargically across the plain.

But the sight spawned a sudden idea in Bolan. Perhaps they, or men like them, could prove valuable in gaining their own independence from the warlords.

Khalid dropped the helicopter a few hundred feet as the river appeared in the distance. He slowed as they neared the coordinates the Executioner had given Elliot and Barkari. "They haven't arrived yet," Khalid said.

Bolan nodded, hardly surprised. They were traveling on the ground over the rough and bumpy paths that passed for roads in this part of the country, and would not be expected for some time. "Turn down the river," he said. "As long as we have to wait, I want to get the feel of the countryside."

Khalid cut the chopper to the south. As they began to follow the winding curves of the river below, Bolan turned to Aziza. She had discarded the blond wig and rubbed most of the makeup from her face as soon as the Astar had leveled off.

Bolan cleared his throat, and Aziza faced him. "I hate to ask this," he said, slightly embarrassed. "But I have to, and I'd rather do it when Friday isn't around."

Aziza's smile was thin, sad. "If that is the case, the question must be—have I slept with Colonel James?"

"Yes."

"No," Aziza said. "We have met, of course, but James is the only one of the five that I have never been with. Let me tell you the whole story quickly to get it out of the way. I was first with Morris. Then General Ham took me away from him, more to show Morris that he *could,* I think, than because he actually wanted me. At least at first." She paused, drew a breath, then went on. "On one occasion I was given to General

Jabbar as a gift, and on another to Field Marshal Salih. After that, I think, is when Ham began to fall in love with me. He has kept me for himself since."

Bolan nodded as they passed over more corn fields and banana patches along the river. "But you inferred earlier that you thought you would have no trouble getting to James. If you haven't slept with him, what makes you think—"

Aziza smiled tiredly. "Put yourself in James's place," she said. "Now that Salih is dead, he is the weakest of all the warlords. And he is the only one of them who hasn't slept with me at least once." She turned to face Bolan fully. "These men invented the term *macho,* Mr. Pollock. Even if James didn't find me attractive, he would want me in order to be 'one of the boys,' as you Americans say."

"You know where his compound is located?" Bolan asked.

"Oh, yes," Aziza said. "He has little cover, so he has been forced to rely on other means of protection. James has built a fort, more or less, between Afmadu and Liboi, on the Kenyan border. He has friends in Kenya, and I'm sure he plans to flee there if he is ever overrun by Ham or one of the others."

"How far is it from here?" Bolan asked.

Aziza anticipated the question that would follow this one, and answered both at the same time. "If we fly there now," she said, "Ben and Elliot will have arrived at the meeting site long before we get back."

Bolan and Aziza lapsed into silence. Bolan knew it would be better to wait and then scout out James's compound with Elliot and Barkari in tow. He hadn't yet formulated a strategy, but he knew the two men in the Land Cruiser would play a part. And they needed to see the place firsthand rather than just hear about it from him.

As the Astar flew on, Bolan continued to watch through the window, studying the sharp twists and turns in the river. Small inlets and outlets and a few tiny islands appeared.

Eventually he checked his watch. "Turn her around, Khalid," he said. "They should be there by the time we get back."

As the Astar turned and headed back, Bolan felt an uneasiness come over him. Something had changed. What was it?

The hot African sun had begun to fall by the time Bolan realized that the men tending the bananas and corn had disappeared. He spotted the Land Cruiser parked along the river a moment later. In front of the vehicle, he saw two tiny specks—one white, the other darker. As the Astar drew closer, he raised the binoculars to his eyes. Elliot and Barkari had spread a blanket over the grass along the shore. They appeared to be sleeping.

A flicker of movement on the other side of the Land Cruiser caught Bolan's eye as the Astar began its descent. He raised the binoculars slightly, looking over the roof of the vehicle. More man-shaped specks were creeping toward the Land Cruiser. Parked a mile or so down the river, behind the approaching men, several vehicles reflected the falling sun in their glass and metal.

Khalid had seen the movement, too. "James's men," the pilot said, his voice strained. "They've parked and are sneaking up on them. I don't think Ben and Elliot have seen them." He gunned the chopper forward. "But we'll never get there in time."

Bolan climbed into the front and strapped himself into the passenger's seat. Drawing the Beretta from shoulder leather, he said, "Yes, we will. Move it." As he opened the Astar's door, his eyes narrowed, focusing on the creeping men below.

At least twenty of them. And they were now less than fifty yards from Don Elliot and Benjamin Barkari.

CHAPTER ELEVEN

Don Elliot was surprised that the helicopter wasn't there when they reached the meeting site on the Juba River. If there was one thing he had learned so far about Rance Pollock, it was that he decided what needed to happen, then *made* it happen that way. The guy was good, *damned* good. During his years with the CIA, Elliot had worked both with and against the best in the business. Some operatives relied on brains. God had given others far more than their share of brawn. A few had both, and they comprised the best of the best.

Elliot slowed the truck as they neared the water. But Pollock...he was...well, he was just in a different class altogether. He had the brains *and* he had the brawn. And he was as brave as they come—he had to be to go after the helicopter at the cannery although outnumbered maybe a hundred to one.

The former CIA man pulled the vehicle to a halt, staring out over the water. So why wasn't Pollock here yet? They'd had plenty of time. Had something gone wrong at the cannery? Had Pollock, Khalid and Aziza been captured? Killed?

Elliot watched the river as it flowed peacefully toward Kismayu. Part of him wanted to turn around, drive back to Mogadishu and find out. The other part told him not to worry. They'd be here.

Elliot looked at Friday in the front seat next to him. The big Swahili was staring quietly at the river, his thoughts a thousand miles away. Elliot felt there was nothing he could do to help his friend with the pain that radiated from those dark brown eyes, and that certainty brought on the former CIA man's own anguish.

Elliot was concerned about Pollock, Aziza and Khalid. But Friday's concern was *personal*. It was *family*. Instead of worrying about two friends and a near-stranger like Elliot, the Swahili saw it as a brother and the woman he loved who might be lying dead back at the fish cannery. And the emotional roller coaster Friday had been riding since seeing Aziza again practically ensured that the alarm he felt now would be blown out of proportion.

Elliot realized that he needed to keep Friday busy somehow. "We're going to be hell-bent for leather once this gig gets rolling," he said, breaking the silence. He opened the door and started to get out. "Let's stretch out while we can."

Elliot got out, shut the door, then turned back to rest his arms on the open window. The warm African sun beat down on the back of his neck as he spoke. "Come on, Friday. Help me spread the blanket out. We'll take a nap."

Friday didn't take his eyes off the river. "I'm not tired, Don. Got a lot of sleep last night."

"No, you didn't, and neither did I," Elliot said. "And we'll be getting even less from here on in unless I miss my guess." He opened the back door and rustled through the gear they had borrowed from Mrs. Mnarani, finding a blanket. "Come on, Friday," he said. "The sun's out." He chuckled. "If you're not sleepy, you can at least work on your tan."

With seeming reluctance, Barkari got out.

Elliot spread the blanket on the ground next to the vehicle and stretched out, looking up at the sky. Friday dropped down next to him, and Elliot suddenly felt like a twelve-year-old boy on a camping trip with his best friend. If it was night, they'd be looking for the Big Dipper.

The two men lay quietly for a few minutes, then Friday broke the silence. "What do I do, Don?"

Elliot didn't answer right away. There wasn't any good answer, but he wanted to be sure he had the best one possible before he spoke. He was on the outside of Friday's turmoil looking in, and from that point of view, the answer looked simple. Either understand why the woman he loved went to bed with the warlords, accept it and forgive her. Or dump her.

But Don Elliot knew that Friday was on the inside looking out. That made the situation a lot more complex.

"Only you can decide that," Elliot said.

"That's a cop-out."

"I know," Elliot said. He rose to his elbows, pulled a dry blade of grass from the ground and stuck it between his teeth. "But I was hoping *you* wouldn't know."

After another moment of silence, Elliot said, "Okay, are you asking me what *I'd* do if it was me?"

"Yes."

Elliot shrugged. "If I was in your shoes, I'd have the same hurt inside that you do. But I can tell you that I think it would be a damned shame to lose a woman like that because of *anything.*"

Friday rolled to his side, balancing himself on one arm. "The rape wasn't her fault," he said. "I know that. I'd like to kill the bastards with my bare hands, and if they weren't already dead I would."

Elliot nodded. "I'd consider it a privilege to be invited along on that one, buddy."

"And I can understand why she didn't tell me about it," Friday continued. "She knew that's exactly what I'd do and she was afraid I'd get killed."

Elliot nodded again. "You need to think about that one long and hard, old friend. It takes real love to do something like that—to give up someone you love for their own good." He glanced at the tortured face of his Swahili friend.

"The part that gets me, Don, is why she did what she did afterward. She went to bed *willingly* with Morris—the very man whose lawless society had allowed the rape in the first place."

"She was after revenge," Elliot said. "And she got part of it. Like you said, the bastards who raped her are dead."

Friday sat up and turned to face Elliot straight on. "But why... why like that?"

Elliot shrugged. "She used the only weapon at her disposal. In case you haven't noticed, women in Somalia aren't exactly parading down the streets burning their bras. They're pretty damned limited in what they're able to do around here."

"You sound like Pollock," Friday said.

"You talked to him about it?"

"More like *he* talked to *me* about it. He's worried that I'll get everybody killed."

"He has good reason to be," Elliot said. "I'd say right now you're operating at about seventy percent efficiency."

Friday sat up restlessly. "Pollock told me to stay behind if I couldn't handle it," Friday said. "If you felt the same way, why didn't *you?*"

Elliot laughed softly. "Pollock hasn't put up with your moodiness for the last twelve years like I have," he said. "And he hasn't worked with you long enough to know that when it comes to fighting, seventy percent of you is still a hell of a lot more than most men.

"Listen, you stupid Swahili," Elliot continued. "We're getting nowhere and I'm really tired. I'm going to try to catch a few more winks while I can."

Elliot twisted to look at Friday. Benjamin Barkari had closed his eyes. Soft snores drifted up from his clenched lips. He might not have been physically tired, Elliot realized, but emotional exhaustion brought its own need for sleep.

Elliot lay back down, drifting into a light half sleep, then a doze. A few moments later his eyelids suddenly popped open, fully awake.

A man—no, *men*—were moving in on them on the other side of the truck. He had heard something. Maybe he'd just sensed it. But they were coming.

Slowly, quietly Elliot reached across the blanket, grabbing Benjamin Barkari by the arm. "Friday," he whispered. "Friday, wake up."

The big Swahili's eyes opened.

The former CIA man pointed toward their truck, then raised his arm and made a dipping motion over it.

Friday got the message. His eyes shot right and left.

Elliot rolled to his stomach, resting his head on his arm as if still asleep but peering between the Land Cruiser's tires with half-open eyes. Through the tall stalks of green-and-yellow grass along the river, he saw a variety of colors that didn't belong there. Spots of blue. Here and there a splotch of tan. Even a patch of red.

Clothing. And the spots of clothing were moving slowly toward them.

Friday rolled over next to him. The big Swahili kept snoring lightly as he peeked beneath the undercarriage.

"Any idea who they might be?" Elliot asked.

Friday shrugged. "James's men, most likely. Probably patroling the river. They must have spotted the Land Cruiser and recognized it as one of Ham's— James is bound to be scared of the bastard. They think we're Ham's men."

"Think they'll talk?" Elliot asked as the spots grew larger through the grass.

"Sure," Friday answered. "To each other. Just as soon as they've killed us."

Both men drew their .45s.

Elliot kicked himself mentally for the lapse in judgment. The AK-47s were within reach inside the truck, but to get to them he'd have to open the door. The way the men in the grass were moving meant they'd seen the vehicle with no one inside. They might or might not have seen him and Friday asleep on the ground. But in any case, opening the door would alert the enemy that they were awake. No, the pistols were a better choice. At least for now.

Behind him, far in the distance, Elliot heard the clop of helicopter blades. He turned quickly, glancing over his shoulder to see his old Astar barreling through the air toward them. Pollock, Khalid and Aziza were inside. Maybe their approach would scare James's men off. He hoped so. Because at that distance, they weren't likely to get here in time to help with the gunfight.

Elliot thumbed the safety on the .45 and felt the cool silver-and-turquoise grips on his fingers. He aimed between the tires at the spot of blue that was leading the other spots.

He pulled the trigger and a 185-grain .45 hollow-point exploded from the barrel of the Colt. The blue spot stopped moving, then fell out of sight in the tall grass. A moment later a barrage of rifle fire answered Elliot's shot, pelting the Land Cruiser with the ferocity of a hailstorm.

BOLAN STRAPPED the seat belt around his knee. Grasping the roof of the helicopter with his left hand, he leaned out the door as the chopper descended.

He could make out the forms on the ground more clearly now. The men stalking the truck were led by a man in a blue T-shirt. Elliot and Barkari had rolled to their bellies to look under the vehicle at the approaching enemy. Good. At least they were aware of the threat.

As the chopper dropped lower, Bolan saw Elliot roll to his side, looking over his shoulder. The customized .45 in his hand glistened in the sunlight. Elliot rolled back, aimed the weapon between the tires, and Bolan heard a distant explosion below. The man in the blue T-shirt took the round in the chest.

As the helicopter neared the surprised men along the river, Bolan tried to drop the Beretta's sights on the chest of a man wearing a khaki BDU blouse. The chopper bobbed and jerked through the air, throwing the sights to the left, then the right, then high.

Bolan waited. As soon as he saw tan in his front sights, he pulled the trigger. A 3-round burst of 9 mm slugs zipped over the roof of the Land Cruiser, at least one of them finding its mark. Blood exploded from the khaki blouse, and the man looked up, then slithered into the tall grass.

Khalid guided the chopper over the truck, then over the group of James's men on the other side. From above, the creeping forms were clearly visible.

A gunner toting an AK-47 aimed skyward at the Astar. Bolan pointed the sights straight down as they passed, getting off another 3-round burst that felled the man next to his comrade.

He leaned farther out of the chopper, the wind whipping through his hair and threatening to suck him from the tenuous restraint afforded by the seat belt. All of James's men were staring up now, surprised at the sudden appearance of the Astar. They were all in the open. But in another second the helicopter would be out of pistol range, so Bolan chose his next target carefully.

A tall, thin man wearing a ripped dress shirt turned back toward Elliot and Friday, an AK-47 dancing in his hands.

Bolan's first two rounds stitched into the man's belly and neck. The third 9 mm burst into his rifle, singing tinnily.

Khalid dipped the chopper sharply, cutting back and dropping even lower as he prepared to make another pass. They were less than twenty feet in the air as they neared the firefight again.

The men in the bush had turned back toward the truck again. Bolan heard a barrage of return fire from Elliot and Barkari. Again the two men were proving their competence. They knew that the chopper couldn't just hover above the fight without presenting an easy target; it had to keep moving. But if the Astar kept passing over, they would have the warlord's men in a cross fire half of the time. So now was the time to keep them busy.

The AK-47s in the hands of James's men continued to boom below. Still half out of the helicopter, Bolan stared ahead. From the angle at which they now flew, only the heads of the men in the grass were visible.

He turned, yelling back into the chopper over the noise of the blades and engine. "We're too low, Khalid!" he said. "Take us up!"

The Astar shot suddenly toward the heavens.

Hooking his knee deeper into the seat belt, Bolan hung on for dear life as the laws of physics tried to pull him from the cabin. "There!" he yelled when he could see most of the men along the river. "Hover a second!"

The helicopter stopped in midair, its blades cutting circles through the sky. A few men on the ground looked up, aiming their rifles skyward. Again Bolan fought the bouncing chopper, trying to align the bobbing sights at the end of his outstretched arm.

Another trio of rounds coughed almost silently from the Beretta 93-R. A man in ragged fatigues fell in a dance of death. Bolan squeezed the trigger again, and a gunner wearing a black T-shirt performed similarly.

Wind caught the chopper, swinging it to the side. Bolan took advantage of the new angle to drop another of the warlord's men who was still firing at the truck. The burst caught the gunman in the back, and he slunk out of sight into the tall reeds.

Return fire forced Khalid to move again, and a second later Bolan found himself out of effective range. The Beretta was almost empty now, but rather than reload, he shoved the weapon back under his arm and drew the Desert Eagle.

Colonel James's men were second-class warriors compared to those of the other warlords. There was a good chance that the near-deafening roar of the big .44 Magnum from above would create panic among them.

As the Astar flew forward again, Bolan saw a man wearing a straw hat. The bright white color provided an excellent contrast to the grass, and zeroing in on the hat, Bolan aimed slightly below it. He hammered out a duo of Magnum rounds that made another man disappear below the reeds along the river.

Bolan fired repeatedly. Two more men fell as the mammoth Magnum boomed from above.

The Desert Eagle's enormous eruptions seemingly terrified three men near the water. As if on cue, the trio foolishly left the relative concealment of the reeds and sprinted into the open plain away from the river.

Khalid saw the men and turned the Astar. Bolan fired twice more, dropping a barefoot gunner wearing blue jeans. He shoved a fresh magazine into the Desert Eagle and chambered the first round. Steadying his arm on the door frame, he dropped the other two men with a pair of .44 missiles.

Below, Bolan saw another man break from the bush and fall to a shot from under the truck. He swung the Desert Eagle toward a man in a soiled floppy hat, shooting the frightened gunner between the shoulder blades, sending him plummeting to the earth.

As the chopper twisted back toward the river, a final shot echoed, then silence reigned. Khalid flew over once, then again, and both times Bolan saw the corpses of James's men in the grass.

None of the men was left standing.

Elliot and Barkari hurried to the front of their vehicle. They pulled rifles from the truck, then waved the chopper to the ground.

Khalid found a spot twenty yards from the river and set the helicopter down. Elliot and Barkari came sprinting up to the Astar. "One of them got away!" the former CIA man shouted, out of breath. "He's keeping to the grass, headed along the river." He pointed north.

Bolan looked over to Khalid and pointed at the roof of the Astar. A second later the chopper was rising again.

Bolan stared down as Khalid guided the Astar north, following the grass. He had to find the man. If anyone escaped to warn Colonel James about the gunfight along the river, the warlord would know something was up and double his security. Even Aziza wouldn't be able to get them through the door.

Bolan's trained eyes scrutinized every opening in the cover. But the brush was too thick, and he saw no trace of the fleeing gunman. When they had gone half a mile, he ordered Khalid to set the chopper down.

"He can't have gotten this far," Bolan said. "He's hiding somewhere between here and the Land Cruiser. Take the chopper back and forth so he'll think we're still searching from the air. Keep his mind on *you*."

Khalid smiled as Bolan got out of the Astar. The chopper rose back into the air.

Bolan dived into the grass. Rising to a crouch, he moved through the reeds. He was backtracking on the man, and there would be no trail to follow. The guy would be holed up somewhere in good cover, hoping to wait them out.

In short, the warlord's gunman had all the advantages. And if he saw Bolan before Bolan saw him, the warrior would become the executed rather than the Executioner.

Bolan moved on, the Beretta leading the way.

THE COUGH WAS QUIET, the sound of a man who has fought the urge to clear his throat for a long time, finally giving in. It was low. Muffled, and nearly inaudible.

But it was enough.

Bolan froze in place like a panther sensing the nearness of his prey. His knees sank deep into the muddy riverbank. The light filtering though the tall grass had faded as the afternoon wore on, and there was a gradual loss of visibility.

He remained motionless, the Beretta gripped in his right hand, his left deep in the mud in front of his knee. Only his eyes moved as they scanned the thick growth ahead.

There were two basic theories of search. The "bands" technique involved investigating the surrounding area side to side, and Bolan had employed this method during the hour and a half since he'd left the helicopter. But now, with the fading sunlight and mounting tension, he switched to the doctrine of "rays," his trained eyes moving in and out, then over to a new sector of vision. The change in routine refreshed his mind and forced him back to a peak awareness that overcame the fatigue of tension.

On the third visual search, Bolan detected a slight movement. Roughly ten yards ahead and slightly to his left, a tiny patch of black showed through the thick reeds of green, brown and yellow. The movement stopped, but Bolan's eyes remained glued to the spot, waiting. Seconds turned to minutes. Finally the small splotch of black shifted again, ever so slightly.

Skin. Black skin. Bolan was sure of it now.

With excruciating slowness, Bolan lifted his knee from the mud, shifting an inch to his right. His head moved just as slowly as he leaned that way, trying to find another break in the reeds. Another spot of black appeared, then a tiny patch of gold a shade lighter than the yellow stalks growing along the river.

A shirt? Either that or pants, but more likely a shirt. And a short-sleeved one—few men wore long sleeves in this climate. So if it was a yellow short-sleeved shirt, the black skin he saw next to it had to be the skin covering an upper arm or neck.

Bolan shifted his knee again, stopping halfway through the movement when the mud below began sucking. His knee had created a vacuum, and he dropped his speed to the point of imperceptibility. His free hand moved next to his leg, shifting mud into the hole. After what seemed like an eternity, the vacuum filled.

Another small break appeared in the foliage. This time Bolan saw not only black and yellow, but also a tiny round spot of white on the yellow shirt.

A button. But was it on the chest, or were buttons on the sleeves common to the shirts worn by the natives in Somalia? He didn't know, and if he shot before he was sure, he ran the risk of simply winging the warlord's man and giving away his position for return fire.

Bolan was about to move again when the gunner did his work for him. As the image ahead shifted slightly, the patch of black above the yellow shirt and white button formed a near-perfect V. Curly black hairs began to fall into focus. The chest, Bolan realized. He was looking at the man's chest. The gunner had unbuttoned the top three buttons of his shirt against the heat, and the black V now afforded Bolan with a target that might as well have had a bull's-eye in the center.

Still moving at a pace that made a turtle look like a racehorse, Bolan steadied himself on his left hand and began raising the Beretta. His thumb flipped the selector to semiauto. The tiny click sounded like a cannon in his own ears, but he knew it wouldn't travel far in the thick grass.

Bolan aimed down the top of the barrel, his eyes glued to the round white spot on the front sight. It fell over the gunman's chest, looking like another white button that had somehow risen from the shirt onto the skin.

Bolan shifted the Beretta slightly, and the white dots on the rear sight fell into place to the sides. His finger moved slowly backward on the trigger.

It was halfway there when the freight train hit him in the back.

The half breath Bolan had been holding blew from his lungs as he was knocked forward facedown in the mud. The Beretta flew from his hand as a fist struck down into his spine. Sharp pains shot up and down his spinal cord as a dozen questions and answers raced through his brain.

What had hit him? Another of James's men? Bolan reckoned he must have seen or heard Bolan earlier and circled through the brush. But why had he tackled Bolan instead of shooting him? He must have run out of ammunition or lost his weapon somewhere during the skirmish.

Bolan rolled to his side as a second fist shot down, striking his jaw. He caught a quick glimpse of the man above him before the blow landed. Big. Fat. At least two-hundred-fifty pounds.

The force of the blow proved there was muscle beneath the fat, and the punch drove Bolan's head back down into the mud. Dirty brown water sloshed up over his face as a hand rose instinctively to block the next blow. The next fist struck his forearm. Then more rained down in a flurry of punches. Bolan blocked some as he struggled to free himself from the sucking grip of the mud. Others blew through his defenses, landing on his ribs, shoulders, chest and face. A hard knuckle struck his jaw, and for a moment his vision went black.

A wild roundhouse blow skimmed across the top of his head as Bolan ducked. The missed punch broke the heavy man's balance, throwing him slightly to the side.

It was the break Bolan needed.

He pushed the man in the direction the punch had thrown him, at the same time rolling to the other side. The roll brought him up out of the mud hole, facing away from his attacker. Blindly Bolan threw a backfist and felt it connect with something hard.

A scream penetrated the mud in Bolan's ears. But whatever he had hit, it wasn't a vital point. The next second he felt the heavy man fall over him again. Pudgy fingers wrapped around Bolan's throat. Again his vision dimmed. He reached for the wrists at his neck, but the man had the better leverage angle, and his hands stayed firm.

As his eyes continued to cloud, Bolan pulled his right arm away, then drove it in an arch against the elbow as the man tried to strangle him. He heard a sharp crunch, then another painful scream, as the joint snapped.

Bolan rolled out from under the man to his knees. A flash of yellow to the side caught his eye, and he saw the man he had stalked less than five feet away. As the man brought the barrel of his AK-47 up into play, Bolan drew the Desert Eagle from his hip holster.

Bolan threw his upper body back, firing from the hip as soon as the .44 cleared leather. A jacketed hollowpoint shot from the barrel, and mud flew from the frame and slide as the Desert Eagle's action chambered another round.

The 240-grain missile left the Magnum automatic at 1,180 feet per second. It had lost very little of that velocity as it blew through the chest of the man holding the AK-47.

Bolan turned and saw the man with the broken arm digging through the mud. His hand suddenly appeared holding the Beretta 93-R. He turned toward Bolan.

A second .44 Magnum round caught the man under the chin, exiting out the back of his head. He dropped to his face in the mud.

Bolan stayed low, executing a quick 360-degree turn. Elliot and Barkari had seen only one of James's men flee along the river. There had been at least two.

Which meant there could also have been three, or four, or...

Bolan stayed in place for nearly five minutes, his eyes scanning the reeds. He heard the chopper overhead and looked up to see it drop out of sight behind the grass.

Finally satisfied no more of the warlord's men were lurking in the reeds, Bolan rose and walked to the fat man. As he pried the muddy Beretta from the chubby hands, the man's open eyes stared up at him in death.

Then a wave from the river washed through the reeds. Mud covered the fat man's face, hiding the eyes in a mask of death for all eternity.

THROUGH THE TINTED windows of the three-quarter-ton Chevrolet Suburban, General Fajir Ham watched the long line of Land Cruisers ahead. Already the sun was falling. It would be dark long before he and his convoy reached the meeting site. He and the light-skinned man had planned the arrival of the first shipment of weapons at night to avoid the American troops. The Americans were preparing to pull out as agreed, and had stopped patroling along the Somalian shore.

Now Ham wondered if Abu-Iyad might not have had another reason for darkness.

Ham's thick eyebrows fell low on his forehead. Abu-Iyad's respect, which bordered on subservience, was an act—Ham knew that, always had. After all, the man represented Iraq, a nation far stronger than any of the warlords. But would Saddam Hussein go as far as a double cross? It didn't seem likely. Already Iraq was under UN sanctions. By secretly trading arms for the desired sea port, and forming a public alliance with

Ham's new Somalia, Iraq would not risk further UN action.

No, Saddam Hussein would not double-cross Ham. At least not on this shipment, which contained only a few thousand assault rifles and pistols.

The sun continued to fall as the convoy moved on. If trouble did come, it would be after the Americans had gone and Ham had destroyed the other warlords. There was always the chance that Hussein would then decide he wanted all of Somalia instead of just the port. But that wasn't likely, either. Somalia was not oil-rich like Kuwait, and Hussein would never risk more Western action by trying to take the poverty-stricken country. Hussein wanted a naval base like the one he had sought in Kuwait. And a new site from which to launch Scud missiles on Saudi Arabia and Israel. Taking the rest of Somalia would not be to his advantage.

Ham glanced into the rearview mirror at the vehicles following his Suburban. He had over a hundred bodyguards with him, but still he was worried. It wasn't the men from Iraq he was about to meet who scared him, but the people of Somalia.

Flashbacks of Benito Mussolini as he was dragged through the street sent shivers down Ham's spine. If the people of Somalia were to somehow organize...

Only one in three of his men currently had weapons. The rest had been turned in to the Americans.

A cold sweat broke on the warlord's forehead. If the people accidentally stumbled on a leader—someone behind whom they could unite...

Ham wiped his forehead with the back of his sleeve. No, it would not happen. There wasn't enough time. Tonight he would be rearmed. Soon he would use those arms to subjugate the people of Somalia even further, and they would have no opportunity to find a leader and consolidate against him.

The truck slowed as it rounded a steep curve, and Ham turned his thoughts to General Morris. Morris had been gunned down by assailants outside one of his cafés in south Mogadishu. Some said the Americans had done it. Others pointed toward James and Jabbar, and some said Ham himself had been behind the assassination. But others said the shooting had been carried out by Somalian natives who had stumbled upon weapons. Ham's thoughts suddenly returned to his worst nightmare.

The people. The tribesmen.

No, they had not killed Morris. And they would not kill him. He would give them no opportunity to organize.

The convoy rounded another curve and the water of the Indian Ocean appeared ahead. The lead vehicle reached the shoreline and turned north, driving slowly along the narrow coastal road.

When the convoy stopped, several Land Cruisers formed a protective circle around Ham's Suburban. A half dozen transport trucks that had been at the convoy's rear now passed through and parked by the water.

Ham turned to the sea and saw the ship anchored a hundred yards from shore. A small rowboat under the power of a tiny engine was making its way toward him. As it drew nearer, he saw that it was guided by a man holding the tiller behind him.

Ali Abu-Iyad was the only other passenger.

The boat hit the sand. Ham nodded toward several of his men, who helped the driver slide the craft up out of the water.

Abu-Iyad stepped over the side of the boat and walked up to Ham. He bowed slightly, then wasted no more time with formalities. "We are ready to unload when you are, General."

Ham looked him in the eye. "You have brought the rifles, then?"

The light-skinned man hesitated. Finally he said, "Some of them."

Ham felt the anger flood his soul. He'd had a premonition that something like this would happen. Four hundred rifles would still mean less firepower than before he'd turned the AK-47s over to the Americans.

"Exactly what *have* you brought?" the warlord demanded. Darkness had fallen completely now, and the waters of the Indian Ocean sparkled under the moon. The night wind whipped his robes against his body as he awaited an answer.

"Two hundred FALNs," said the man with the light skin. "And one hundred Heckler & Koch G-3s." He paused. "But the H&K MP-5 submachine guns have arrived also. There are fifty. And two dozen Browning Hi-Power pistols."

Ham stared him in the eye. It was not so bad. Almost all of his men would now have a weapon. "How much ammunition?" he said.

Abu-Iyad looked out over the sea. "The ammunition has not yet arrived," he said.

Ham grabbed the man's throat. "What do you mean, it has not arrived?" he screamed. He shook the other man uncontrollably. "What good are guns without ammunition?"

Abu-Iyad reached up, prying Ham's fingers from his throat. He stepped back from the enraged warlord, his face turning an angry red. He took several deep breaths to regain control, and suddenly the disciplined smile was back on his face. "You must realize, General," he said, "that what you requested is coming from several countries. And it must avoid trade blockades around both of our nations. The rest of the weapons and the ammunition should be here within a few days."

Ham knew that what Abu-Iyad said made sense. But the warlord was being stalled—he could sense it. "We will take what you have, then," he said quietly. "Unload it."

The pilot of the small boat started the motor. Two of Ham's men jumped into the craft as it started back toward the ship.

"We must talk," Ham said, taking Abu-Iyad's arm and leading him toward the Suburban. He nodded toward two more of his men with rifles, and the pair followed. "I had planned to invade Ethiopia tomorrow," he said to the man on his arm as they walked. "Jijiga."

"Jijiga?" Abu-Iyad said. "But there is nothing there to be gained. Old men, women and children...."

Ham shrugged. "Their bodies will serve as a warning to other villages," he said as they reached the vehicle. One of the men opened the door, and Ham slid into the front passenger seat as Abu-Iyad got into the back.

Ham turned to face him. "I am unable to begin my conquest of Ethiopia as I had planned, because of your delays," he said. "Please explain it to me."

Abu-Iyad smiled, but even in the semidarkness of the truck Ham could see it was the smile of a predator. "Please, General," he said. "Even as we speak, I suspect many of the remaining weapons have already arrived in Baghdad. Perhaps even the ammunition. If not, they will be there soon." He paused. "These things take time, you must realize."

Ham nodded. "I understand. But I am ready to take over an entire country, then move on into others. I cannot do this until I am adequately armed. At the moment even the old men, women, and children of Jijiga outnumber me, and I am forced to stay in hiding. *Hiding.* Do you know what that is like for a man such as myself?"

Abu-Iyad's head bobbed slowly. "I can appreciate your frustration, General," he said. "But you must also appreciate mine. I have worked hard for you and I am tired. My greatest desire now is to deliver the rest of your arms, collect my fee from Mr. Hussein and disappear somewhere on the other side of the world."

Ham smiled as Abu-Iyad's words brought into perspective an unconscious suspicion he'd had all along. Perhaps Abu-Iyad wasn't the loyal Iraqi he made himself out to be. Perhaps he had his own agenda.

Ham eyed the man as the situation grew clearer. The meager number of weapons this Iraqi had brought tonight were a sacrifice, a way of buying time. Abu-Iyad had the rest of the weapons and the ammunition; Ham was sure of it. But Abu-Iyad had other customers in mind, and he believed a few FALNs would get the head start he needed without arousing suspicion.

"I *do* appreciate your frustration, dear friend," Ham said. "Have you any idea where you will go when this is over?"

Abu-Iyad answered so quickly that Ham knew it was a well-rehearsed lie. "I have been considering Bermuda," he said. "At least some place where I can lie back in the sun, look at the sea and not worry that the footsteps I hear behind me might be American Marines."

Ham nodded. "A good plan. And since I *do* appreciate your frustration, I will arrange for you to achieve at least a part of your plan immediately. You will accompany me back to my compound. There, on the plateau, you may lie in the sun all you want. You may rest assured that any footsteps you hear will be those of my men. The only thing missing will be the ocean."

"Thank you for the offer, General," said Abu-Iyad. "But I am afraid I must return to oversee the rest of the shipment."

Ham chuckled softly. "Perhaps I should rephrase my words," he said. "They were not an offer. They were an *order*. I no longer feel I can trust you, dear friend, so you will remain here until the rest of the weapons arrive."

"General, please be reasonable," Abu-Iyad said, and for the first time Ham thought he heard a note of insecurity enter the voice. "There are arrangements I must make personally. I must..." His voice trailed off.

Ham smiled. Yes, he thought, you must contact whoever you have left in charge of the weapons and tell them your plan hasn't worked. "I have telephone lines at the compound," Ham said. "You will be free to use them."

"General, surely you must realize how delicate this operation is. I *must* make the final arrangements in person. I simply cannot get it all done over the phone."

After several seconds Ham said, "You had *better* get it done over the phone, my dear friend. For if you do not, you will never leave my compound alive."

General Fajir Ham turned back to the front of the truck, his hand moving to the electric window control in the door. Pushing the switch, he lowered the rear windows, then watched in the rearview mirror as rifle barrels protruded into both window to press against the cheeks of the man in the back seat.

CHAPTER TWELVE

The Astar rose higher into the air as Bolan, Aziza and Khalid Barkari neared Colonel James's compound near the Kenyan border.

"Will they be able to see us?" Aziza asked from the back.

"Perhaps," Khalid said behind the controls. "But it will not matter. We are in the flight lanes from Mogadishu to Nairobi. No one will pay much attention."

Settling back as they flew on, Bolan watched as a tiny rectangle appeared below in the distance, gradually growing in size as the helicopter neared. He lifted the binoculars to his eyes, leaning forward to study the stronghold as Khalid cut the Astar's speed.

Bolan studied the compound through the twin lenses. Although of modern construction, it had followed the style of ancient Roman fortresses. That made sense, since this portion of Somalia had long been under Italian rule. The thirty-foot walls were of concrete blocks. Pillboxes at the four corners were even higher. The Astar was approaching what appeared to be the front of the installation, and Bolan could see that the main entrance was large enough to accommodate a large supply truck.

Bolan turned the binoculars to the pillbox on the right front corner of the compound. Rising perhaps ten feet higher than the walls, it and the other three lookout stations would contain men with assault rifles.

There might even be machine guns mounted on turrets.

The chopper hit an air pocket and bounced upward as they drew even with the front of the compound. Looking straight down, Bolan spied a large mansion slightly offset in the center of the rectangle. Around the mansion were various outbuildings, including a structure slightly smaller than the house: barracks. Cars, supply trucks and various other vehicles were parked throughout the grounds.

"Cut to the side, Khalid," Bolan ordered. "Get me an angle where I can see the back."

As the Astar headed east, Bolan twisted in his seat. An Olympic-size swimming pool was visible just behind the house, along with a deck and cabana. There were a few other unidentifiable outbuildings, and a rear entrance identical to the one in the front wall.

Bolan frowned, contemplating the fortress as the Astar flew on toward the Kenyan border. Simple, even antiquated by the standards of modern warfare, Colonel James's compound would offer little resistance to a modern army. The concrete walls would fall easily to a few mortar rounds, after which as few as a dozen special-forces soldiers could probably storm the grounds and take control within minutes. Or they could sit back and keep firing mortars until the place looked like the bombed-out sections of Mogadishu.

Bolan faced forward again. The problem was, he didn't have a modern army. And even if he had, his mission called for a strategy far more subtle.

A small guard shack along the road into Kenya appeared a few miles later, and Khalid cut south toward the ocean. They circled back to the Juba, then dropped low enough to follow the road between Gelib and Afmadu.

Bolan lifted the binoculars again and studied the pitted asphalt. A tiny black speck finally appeared, bumping its way toward a shallow valley on the plains. "This is it," he said. "Take her down."

A few seconds later the chopper set down in the valley. Hidden from all four sides, Khalid left the engine running as they waited. Bolan turned and looked over the back seat at Aziza, who had changed into a long white dress. The white presented a startling contrast to her smooth caramel skin. The dress had become wrinkled from packing, and she had strategically torn the strap on one shoulder and ripped the slit in the side a little higher. Her hair was ruffled and windblown, and her overall appearance was exactly what the next step of the mission called for.

Aziza Mnarani looked disheveled in a singularly erotic way.

Bolan chuckled silently. He'd needed to do little to make his own appearance look unkempt. After the fight with the two men along the river, he had done his best to wash the mud from his clothes while Elliot and the Barkari brothers drove the men's vehicles into the river and sank the bodies. Bolan had been left with dirty pants and jacket, and a face that bore the cuts and bruises put there by his overweight attacker.

Both Aziza and Bolan looked exactly the way he wanted them to look: like a man and woman who'd been running at breakneck speed across Somalia with General Ham and his men close behind.

"You've been here before?" Bolan asked, breaking the silence.

"Only once. With Morris. We had dinner with Colonel James, and they talked of some border dispute that they were trying to settle peacefully."

"Tell me about the security," Bolan said.

"You will be searched," she said. "They will take all weapons while we are in the compound."

Bolan nodded. He had expected as much. "But no metal detectors?"

"No, at least not here," Aziza said. "Ham and Jabbar seized the ones from the airports when Barre first fell, and I doubt James has found one anywhere else. Remember that James is the weakest of the remaining warlords." She smiled widely, showing an even row of white teeth that matched her dress. "His methods are primitive compared to Ham and Jabbar. James is your basic bargain-basement warlord."

The fact that James's security was not on a par with Ham's or Jabbar's was the reason Bolan had chosen to strike the southern warlord. By the time they were done at James's compound, Grimaldi should have arrived over Somalia and made the drop. The plastic-and-ceramic Glock, and the equally metal-less Hellweg speed rig, should get Bolan through the metal detector to Jabbar. But that trick was only likely to work once, and when he came to Ham, he would need a new approach.

Although he hadn't quite worked the details out yet, the Executioner had mapped out his basic strategy.

Bolan turned his attention to James's compound. Aziza would serve as a first-class ticket, but once they were inside, it would be up to him to find a time and place to take James out. It wouldn't be easy by any means, but it shouldn't prove too difficult if the same security weaknesses he had seen outside the compound were present inside, as well.

Bolan removed his jacket and slipped out of the shoulder rig. Getting away—that was where the problem lay. And there were only two possible answers. Killing James privately, then slipping out without any of his men knowing what had happened, was the preferable course. But if that chance didn't present itself, they would have to just take the man out and make a run for it.

Bolan unfastened his belt buckle and removed the Desert Eagle and extra magazine caddie from his belt. He knew they would be taken from him, anyway, and that he would probably still be without them when the time came for a quick escape. He would get replacement weapons from the package Grimaldi would soon be dropping through the sky.

A car engine sounded in the distance. Looking up, Bolan saw the Land Cruiser appear on top of the rise to his right. Elliot sat behind the wheel with Benjamin Barkari beside him in the passenger's seat. Slowly the vehicle made its way over the grass and down into the valley.

Bolan saw a frown on Barkari's face as the truck drew near. The Swahili warrior was struggling with something in his lap.

Bolan helped Aziza out of the Astar as the truck stopped twenty yards away. They ducked under the flying blades and hurried toward the vehicle.

Barkari stepped out and offered an AK-47 to Bolan. "One of them we picked up at the river," he explained. "Looks like a bullet hit it. It'll take the magazine, but I can't get it to chamber a round. You want it?"

Bolan knew what he meant. Their cover story was to be that they'd been on the run. But they had *survived*. If they arrived at James's compound completely unarmed, it would raise a few eyebrows as to just how they'd accomplished such a thing.

Bolan took the rifle and tossed it into the back of the truck. He nodded to Elliot. "Come with me," he said.

Retracing his steps to the Astar, Bolan adjusted the radio to the frequency he knew Grimaldi would be using. "The package I ordered will get here while we're with James," he said. "Go back to the river and pick it up for me."

Elliot nodded. "How is your man going to know to trust me?"

Bolan needed a quick code that Grimaldi would immediately recognize, but wouldn't give away any info about Stony Man Farm. "Tell the pilot he executes a lot of fine flights," Bolan said. The word *execute* was incongruous enough to catch Grimaldi's attention.

"He executes a lot of fine flights," Elliot repeated, then shrugged. "Whatever the hell that means."

When Bolan got back to the Land Cruiser, Benjamin Barkari had taken Aziza in his arms. He held her at arm's length, staring into her eyes, his own face a mask of worry. "Please be careful," he whispered.

Aziza nodded. "You, too," she said. She rose suddenly on her toes, bringing her lips up and locking them with the Swahili's.

Elliot and Barkari moved to the Astar as Bolan twisted the truck's key and started the engine. The door next to him opened, and the beautiful black woman took the seat next to him.

A moment later they pulled up out of the valley and onto the road, on their way to kill the next of the Somalian warlords.

DUST BLEW UP as Bolan skidded to a halt ten yards in front of the compound's front entrance. He looked upward through the windshield to the row of men leaning over the top of the concrete wall.

At least three dozen Ak-47s were aimed downward.

Bolan then glanced to the pillboxes at the corners of fortress. He had been right. The lookout stations were equipped with machine guns—Egyptian versions of the Spanish 7.92 mm Alfa 44. He could see the distinctive cooling fins on the barrels.

Barrels that, like those of the AK-47s, were ready to smother Bolan and Aziza in fire at the slightest provocation.

A flicker of movement in the rearview mirror brought Bolan's eyes up, and he saw a half-dozen men suddenly appear behind them. The doors of the vehicle were ripped open, and he and Aziza were jerked out.

All of the men seemed to speak at once. Questions assaulted Bolan and Aziza in a tongue he couldn't understand. Then two men grabbed him by the shoulders, spun him back toward the truck, and pushed him.

Bolan placed his hands on the roof of the vehicle as hands searched him for weapons. Directly across from him, he could see Aziza going through the same process. A tall, reed-thin man with a thick, curly mustache and goatee ran his hand along her waist. Sweat glistened on his forehead and upper lip as his hands moved upward to her shoulders. The hands slid down under Aziza's armpits, and moved around her sides and inside her neckline. The man giggled as he stroked Aziza's breasts.

Aziza stared past Bolan, emotionless.

Bolan gritted his teeth, resisting the urge to jump the compound guards right then and there.

Finished with their search, the men behind Bolan pushed him harder into the side of the truck. More questions assaulted him.

Bolan shrugged the fact that he didn't understand. On the other side of the vehicle, the skinny man tired of his sexual battery and spun Aziza back to face him. The two conversed in their native tongue.

Suddenly the leer on the thin man's lips was gone, and his black skin paled to a sickly gray.

Bolan knew what it meant. Aziza had just told him who she was. He had recognized the name and realized his treatment of her might bring punishment.

The thin man pulled a walkie-talkie from his belt. His voice took on a respectful tone that bordered on reverence as he spoke into the instrument. A voice answered, then the airwaves were silent.

Bolan, Aziza and the men holding them waited. Several minutes later a low, gravelly voice came over the walkie-talkie. Even though he couldn't understand the words, the tone told Bolan that orders were being given.

A moment later the thin man with the goatee opened the back door of the Land Cruiser and pulled out the AK-47. He spoke excitedly as he lifted the rifle.

The warlords had turned in most of their weapons in compliance with the recent agreement, and Bolan suspected that the guns he saw ringing the top of the compound were most of what James had left. Until they could rearm, every new rifle they came upon was valuable.

Bolan smiled. He hoped the man with the goatee chose to use the disabled AK-47 for his personal weapon.

Bolan was shoved into the back seat. The door on the other side was opened, and Aziza got in. "The last voice was Colonel James," the beautiful black woman whispered as the thin man slid behind the wheel. "They are taking us to him." She paused, then added quickly in a voice even lower, "I told them you were a mercenary who helped me escape Ham. I think they believe me."

Bolan nodded. He wanted to ask how much more of their cover story she had already gotten out, but this was hardly the time or place. There was no way of knowing which, if any, of the guards spoke English.

The heavy wooden gate slid open and the procession started forward. The man who had molested Aziza drove slowly, allowing the men with the AK-47s to keep up on foot to both sides of the truck. The gate closed again behind them, and they drove directly to the mansion Bolan had seen from the air.

Bolan was jerked from the vehicle and frisked again by two men who'd been standing guard on the front porch of the house. Aziza, he noticed, was treated with far more respect now, and when she spoke angrily to the new guards, they stepped back from Bolan, as well.

Colonel James was waiting in the antechamber just inside the front door. Approximately six feet tall, he wore carefully tailored European slacks and a red-and-gold smoking jacket. An ascot circled his throat beneath the jacket, and soft leather slippers covered his feet.

Bolan looked at the man's face. He had the sharp, eaglelike features of the native Somalian. His expression was a well-rehearsed look of confidence. Only the haunted eyes betrayed that self-reliance, and Bolan looked inside them to see the soul of a true paranoid.

Bolan knew he would have to be careful; *very* careful. News of Morris's assassination would have reached here by now and intensified James's paranoia.

James stepped forward, taking Aziza's hand. Raising it to his lips, he kissed it, then stepped back. Ignoring Bolan, he spoke to Aziza.

Aziza answered, nodding at Bolan several times, and finally James turned to face him. Switching to English, the warlord said, "I must thank you for rescuing my wonderful friend from General Ham," he said. "Let me extend the hospitality of my humble home. Please feel free to take sanctuary here for as long as you feel it is necessary."

Bolan watched the tormented eyes. Right. He could stay here as long as he liked—unless Ham found out. James might fight for Aziza, but Bolan knew where he stood if the stronger warlord learned where he was hiding.

"General Ham," James continued, "is also my friend, of course. But I am afraid he had no idea how a beautiful woman like this should be treated." He stopped talking long enough to eye Bolan's muddy condition head to toe, then said, "I am certain you would like to refreshen yourself. I will have my men show you to your quarters." He brought his arm up and glanced at the gold Rolex on his wrist. "You should have just enough time before dinner."

James turned to Aziza and offered her his arm. "I will escort you to your rooms personally, my dear," he said.

Aziza slipped her arm through the warlord's and smiled up at him. "I cannot tell you how much I appreciate your protection," she said, her eyes growing wide, like those of a little girl.

Bolan glanced at James. Aziza was obviously having the desired effect. The man's eyes had lost their haunted look and were now portholes to the lust in his heart.

Aziza turned to an angle where neither James nor his guards could see, gave Bolan a quick wink, then disappeared down the hallway on the arm of the warlord.

THIRTY MINUTES LATER, Bolan twisted the knobs and turned the shower off. Reaching out of the stall, he pulled a large bath towel from the rod. Drying himself, he noticed the empty rod.

The towel holder, like all the plumbing accessories in the bathroom, were of pure gold. The cabinet tops were constructed of tiny square ivory tiles from the tusks of poached elephants, and the cabinets were constructed of the smoothest marble Bolan had ever seen.

The bedroom was as elaborate as the bathroom. As he walked to the ornately carved oak bed where fresh clothes had been laid out, he saw the silk-and-leather love seat against the wall, the expensive lamps on the small tables that matched the bed and the chandelier hanging from the ceiling.

Bolan was no interior decorator, but even he knew the chandelier belonged in a dining room. None of the other furniture went together, either, and appeared to have been chosen only because of its gaudiness. His eyes fell on the wood-burning fireplace in the corner. Somalia was hot and humid during the rainy season, rarely dropped below eighty degrees the rest of the year, and he couldn't help wondering just how many fires needed to be built.

The fireplace was symbolic of the entire mansion—James's entire philosophy, actually. While the people of Somalia scraped for every bite of food, the warlords grew rich. But immense wealth never had, and never would, automatically bring class or taste.

Bolan lifted a bright red pullover shirt from the bed and pulled it over his head. It was at least two sizes too small and stretched tightly across his chest. The khaki pants fit in the waist but clung to his thighs, and the cuffs made a line halfway up his calfs.

Bolan pulled on his hiking boots. Someone had cleaned the mud and grit from them as he showered, and given the tanned leather a new coating of oil. He wouldn't be asked to pose for *GQ* in this getup, but he'd get by.

The telephone next to the bed rung shrilly as Bolan laced his boots. He lifted the receiver. "Hello?"

A quick phrase in Cushitic met his ears.

"I don't understand," he answered.

"I am sorry," the voice said in English. "I forgot. Dinner is about to be served. Colonel James requests your presence. An escort will be sent for you." The line went dead.

A moment later there was a knock on the door. Bolan twisted the knob to find a ravishing black woman standing in the hall. She had the sharp features Bolan had grown accustomed to in Somalians, and her pouty lips wore a coat of bright pink lipstick. She was dressed in a white mini-skirt and matching tube top, with a pair of white high heels, and the fact that she wore no bra was as evident as the nose on her face.

"I am Zahra," she said, smiling. "Are you ready?"

Bolan smiled and nodded, stepping into the hallway and offering his arm.

Zahra led him to the elevator. As they waited, he discretely studied the woman. It was obvious she had been sent to him as a gift from James, but the reason behind the gift was hardly generosity.

James wanted Aziza for himself. Which meant he wanted Bolan busy and out of the way.

A few minutes later Bolan found himself seated in a huge dining area between Zahra and James, who was on his right at the head of the table. Aziza sat across from him, and Bolan had to smile at the arrangement.

The term *right-hand man* originated with the ancient Romans, where the custom was that Caesar would seat his most trusted confederate to his right. The man to his left would be Caesar's second most trusted. Both were close enough to get to their ruler with the short daggers hidden beneath their cloaks, but assuming both were right-handed, the man to Caesar's right had a straight shot. Stabbing from the ruler's left involved a rather awkward twist before it could be delivered.

James might be many things, but he was no fool.

Bolan had been seated to his left.

That wasn't the only precaution the warlord had taken, Bolan realized as two waiters dressed in formal

Somalian robes brought in the first course of the meal. Standing nonchalantly around the walls, and thereby covering the table from all sides, were four hard-faced men. They showed no weapons, but as Bolan took his seat he saw one of the men—a tall, broad man sporting a full beard—twist to speak in a low voice to one of the waiters.

Bolan couldn't help but notice that a telltale bump beneath the man's robe, on the right side, could only be the grip of a pistol.

Bolan noted the information. He had considered several plans of action while in the shower, but had not as yet settled upon a way to eliminate Colonel James. He would have to keep his eyes open and be ready to take advantage of whatever opportunity presented itself.

The long table was quiet as the two waiters set large platters filled with tomatoes, bananas, grapes and grapefruit in the center. Beneath the table Bolan felt a soft hand move to his thigh, then upward. He turned to see Zahra smiling up at him. He smiled back. "Later," he whispered, and the hand was removed.

Aziza grinned at him from across the table, stifling a laugh. She could not have seen Zahra's hand beneath the table, but she had seen Bolan's reaction to it.

James smiled as the waiters disappeared. "It is good to have guests," he said. Holding both arms out, the palms of his hands up to indicate the food, he said, "Please partake of my humble offerings."

Bolan waited as Aziza and Zahra took fruit from the platters onto their plates. *Humble* was hardly the word for it. He had seen only the first course so far, but it already consisted of more food than the average Somalian peasant family ingested in a month.

James tore several grapes from their stems and dropped them into his mouth. As he turned to Aziza, Bolan saw that the lust on the man's face hadn't diminished during the hour or so that they'd been at the compound. If anything, it had increased.

"So you would like to remain here?" James said. "In sanctuary from General Ham? Both of you?"

Aziza peeled a banana, then slowly, deliberately pushed it past her lips. Looking up at James with wide brown innocent eyes, she nodded. Pulling the banana back out of her mouth, she said, "Please. Ham will kill us both if he finds us."

James set down his grapes. "I understand why," he said. "I doubt that I could stand the loss of such a beautiful woman, either."

Bolan felt movement at his side and turned to see Zahra holding a grape up to his mouth. He opened his lips and a began chewing as James turned to him. "And you, Mr...."

"Pollock," Bolan said. "Rance Pollock."

"I am still not clear exactly where *you* fit into the picture."

Bolan shrugged. "A gun for hire," he said simply. "I could tell you how I became acquainted with Miss Mnarani, but it's a long, boring story. The short version is that when she'd had enough of Ham, she hired me to get her out." He took another grape offered from the side.

James had started to speak when the waiters appeared with steaming bowls of the spaghettilike dish known as *basta*. The colonel waited until each person had been served and the waiters had ladled a large measure of sauce into the bowls, then said, "Yes, I see. But what are your plans now, Mr. Pollock?"

Bolan shrugged. "I'd like to remain here a day or two until the heat dies down. Then I'm out of Somalia as fast as these legs will carry me."

James smiled and nodded. "Yes. But I suspect the 'heat,' as you say, will get hotter before it lessens. I can arrange your departure from the country immediately, tonight, in fact, and it will be safer than waiting until Ham follows your trail."

Bolan forced a smile. James wanted him out of the way, and *now*. He didn't want Ham to find out he was harboring a man the stronger warlord wanted dead. And that didn't give Bolan much time. "That would be great," he said. "Do we have time to finish dinner?"

James and the others around the table laughed.

Zahra offered Bolan a fork rolled with *basta,* but he shook his head. Picking up his own utensil, he began to eat as the table lapsed again into silence. When they had finished, the waiters replaced the bowls with fresh plates. Huge platters of mutton, goat and even beef— a nearly unheard-of delicacy in the country—were set on the table. They were garnished with roasted potatoes, onions and peppers. There was enough food to make the average peasant faint in disbelief.

Zahra tried to feed Bolan once more, but he declined.

Bolan cut a piece of mutton and began chewing. The conversation changed to small talk. Bolan entered in when appropriate. He finished his meat, then waited until James was busy talking to Aziza.

The steak knife slipped unseen up his right sleeve.

As soon as everyone had finished, the waiters cleared the table again and brought in platters containing more fruits, nuts and cheeses. Bolan shook his head when Zahra offered them to him.

James saw the movement and turned to him, the smile on his face now an undisguised sneer. "You have had enough?" he said.

Bolan nodded.

"Then it is time that I helped you, as I promised earlier," the warlord said. "I am sorry, Mr. Pollock, perhaps your story is true. But I cannot afford to take chances at this stage of the game." He clapped his hands, and the bearded man behind Bolan suddenly appeared at his side. "I am afraid I must hold you for my good friend General Ham."

Bolan studied the man's crazed eyes. What James planned to hold for Ham was a dead body. He couldn't turn Bolan over without some story about Aziza, and a dead man couldn't contradict whatever tale James came up with.

"Please do not resist," James said. "I would not like to have you killed in front of a beautiful woman."

Aziza shook her head violently. "What is this?" she demanded. "This man saved my life! He brought me to you! And this is how you reward him?"

James shrugged.

Aziza stared at him. "This man is my friend. If he is to be held as a prisoner, then hold me, as well."

"I am," James said simply. "But your cell will be my bedroom."

Bolan felt the guard's firm grip on his right arm. This was hardly an ideal time to strike, but in a few minutes he'd either be dead or locked up in some part of the mansion.

It was now or never.

The bearded guard pulled upward on Bolan's arm. Bolan rose as if surrendering to his fate, but when he was halfway to his feet, his left hand snaked into his right sleeve. The steak knife appeared and a second later penetrated the robe of the bearded man and entered his heart.

Zahra let out a startled gasp as Bolan twisted the blade, then jerked hard on the handle. Wet sucking sounds filled the room as the knife came out of the bearded guard's chest. Turning immediately to James, Bolan drove the bloody blade into the warlord's throat.

The Roman philosophy of "right-hand men" had one fatal flaw: not all men were right-handed, and some—like the Executioner—were equally adept with their left.

James's eyes opened wide in disbelief as Bolan's blade struck the back of his neck and lodged in his spine. Bolan knew the shocked guards around the room were returning to their senses. Abandoning the steak knife, he turned back to the bearded guard who was just now starting to fall over the table.

With one smooth movement Bolan parted the man's robes and jerked a 9 mm CZ75 from his waistband.

Bolan turned. To his side he saw a flash of silver in Zahra's hand. Lifting the weapon, he double-actioned the first shot into the bearded guard behind him as his free arm brushed Zahra's silver streak away. His round caught the man as a smaller explosion sounded on Bolan's other side.

He swung the 9 mm weapon toward the wall behind Aziza as she dived protectively over the table toward him. He dropped the CZ's sights on the guard directly behind where she had sat, squeezed the trigger twice and caught the man in the face and neck.

Landing on the table, Aziza reached up and grabbed Zahra by the throat. A small nickel-plated automatic went clattering across the table as the two women fell out of sight to the floor.

Recovering, the guard against the far wall fired a double-tap of 9 mm slugs at Bolan; they flew past, singing in his ear. Bolan faced the man as Aziza and Zahra came back into view at his side. Aziza was on top of the other woman, pummeling her with her fists.

Bolan pulled the trigger twice. The first round caught the guard in the upper chest, spinning him to the side. The next round entered the side of the man's head, blowing out the other side in a rainstorm of blood and brains.

The last of the four guards fell to the floor.

Bolan turned to the floor in time to see Aziza punch Zahra one last time, then wrest a small dagger from the other woman's hand. Without preamble, Aziza raised the double-edged blade, then drove it down into the other woman's breast.

Bolan reached down, grabbing Aziza by the shoulder and hauling her to her feet. "The others will have heard the gunshots," he said. "We've got to move." He paused. "You shoot as well as you stab?"

Aziza grabbed the nickel-plated automatic off the table. "Stick around and you'll find out," she said.

Bolan circled the room quickly, picking up another CZ75 from a downed guard and dropping four extra 15-round magazines into his pockets. He moved to the door the waiter had used, then turned to Aziza behind him.

The beautiful black woman had added another of the Czech 9 mm weapons to her personal arsenal, and now held it in her right hand. She gripped the nickel-plated pistol, a Baby Browning .25, in her left. Bolan studied the woman a moment. Aziza's white gown had been ripped all the way to the waist in her struggle with Zahra, and even more of the smooth caramel skin was exposed. Bolan didn't have time to admire the beauty. As he turned back to the door, it burst open and a waiter toting an ancient Italian OVP submachine gun burst into the dining room.

Bolan dropped the man with a quick double-tap of rounds from the CZ75, then uncocked the hammer and shoved the pistol into his belt. As old as the subgun might be, if it worked, it would be a far sight better than any pistol.

Kneeling by the waiter, Bolan lifted the weapon. It looked little different from a short hunting rifle, except for the magazine protruding conspicuously from the top. He pulled back the knurled sleeve around the receiver, checked the chamber and found a live round. He let the bolt fall back.

He turned as another waiter came through the door. The man fell to a quick burst of fire from the OVP. Bolan stepped over him, motioning Aziza to follow.

The kitchen, on the other side of the swinging door, was empty. The Italian subgun held ready, Bolan made his way to another door.

They met no resistance as they hurried quietly down a hallway, searching for an exit. There were more guards in the house, Bolan knew—he had seen them. The fact that they had not come running into the dining room could only mean they had elected to cover the exits instead.

They would be waiting.

Bolan entered the room at the end of the hallway and found himself in a den. A sliding glass door looked out over the swimming pool. Looking through the glass, he saw a wooden deck running the circumference of the water. A large concrete patio surrounded that. Lounge furniture, imitation waterfalls and huge stone statues of ancient African tribal warriors decorated the area. A short walk led past two palm trees in iron planters to the pool. The area seemed deserted.

Bolan's survival instincts went on red alert. The rest of the house guards had to be somewhere. Were they hiding behind the statues, plants or other decorations?

He hesitated. They had to be, at least some of them. Accidentally coming out of the house at a point no one was covering was simply too much good fortune.

Bolan reckoned he had two choices. He could lead Aziza out of the house here and be prepared for the attack he knew would follow, or make his way back through the house and try to find another way out.

The Executioner didn't have to make the choice. It was made for him.

Running footsteps suddenly sounded behind Bolan and Aziza. He turned as two men with rifles entered the room. Behind them, still in the hall, were more shadowy figures.

The two men already in the room dived for the floor as Bolan fired a quick burst from the OVP, then ripped the sliding door back along its rails. He shoved Aziza out onto the patio, then followed.

A moment later the pool area came to life. Men armed with a variety of pistols, submachine guns and short-barreled shotguns suddenly appeared from behind the statues, waterfalls and other decorations.

The thin man with the goatee who had taken such pleasure in frisking Aziza now stepped forward. "Drop your weapons, Pollock," he said in English. "Or you will die."

CHAPTER THIRTEEN

Seated behind the controls of the landed Astar 1450 TT, Don Elliot stared out into the night, watching the waters of the Juba River glide softly by. Out of the corner of his eye, he could see Benjamin Barkari beside him.

Friday's hands were in his lap, and he clenched both fists tightly, then straightened his fingers. He performed the movement repeatedly.

Elliot looked out the side window, clearing Friday from his peripheral vision. Waiting was hard on the nerves—his, as well as Friday's—but watching the Swahili's overwrought performance only made things worse.

Finally Friday let out a deep breath. "I don't like it, Don. I don't like it at all."

Elliot let his fingers tap a melody across the control column. "Of course you don't, Friday," he said, careful to keep his tone humorous. "The woman you're in love with is out with another man. And while I'm a poor judge of looks in the male of the species, I suspect more than one member of the fairer sex has fallen for our Colonel Pollock." He watched for Friday's reaction.

Barkari shook his head. "You know what I mean, Don," he said. "They're out there on their own. No backup. If something happens, we'll never even know what." He paused. "They just won't ever come back."

"Tell you what," Elliot said. "As soon as we make the pickup here, we'll do another quick fly-over. Think that'll make you feel any better?"

"I doubt it," Barkari said. "But I suppose it'll have to do."

As if the mysterious pilot Pollock had been awaiting had heard their conversation, a voice came over the chopper's radio. "Birdman One to Bird Watchers. Come in, Bird Watchers."

Elliot leaned forward, pulling the microphone out of the clip mounted to the control panel. "Bird Watchers here," he said. "Come in, Birdman."

After a pause the voice said, "I'm not talking to the chief Bird Watcher."

"Negative," Elliot said. "He's soaring with the eagles at the moment. But he said to tell you you've executed some fine flights...whatever that means."

Elliot heard a soft chuckle over the airwaves. A moment later the voice said, "Affirmative, Watchers. I'm laying my egg now." The radio went silent.

Shortly Elliot heard the hum of unseen engines overhead. Then the sound faded, and a bright, iridescent green glow appeared in the night sky. As it fell toward the earth, it took on the conelike shape of a small parachute.

Friday was already out of the Astar and halfway to the landing spot by the time the chute hit the ground a hundred yards away. He came sprinting back with a hard plastic case and jumped back into the helicopter.

Elliot let the Astar warm up, then took them back into the air, pointed south. Soon they were sailing over southern Somalia once more.

When the lights of the compound appeared in the distance, the former CIA operative glanced to his side. "We can only afford one pass, Friday," he said. "So take a good look."

Elliot slowed, knowing he was taking a chance by going over at all. Too much extra air traffic, combined with surprise visitors, would add up to only one thing in Colonel James's mind.

Surveillance. Surveillance that could get both Pollock and Aziza Mnarani killed real quick.

"I'll take the left side, you watch the right," Elliot said as they drew even with the front wall. "If you see any—"

He stopped in midsentence as they moved over the mansion. Below he saw at least thirty armed men suddenly step out from cover around the pool.

"They're down there!" Benjamin Barkari shouted. "Aziza and Pollock! I just saw them come out the back of the house!"

Elliot whirled the Astar around. "Here's another fine mess you've gotten me into," he said as he lowered the chopper down hard. He turned to his partner, but Friday had already opened the chopper door and was hanging out into the air very much like the man they knew as Rance Pollock had done earlier that day at the Juba River.

"DROP YOUR WEAPONS!" the man with the goatee screamed. "This will be your final warning!"

Bolan halted by a large iron planter. He glanced to his side. Standing next to him, by the other palm-tree planter, was Aziza, her face showing no fear. The beautiful black woman was ready to die in her pursuit of justice—probably had been ever since that first night over a year ago when Morris's men had raped her.

But Bolan knew that if he and Aziza went down now, it would be in a blaze of fire whose flames led toward no good end. Morris and James were dead, but unless Ham and Jabbar were taken out of the picture, they would quickly take over their areas and continue the subjugation of the Somalian people.

And Bolan couldn't stop them if he was dead.

He studied the man with the goatee. No, it would be better to drop the guns now and hope that another lapse in security would provide a chance to—

The sudden noise of helicopter blades overhead cut into Bolan's thoughts. The sound was coming from the front of the compound—the direction from which Elliot and Barkari would come, and within a microsecond Bolan had decided on a different course of action.

Slowly, milking every split second he could out of the movement, Bolan started to lay down the OVP. The weapon was halfway to the ground when the chopper suddenly appeared above the mansion.

For a split second James's men gave in to the temptation to look up. It wasn't much. But it was enough.

Bolan dropped to one knee, snapping the barrel of the aged subgun back up as he fell. Firing from the hip, his first rounds caught the man with the goatee in the lower abdomen. A shrill shriek of agony exited his lips.

A second later two pistol rounds sounded next to Bolan, and he saw the top of the man's head fly away. He turned in time to see Aziza's CZ75 falling back from the recoil of the second shot.

Bolan reached out, shoving the beautiful black woman behind the iron planter to their right. As the other men opened up with return fire, he dived behind the other iron planter. Bullets struck the iron in front of him, singing off across the pool area and ringing in his ears. Shredded pieces of palm leaves rained down over his head from high rounds. Behind him the sliding door shattered, and tiny pieces of glass blew through the air like hail.

Bolan dropped low behind the iron planter, moving on all fours to the edge. He heard the sound of the helicopter blades approaching again and waited until the sounds of fire on the other side of the planter were directed overhead. Then, leaning around the edge of cover, he sent a quick burst into a guard aiming an AK-47 at the Astar.

Bolan glimpsed the chopper, a hundred feet over the pool, then the return fire from James's men sent him diving back behind the iron.

He rose slightly until his eyes cleared the rear of the planter. The chopper flew directly overhead now, bobbing and weaving in the air like a well-trained boxer.

Bolan saw that Benjamin Barkari was hanging out of the chopper's open door. The Swahili held the top of the door with one hand and fired a pistol down into the melee with the other.

Bolan took a deep breath. Barkari had seen him use that technique earlier along the river. It was far more complex than it looked, and Bolan silently prayed that Friday had practiced it before, not just picked it up from watching.

As the gunfire on the ground continued, Bolan dropped low again and moved to the edge of the planter. He shifted the OVP to a left-handed grip, angling the barrel in front of him.

Seeing a guard in blue jeans and a tattered red shirt, he squeezed the trigger and let the Italian subgun stitch new button holes in the shirt.

Bolan ducked behind cover again as James's men picked up on his new location and fired. Moving to the center of the planter, he raised his head. He could see the chopper, darting down, jerking up, darting and jerking again and again.

With each new dive, Benjamin Barkari cut loose with a round or two, his intense face visible in the lights of the compound.

The gunfire on the other side of the planter still raged as Bolan moved on all fours back to where he could see Aziza. She was crouched behind the planter on the other side of the walk, the CZ75 gripped in both hands.

A still-bleeding corpse lay on the sidewalk just to her side. Aziza saw Bolan, glanced down at the dead man and nodded. She looked ready for more in case any of the other men were foolish enough to try to round the iron planter.

Bolan leaned around the edge, firing again, this time dropping a gunman in khakis and another wearing flowing native robes. The OVP's 25-round magazine ran dry and he ducked, dropping it to the ground and snatching the CZ75 from his waistband.

He took another deep breath. The intensity of fire from the other side of the planter had lessened considerably. Unless he missed his guess, the work he had done, combined with Elliot and Barkari's air attack, had downed at least half of the men who had been in the courtyard.

Bolan moved back to the center of the planter. So far, he had gone right and left to take men out. Each time he did, he increased the enemy's awareness, and sooner or later a bullet would be waiting.

He looked at the top of the planter—maybe four feet off the ground. His jaw set firmly.

It was time to go over the top.

Suddenly Bolan dived up over the iron. Falling a good two feet below the rim, he landed in the dry dirt next to the trunk of the palm tree. He rose slightly, peering over the front edge of the barrier now.

Some of the remaining men were firing at the helicopter. The others had their eyes glued to the sides of the planter. None of them seemed to have seen him vault the side.

Bolan dropped back, reorganizing his plan of attack. His first few shots from inside the planter would give away his new position, so he had to make the most of them.

Rising again, he scouted the area. Two men were huddled together ten yards to his left, their heads visible through the open areas of a sculpture that portrayed a hunter about to spear a leaping lion. Moving clockwise around the pool, he saw another man beside what appeared to be a housing for the pool pump.

Two more leaned out from the stone sides of twin warriors with bows, and another crouched behind a large statue of an elephant.

Bolan inched the barrel of the CZ-75 over the side of the planter. As some of the men waited behind cover and others fired at the helicopter still dancing through the sky, he took the pistol through a dry run.

Bolan dropped the sights on one of the two heads visible behind the stone hunter and lion. Mentally pulling the trigger and riding the recoil, he brought the weapon back down on the head of the second man. He moved on through his practice drill, moving to the man behind the pump house, then swinging the pistol on to the warriors with bows.

As he twisted the pistol toward the elephant, he heard a crack from the sky and saw the man collapse over the tusks of the stone beast.

He quickly returned the sights to the men behind the hunter-and-lion sculpture. His first live round drilled between the hunter's stone legs and into the lower jaw of the man behind them. The second shot passed an inch in front of the lion's bared teeth and entered the brain of the other man.

Less than a second had passed when the CZ75's sights fell on the man behind the swimming-pool pump house. Another quick squeeze of the trigger sent him tumbling from cover.

By now the only remaining enemy in the pool area had pinpointed Bolan. The man turned away from the helicopter and fired a burst of 7.62 mm autofire from one of the ever-present AK-47s, forcing Bolan to drop below the edge of the planter.

Landing with his back against the trunk of the palm tree, Bolan saw the final gunman return his attention to the helicopter. The chopper had come in low and several rounds struck the Astar's door, one of them sending sparks through the night as it glanced off the steel next to Benjamin Barkari's hand.

The Swahili lost his grip. Suddenly he was falling through the sky beneath the Astar. But ever the warrior, Benjamin Barkari continued firing as he fell, and Bolan heard a scream of death from the man still behind the statue.

The big Swahili warrior plummeted out of sight beneath the rim of the planter.

Bolan rose to his knees. Looking over the side of the planter, he saw the horror on Aziza Mnarani's face.

She had seen her lover's fall, as well.

Aziza sprinted from behind her planter as Bolan vaulted the side of his. "Ben!" she screamed into the night. "Ben ... Benjamin!"

Bolan hurried after the running woman, his eyes scanning the courtyard for Friday's body. More men would be coming from other parts of the compound. The sooner they boarded the helicopter, the better. Benjamin Barkari had fallen a good fifty feet, and Bolan doubted that he or Aziza could do anything for him now.

Bolan caught Aziza by the arm halfway between the planters and the swimming pool. She tried to twist away but when she couldn't break his grip, she looked up at the sky, her mouth opening wide in agony.

"Ben!" Aziza Mnarani screamed again.

The helicopter blades beat loudly as the Astar 1450 TT dropped through the air settled next to the pool. Bolan tried to guide the grief-stricken woman toward the chopper, but this time she broke free from his grip and ran back toward the pool, again screaming, "Ben! Ben, I love you!"

There was a sudden sound of movement in the water, and Bolan tightened his grip on the CZ. Then a dazed Benjamin Barkari pulled himself up out of the deep end and fell to his back on the concrete. He looked up at Aziza.

"I love you, too," he said, spitting water while more ran from his nose. "But let's talk about it another time, okay?"

THE NIGHT AIR blowing through the open windows of the Astar was cooler than usual as Bolan, Aziza, Elliot and the Barkari brothers made their way across the Ogaden Desert. Upon leaving the compound, they had cut east to Gelib to refuel, then started north for their next stop—Djibouti.

Bolan took a final look at the desert racing by a few feet beneath the chopper's skids, then opened the hard vinyl case Grimaldi had dropped from the sky a few hours earlier. Elliot was still piloting the Astar and had kept them well below Ethiopian radar since they'd clandestinely crossed the border.

Bolan didn't expect any problems from the Ethiopian authorities. But if they came, the Astar was still close enough to Somalia to slip back into the country.

Bolan reached overhead, flipping on the map light. Inside the case he found a smaller plastic box labeled Glock. It was a high-tech, mostly polymer pistol that, in the few short years of its existence, had already found favor with police and military units the world over.

Bolan opened the lid. Inside he found a Glock Model 21 .45-caliber pistol and several spare magazines. He lifted the weapon out of the box.

The first thing to catch his eye was the small, nipplelike protrusion on the front of the trigger guard. Aiming at the floorboard, he pressed the button on the Glock's wide backstrap, and a bright red laser dot appeared between his feet. The circuit wiring of the Aro Tech LAW-2000 laser sight ran through the trigger guard to the power source behind the magazine well. No external cables existed that could catch on clothing or other objects and disengage the system.

Bolan nodded his approval in the dim light. Cowboy Kissinger had outdone himself this time.

Bolan let up on the button, and the red laser spot disappeared. Removing the empty plastic 13-round magazine, he dropped it back into the box with the spares. The chamber proved to be empty, and he pulled the trigger, moving the striker into the forward position.

Bolan pulled the slide slightly back, then used his other hand to pull down the serrated tabs of the takedown latch. The slide moved forward off the frame. The barrel and recoil spring guide came out easily, and he spread the parts across his lap for examination.

This modified Glock 21 was metal-detector-proof, as he'd requested. Many Glock pistols were already plastic, and Cowboy had replaced the parts that weren't with ceramic. The Glock had no safety with which to fumble, and fired from a more or less halfcocked position with each stroke of the trigger.

Bolan reassembled the weapon and opened the plastic ammo container. Inside he found four hundred rounds of hollowpoint ammunition that again employed ceramics instead of lead or steel. Bolan loaded thirteen of the space-age .45s into the plastic magazine, shoved it into the gun and chambered a round. Removing the magazine once more, he topped it off, then filled the spares.

Setting the Glock 21 and extra magazine back in the case, Bolan turned to the small cardboard box next to it. Lifting the lid, he found a new black dress belt in his size, a holster that looked as unorthodox as the pistol it was designed to carry and extra magazine carriers. He glanced at the tension screws in the leather. Again Cowboy had replaced the steel, this time using nylon.

Bolan leaned forward as the Astar continued to skim over the desert. He removed the belt he was wearing and threaded the thick piece of leather from the box through the first two belt loops on his left side. After adding three magazine carriers, he worked the belt on through the loops to his strong-side hip. The holster slid on next, before he buckled the ends together.

Bolan reached back in the box, pulling out a small screwdriver. With most holsters—even from top-of-the-line manufacturers—he'd be done as soon as he dropped the weapon into the hole. But with the Hellweg speed rig, that was just the beginning.

He twisted and began tightening the holster screws above and below the belt. When he'd gotten it semitight, he let his hand fall as if to draw, then shifted the rig slightly and tightened it the rest of the way. He completed the same lengthy process of trial and error with the magazine caddies, before finally inserting the Glock and extra rounds into their proper places.

Bolan leaned forward suddenly, his hand falling on the grip of the Glock. Even in the cramped space of the helicopter, the draw was smooth and perhaps two-tenths of a second faster than what he could do with a different rig.

The speed rig was far more trouble than most holsters. But it was also much faster and was more secure, as well. It served as a metaphor for most things in life: you could have convenience or you could have competence.

But you rarely found both in the same package.

No, Cowboy had worked hard to get the Glock, the ammunition and the speed rig to the point where they would slip undetected through a metal detector and still function. And Bolan would put in extra work every time he took the rig off and had to put it on again. But when all the work was done, Bolan reminded himself, he would still have not taken more than two-tenths of a second off his draw.

Bolan thought of Jabbar and Ham and the situations twoard which he, Elliot, Aziza and the Barkari brothers were racing.

Two-tenths of a second just might mean the difference between life and death.

HASSAN GOULED APTIDON, the leader of People's Progress Assembly, had become president of Djibouti when the French granted the country's independence in 1977. He had remained in charge of the tiny North African nation ever since. But since the

Gulf War, Djibouti's real power had been in the hands of General Jabbar, the warlord.

The war had placed Gouled between a rock and a hard place. Shortly before the invasion of Kuwait by Iraq, he had signed a military pact with Baghdad and received coastal patrol boats and various other armament. But Djibouti had also had a long-standing pact with France, and was currently accepting an annual grant of nearly two million dollars from the U.S.

So Gouled did what most politicians do when they find themselves in a conflict. He talked out of both sides of his mouth just as fast as his lips would move and hoped everyone heard what they wanted to hear and nothing more. He immediately went on record opposing the buildup of French, Italian and American military forces in the gulf. At the same time he invited their warships to use the Djibouti naval base and suggested his nation as temporary quarters for the troops preparing for war.

The people of Djibouti saw the contradiction, and he began to lose support. Ahmed Jabbar, then a wealthy businessman, saw his opportunity and took it. Massive amounts of money were spent in an even more massive image campaign. The right palms were greased to avoid any thought of impeachment.

Gouled retained the presidency, at least officially. But by the time Kuwait was back in the hands of the Kuwaitis, General Ahmed Jabbar held the power within Djibouti and ruled from his estate on the coastal plain.

As he sat quietly in his second-class seat on the bumpy train from Dire Dawa, Ethiopia, Mack Bolan knew this. He had read all about it in the Stony Man

Farm intelligence file during his flight over almost a
week earlier. And now, as the train slowed as it neared
the city of Djibouti, he vowed that the reign of Ahmed
Jabbar, the warlord masquerading as a businessman,
would come to an end by nightfall.

Next to him he heard Khalid Barkari snoring softly
as they entered the city. He looked at the seat across
from him. Elliot sat next to the greasy window, his
eyes fixed to the glass. To his side, Aziza had fallen
asleep with her head on Friday's shoulder. The blond
wig covered her head again, and she had reapplied her
makeup.

Benjamin Barkari sat next to the aisle, his arm
wrapped tightly around Aziza's shoulders as if he were
afraid he might lose her again.

As dawn had broken over northern Africa, Elliot
had landed the Astar near the point where the Somalian, Ethiopian and Djibouti borders met. They had
reluctantly abandoned the helicopter and made it to
the nearest frontier train stop just as the express pulled
in. Each of them carried a passport—none but Aziza's
in their real names—and the customs officers at the
border had given them no trouble.

Bolan sat back against the wooden seat and rubbed
his face. Two down, two to go. Morris and James had
fallen. Jabbar would be next.

Then the man known as General Fajir Ham.

The train slowed further as it crossed the intersection of the Boulevard de la République and Avenue
M. Lyautey. Bolan turned his attention to the window. The sight he saw outside reflected both Djibouti's African heritage and the Western and Mideastern
influence of the past and present. On the streets and

sidewalks he saw people dressed in African, Arabian, European and American styles—as well as every possible combination in between.

Bolan knew the majority of Djibouti's half-million residents were either Issa or Afar tribesmen. But there were also transplanted Yemenis and French left over from the occupation. In addition, close to a hundred and fifty thousand refugees from the civil wars in Somalia and Ethiopia had fled to Djibouti over the past few years.

Like America herself, Djibouti had become a melting pot of unsatisfied humanity.

The train rolled into the station, and Bolan got up, pulling his pack out from under the seat.

"I'd recommend we split up," Elliot said in a low voice. "You and me, Pollock. Khalid, Friday and Aziza. Ham and Jabbar will be looking for white Americans traveling with blacks."

Bolan nodded. "Everyone know where to meet?"

Aziza and the Barkari brothers' heads nodded.

Friday lifted both his and Aziza's bags. "Bigot," he whispered over his shoulder to Elliot, then ushered Aziza and his brother down the aisle.

Bolan smiled wryly. Benjamin Barkari might not be back to a hundred percent awareness or fighting ability quite yet, but he was on his way. The return of banter between him and Elliot was a good sign.

Bolan led Elliot out of the station and across the street to Rue Pasteur. They flagged a cab, threw their bags in the front seat next to the driver and slid into the back.

"African quarter," Elliot said.

As the cab made a U-turn, Bolan saw Aziza and the Barkari brothers getting into another cab. He glanced up to make sure the driver wasn't looking into the rearview mirror, then let his hand drift to his side. The speed rig was doing its job well. It hadn't budged a millimeter since he'd tightened down the nylon tension screws, and the Glock would be ready for a quick presentation—from the same place each time—whenever he needed it. He adjusted the navy blue blazer over the gun, then returned his hand to his lap. He had taken the jacket, a fresh shirt and new khakis from his pack during the flight. The bush jacket and pants he'd worn during the battle along the Juba River were now soiled to the point where they attracted too much attention.

The cab drove quickly past the cafés and souvenir shops along Place Muhamoud, then entered the African quarter. Elliot directed the driver to a corner building.

The man pulled in next to the curb, turned in his seat and opened his mouth in a wide, brown-toothed leer. He said something in Cushitic.

Elliot chuckled, paid him and they got out.

The former CIA man turned to Bolan. "He told us to have fun," he said.

Needing a base of operations in Djibouti, they had chosen one of the hotels Khalid Barkari knew in the African Quarter. Anything and everything went on in this part of town, and the sight of two American men entering one of the hotels—which invariably doubled as brothels—would attract no attention.

Bolan led the way up the steps and into the dingy lobby. Elliot waited behind him as he registered, paid the shriveled old woman behind the desk, then turned to look at the former CIA man when she asked a question in her native tongue.

Elliot chuckled again. "She wants to know what kind of woman you want," he said.

"Tell her I don't want a woman," Bolan instructed politely.

Elliot and Bolan headed for the rickety elevator in the corner of the lobby. When the door opened, the two entered in silence.

After their long trip, it would feel good to freshen up and relax, but only for a short while. After all, Bolan had other things on his mind. He had to fabricate a plan, then execute it.

The Executioner still had two warlords to kill.

CHAPTER FOURTEEN

Benjamin Barkari watched the old woman behind the hotel desk as she answered his question. Her face was hard and unfeeling, like the man who had given them a quick glance on the sidewalk.

"Room 212," she said.

Barkari started for the elevator when a bony hand reached out and caught his sleeve. "Three more people," the woman said coldly. "Five hundred more francs."

Barkari reached into his pocket and dropped several bills on the counter. He didn't know what the current rate of exchange was, but that would more than cover it.

The woman scooped up the money, and it disappeared beneath the counter. She turned away, her face still devoid of all emotion. Like the man they had seen leaving the hotel, and the other people who had passed Friday, Aziza and Khalid on the street after they'd left the cab, the old woman didn't care that they were on their way upstairs to join two white men and perform God-knew-what perversions on a whore in a blond wig.

Lust, depravity and degradation—they were simply part of life in this section of Djibouti. It reminded Barkari too much of Aziza's former situation.

The elevator arrived, and Khalid led the way on board. Friday squeezed Aziza's arm, and she squeezed back. He stared silently at the paint-chipped wall as the car rose, banging and clanking and threatening to break with each new turn of the cable crank.

The fury that had filled him when he first learned of Aziza's rape had become manageable. He was thinking straight again, not letting the pain influence his judgment—at least not all of the time.

The elevator stopped, and Friday ushered Aziza off the car and down the hall toward room 212. Khalid knocked softly on the door and Elliot answered.

When they entered the dingy room, the man they knew as Pollock was sitting on the bed reassembling one of the M-16s they had broken down to hide in their luggage.

Elliot pulled three chairs from under a splintered wood table against the wall, and Friday, Khalid and Aziza took seats. Bolan finished assembling the rifle as Elliot dropped down on the opposite side of the bed.

Bolan set the M-16 down and looked up. "Okay," he said. "The plan here is going to be similar to the one we used with James. Not because it's all that great, but because it's all we've got." He looked at Aziza. "I want you to call Jabbar. Tell him you've run away from Ham for whatever reason you think he'll buy, and that you need protection."

Aziza nodded. "He knows Ham and he will believe me," she said. "The problem lies in the fact that he and Ham are allies. He will not want Ham to know I am here."

Bolan frowned, rubbed his chin, then stopped. "Then the best bet is to beat him to the punch. Tell him you know that. But you had no place else to turn. Appeal to his manhood and tell him all you're interested in is a safe place to hide until you can get out of the country. Think he'd go for that?"

Barkari turned to watch the wheels turning in Aziza's head as she considered the possibility. "I think so," she finally said. "All he will be interested in is having sex with me again, he will know I will give him that in appreciation for protection. I will suggest that he might want to keep me in an apartment some place out of the country, but nearby. Yemen or Oman." She paused. "What do you think?"

"I don't know the man. You do," Bolan said.

Friday's chest tightened again.

"It will work," she insisted. "As I said, he doesn't love me like Ham and Morris did. But he does love sex. That is all he will want."

Barkari's heart felt as if it might explode in his chest. "Will you give it to him?"

Bolan, Aziza, Elliot and Khalid turned. An uneasy silence fell over the room.

Aziza looked at the floor. "I will do what is necessary to ensure his death," she said softly. "Nothing more, nothing less."

Benjamin Barkari listened as silence fell over the room again. He would have preferred a knife to slice his flesh than to have the woman he loved sleep with any other man again.

Bolan took charge suddenly. "It won't be necessary if we don't give him the opportunity, Friday," he said. "We'll get in, get the job done and get out, just like we did with James."

"But what if you do not?" Friday argued. "And even if it works with Jabbar, then what of Ham?" He turned to face Aziza full on. "Will you sleep with them? Will you?"

"Friday, old friend..." Elliot said tentatively.

Benjamin Barkari looked at him.

Elliot's smile was hard. "Just shut up, okay?"

For the first time in his life Benjamin Barkari wanted to kill the man whose life he had saved and who had saved his. But as he continued to stare, Elliot's words sank in and began to bring him back to reality. He closed his lips tight against his teeth.

Bolan quickly changed the subject. "Jabbar won't tell Ham you're there," he said, looking at Aziza. "But once the hit goes down, his men might. They'll need jobs, and Ham will be the only show left in town. So we've got to take out the phones and any other comm setup we find." He paused. "That also means none of Jabbar's men leave the house alive."

Aziza, Khalid and Elliot all nodded their understanding. Benjamin Barkari felt himself nodding, too.

Bolan turned to Elliot. "Does Jabbar know you and Friday by sight?"

Elliot shrugged. "Impossible to say. We aren't exactly movies stars around here, but the fish cannery did well. He might recognize us and he might not."

Bolan let out a deep breath. "We can't afford to take the chance, then." He turned back to Aziza. "Okay, you and I go in alone again. Same song, second verse. I'm a merc you hired to help you get away."

He stood up, turning to Elliot, Friday and Khalid. "You three stay outside. Work in as close as you can without getting spotted, and be ready to move in with the big guns as soon as you hear shots."

Benjamin Barkari clenched his fingers into tight fists, remembering the agony he'd experienced during the period when Pollock and Aziza had been in James's compound. He would have to go through it again here in Djibouti. And then again with Ham.

If the woman he loved wasn't killed right here by General Jabbar first.

Bolan moved to the ancient black rotary phone on the table and lifted the receiver. Without speaking, he held it out to Aziza.

Benjamin Barkari watched the woman he loved stare at the floor as she dialed the number. A dark, cloudy numbness moved over him as he listened to her speak softly into the receiver, identifying herself and then asking to speak to Jabbar.

Aziza looked up, pressed the phone to her breast and turned to the men in the room. "Jabbar is there. They are transferring me."

A moment later she began speaking again, gradually letting her voice become more emotional until she was crying by the time she hung up.

Aziza Mnarani wiped the false tears from her eyes and turned to face Bolan. But her eyes were on Benjamin Barkari when she finally spoke. "He has agreed to meet with me," she said. "He is expecting both me and my hired bodyguard at his new summer house on the coast in one hour."

WITH FIVE PEOPLE INSIDE, the taxi seemed crowded
compared to a big all-terrain vehicle.

It would have been even more crowded, Bolan
knew, if the driver had come along. But the man who
had been sitting behind the wheel of the cab parked on
Avenue de Large wasn't going *anywhere*. At least not
until he worked his way out of the ropes Bolan had
knotted around his wrists and ankles and crawled out
from under the bed of the hotel room they had just
abandoned.

As the cab left Djibouti proper and started north
along the glistening white sands next to the coastal
road, Bolan sat back in his seat directly behind Benjamin Barkari. Friday was driving, wearing the cap he
had taken from the driver. From where he sat, Bolan
couldn't see the Swahili's face in the rearview mirror.
But he wished he could.

Benjamin Barkari was getting a handle on things,
although it was taking time. He still drifted into
periods of anger, and his emotional state needed constant monitoring. Elliot was doing a good job of
keeping his friend on the right track, though.

The cab rounded a curve in the road, and a new gray
Victorian-style house appeared in the hills ahead. The
house faced the sea and was encircled with a thirty-
foot iron fence topped with concertina wire.

"Pull over," Bolan ordered Barkari.

The Swahili pulled to the side of the road next to a
small grove of palm trees.

"This is no time to start taking chances," Bolan
stated. "Elliot, you and Friday wait here. Khalid, grab
the hat and the wheel and take us on in, then come

back for them. Like we said before, work your way in as close as you can but don't get caught."

Elliot and Barkari got out as Khalid slid into the driver's seat. The two men moved out of sight behind the trees as the cab took off again.

"You ready?" Bolan asked Aziza.

She placed a hand on his arm and nodded.

A winding path led off the main road into the hills past large boulders, banks and outcropping of rock. The house would appear for a few seconds, then fade away again each time the cab fell behind a new barrier. Finally Khalid took them into a straightaway, and a gate appeared ahead. "Here we go," the younger of the Barkari brothers said with a deep breath.

The cab stopped at the gate, and four men with rifles appeared and circled the cab.

Khalid spoke to them in Cushitic, and then Aziza leaned out. Her words were angry and scolding. Whatever they meant, they had the desired effect.

The men stepped back, the gate parted and the cab drove on.

Bolan saw the signs of recent construction as they neared the two-story house. Stacks of plywood, wallboard and scraps of used material lay in heaps across the ground.

Jabbar had told Aziza the house was new, which meant he was proud of it. That in turn meant the first thing he would want to do was show it off to his potential bedmate.

And that gave Bolan an idea.

Khalid stopped outside the front door, and Bolan helped Aziza out of the cab. "Get out of here before somebody you grew up with sees you," Bolan whispered out of the corner of his mouth. "Go get Elliot and your brother and start making your way back on foot."

The two-story Victorian house had a large upstairs deck just above the front door. White cast-iron patio furniture reflected the sunlight. On the ground floor a redwood porch ran across the front of the house, separating it from the detached garage. A large courtyard lay in between. Grass had recently been planted just beyond the white picket fence that enclosed the yard, and bushes and several young trees sprouted from the flower beds.

Bolan glanced over his shoulder and saw a breathtaking view of the ocean.

A dozen or so men worked around the grounds, planting shrubs and trees, loading scraps onto a flatbed dump truck and painting the trim around the windows and doors. All wore work clothes. But a pistol hung from each hip.

Bolan opened the gate in the white picket fence, and Aziza stepped through. He scanned the area casually as he followed. He saw what he was looking for just to the side of the house.

A metal telephone housing box stood ten feet from the exterior wall, which meant the underground cable lay on that side of the house.

Bolan and Aziza had made it to the edge of the deck when the front door opened and a muscular black man stepped into the doorway. He wore leaf-pattern cammies and brown jungle boots, and a stainless-steel Smith & Wesson .357 Magnum hung low from a gun belt on his right hip. A sheath knife with a bright pearl handle balanced the revolver on his left, and the bright yellow patches on both shoulders and the front of his black beret bore the words Jabbar Security.

Bolan nodded to himself as he and Aziza stopped in the middle of the porch. With no official government currently operating in Somalia, the warlords operated freely. But here in Djibouti things were different, and Jabbar was keeping up his respectable-businessman image by costuming his hired killers as security guards.

"Please," the sergeant said in heavily accented English, "the general awaits you." He stepped back from the doorway to allow them to pass, revealing four more similarly dressed men standing in the hallway. These men not only wore pistols but had AK-47s slung over their shoulders.

Aziza entered first. Bolan followed, feeling the temperature drop a good thirty degrees as the air-conditioning hit him in the face.

"Follow me," the stocky sergeant said. Turning on his heels, he led them down the hall, the other security men following.

The leader of the guards led the way briskly around a corner. Bolan turned to see what he'd been expecting—a metal detector.

It was time to find out just how well Cowboy Kissinger had done with the Glock and Hellweg rig.

The sergeant didn't break stride as he stalked through the security device, his weapons tripping the alarm and sending a loud buzzing sound along the passageway. He turned abruptly and held up a hand, stopping Bolan and Aziza in their tracks. Waiting a moment for the detector to reset itself, he waved Aziza on through.

The beautiful black woman passed through the metal detector quietly.

The sergeant held up his palm again, and Bolan waited. As soon as he got the wave, he stepped between the arches.

The buzzer hummed loudly.

Bolan didn't hesitate. Stepping back through the arches, he reached into his pocket as the barrels of four AK-47s and one S&W Model 66 pointed his way. "Keys," he said, smiling, slowly producing the key ring from the truck they'd driven earlier. He handed it to the man behind him and turned back to the metal detector.

Bolan had carried the keys on purpose, knowing full well that most men carried enough metal to trip a detector. The exception was when they *knew* ahead of time that they'd be going through such a device and wanted to avoid the small inconvenience.

Bolan had known, of course, that Jabbar employed the apparatus he had stolen from the airport. But he needed to create the illusion that he had no idea of any of the inner workings of the warlord's operation.

This time Bolan passed silently through the machine.

The sergeant stepped in front of him suddenly, forcing him to stop. Bolan knew immediately why.

All plans had flaws, and the fly in this ointment had been the possibility that the guards would insist on a manual search for nonmetallic objects. It was a chance he'd been forced to take; there had been no way around it.

"With my apologies, sir," the sergeant said. "I am afraid I must submit you to the small inconvenience of a brief body search."

Bolan shot him an annoyed look, which slowed the man for a second.

Aziza stepped between them. "What?" she said, her voice filled with irritation. "This man saves my life and delivers me to your general and you would submit him to such humiliation?" She looked up into the sergeant's eyes. "Where is General Jabbar?" she demanded. "I wish to speak with him *immediately.*"

"And so you shall," a voice suddenly said from the other end of the hall.

Bolan looked up to see a man wearing colorful robes walking toward them. Jabbar had a flatter nose than most of the Issas and Afars he had seen, and Bolan suspected he had ancestry among the other tribes of northern Africa.

Jabbar stepped up to Aziza, reached out and took both of her hands in his. "My dear," he said, smiling widely.

"My General," Aziza said, her voice low and purring like a kitten.

"What is the problem?" Jabbar said.

Aziza looked up at him innocently, her face pouting like a little girl's.

Aziza Mnarani was *good.* She could play men like fiddles, and he watched the strings inside Jabbar's heart launch into a concert as the warlord looked back down at her.

"This man, Mr. Pollock," Aziza said, glancing to Bolan, "saved my life. We have both gone successfully though your metal detector, and now your ser-

geant wishes to subject him to the embarrassment of
a body search.''

Jabbar turned without hesitation and slapped the
sergeant across the face. Then he extended the same
hand in friendship to Bolan. "I am grateful to you,"
he said. "And you shall be rewarded."

Bolan shook the hand. "No reward is necessary,
General," he said. "Miss Mnarani already paid me."

Jabbar smiled and turned back to the beautiful
woman in front of him. "As you have no doubt noticed, we have just completed my new country home.
Would you and your friend care for a tour?"

"I would love one, General," Aziza said. She
glanced over to Bolan.

Bolan nodded.

Jabbar took Aziza's arm, nodded to his security
men, then turned down the hall. Bolan fell in behind
the two and heard the footsteps of the guards following behind him.

Jabbar was no fool. He had aborted the body search
to impress Aziza, but he was well aware that General
Morris and Colonel James had both been assassi-
nated. His men would remain handy.

The warlord led the way through an eclectic living
room decorated in a combination of European and
American styles, with several African sculptures and
paintings added. They moved from there into a dining area.

Jabbar had been around a while and no longer felt
the need to shout out his success. The six ground-level
bedrooms reflected subtle taste rather than preten-
sion. The party moved quickly in and out of each
room, with the guards carefully circling the room each

time to make sure their master was ringed with protection. The warlord pointed out items here and there with the grace of the practiced host, but as the tour progressed, it became increasingly evident that he wanted it over.

Finally the general led the way to the stairs, talking softly and explaining the finer points of how he had chosen the color for the wallpaper and the fact that the indoor waterfall he had wanted for the parlor had proved impractical due to the high humidity. Jabbar was particularly proud of the natural-gas-powered air conditioner—a rare luxury in this Third World country.

Bolan took careful inventory of the house during the tour—from the point of view of a warrior rather than an aficionado of fine homes. No other guards— in fact, no one else at all—appeared to be in the house, at least downstairs. Almost every room had a telephone, so the fastest way to abort contact with the outside world was to cut the main line outside. He had seen no two-way radios or any other form of communication.

Halfway up the stairs, Bolan saw Aziza squeeze the warlord's arm. "You have told me nothing of Mrs. Jabbar, General," she said in a teasing voice. "Surely she helped you decorate much of this lovely home. Tell me, is she home?"

Jabbar chuckled softly. "Unfortunately, no," he replied. "She received a call and had to leave earlier in the day. The call, coincidentally, came right after yours."

Aziza's giggle would have melted plutonium.

When they reached the second floor, Jabbar led them outside onto the deck Bolan had seen from the ground. The breeze blew hot over their faces, and the warlord said, "It is more pleasant in the evening. During the day, far too warm. We will come back this evening."

"Yes," Aziza said. "It has gotten *warm*." She and Jabbar exchanged knowing glances as the warlord led the party back inside.

A study, game room complete with the newest video games from America and a library followed. The upstairs, like the floor below it, was as elaborate and tasteful as any of the world's finest palaces or government buildings. They toured three more bedrooms, then came to the most elegant of all—the master bedroom.

"So, this is where you and Mrs. Jabbar sleep," Aziza said quietly. "Where little warlords are created."

Jabbar laughed, then turned to face her. He seemed for the moment to have lost sight of the fact that his security guards and the man he knew as Pollock were in the room. Lust poured from his eyes as he looked down into Aziza's. "She will not be back for several days," he whispered.

From the angle at which he stood, Bolan could see Aziza look up at the warlord. Her brown eyes opened wide again as she affected the look of an innocent little girl. Softly she said, "General, I believe I have changed my mind."

Pure, unadulterated fear suddenly covered Jabbar's face. "What?" he whispered. "You do not—"

Aziza reached up and placed her fingers over his mouth. Slowly her lips curled up in a sexy smile. "About the body search," she said, her voice low and seductive. "But I think it is *I* who should have one. A *complete* search, General. Very...very...complete."

Bolan watched the warlord's face tighten. He was totally mesmerized by the beautiful woman now offering herself to him. He glanced behind him to see that the guards were nearly as overcome by the raw sexual energy Aziza Mnarani could dispense upon command.

Bolan hesitated only a second. He had five heavily armed men and one warlord to kill before any of them killed him. Right now they were preoccupied, but that would last for only a second.

He would get no better chance.

Turning, he took a half step back and let his hand sweep the tail of his blazer away from the Hellweg speed rig.

The Glock 21 came out fast and smooth as the men in the camouflage uniforms gaped at the woman before them. Bolan felt the LAW-2000's activator button hit the web between his thumb and trigger finger on the backstrap of the weapon.

The small red laser dot appeared first on the sergeant's knee as the .45 cleared leather. It skipped up his pants, then shirt, finally lighting on the center of his forehead.

Bolan squeezed the trigger, and the Glock exploded in his hand.

The man in the security uniform died thinking of Aziza Mnarani.

Bolan had swung the .45 to the next guard before the other the men in the room realized what had happened. He, too, died with happy fantasies of the beautiful black woman.

The third of the five guards had time to see what killed him. But what he thought about it, Bolan would never know.

The final two men in camouflage both stood to the left of where the first guard had fallen. Bolan raised the Glock slightly as he swept the bright red beam their way. The taller of the two men was ill trained and died stupidly trying to decide between the pistol on his side and the AK-47 slung over his back. He had a hand on both weapons when the next all-ceramic .45-caliber hollowpoint split through his nose and threw him back against the wall.

The last guard standing had no such problem with decisions. He had drawn a bright blue revolver by the time the dancing red dot fell on his chest. He even had it halfway sighted when Bolan pulled the Glock's trigger and sent another round blazing into his heart.

Bolan turned to Jabbar.

The warlord stood frozen, his lower lip halfway to the floor.

The Executioner dropped the laser sight spot to halfway between the man's eyes.

"Wait!" Aziza screamed.

The Glock's trigger stopped at the end of the trigger creep.

Aziza squatted quickly next to the nearest man on the floor and jerked the .357 from his holster. Rising again, she turned to Jabbar and shoved it under his nose.

The warlord's eyes opened wide with terror. "You..." he sputtered. "You?"

"Yes, me," Aziza said as she pulled the trigger.

The stench of cordite filled the room as the noise from the rounds died down. But Bolan didn't kid himself. The shots he'd just fired, and particularly the .357 Magnum Aziza had just used to blow the better part of General Jabbar's head from his shoulders, weren't quiet.

The men dressed as workers outside would have heard the gunfire. And if they weren't already inside the house, they were on their way.

Bolan tapped the magazine release and jerked the partially spent box from the Glock with his free hand, dropping it into his coat pocket before replacing it with one from the magazine carriers on his side. "Let's go," he said. He grabbed Aziza's arm and headed out the door.

They were halfway down the stairs when they heard the front door slam open against the wall.

Bolan grabbed Aziza's arm again as they hurried down the rest of the steps. They had reached the landing when a workman turned the corner of the hallway, gripping a Model 66 in both hands.

Bolan didn't wait for him to take aim. Letting the red dot dance up the man's sweat-stained work shirt, Bolan squeezed the trigger and sent two .45s rocketing into the chest. As the workman fell to the floor, two more charged around the corner.

The first man was dressed in khakis and held a Browning Hi-Power in his fist. But he tripped over the gunman Bolan had just downed and tumbled to the floor.

Bolan let him roll as the second man saw what was happening in time to leap over the body on the floor. He was in midflight when two ceramic hollowpoints blew through his shoulder and throat.

The rolling gunner now came to a halt on his face at Bolan's feet. As he struggled to his knees, Bolan drew the red dot back down and gave him a lone .45 in the teeth.

A boom sounded behind Bolan, and he turned to see another workman clutching his chest in surprise.

Aziza faced the man, gripping the .357 in her hands.

Bolan motioned for her to follow him and made his way cautiously over the bodies in the hallway. He stayed back from the corner, moving slowly out an inch at a time. Two inches out he saw a flicker of movement just around the corner. Aiming about a foot into the wall, he tapped the Glock's trigger twice. The rounds drilled through the thin wallboard, and a scream sounded from the other hall.

A man wearing faded jeans and a paint-spotted shirt tumbled into the intersection of the two halls.

Bolan moved out into the hall, seeing a clear path to the front door. He reached behind him, taking Aziza's hand and sprinting that way. What he had to do now was cut the phone lines before anyone awakened to the fact that their warlord was dead and decided to alert Ham.

Bolan halted at the end of the hall. Slowly he opened the door.

Two men, one of them reaching for the doorknob, were about to enter the house. They both fell in a flurry of blood and screams as the red dot of the LAW-2000 danced back and forth between them.

Bolan scanned the length of the redwood porch, left and right. Clear. Pulling Aziza outside, he turned toward where he'd seen the phone box earlier.

A sudden burst of automatic rounds splintered the wood next to his face, and he dived to the redwood deck, drawing Aziza down on top of him. Rolling out from under the woman, he came up in the prone position, the Glock aimed in the direction from which the shots had come.

Six men sprinted toward the porch. Four had drawn pistols from their work clothes. The other two carried AK-47s that they had located somewhere around the grounds.

Bolan pointed the Glock at the nearest man with an AK. The laser was useless now that they were in direct sunlight, and he waited for the white paint on the front iron sight to fall behind the two dots at the rear. A double dose of Kissinger's special hollowpoints dropped the man to the ground.

Bolan swung the .45 toward the other rifleman. But before he could fire, another Magnum boomed in his ear, and the other AK-47 bearer fell with a .357-caliber hole in the side of his head. Bolan glanced to his side to see a tiny wisp of smoke rise from the revolver in Aziza's hands. Then he turned back to a gunner wearing a sweat-drenched plaid shirt.

The man fell next to the two with the assault rifles.

Bolan fired again, hitting two more workmen who were desperately seeking cover. Another big revolver round exploded, and the last of the six men fell to Aziza's long-awaited vengeance.

Up and running again, Bolan and the black woman turned the corner of the house and leaped from the porch. Bolan sprinted toward the telephone box. Halting in his tracks, he lined the white dots up on the cable and pulled the trigger three times.

The main telephone line snapped in half.

More AK-47 and pistol rounds drove him behind the cable housing. Aziza hit the ground and rolled toward him. As he turned toward the attack, he heard the familiar noise of .223-caliber autofire coming from a distance.

Four more of Jabbar's gunners were firing toward the telephone box. But as he raised the Glock to return that fire, two of them fell.

Bolan saw Don Elliot and Benjamin and Khalid Barkari racing through the gate.

Before Bolan could join in the attack, a new threat boomed from the side. He turned to see three men diving behind the cover of building scraps as they fired. Grabbing Aziza, Bolan hauled her to her feet and took off again amid a hailstorm of bullets, rounding the front of the house again and cutting across the redwood porch.

Something ripped through the top of his blazer, and Bolan felt the burn as lead skimmed across his skin. He twisted as he ran, tapping the Glock's trigger twice and letting the ceramic rounds take out a gunner who had rounded the house from the other side. When he reached the picket fence, he turned, grasped Aziza by the waist and hoisted her over.

Newly planted grass and dirt blew over Bolan's ankles as a volley of autofire spattered into the ground next to his feet. He twisted at the waist, snapping off another .45 round that caught a man wearing a soiled white shirt squarely in the breast bone.

Bolan turned back, vaulted the short fence, then pushed Aziza toward the open garage. More rounds chased them through the door, and he shoved the woman to the floor, then moved to the side of the opening and dropped to one knee.

A man wearing a red bandanna as a sweatband ran foolishly toward the garage, spraying the opening with 7.62 mm lead. Bolan took his time, sending a single round into the man's face.

The .45 struck just under the chin and exited through the back of his head. The energy of the round blew the bandanna off the gunner's head as the Russian assault rifle fell from his hands and clattered across the driveway.

Bolan ducked back as more bullets assaulted the wide garage door. He heard more .223-caliber fire from the other side of the house. No new targets presented themselves through the doorway, and with Aziza now safe, he rose to his feet and turned toward her.

His eyes skimmed the room. The garage had been used as a storage area during the building of the house. Unused two-by-fours, patio blocks and cans of tar, paint and other liquids were stacked along the wall. "Stay here until one of us comes back for you," he said as he reloaded the Glock once more. "How many rounds you have left?"

"Four," Aziza said.

"Use them wisely," Bolan said, and darted back out into the fight.

Bolan sprinted once more to the redwood deck. He dropped to a roll at the corner, letting the burst of fire he suspected would greet him sail over his head before rising to a knee and ending it with a quick 3-round burst.

Two more autobursts sounded as he rose to his feet and headed for the back of the house.

But by the time he reached it, the war was over, at least for now. Bodies littered the backyard, and Elliot, Khalid and Benjamin Barkari walked toward Bolan from three different angles.

"We've run out of targets," Elliot said, grinning.

Bolan nodded. "Good. Go find us something to drive."

Elliot was still grinning when he jogged off.

Bolan turned to Benjamin Barkari. "Aziza's waiting for you in the garage."

Fear covered the Swahili's face.

"She's fine," Bolan said. "Go get her."

Benjamin Barkari took off to the side of the house.

"Khalid," Bolan said. "I'm going back in to make sure we didn't overlook anybody and make double sure the phones are dead. There are cans of paint and other supplies in the garage. See if you can find some paint thinner and bring it inside."

Bolan turned and hurried back into the house. With the red dot of the laser sight leading the way, he checked every room, closet and nook and cranny of the house General Jabbar had just built, trying all the phones along the way.

They were as dead as the gunmen littering the floors.

Bolan finished upstairs, knelt next to the security guards he had shot first and tore the camouflage blouses from their backs. He hurried back down the steps to the utility closet in the hall where Jabbar had shown them the air-conditioning unit.

Khalid arrived with a can of paint thinner in each hand as Bolan opened the door.

As he tore the shirts into strips, Bolan pictured Ham in his mind. Word of this attack would reach Ham before they could; there was no doubt about it. Which meant they weren't likely to pull off a similar infiltration. Another plan was called for.

And as he soaked the strips of cloth with paint thinner, that plan began to formulate in his mind.

Stretching the wet rags out across the floor from the air conditioner, Bolan knelt next to the end and pulled a book of matches from his pocket. "Get ready to run," he told Khalid.

He struck the match, dropped it on the end of the makeshift fuse, stood up and raced toward the front door behind Khalid.

As they vaulted off the redwood deck, then leaped over the white picket fence, a white Lincoln Town Car pulled up near the gate. Elliot sat behind the wheel.

Khalid led the way, diving into the car as Benjamin Barkari opened the back door from inside. Bolan dived in on top of him and the Lincoln spun away.

"Where to, sir?" Elliot said, adopting the accent of a British chauffeur.

"Drop the lady and me off at the Djibouti airport," Bolan said. "You two are going on."

"Where?" Barkari asked as they crossed the gate and left the grounds.

Before Bolan could answer, an explosion rocked the car, threatening to throw it to the side of the road.

As Elliot regained control of the vehicle, Bolan looked over his shoulder and saw General Jabbar's new home go up in a fireball.

CHAPTER FIFTEEN

Ali Abu-Iyad had known all along he was dealing with a madman. He just hadn't realized the extent to which Fajir Ham's brain had deteriorated.

Leaning back on the woven plastic straps of the aluminum-framed recliner, Abu-Iyad cupped his hand over his eyes against the hot afternoon sun. Next to him a pitcher of lemonade and several paper cups rested on a small table that stood in the sand. The table also held a bottle of suntan lotion, a paperback novel and a towel.

More mockery. As Ham had said, the only thing missing was the sea.

Abu-Iyad lay back and closed his eyes, feeling utterly ridiculous. Ham had taken keen delight in setting up this humiliating little plateau parody above the underground compound. And the warlord's inherent viciousness had been compounded by the news that now General Jabbar, too, had been killed. The warlord's nerves had now stretched to the breaking point; there was no longer any doubt that whoever had killed James, Morris and Jabbar would now come after him.

Abu-Iyad shifted on the recliner, wondering how much longer the general would demand he play this ridiculous sunbathing game. The news of Jabbar's death had come shortly after they had returned to the compound, and Ham had grown even more paranoid than usual.

He had shoved the telephone in Abu-Iyad's hand and demanded he call for the weapons immediately. He insisted the Iraqi inform his "partners in crime" that they had been found out, and tell them they must send the rest of the weapons and ammunition immediately or Abu-Iyad would be killed. And Ham would not pick them up from the ship this time. The Iraqis must deliver them to his stronghold, here.

Abu-Iyad had done as he'd been told. Which had confused the hell out of his "partner in crime", Thabit Habash, the Iraqi colonel in charge of loading the guns for transport to Somalia.

Abu-Iyad raised himself up on his elbows and stared across the lifeless plateau. "You see, you stupid, paranoid warlord," he said out loud. "There was no crime. There did not need to be. The port you are giving us is one hundred times more valuable than the weapons you will be receiving."

The Iraqi flopped back on the recliner in disgust. "And did you really think I would choose to live the remainder of my short life dodging the assassins Saddam would send to track me to the moon if necessary?"

A loud screech of metal came from the large rock twenty feet from the recliner as it began to shift to the side. Abu-Iyad stood up. Perhaps Ham had finally tired of this childish game. If so, it was time Abu-Iyad put his anger and contempt on the back burner. At least for a little while longer.

A man wearing the familiar blue arm band that Abu-Iyad had grown to hate over the past few weeks stuck his head up out of the ground. "The general wishes to see you," he said, waving him forward.

Abu-Iyad stood up as two more men in blue arm bands hurried up out of the hole and retrieved the table, lemonade and other props of Ham's asinine melodrama. The Iraqi folded up the recliner himself and carried it to the stairs.

Clad only in the swimsuit the madman had provided, Abu-Iyad followed the soldiers through the metal detector just inside the compound, the buzzer chirping irritably as the aluminum furniture crossed between its beams. They walked the winding halls to Ham's office, where one of the soldiers opened the door and ushered Abu-Iyad inside.

General Fajir Ham held his war club in one hand and the phone in the other. He glared at the wall, looking as if he might explode any second.

And as Abu-Iyad watched, he did.

"Who has done this to you!" he suddenly screamed into the phone. "I will cut their testicles off slowly and stuff them into their mouths!" He pounded his war club on the floor, then his voice calmed. "Yes...I will send the helicopter...for both of you...tell him he will be rewarded." There was a pause. "Yes...I love you, too, my sweet."

Ham slammed the phone down, then looked up, for the first time aware of Abu-Iyad's presence. His face paled to an embarrassed gray. "Aziza was kidnapped!" he screamed.

Abu-Iyad frowned. "Are you certain?" he asked.

"Of course, you fool!" Ham screamed again. "She was in the clutches of General Morris's men for two days and I did not even know it!'' He looked down at his desk, shaking his head in disbelief.

"But General Morris is dead," Abu-Iyad said.

Ham looked back up, striking the floor with his club again. "Apparently he learned she was returning to her mother's house and gave the orders before his assassination. The men who took her hid her in Djibouti." He stopped suddenly, his mouth falling open. "Morris!" he screamed at the top of his lungs. "Morris sent his men there to hide her from me. He must also have been behind the attack that killed Jabbar!"

"General," Abu-Iyad said. "With all due respect, if it was Morris who killed Jabbar, then who killed Morris?"

Ham shook his head. "I don't know, I don't know...."

Abu-Iyad didn't respond. Morris couldn't have been behind Jabbar's death, but the Iraqi didn't plan to be the one to point that out. Ham was losing it, clearly coming apart at the seams.

Well, Abu-Iyad didn't care if that happened—as long as he wasn't around when it did. Ham would cut his own nose off to spite his face, and when the last drop of sanity and restraint finally dripped from his afflicted brain, other heads would roll with the warlord's. When that happened, Ali Abu-Iyad planned to be safely out of this backward Third World hell.

"Yes, I am certain you are right," Abu-Iyad said. "Is Aziza all right?"

Ham nodded. "Yes, thank Allah. She somehow attracted the attention of an American who helped her escape." He paused. "I do not know all the details. She will tell me when they arrive."

Abu-Iyad frowned inwardly, careful to keep the expression off his face. Chance help from a passing Good Samaritan American? Perhaps the details *would* make the story more plausible. As it stood now, it ranked right up there with the most farfetched tales the Iraqi had ever heard.

The inner frown turned to a secret grin. It sounded far more as if the gorgeous black woman needed a cover story for a few days' romp with some other man. Maybe even this American she claimed had rescued her.

Ham snatched the phone from his desk again and jabbed several buttons with his thick black fingers. "Ilaoa," he ordered. "Take the helicopter immediately and go to Djibouti. Miss Mnarani and an American will be at the airport." He slammed the phone down again.

Abu-Iyad continued to repress the smile that wanted to engulf his face. "I, too, thank Allah that Miss Mnarani was not hurt," he said. He leaned over the desk, lowered his voice and whispered, "Surely her captors would not have dared to force themselves on her in any way."

Ham looked up, horrified, the idea obviously not having occurred to him.

"No, I think not, General," Abu-Iyad said. "Morris would not have allowed such a thing." He paused, frowning, this time letting the expression show. "Of course, after the men learned of their leader's death and realized that there would be no retaliation for their actions...." His voice trailed off.

Ham's black face nearly turned white.

Abu-Iyad straightened up, pursed his lips and shook his head. "No, *probably* not even then." He smiled now. "If you please, General, I will go get dressed and prepare for the arrival of the rest of the weapons."

He turned to walk out of the room, pleased at having returned at least part of the humiliation he had suffered, when an idea struck him. An idea that if it proved to be true, would affect him before he was safely back in Baghdad.

Abu-Iyad turned back to Ham. "This man . . . this American, General . . . did she say what he looked like?"

"No," Ham said. "Why?"

"The American who supposedly teamed up with Elliot and Barkari. You do not suppose—"

Ham shot up from behind his desk. "What? That it is him? That he has somehow tricked Aziza and gained her confidence?"

"Well," Abu-Iyad said. "That, or. . . ."

Ham waved the war club in his hand, his face taking on the countenance of a wrathful demon. "Surely you do not suggest that she has betrayed me?"

Abu-Iyad began to backtrack as fast as he could. In Ham's current state of mind, a suggestion like that might well get him killed. "Of course not," he said quickly. "But perhaps this man bears checking into. In case he has tricked her."

The Iraqi turned and left the room quickly, anxious to get away from the madman who grew more deranged by the minute. Soon the weapons would arrive. When they did, he would leave. And after that the warlord could take his insanity out on the old men, women and children in Jijiga, and then the entire nation of Ethiopia for all Ali Abu-Iyad cared.

Ali Abu-Iyad wanted only one thing.

To have General Fajir Ham out of his hair for good.

FROM INSIDE the small restaurant of the Djibouti airport, Bolan watched as the big Hughes 500D descended.

"That's it," Aziza said, taking a deep breath.

Bolan nodded. "I'm ready."

He ushered the young woman out the door and toward the chopper as a man wearing one of the familiar blue arm bands ducked under the blades and approached them. He stopped when he saw Aziza and offered a few anxious words in her language. Aziza nodded.

The man switched to English as he turned to Bolan. "You are the gentleman who has saved Miss Mnarani?" he asked.

Bolan nodded.

"Come," the man ordered, pivoting back toward the Hughes. "The general wishes to reward you."

Bolan and Aziza followed him to the open door of the helicopter. As he climbed into the back seat, Bolan saw another man with an arm band seated against the window, his face turned the other way. Something—Bolan couldn't put his finger on what—was vaguely familiar about him.

Then, as he settled into the seat, the face turned toward Bolan and he saw the scab still healing on the man's chin.

Ilaoa. The man who had tied him up and tried to beat Elliot and Barkari's whereabouts out of him at the safehouse.

The little man's face twisted into a wicked smile as he shoved a Browning Hi-Power into Bolan's ribs. "This reminds me of an American movie I once saw," Ilaoa said as he patted Bolan down with his free hand, jerking the Glock from the Hellweg rig. "I am tempted," he said as he stuffed the gun into his waistband, "to say, 'So! We meet again, Mr. Pollock.'"

Bolan stared at the little man. "Say whatever you like," he said. "By the way, it looks like your face is healing."

The good humor faded from Ilaoa's face and was replaced with a scowl. "And yours, as well," he said. "But do not worry. I will open fresh wounds soon." He looked up into the front seat. "Take us up!" he ordered the pilot.

Aziza had twisted around from the front seat. "What are you doing, Ilaoa?" she demanded. "This man saved my life!"

Ilaoa shook his head. "If he did, it was only to win your confidence. He is in league with Elliot and Barkari. I suspect we now know who is behind the assassinations of the other warlords."

"Impossible," Aziza said, but her words had no effect on the little man. She glanced quickly to Bolan for instructions.

The game had changed. And it was time they changed with it.

Almost imperceptibly Bolan nodded, mentally willing the order and praying the woman would pick up on it. If Ilaoa had time to think, he might well realize that there was always the chance that Aziza, too, was in on the assassinations.

If he did, their last chance would be lost.

Aziza twisted suddenly in her seat. "You bastard!" she cried, slapping Bolan hard across the face. "You *used* me?"

Bolan didn't answer.

The helicopter rose into the air, banked sharply to the southeast and started toward the plateau as Ilaoa pulled a set of handcuffs out of his pocket.

FLANKED BY TWENTY MEN armed with what remained of the AK-47s, General Fajir Ham leaned on his war club and looked out over the plateau at the oncoming convoy of trucks. He turned to Ali Abu-Iyad next to him. "Amazing what can be done when one tries, eh, my friend?"

"General," Abu-Iyad said. "As I told you before, *I did not have plans to steal your weapons.* By coincidence they arrived at this time."

Ham turned away. He had grown tired of the man's ineffectual attempts at double-dealing, and he would have killed the Iraqi as soon as the shipment arrived if the alliance with Saddam Hussein was not so important. Who knew when he would need more help from his Arabic brother? Somalia, Ethiopia and Kenya were only the beginning. So sooner or later he was bound to run out of bullets again.

The first of the six trucks stopped within twenty yards of where Ham stood, the other trucks drawing to a halt behind it. A man wearing gray BDUs, a standard Soviet-design helmet and black boots with high gaiters dropped down from the passenger's side of the cab. A Makarov pistol dangled from his web belt as he walked forward. He nodded to Abu-Iyad, then turned to Ham and without preamble, said, "Where do you wish your weapons, General?"

Ham stepped past the false rock and tapped his Issa war club on the steps. "Open the armory entrance!" he shouted down the stairs.

A second later a huge section of earth began sliding to the side a hundred yards away.

"There will be room for two trucks at a time below," Ham said. "My men will help you unload."

The man in the gray BDUs nodded and returned to the truck, and the convoy started toward the huge opening.

Ham pointed to the steps by the rock, and Abu-Iyad preceded him down. Soon, they were in the general's office once more.

Ham leaned his cane against the wall and flopped into the chair behind his desk, conflicting emotions flowing through him. But for the first time in several days, he had begun to see the light at the end of the tunnel. Aziza would be here in a few more minutes— the pilot had already radioed in their position. She had told him she hadn't been harmed. Abu-Iyad had been toying with him. He knew that. And he knew the man would pay for that, as well.

The rest of the weapons and ammunition had finally arrived. And now that someone had killed James, Morris and Jabbar, he could take over their regions even easier than he had planned. In fact, that could be done at any time.

Ham lifted the phone. "Suberi!" he shouted.

A voice said, "Yes, General?"

"Prepare the men," Ham said. "Be ready to march on Jijiga as soon as the Iraqis leave." He hesitated, thinking of Aziza. "No, I will require a little time. Make it one hour after their departure."

"Yes, General," Suberi said.

Ham hung up. He felt the excitement mount in his soul, and felt also a stirring in his groin. Yes, first he would have Aziza. *His* way. Then the people of Jijiga would bring him as much pleasure as the woman who was about to become his. The warlord looked over to Abu-Iyad. He wanted the man out of the way. But as he reached for the phone again, it buzzed.

Ham lifted the receiver to his ear. "Yes?"

"The helicopter, General," he heard the voice say on the other end. "It is arriving."

DUSK WAS FALLING over the plateau as Bolan saw the trucks parked below. Aziza had explained the layout of Ham's underground compound, and as the Hughes dropped toward the plateau, he saw two of the trucks disappear down a wide ramp he knew led to the armory at the rear of the subterranean offices and sleeping quarters.

The pilot spoke into the radio headset as the skids hit the ground next to the large rock Aziza had told him hid the front entrance. Bolan watched it slide to the side as Ilaoa pulled him from the chopper.

The little man had produced not only handcuffs, but a belly chain and leg irons during the flight. He had dealt with Bolan before and was taking no chances. Even with Bolan bound as he was, Ilaoa kept the cocked Browning Hi-Power jammed into his ribs.

With his other hand Ilaoa jerked on the chain between Bolan's wrists. Bolan hobbled forward toward the opening where the rock had been. Aziza walked to his side, sending a constant barrage of words his way in a language he couldn't understand.

But Ilaoa liked the words, whatever they were. He nodded his agreement and even laughed when the beautiful black woman's insults became exceptionally colorful.

Ilaoa pulled him down the steps and through the buzzing metal detector. They were met by four more armed men, and the procession moved on through a labyrinth of halls. Few others were visible in the underground quarters, and Bolan guessed they'd been sent to the armory to help with the unloading.

Ilaoa came to a halt at a closed wooden door and knocked.

"Enter," came a voice Bolan guessed must be Ham's.

General Fajir Ham rose from behind his desk and came around the side, immediately taking Aziza in his arms. He kissed her face over and over, hugging her, holding on like a little boy to a stuffed animal he thought had been lost.

Bolan took in the rest of the room, noting a man of Arabic descent who had risen from the couch against the wall. The man wore only a swimsuit.

The light-skinned man. Ham's link to Iraq.

Finally Ham turned away from Aziza and saw Bolan. "Why is this man being treated like this?" he demanded. "He saved Aziza!" He raised a hand to strike Ilaoa.

Ilaoa shrank away.

"No, my General!" Aziza said, grabbing the hand.

"He is the man I told you about," Ilaoa said. "The same man who escaped us at the apartment in Mogadishu."

Ham looked to Aziza.

Aziza nodded. "I do not know exactly what he had planned," she said. "But it is obvious he would have used me to get to you." She smiled wickedly up at the warlord. "But I suspect we can find out what he was planning, don't you, my General? Perhaps we can find out together."

Bolan saw the lust that suddenly came over Ham's face. Torture with a beautiful woman like Aziza Mnarani? What more could a demented soul like Ham ask for?

The light-skinned man cleared his throat. "General," he said.

Ham looked toward him. "What, Abu-Iyad?"

The man in front of the couch looked at Bolan, then at Aziza. His voice trembled slightly as he said, "General, did you ever consider..." His words trailed off.

"What?" Ham demanded. "Did I consider what?"

The man called Abu-Iyad turned to the side. Bolan could see his face, could tell he was debating exactly what to say next.

"I am not saying that this is the case, General," the light-skinned man finally said. "But... is it not possible that this man was not alone in his plot?" Again he looked to Aziza.

It took a second for the words to sink in. But when they did, Ham also turned to look at Aziza. His eyes narrowed, his face becoming a mask of careful scrutiny. For what seemed like hours, Bolan watched him study the woman, searching for any sign of deceit or betrayal.

Finally Ham turned to Ilaoa. "It appears we will have more than one prisoner today," he said.

The room fell silent.

Ham turned so swiftly that his robes swirled around him. Grabbing the Iraqi by the throat, he held him up in the air in one powerful hand. "This is the woman I *love!*" he screamed at the terrified Iraqi. "Do you suggest that she has betrayed me?"

Abu-Iyad tried to speak, but his words were choked off by Ham's fingers. His face turned red, then gray.

Still holding him with one hand, Ham reached for a war club leaning against the wall. The warlord brought it over his head, then down across the Abu-Iyad's skull with a sickening thud.

Ham stepped back and let the man fall to the floor. "I was wrong," he said evenly. "It is one more *body* we will have."

Aziza wasted no time. Turning as swiftly to Bolan as Ham had to the Iraqi, she slapped him again, then reached up and grabbed him by the collar with both hands. "You!" she screamed at the top of her lungs. "Did you think you, too, could deceive my general? You, as well, will soon be a body! But you will die much slower than this man!" She released his collar and stepped back.

As her hands moved away, Bolan felt something fall lightly down his neck beneath his shirt.

Aziza moved to Ham's side and pressed her body against him, her eyes still glued to Bolan. "Your death will be slow and painful," she whispered in a husky voice. She looked up into the warlord's eyes. "It will be something my general and I devise together."

Ham stared at the woman, looking like some ravenous animal. "Lock him up," he said, his voice filled with passion. "We will get to him . . . when we can."

As Ham spoke, Bolan watched for Aziza's reaction. For a moment the beautiful black woman broke character in the part she was playing. And her face became a mask of terror.

IT WASN'T A CELL by any means. Just a room. And even with the door locked, it wouldn't have been hard for Bolan to kick it down.

Except for the fact that his feet were still bound together by the leg irons. And his hands were still cuffed to the thick belly chain around his waist.

Ilaoa shoved Bolan into the semilit room and paused in the light from the doorway, taking great delight when his prisoner struck the wall before falling to the floor. "It will get worse." He smiled. Then, cackling with glee, he closed the door behind him and turned the lock.

Bolan didn't waste time. His hands strained up his chest, trying to reach whatever it was Aziza had dropped down his collar. But the object had caught between his skin and the T-shirt he wore under the dress shirt. He could feel it. And the restraints around his wrists and waist held him back.

A soft whimper sounded across the room.

Bolan rolled to his side, seeing for the first time that he wasn't alone. Two other prisoners—women, it appeared in the dim light—lay with their backs against the wall. As his eyes grew more accustomed to the semidarkness, he saw that both women were nude. One was black, the other seemingly Caucasian.

"Who are you?" Bolan asked.

He got no response.

Rolling to his side, he came up in a sitting position and studied them more closely. Ancient scars and fresher welts covered their bodies. Here and there he saw circular burns that had come from cigarettes. Both of the women stared back at him, their eyes dead to the world.

"Who are you?" he asked again.

Again they didn't answer.

When he leaned in closer, both women screamed.

"Shh," Bolan whispered quietly. "I'm not going to hurt you. I need you to unbutton my shirt."

The black woman shook her head violently back and forth. "No..." she moaned. "No..."

Bolan clenched his fists, an even stronger fury than he'd felt before flooding him. Aziza had mentioned Ham's depravities. These women looked like two of his victims. God only knew what they'd been through. But whatever it was, it had reduced them to whimpering heaps of flesh that expected only pain and degradation.

He had to overcome that or they'd all die.

"Listen to me," Bolan said gently. "I'm not going to hurt you." He held the handcuffs up as far as he could. "See? I'm a prisoner, too. But I can get us out of here. I have something down my shirt that will help. But I can't reach it. I need you to help me."

A flickering of recognition flashed in the black woman's eyes. "You won't... hurt me?"

Bolan held the cuffs up again. "I couldn't hurt you if I wanted to," he said. "Now help me. And then you have my promise. I'll help *you*."

Slowly the woman reached forward. She touched his shirt as if it might be a snake about to strike.

"It's trapped just under the collar of my T-shirt," Bolan instructed.

The woman's eyes were still fearful, but she forced her fingers under his shirt. They came back out holding a small black object. "A...hairpin?" she said.

Bolan nodded. Aziza was smart. Streetwise. She knew what it could be used for. "Carefully, now," he said. "Put it in my hand. Don't drop it or we'll never find it again in the darkness."

The woman slowly handed him the pin.

Bolan moved his hands together, bending the tip of the hairpin into a makeshift handcuff key. A moment later the cuffs sprang open. The leg irons took the same type of key, and he opened them next. Then, unwrapping the belly chain from around his waist, he stood up.

"Take us with you...please," the black woman said.

Bolan helped both women to their feet. They wrapped their arms around each other, crying softly.

"Stay close to me," he said. "As soon as we can find a place, we'll hide you."

Bolan grabbed the belly chain and moved to the door. It opened outward, which meant it would be easy to kick. But there was no window, and he would have to move into the hall with no prior knowledge as to what was out there.

He wrapped the ends of the belly chain around his hands, leaving a loop of a foot in between. With a deep breath, he kicked the door.

Wood splintered as the door flew open. As Bolan shot through the opening, a man holding an AK-47 looked up from the hallway.

With one giant leap, Bolan looped the chain around the barrel of the rifle. It flew from the guard's hand, clattering to the floor as Bolan moved in, switching the loop to the man's neck. A few seconds later the man lay next to the weapon on the floor.

Bolan grabbed the AK-47 and started down the hall, the women at his heels. Most of the guards were still in the armory. They made three turns, then encountered four armed men.

With AK-47s in their hands, the guards suddenly appeared around a corner twenty feet away.

Bolan didn't like the noise he knew he was about to make. But he had no choice. He cut a figure-eight back and forth across the hallway, and the men toppled to the ground.

"Come on!" Bolan yelled over his shoulder, reaching back to take the hand of the nearest woman. He sprinted forward, leaping over the men on the floor and pulling the women on. He recognized the hall to Ham's office as he turned the next corner, so sprinted that way.

The door was shut. Bolan dropped the hand behind him, lowered a shoulder and knocked the door from the hinges. He fell to his knees, bringing the AK up as he took in the room before him.

His stomach rolled over at what he saw. Aziza's dress lay in shreds on the floor. General Fajir Ham stood above her, his robe pulled to his waist. The war club was in his hand as he turned to Bolan in shock.

Bolan dropped the front sight of the AK-47 on the warlord's chest and pulled the trigger.

A loud metallic click echoed through the room.

Ham dropped his robe and bolted through a door on the other side of the room as Bolan cursed under his breath. There had been no time to check the AK-47 he'd taken from the guard outside the room, and the rifle hadn't carried a full magazine.

Rising to his feet, Bolan hurried to Aziza. "Are you all right?" he asked.

"I am fine," she said, shuddering. "He was not... ready yet."

"You have some other clothes here?" Bolan asked.

Aziza nodded toward another door.

"Get dressed and get these women something to wear," he ordered. "Then stay put. I'll be back for you."

"Where are you going?" Aziza asked.

"To end it," he answered.

Bolan dropped the empty AK-47, glancing around the room for another weapon as he started for the door through which Ham had disappeared. Seeing nothing, he pushed on into another of the underground hallways.

But this hall was different. Instead of winding, it ran straight for perhaps twenty yards before coming to an abrupt halt at a gray metal door with a small glass window near the top. As he sprinted that way, Bolan saw no other doors leading off to the sides.

He knew the door had to lead to the armory, where the Iraqi troops were still unloading the general's new "toys."

Slowing as he reached the door, Bolan stepped to the side, dropped beneath the window and peeked into the nearest corner. Ham stood less than ten feet away on the other side of the door, waving the war club wildly in the air as he screamed at several men with crates in their hands.

Beyond Ham and the men in the blue arm bands, Bolan could see two Iraqi trucks. Men in gray BDUs were helping the men with blue arm bands unload more crates.

The men listening to Ham suddenly dropped their crates. Breaking one crate open, they withdrew several new Heckler & Koch G-3 assault rifles and began filling the magazines.

Bolan watched for only a second more. Spread throughout the large armory were at least a hundred of the enemy. He wasn't going to take too many of them out. Not without a weapon.

Ham was going to have to wait.

Reluctantly Bolan sprinted back down the hallway, turned into Ham's office and burst into the room to the side.

Aziza and the two women Bolan had brought from the locked room stood in the center of the bedroom. All three wore blue jeans and were in the process of pulling T-shirts over their heads.

"Hurry," Bolan urged. "Ham's just inside the armory and he's got men loading up to come back. We've got to get topside before—"

Footsteps pounding in the hallway cut him off in midsentence. Grabbing the black woman who was nearest him, he shoved her toward the door to the office, then out into the hall.

Aziza followed a moment later with the white woman in tow. She had quickly recognized the emotional state of the other two women, knew they needed leadership and accepted the job as readily as Bolan had.

Bolan pushed the black woman down the hall, through the twists and turns back to the metal detector. He stopped long enough to flip the switch and start the rock moving outside, then hurried up the steps.

By now the entire compound would be aware that he was loose. Even in the darkness he stood little chance of making it across the plateau on foot with the women. But if he could make it to the Hughes, or even to one of the trucks, there might be a chance of getting the women to safety, then returning in time to join Elliot and Barkari when—

The door above them opened, and moonlight shone down into the staircase. Bolan pushed the black woman to the top of the stairs and stepped out onto the plateau, catching a flash of the Hughes parked a few yards away before turning to pull Aziza and the white woman up the steps.

If he could make it to the chopper, he might just get the engines warmed up before—

Bolan knew something was wrong even before he turned back around. For as he pulled Aziza through the doorway, her face turned to a grimace of horror.

Twisting back toward the helicopter, Bolan saw at least thirty H&K G-3 assault rifles pointed his way. Then thirty men worked the bolts to chamber their first rounds, and the dull metal clanks echoed across the plateau.

General Fajir Ham stepped forward out of their midst.

Bolan stared at the man. He had brought his troops up the ramp and around, knowing Bolan would head that way.

Ham's face was a mask of hatred as he grabbed a rifle from the man next to him, shoved it under Bolan's chin, then paused. "No," he said softly. "Ilaoa, you may have this one. I will take my *loved one.*"

Ham turned toward Aziza as Ilaoa stepped up and rested the barrel of another G-3 on Bolan's nose. The little man still carried the Glock 21 in his belt.

Ham jammed his own weapon between Aziza's breasts. "You betrayed me," he said, his voice growing low. Tears formed in the corners of his eyes. "Do you have anything to say before I kill you?"

Aziza paused, then slowly, softly pursed her lips. "Fuck you, you bastard," she whispered.

The general screamed in rage. His finger fumbled for the safety on the weapon.

"Say goodbye," Ilaoa told Bolan, as he did the same.

Somewhere in the darkness, a shrieking war hoop broke the stillness, reverberating across the rocky plateau. Another similar cry quickly followed, and then suddenly the area to the right of the compound entrance lit up with a hundred tiny fires.

Bolan turned toward the fires as the sounds of running men pounded over the rocks toward where they stood. In the ghostly light of the torches, he could see perhaps five hundred Issa warriors carrying not only torches, but spears, machetes and clubs.

Benjamin Barkari had found the men of the villages and persuaded them to accompany him. Now the big Swahili ran in front, an AK-47 in hand, as he led his army in their sprint across the plateau.

New war cries screamed through the night from the opposite direction. Bolan and the others turned that way and saw another line of torches ignite. The men running toward them from the left looked little different than the Issas in the firelight. They wore the same worn-out clothes, had the same emaciated bodies from years of starvation and abuse at the hands of General Ham and the other warlords.

But these were the Afars. And at the front of the pack of running black forms, Bolan saw a white spot—the face of Don Elliot.

BOLAN SWEPT the G-3 to the side as Ilaoa pulled the trigger. A .308 NATO round exploded from the barrel, striking the concrete behind him and ricocheting. Bolan heard a scream as the flattened soft-point slug struck one of the men in the blue arm bands in the knee.

Bolan grabbed the rifle stock and twisted hard to the side. Now it was Ilaoa's turn to scream as his index finger snapped inside the trigger guard.

Twirling the rifle in his hands, Bolan jammed the barrel against Ilaoa's forehead. He pulled the trigger, and the top of the man's head sailed away.

Bolan turned the G-3 toward Ham, but he was a split second too late.

The warlord had grabbed Aziza around the neck and now held her in front of him as a shield. "Stay back!" he screamed into the darkness. "And do not follow or I will kill her!"

Walking backward, he pulled her into the opening to the compound and disappeared down the staircase as more gunfire broke out and the war above ground got under way.

Bolan ducked a full-auto burst of rifle fire, then returned the favor with a short stutter of rounds into the chest of one of Ham's men. Twisting away from the stairs, he saw several of the advancing Afars fall. But the warriors behind them leaped into the air, vaulting the bodies of their fallen tribesmen with more of their bloodcurdling war cries.

Elliot, still leading the pack, shot from the hip with his customized Colt .45, downing one of the gunmen near Bolan with a lung shot.

Two dozen spears arched though the blue-black sky, their silhouettes crossing the moon before their tips found homes in the chests of men wearing blue arm bands.

From farther down the plateau, near where the Iraqi trucks were parked and waiting to drive down into the bowels of the armory, Bolan heard more gunfire. He glanced that way to see Benjamin Barkari leading the Issas toward the opening. Several of the Iraqi soldiers who had gotten out of the trucks now fell to the ground beneath the spears, arrows and machetes.

But now Ham's men poured forth up the ramp, firing in panic as they ran. Some of their bullets struck home and sent Issas to their graves. But the brave Somalian natives fought on, closing the field of battle to impale their spears into chests and pound skulls with their war clubs.

A detachment of archers suddenly flanked out to both sides of the main contingent, halted and sent arrows twisting through the night to fell even more of Ham's men.

Bolan knelt next to Ilaoa and jerked the Glock 21 from the man's belt. The G-3 might be a top combat rifle in some theaters of war, but it was big, bulky, long and heavy—not what he wanted when maneuvering down the narrow halls of the compound below.

More men in the blue arm bands fell to the primitive weapons of the Afars and Issas as Bolan dropped the rifle and sprinted toward the stairs. Out of the corner of his eye he saw Elliot shoot his .45 dry, shove it into his holster and scoop up one of the fallen G-3s. Glancing the other way, Bolan watched Benjamin Barkari jam another magazine into his AK-47.

The sharp cracks of rifle fire changed to dull thuds as Bolan descended the concrete stairs. By now he knew Ham would be well into the compound. The warlord would have had time to get set up, and could be waiting around a corner ready to ambush anyone who came along.

The Executioner reached the bottom of the steps and darted through the buzzing metal detector again. With the Glock's laser beam dancing in front of him, he hurried through the halls, checking offices and rooms.

Bolan reached Ham's office and burst inside, seeing no one. He stuck his head down the hallway to the armory. Empty, as well. Had Ham taken Aziza that way?

The question was answered as Bolan heard a noise to his side. Turning, he saw a closet door fly open.

The red dot of the LAW-2000 dropped on the chest of Aziza Mnarani. Her arms were extended over her head, her wrists tied to a beam above the door.

Bolan heard a sharp crack as a heavy object came down on his wrist from the side. The Glock fell from his hand. He turned, stepping back, to see General Fajir Ham bringing his war club over his head in preparation for another blow.

Bolan backpedaled across the room, his paralyzed right arm hanging limp at his side. Ham stepped in, bringing the war club straight down and missing Bolan's scalp by an inch. The warlord raised the club again, to the side this time, swatting right to left like a batter slamming a baseball.

Bolan ducked, the heavy bludgeon again narrowly missing him. He dropped onto the floor, slamming a forearm into Ham's knee and sending the warlord to his back. Rising over the man, Bolan drew back his good arm as the war club drilled into his sternum.

Bolan froze over Ham, the air rushing from his lungs as from a punctured air balloon. He coughed, pressing out, trying to relieve the vacuum in his lungs.

Ham rolled deftly to his side, bounded to his feet and hoisted the war club high again.

Bolan dived toward the door, hit the ground and rolled away from the club as it split the air behind him.

He rose back to his feet, still struggling to catch his breath. He turned as the club whisked by again.

Bolan ducked out of the office into the hall, back-pedaling again as the air pressure in his lungs began to equalize. Ham plodded steadily toward him, stepping, swinging, stepping, swinging, like some giant windup toy gone berserk. Deranged rage covered his face. Mucus blew from his lips and nostrils each time the war club missed its mark. Finally, in total outrage, he drew the club back over his shoulder and hurled it at Bolan.

The war club struck Bolan on the side of the head, and he was thrown against the wall.

Bolan's vision clouded from the blow as his arms flailed against the wall for a grip. He heard an inhuman bellow as he slid slowly down the wall, then was driven to his back as General Fajir Ham's full two hundred fifty pounds struck him broadside.

The force of the blow drove Bolan beyond Ham's outstretched arms, and he skidded down the hall on his side. He raised his head in time to take a kick to the jaw that somersaulted him backward.

Ham pressed on, aiming more kicks at Bolan's ribs, legs and shoulders. Pain racked his body, and Bolan fought for consciousness as he rolled around a corner of the underground hallway and rose to his knees.

The next kick came straight up, its purpose to land under the chin and end the confrontation. Through blurry eyes, Bolan saw it coming. He willed his body to the side, and after what seemed like an eternity, the weary, battered muscles answered the command.

The kick skimmed up his torso and over his shoulder, meeting little resistance and throwing Ham off balance to the floor.

Bolan rolled on top of the man, straddling him, his left arm moving up as his right continued to hang useless at his side. His fist came down like a hammer, pummeling the screaming face below and sending bright white teeth popping from Ham's mouth like popcorn. Bolan raised his fist again, feeling the warlord's hawklike nose crack beneath the blow as it descended. His fist rose again then again, and again, slamming into the screaming red lips until Bolan's left hand was as numb as his other arm.

Bolan paused, catching his breath and looking down at the battered face before him. One of Ham's eyes had swelled over. The other stared back with the hatred, fury and madness of all the demons in hell.

Out of the corner of his eye Bolan saw the war club, which had rolled to a halt against the wall. He rose to his feet, stumbling over to the weapon, then moving back to raise it over Ham's head. As he was about to bring it down, he heard footsteps in the hall.

Bolan looked up to see an Afar warrior carrying a machete round the corner. Another tribesman followed, carrying a spear. More of the emaciated warriors appeared, until the hallway was packed wall to wall.

A sound from the other end of the hallway drew Bolan's attention. Three dozen Issas had made their way down the armory ramp, found the hall to the warlord's office and were now walking slowly toward Bolan and Ham.

Bolan lowered the club in his hand as the Afar in the lead came to a halt in front of him. The man had painted his thin, starving face after the fashion of his forefathers, and he now stood staring down at General Fajir Ham.

He glanced up at Bolan.

Bolan knew what he wanted. And he'd get it, as soon as Bolan made sure Aziza had been freed. When he checked the closet where she'd been tied up, one of the warriors gestured down the hallway, indicating that Aziza was okay and had been escorted outside.

The Afars parted as Bolan walked silently through them toward the entrance to the underground tunnel. As he passed a final time through the metal detector inside the door, the metal studs in the war club sounded the buzzer.

But far louder behind him, the Executioner heard the wet sounds of thrusting spears and chopping machetes.

A new dawn was breaking over the central Somalian plateau as Bolan dragged the sole surviving Iraqi soldier across the ground to the truck.

The truck, too, was the only one of its kind to see the new day arrive. The others stood a hundred yards away, smoke still rising from their exploded gas tanks and skeletal chassis, a few flames still licking up toward the sky and melting the weapons inside past the point of serviceability.

Don Elliot opened the door to the truck, and Bolan lifted the frightened Iraqi off his feet and threw him behind the wheel. "Tell your boss to sleep lightly," Bolan said as the man's shaking hand twisted the key in the ignition. He paused, staring steadily at the terrified face. "Tell him some day I plan to come visit him."

Bolan slammed the door and the truck drove off.

Shading his eyes with his hand, Bolan looked out over the plateau beyond the truck to see the last of the Afar and Issa warriors returning to their villages. The black woman he had rescued hours earlier had been an Issa, and the men of the tribe had taken her back to her village. The white woman was being taken by the Afar chief to Mogadishu, where she would be reunited with her family and try to put her life back together.

Bolan would never forget the painted faces that had smiled at him before leaving. Still emaciated, they had nevertheless radiated new hope as the warriors turned and headed out across the plateau.

The roar of engines sounded overhead, and Bolan looked up to see the Panavia Tornado F2 approaching from over the mountains to the north. He had called Stony Man Farm just before the tribesmen had set fire to the underground compound, and was informed that Grimaldi had stayed in the area, anticipating that he'd soon need a lift.

Footsteps behind Bolan made him turn, and he saw Khalid walking up to join him and Elliot. Then Benjamin Barkari and Aziza Mnarani appeared, strolling hand in hand to meet them. The three stopped in front of Bolan.

Friday cleared his throat nervously. He started to speak, then stopped.

Aziza elbowed the Swahili in the ribs. "Go on," she prompted.

"Well," Friday said, his eyes moving from Bolan to his brother and finally to Elliot. "We, uh, we've got an announcement to make." He paused. "We're... we're getting married."

Elliot and Khalid laughed, then clapped. "It's taken you long enough," Elliot said.

"Don," Friday said. "I don't...I mean...you and I have...we've..."

"We've been together a long time," Elliot finished for him. He laughed again. "Maybe too long. People were beginning to talk." Then his voice grew serious and he said, "Let me tell you something, Friday. During all those years we spent together, if I'd have stumbled on a woman like this—" he leaned forward and hugged Aziza "—I'd have dumped your mangy ass for her so fast your head would still be spinning." The former CIA man stepped back, still grinning.

"But what are you going to do?" Friday asked. "Where will you go?"

Elliot pulled a folded piece of paper from his back pocket. "Remember last time we were in Mexico?" he said.

Friday looked at him incredulously. "That map of buried treasure you bought?" he said. "Don, you got that from a Yaqui Indian who sold four or five of them every day. There's nothing to it. You'll never find—"

Elliot shook his head. "*Finding* treasure doesn't matter," he said. "The important thing is that you never quit looking for it. I know that now."

Friday still frowned. "You'll get over there and get killed by *banditos* without me to look after you. Scorpions will poison you. Tarantulas—"

"Oh, cut it out," Elliot said. "I need the help of an old, broken-down mercenary like you about as much as I need another run-in with four or five warlords. Besides, I've got a new partner."

"A new partner?" Friday said. "Who?"

Elliot laughed again. "Sort of a younger version of you." He glanced over to Khalid. "Think maybe I'll call him Thursday."

Khalid Barkari smiled. "I've always wanted to go to that cantina I've heard so much about." The younger Barkari chuckled. "I suspect the story about it has been highly exaggerated over the years."

As the Tornado's wheels hit the flat plateau and skidded to a halt, Benjamin Barkari turned to Bolan. "Pollock, or whatever your real name is, I want to thank you." He wrapped an arm around the beautiful black woman at his side and pulled her close to him. "Not just for what you have done for my people. But also what you have done for Aziza and me."

Aziza broke away from Friday, rose to her toes and kissed Bolan on the cheek, then ducked back under Friday's arm. "How do you look in a tuxedo?" she asked.

Bolan laughed. "Like a mob prize-fight promoter," he said as he started toward the plane and Elliot, Aziza and the Barkari brothers fell in step to his sides.

"No, really," Friday said. "Any chance you could come back for the wedding?"

Bolan turned. He shook Elliot's hand first, then Khalid's. When he got to Benjamin Barkari, he said, "We'll see." He smiled at the three men and the woman who had all proved to be such able soldiers against the warlords of Somalia. Then, with no further words, he boarded the plane.

As the Tornado F2 lifted into the air, Bolan took his seat and leaned back, closing his eyes. He wouldn't return for the wedding; he knew that. There wouldn't be time. While they might not call themselves warlords, and might not operate exactly the same as James, Morris, Jabbar and Ham, the world was full of other men who preyed on the weak and helpless. And it was in fighting them that the Executioner would spend his time.

Bolan had fallen into a semisleep when Jack Grimaldi's voice jerked him back to consciousness.

"Almost forgot, big guy," the Stony Man pilot said, lifting the radio mike. "Hal wanted you to touch base as soon as we took off. Something about Bosnia, I think he said...."

The wheels of retribution are turning in Somalia

STONY MAN™ 17
VORTEX

Sanctioned to take lethal action to stop the brutal slaughter of innocents, the Stony Man team challenges the campaign of terror waged by two Somali warlords. But in the killing grounds the Stony Man warriors are plunged into a full-blown war fueled by foreign powers with a vested interest in the outcome of this struggle.

In June, don't miss the second
fast-paced installment of

D. A. HODGMAN

STAKEOUT SQUAD
MIAMI HEAT

Miami's controversial crack police unit draws fire from all
directions—from city predators, local politicians and a
hostile media. In MIAMI HEAT, a gruesome wave of cult
murders has hit Miami, and Stakeout Squad is assigned
to guard potential victims. As panic grips the city, Stakeout
Squad is forced to go undercover...and dance with the
devil.

Don't miss MIAMI HEAT, the second installment of Gold
Eagle's newest action-packed series, STAKEOUT SQUAD!

Look for it in June, wherever Gold Eagle books are sold.

Blazing a perilous trail through
the heart of darkness

JAMES AXLER

DEATH LANDS®

Ground Zero

Ryan Cawdor and his band of survivalists search for a better future
in the devastated ruins of a city once called Washington. Facing
double jeopardy posed by a barbaric baron, and the indifferent
wrath of nature, Ryan Cawdor and his band of warrior survivalists
are determined to persevere against predatory foes.

In the Deathlands, everyone and everything is fair game, but only
the strongest survive.

Remo and Chiun come face-to-face with the
most deadly challenge of their career

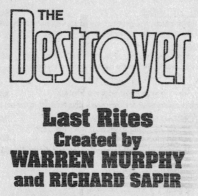

THE

Destroyer

Last Rites
Created by
WARREN MURPHY
and RICHARD SAPIR

The Sinanju Rite of Attainment sounds like a back-to-school
nightmare for Remo Williams. But as the disciple of the last
Korean Master, he can't exactly play hooky. Join Remo in
LAST RITES as Remo's warrior skills are tested to the limit!

Don't miss the 100th edition of one of the biggest and
longest-running action adventure series!

SURE TO BECOME A COLLECTOR'S ITEM!

Look for it in August, wherever Gold Eagle books are sold.

Don't miss out on the action in these titles featuring
THE EXECUTIONER®, ABLE TEAM® and PHOENIX FORCE®!